WEST OF THE WALL

WEST OF THE WALL

Berlin, 1962. A city ripped in two ... a family torn apart...

Trudy Hulst has no idea if her husband survived his attempted escape past the newly constructed Berlin Wall, but she knows too well the consequences of his actions. Now branded the wife of a defector, she faces a life in prison. With no real choice, she is forced to follow, praying she can find a way to claim their child once she's in West Berlin. Surviving her harrowing break for freedom, Trudy wanders the wall like a ghost, living for brief glimpses of her son, stranded behind barbed wire and surrounded by armed soldiers ... and she knows she will do anything to get him back.

WEST OF THE WALL

by

Marcia Preston

Magna Large Print Books
Long Preston, North Yorkshire,
BD23 4ND, England.

British Library Cataloguing in Publication Data.

Preston, Marcia
 West of the wall.

 A catalogue record of this book is
 available from the British Library

 ISBN 978-0-7505-3004-0

First published in Great Britain in 2008 by Mira
a registered trademark of Harlequin Enterprises Ltd.

Copyright © Marcia Preston 2008

Cover illustration © Rod Ashford

The moral right of the author has been asserted

Published in Large Print 2009 by arrangement with
Harlequin Enterprises II B.V./S.à.r.l.,

Magna Large Print is an imprint of Library Magna Books Ltd.

Printed and bound in Great Britain by
T.J. (International) Ltd., Cornwall, PL28 8RW

All the characters in this book have no existence outside the imagination of the author, and have no relation whatsoever to anyone bearing the same name or names. They are not even distantly inspired by any individual known or unknown to the author, and all the incidents are pure invention.

This book is dedicated to the memory of
Lyn Enz, teacher, fellow traveller and friend,
who provided the impetus for my first
visit to the Berlin Wall.

ACKNOWLEDGEMENTS

I'm deeply indebted to a great number of people and texts that served as resources for this book. Chief among these are Dagmar Rossberg and Dr Klaus Rossberg, who read an early draft and spent hours correcting my misconceptions of the German Zeitgeist and language. Any errors that remain are due to my own failings or licences taken for the sake of story, and not to the Rossbergs' unassailable expertise.

Particular thanks to Andreas Ramos for his firsthand account of the weekend the Wall fell; to Gwen Dobbs at the Max Chambers Library, University of Central Oklahoma; to Dr Ann Hamilton, TA Minton, Suzanne Owens and Jeff Spelman, trusted readers; to my friend and agent Elaine English; to my editor Miranda Stecyk for her wise counsel and insistence on my best work; and as always to Paul – for everything.

PROLOGUE

East Berlin, October 1962

From the shadow of a doorway on the abandoned Muhlenstraße, Rolf watched the Grepo patrol pass along the riverbank for the third time, the echo of their boots fading into the night. Three-ten a.m.; the border guards were precise. Each round trip along their section of the barricades took exactly twenty minutes.

His life depended on those twenty minutes.

Quickly he discarded his boots and jogged across the street, thick wool socks muffling his footsteps. When he reached the barricades bordering the embankment of the River Spree, he dropped to his belly and wormed under the barbed wire that looped in generous spirals around steel frames. He kept his head down, chin scraping the ground. A barb caught the back of his shirt and he stopped and unhooked it carefully, then inched forward again. When his legs were clear of the wire, he rolled down the incline toward the water without a sound.

A three-quarter moon rippled on the river's surface. The night was clear, unlucky for his mission. A cold rain would have disguised his movements in the water, and also made the border patrol less conscientious. But he hadn't the leisure to wait for rain.

At the water's edge Rolf stopped, listening for bootfalls. Nothing but silence and the barking of a dog in the far distance. He took wire cutters from his pocket and clamped the handle in his teeth. Spirals of barbed wire lay submerged in the river, a deadly deterrent for East Berliners who might dare to swim toward freedom. With one last glance in the direction the Grepos had vanished, he murmured a benediction – *Gott hilf mir* – and sank into the frigid water.

After the initial shock, the chill that crept through his clothes felt good against his sweaty skin. The exertion of swimming would keep him warm. The Spree was wide here, nearly a hundred meters, but it was safer than trying to cross the border near Unter den Linden, where the river was narrow but the guards more numerous. Rolf took a deep breath and submerged, pushing off from the bank.

The river at night was ink black. With one hand stretched in front of him to check for obstacles, he made forceful strokes with his legs. He kept going, making good progress, until his lungs ached for air. Then he rolled onto his back and rose slowly so that only his nose and mouth breached the surface. He took a deep, silent breath and sank again.

He was a good swimmer and confident in the water. As a boy he had been on the school swim team and had visions of training for the Olympics – he and his friend Wolfgang.

He thought now of Wolfgang, once closer than a brother, who had become a Party member and a *Volkspolizist*. If Wolfgang were patrolling this street tonight and saw Rolf escaping, would he shoot?

Their lives and their political paths had split apart when they were preteens. After the war they'd renewed the friendship as students at the university, but no amount of late-night debate could change either of their minds about the merits of communism.

The first thirty meters was easy. He took another breath, careful not to create ripples, and swam on.

This time, in the liquid darkness, he saw the faces of his wife and baby son. The image cut him. When would he see Trudy and Stefan again? Or his aging mother who had no other family left? But he'd had no choice; to stay would have put them all at risk.

He'd known it might come to this, ever since that muggy August night last year when he'd watched East German troops barricade the borders and erect the despised wall. The show of Russian military force that backed them had chilled his blood. East Berliners had felt the vibrations of change for weeks, but nobody expected a wall. Not even Rolf, with his ear constantly tuned to political winds. In the last days before the border was sealed, hundreds had fled to the Western sectors with nothing but the belongings they could carry. If he and his family had joined the exodus, he wouldn't be swimming these dark waters now.

He should have known. Should have packed them up and fled. But Trudy was pregnant that summer, and she'd already had two miscarriages. She was under doctor's orders to stay calm and not exert herself. Even after the Wall slashed Berlin in half, he'd thought the boundary couldn't stand. He'd tried to work from within to help liberate his city, but when protests and political appeals failed, his underground organization helped twenty-three people escape to the West before he was identified.

In the end, even Trudy understood that he had to flee. If he stayed, he would be imprisoned, or *accidentally* shot.

In the dark waters before him, Rolf's hand struck the anticipated barbed wire. He almost smiled. His breath running out, he took the cutters in his right hand and carefully groped for the wire with his left. There. It was cut. But there would be more; he had to stay alert. He pumped his legs and rose toward the surface.

As he pushed upward, something sharp caught his trousers and sliced his leg. His lungs burned, but the wire would not let him reach the surface. He cut it quickly. His leg stung and was probably bleeding, but it was free.

Clutching the cutters, he lunged upward, only to be struck sharply across the back of his neck with another spiked strand. The barbs ripped down his spine as he struggled to swim out from under the tentacles. The wire clung to his torn shirt, but he was only inches from a lifesaving breath now and he pushed again.

He broke the surface in a rush and sucked air.

Pain striped his leg and his neck. The wire still tore at his back. He must dive again quickly; he had made too much noise. Water streamed into his eyes and blurred his view of the riverbank, but he couldn't wait for it to clear. He took a deep breath and submerged.

The wire held fast to his shirttail and he could not reach it with his cutters. Finally his fingers closed around the wire behind his back and he wrenched hard, jerking it free. He tried to calculate how long he had been in the water – maybe ten minutes. He must hurry. He was less than halfway across and more wire would be waiting in the water ahead.

He sank down, hoping to swim beneath the wires. His stockinged foot touched something slick and alive, pinning it to the riverbed until it jerked away. He pushed off and swam, staying deep.

The darkness was disorientating. What if he surfaced and found he had gone in the wrong direction? All he could do was swim hard toward what he thought was the western bank. He stayed deep until his chest cramped and his eyes bulged. Then he began a careful ascent, feeling above him for the treacherous wire.

He did not catch it with his hand. He had moved upward through a loop so that when his thigh brushed past, pumping hard for the surface, a barb caught him viciously and ripped a long gash. His mouth opened and the cutters fell from his teeth. He grabbed for them in the blackness and miraculously caught his left thumb between the handles. Lunging upward, he broke the surface in a rush, gasping.

They were waiting for him.

He felt the impact of the bullet before he heard the rifle's crack echo across the water. There was no pain, just an awful deadness in his left arm and shoulder. The cutters were gone. He gulped air and sank.

He pumped hard with his legs and right arm. His left shoulder was numb. He had not even seen who shot him.

A strange warmth washed over him and made him think of sleep. He saw Trudy's face in the water, the brave and angry and betrayed face he had left behind only hours ago.

I am not beaten. I can swim with one arm.

He was moving slower now, afraid to surface although he knew he must. This time he would wipe the water from his eyes and see how far he had to go. He had scouted a clump of low-hanging trees on the western bank where he could pull himself from the water without being seen. One more breath. If he could just get one more breath he was sure he could make it to the West. He had come so far.

The sleepiness was a dangerous sign. He must surface now, quickly check his location and make it across without another breach. And he must do it without splashing.

He felt the coolness of air on the crown of his head and rose just far enough to uncover his mouth. Moving his hand slowly, he wiped water from his eyes. On the eastern bank, the two Grepos and another dark, squat figure stood watching for him. They were looking downstream too far. He turned his head and saw the clump of trees, a shadow, far to his right. Perhaps thirty meters away. They might expect him to surface there, but it was the only possible cover.

He had submerged again, his lungs bulging with fresh air, when the delayed pain speared his left shoulder. He doubled up in the water and waited for the pain to subside. It did not subside, but he adjusted and started swimming again.

His legs were leaden now and his one good arm could barely propel his weight. *Kick. You must kick.* He sent the message consciously to his feet. *Kick and pull. Kick and pull.* He was losing blood from the bullet wound and moving too slowly. He would not make it across without breathing again.

Kick and pull. Finally he knew he must breathe or lose consciousness, and he rolled painfully onto his back, exposing only his mouth and nose above the water. He lay that way a moment, resting, and he could hear the voices of the men on the bank. He expected gunfire at any moment. But the shots did not come and he sank again, forcing his limbs into motion.

Kick and pull. It couldn't be much farther.

Kick and pull. God, let it be there on the next pull. One more. Just one more pull.

And then his dragging foot touched the bottom. He crouched on the riverbed and began to crawl up the slope. He felt ahead of him with his good arm, found the tree branches and grasped one in his hand. He was there!

He opened his eyes just below the surface and saw the overhanging branches silhouetted against the sky. He groped his way under the trees and crawled up the bank, water streaming from his body. His right hand struck something sharp in the darkness. He looked at his hand and saw blood, black in the shadows. The western bank had been covered with broken glass. It crushed beneath his knees and cut into his palms.

Thorough bastards. His face twisted in a smile.

He brushed away glass and lay panting on the bank under the willows. His clothes, his hands, his left side were covered with blood.

Too much blood.

Apparently the guards had not seen him. He raised his head and tried to see them. He blinked hard but his vision was cloudy and he could not focus on the opposite bank. It wasn't safe to rest here; at any moment the guards might empty their rifles into the trees.

He ignored his serrated knees and palms and crawled up the slope below the brush and over the edge of the embankment. He rolled down the other side, oblivious to the pain, and pulled himself along on his stomach.

Rifle shots exploded behind him, riddling the trees and the riverbank. He flinched and laid his head on his arms, breathing hard until the shooting stopped. He had left the trees just in time.

He crawled on his belly, dragging the useless left arm, toward a deserted building on the western side. He looked down the quiet street. There were no policemen patrolling here, no soldiers. Rolf gritted his teeth.

He looked behind him and saw in the darkness a long smear of blood like the sticky trail of a slug. His heartbeat felt faint in his throat. An irresistible sleepiness pulled at him. He thought of the softness of his baby son, sleeping in his crib.

Rolf laid his head on his arm and wept.

A dark pool collected beneath his shoulder. He dipped his finger into the blood and wrote a message on the wall of the building. *Trudy, endlich frei.*

Trudy, finally free.

TRUDY

CHAPTER 1

East Berlin, January 1963

The five o'clock whistle shrilled, and Trudy pulled the lever to shut down the ancient, clattering loom. She had stood on cold concrete since seven that morning, and her legs felt numb and swollen. A persistent ache nagged her lower back.

On the next machine over, her friend Renate was using up the last of her yarns before quitting. If you were close to finishing a job, you were expected to complete it before leaving. Renate was pushing fifty, twenty years older than Trudy, but she never complained about the long hours or her aches and pains. Trudy made a sympathetic face at her, but Renate just shrugged.

When her loom was quiet, Trudy anchored the pattern cards and locked down the machine. All around her in the cavernous, high-windowed building, other machines fell silent one by one. The echo of their rattling bottled up her ears. A parade of unsmiling women crossed the factory floor in rubber-soled silence, too tired to talk. Trudy joined the queue and clocked out, placed her time card in its proper slot in the rack and left the building.

Outdoors, a greasy yellow light hung above the factory roof The low sky smelled like diesel exhaust and possible snow. Trudy rolled her head

23

in a slow circle and felt the burning between her shoulder blades, the crackling in her neck. She buttoned her coat and started the long walk home through gathering darkness.

Twelve weeks today. Stefan's first birthday had come and gone, then Christmas and New Year's. Twelve weeks since Rolf had gone across, and still she'd heard nothing from him. Maybe Gisela had received some word from him today. She quickened her steps as if she hadn't fed herself the same hope every evening.

Lights winked on in the buildings along her route. The pungent aroma of bratwurst and sauerkraut drifted out from an apartment house, and her stomach rumbled. She was always starving by the time she got home. But she was luckier than most of the women on her shift, who still had to cook a meal for their families. Gisela would have dinner ready, and her mother-in-law was a good cook. Trudy pulled her coat tighter and pictured Stefan at home in the warm apartment with his grandmother, waiting for her return. That vision sustained her during the long days at the textile mill.

A few months ago, Rolf would have been there waiting, as well. For a while after the wall went up and cut him off from his job in the western sector of the city, he was at home more than he had been in years. She'd enjoyed those weeks, despite the financial hardship. But because he'd been a *Grenzgaenger* – a border crosser who lived in the East but worked in the West for better pay – he'd found it difficult to get a decent job in East Berlin. As the weeks dragged on, Rolf grew frustrated and bitter. Trudy had taken the factory job to get them by until he found something better. And Rolf had begun to spend hours away from home in other pursuits, dangerous ones that brought tension and arguments between them. And finally his exile.

It was fully dark by the time she climbed the stairs to their second-floor flat. Trudy insisted that Gisela keep the door locked when she and Stefan were alone. Trudy tapped three times before using her key. Behind the door Stefan shrieked, and she knew he was scrambling toward her on all fours, quick as a cat. He'd started walking before Christmas, but he could still crawl faster.

Smiling, she stepped inside and scooped him up, covering his face with sloppy kisses. He giggled and squirmed, his dark curls falling away from his face, and then lifted his shirt so she could tickle his tummy. Was it possible he had grown just since this morning? At this rate he'd soon be too heavy for *Mutti* to lift.

Gisela called to her from her favorite chair, where her knitting was spread on her lap. *'Hallo, meine Liebe.* A long day?'

Trudy carried Stefan and sank onto the sofa. 'No longer than usual.' She sighed. 'Something smells wonderful. Goulash?'

'With boiled potatoes and green beans. It is ready when you are.'

'In a few minutes.'

Stefan slid off her lap and onto the floor, where he'd left a pile of lettered blocks. Trudy slouched back on the sofa and watched the rhythm of Gisela's knitting needles working blue-and-grey yarn. 'What are you making?'

'A cap and mittens for Stefan. I found an old sweater of Heinz's in a drawer and unraveled the yarn. It's pretty, *ja?*'

'Yes, it is.' *Mutti* was a master at making do with what she had, a skill left over from the war in which her husband Heinz had died.

Tonight Gisela's hands seemed tight on the needles, and Trudy noticed extra lines around her eyes. Either the arthritis had settled in her bad leg again, giving her pain, or something else was wrong. Trudy watched her a moment longer.

'Mutti? Did you hear something today?'

The needles kept working and her voice betrayed no emotion. 'I had a call from Wolfgang.'

Trudy frowned. 'Wolfgang Krüger?' News from Rolf should come from one of his associates in the underground, not from the *Volkspolizei.*

'What other Wolfgang do we know?' Gisela looped a double strand of yarn over the needles and took three quick stitches. The cap was starting to take shape, thick and warm.

'What did he say?'

Gisela glanced up, and for a moment her fingers went still. 'He wants to come visit us. He didn't say when.'

Trudy's pulse jumped to her throat. This couldn't be good. She hadn't seen Wolfgang Krüger in months, maybe longer, and she doubted Rolf had either. 'Why?'

Gisela shook her head and said nothing. She resumed her knitting.

Trudy saw in the set of Gisela's jaw that there was more to her conversation with Wolfgang

26

Kruger than she was saying. *Mutti* was worried. She was also as stubborn as an old habit, and Trudy knew it was useless to question her further.

Gisela pushed the yarn back on the needles and folded her work into its faded canvas bag. 'I'll set dinner on now. I'm sure you and Stefan are both hungry.' She pushed herself up from the chair and started for the kitchen.

Now that Rolf was gone, they rarely ate at the big dining table that anchored one end of the living room. The table was one of only two Hulst family heirlooms to survive the war. The other was the rocking chair Trudy used every night at Stefan's bedtime. Tonight Gisela set out their meal on the small table in the kitchen.

There was little meat in the goulash, but *Mutti* was skillful with seasonings. Trudy held Stefan on her lap and let him eat small bites from her plate. She offered him a spoon but he preferred to use his fingers, and she was too tired to insist.

She ate all of her goulash and took another half portion, but *Mutti* picked at her food and had little to say. Trudy listened to the ticking of the kitchen clock and the rhythmic kicking of Stefan's foot against the table leg. She watched him track down green beans and gnash them happily with his three teeth.

When Stefan was full, he squirmed to get down. Trudy and Gisela cleared the table and stacked the dishes. While Trudy washed and Gisela dried, Stefan toddled around their legs, jabbering. His elbow was hooked around the neck of Bebe, the stuffed bear Rolf had given him not long before he left. The bear's brown fur was already matted, the red tongue partly gone.

By the time they'd finished, Stefan's eyelids were heavy and he was starting to fuss. Trudy wiped him down with a warm cloth, changed him into pajamas and let Gisela kiss him goodnight. Then she carried him to the bedroom they shared.

Inside a circle of yellow lamplight, the rocker creaked its familiar song while Trudy's feet pushed against the floor. All day in the cold clatter of the textile mill, she had looked forward to this quiet time. She hummed a Bavarian lullaby her mother had sung to her when she was small. Gisela had rocked Stefan's father in the old chair, and Trudy hoped those memories would somehow pass to Stefan. She wanted him to have the kind of family history that she had lost in the war.

Stefan was her miracle baby, her first and last. The solid weight of him grounded her, and she was thrilled by the bright intelligence in his eyes. Even now, the perfection of his tiny hands left her breathless.

She laid her head back on the chair and closed her eyes. Stefan's nose was stuffy and his breath rattled in his chest. Probably taking a cold.

A child's life ought to be safe and happy. But she couldn't even protect Stefan from catching cold or scraping his knee, let alone from the scary things that happened to children. Her own mother must have lain awake with the same worries, while Germany lunged toward war and Trudy's father was drafted into Hitler's army.

She had been six years old when her father

28

went away, and now the same thing was happening to Stefan, even younger. The only image she had left of her father was a tall, straight man in a handsome uniform. His face had become a blur within a year after he was gone. How long would it take Stefan to forget Rolf? Perhaps he already had.

Humming her mother's lullaby, Trudy tried to remember her father's face. She'd been proud of him on the day he left, not even worried. Her father was invincible, and the grown-ups had talked about Hermann Goering's promise that not a single enemy bomb would fall on the capital of the Reich.

The British RAF proved Goering wrong. The first time the sirens blared in the night, her mother had pulled her from bed in her nightgown and they rushed to one of the bunkers near their home. Trudy had shivered in the damp cave, cradling the puppy her father had given her for her birthday. She clutched a blanket around them both, while her mother prayed and the night exploded.

That night the planes did little damage to Berlin. But that was only the first air raid, followed by many more. There were other dangers, too – looters in the bombed buildings and ruthless armed policemen in the streets. Worst of all, her friend Elsa Hammerstein disappeared along with her whole family, and no one would tell Trudy where they'd gone.

Her father had come home only once, on leave. He was nervous and thin, and there were special ribbons pinned to his chest. His smile could not

29

mask something sad and frightening behind his eyes. She thought the uniform had changed him, made him look like all the others. She wondered if she saw him among a hundred soldiers marching in the street whether she could pick him out of the crowd.

The night before he went away again, she sat on his lap and buried her face in the curve of his neck. He drank one beer after another, and her mother said nothing. Trudy inhaled his masculine smell and he hugged her and stroked her hair.

'What would happen if you didn't go back?' she whispered.

For a few seconds, he was quiet. 'They would come and get me.'

'You could hide.'

His arm tightened around her and she looked up to see him smiling.

'No,' he said, and the smile faded. 'They would find me. Besides, when a man's country is at war, he must defend it.'

Then he looked at her in the way parents do when they're thinking how fast their children have grown. Everyone had told her that lately, and her father hadn't seen her for more than a year.

'You must help your mother all you can,' he said. 'Take care of each other. The war may last a long time, and it will be hard for everyone. Do what *Mutti* says and don't complain.'

'I will, *Vati*.'

'I know you will. You're a good girl.' He touched her face and smiled. 'And you're going to be as beautiful as *Mutti*.'

He left the next morning before daylight, and

she never saw him again. Not even his body.

Stefan snored gently on her lap, his eyelashes a dark fringe against the ivory cheeks. Trudy kept rocking. She touched her fingertip to a sprinkle of cinnamon freckles across his nose, the only feature he'd inherited from her. His eyes and mouth and chin were all his father's.

The father who'd deserted them.

Trudy shivered in the warm room. Only when she was holding Stefan close was she brave enough to consider why she hadn't heard from Rolf. Wouldn't a man who loved his family find some way to contact them, let them know he was all right? Unless he'd been caught.

She understood that he had to leave the East before he was arrested. She also knew this development was a direct result of choices he'd made. Rolf had maintained a life apart from her since they'd first met, when she was a new student at the university. He was two years ahead of her, studying art and history, but political activism was his true career. He had demonstrated against the Communists in the early 1950s and miraculously escaped arrest.

Rolf had rescued her from loneliness, and she loved him for that. She even loved his passion for his beliefs. But during the years of their marriage, the price for that passion was absence. It was Gisela who had held Trudy's hand when she miscarried, and who had taken her to the hospital when her labor with Stefan began. On Stefan's first birthday, Trudy had bought him a set of wooden blocks and *Mutti* borrowed enough sugar for a small cake – but his father was not there. In the end, she thought with some bitterness, politics was more important to Rolf than his wife and son.

On her lap, Stefan snuffled and his thumb found his mouth. Trudy told herself harshly to stop wallowing in the past. She was not the first woman to support a family and raise a child without his father. Stefan had become the center of her life, and she still had him and *Mutti*.

Gradually the knot in her chest loosened. She was almost dozing when she heard the light tapping sound, a knock on the front door. In the small apartment, no noise escaped attention.

She stopped rocking and heard *Mutti*'s uneven footsteps cross the living room floor. The door scraped open and she heard a man's voice. Their conversation was a low hum, the words un-distinguishable through the bedroom door, but she could tell Gisela had let the man in. And something in *Mutti*'s tone told Trudy that the man was Wolfgang Krüger.

CHAPTER 2

Trudy didn't move, listening. Soon she heard the rattle of Gisela's old teapot and the clatter of cups being set on the table.

There was no reason Wolfgang should come here unless he knew something about Rolf. Yet she couldn't ask him, couldn't let on where Rolf had gone. Gisela still thought of Wolfgang as

Rolf's boyhood friend, and that was dangerous. Men grew up and they changed. Trudy had known Wolfgang for years, too, since she and Rolf and Wolfgang were at the university together. Even then he was polite and serious, and a student of Marxism. He and Rolf used to argue social theory endlessly. But Wolfgang went off to some kind of school in Moscow, and now he was not only a Party member but a senior officer with the *Volkspolizei*.

Surely to God *Mutti* hadn't told him anything.

Trudy rose quietly from the rocking chair and lowered Stefan into his bed. A strand of her hair fell against his face and he smiled in his sleep. She kissed his ear and pulled a blanket over his legs, let her hand linger a moment on his warm back.

Beside the door she paused, composing her face before she turned the knob.

Mutti and Wolfgang sat at the round dining table at one end of the living room. She'd forgotten how tall he was. Even seated, he seemed too large for the small apartment, especially in his uniform. He looked up at her with sky-blue eyes she had not forgotten.

'Hello, Trudy.'

She flashed on a memory of herself and Rolf and Wolfgang at a beer garden, toasting her good marks at the end of her first semester. It was a happy memory, but it was a long time ago. She couldn't trust anyone who worked for the People's Police.

'What brings you here, *Herr Vopo?*' she said. 'Are we all under arrest?'

'Sit down, *meine Liebe*,' Gisela said quickly. 'I

33

will pour you some tea. We have no more sugar, though.'

'Thank-you, *Mutti*.' Trudy sank into a chair and kicked off her heavy shoes.

Wolfgang sat sideways at the table, one leg crossed over his other knee. His Vopo hat lay open on the floor, like the caps of out-of-work musicians who played for coins in the U-Bahn stations, before the government declared it illegal. She wondered what Wolfgang was hoping to collect. Information?

'Gisela says you're working at the textile factory,' he said, the old politeness unchanged. 'How is it going?'

She shrugged. 'Long hours. The machinery keeps breaking down, but still we turned out two hundred bolts last week.'

'Stefan is asleep?'

'Yes.'

'I had hoped to see him.' He smiled. 'Gisela says he's walking now. It doesn't seem possible.'

Trudy set her cup down and pushed her hair back behind her ears. She was too tired, and too worried, to be social. 'Why have you come, Wolfgang? Your superiors would disapprove.'

His eyes narrowed, but he answered patiently. 'We're not forbidden to visit old friends.'

'Rolf isn't at home.'

'You and Gisela are.' His shook his head, as if giving up on something. 'Trudy, let's not play games. I know why Rolf is not at home.'

She glanced quickly at her mother-in-law but Gisela looked away. 'He's out drinking beer with some friends,' Trudy said.

A sadness crossed his eyes, and she remembered seeing the same expression on the night before he left for Moscow. She wondered now as she had then: What did it mean?

Gisela reached over and took her hand. 'Wolfgang has news of Rolf.'

'*Mutti!*'

Wolfgang cleared his throat. 'I know Rolf crossed the border, and why. I came to tell you he's been listed as a defector. And as a result, you are under suspicion.'

'Me? I've done nothing.'

'Perhaps not, but you are being watched by the Stasi.'

The special police were infamous for intimidation and spying. There were rumors of ruthless interrogations. The husband of a coworker at the textile mill had been taken in for questioning by the Stasi and never seen again. The woman could not find out what happened to him.

'Any small transgression will result in your arrest,' Wolfgang said. 'And they don't have to arrest you to take you in for questioning.'

She tried to wave away the chill that crawled her spine. 'They won't arrest me,' she said, with more certainty than she felt. 'They need factory workers too badly. And God knows I have no time to do anything illegal.'

'What about the forbidden political meetings you attended with Rolf at the Free University in the West?'

Her pulse skittered. 'That was years ago! How would they know about that?'

He frowned at her as if she were being naive.

'They know everything. It doesn't matter how long ago it was.'

She shook her head. 'And this is the branch of government you work for.' Her mouth twisted. 'The Ministry of State Security.'

'I don't work for the Stasi,' he said sharply. 'And whether or not you approve of my job is irrelevant.' He fixed her with his pale eyes. 'Trudy, *your name is on a list*. You are marked for constant surveillance.'

'You mean harassment.'

He didn't deny it. 'They've been watching to see if anyone from Rolf's underground network contacts you. If no one does, they will threaten you to get information.'

'I know nothing about it. Rolf doesn't want me to know.'

'The Stasi won't believe that. They will demand names.'

Heat rose darkly in her stomach. 'What about Gisela and Stefan?'

'They probably won't bother Gisela because of her age, nor Stefan. But if you don't give them the names they want, they will not hesitate to put you in prison.'

He watched her face, his eyes intense. 'In those prisons, the lucky ones work eight hours a day, seven days a week. They survive on a slice of black bread with lard for breakfast, thin soup for lunch and dinner, if they get dinner. Visitors may be harassed, or not allowed. Packages from the outside are often confiscated or ruined on purpose by the guards.'

'Swine,' Gisela hissed. 'The Stasi are swine.'

'They are accustomed to dealing with criminals,' he said, a weak defense. 'There are interrogations,' he told Trudy. 'There's no special mercy for women. In fact, women may have it worse.'

Trudy looked away, her breath short. *'Gott hilf mir.* This cannot be happening.'

He leaned forward in his chair. 'You must not let yourself be arrested. If you are, there's nothing anyone can do to help you.'

'But how can I stop them? What can I do?'

He waited until she met his eyes. 'Perhaps you should follow Rolf to the West.'

She made a small noise like a yelp. Her voice fell to a whisper. 'You could lose your job just for saying that.'

'Then you understand how serious this is.'

Trudy glanced at Gisela and was shocked to see tears in her eyes. In all the years they'd lived together, she'd never seen Gisela cry.

'This is crazy. I have no idea how to cross the wall. Even if I did, I could not leave my baby. Or *Mutti.*'

'I could make arrangements for you,' he said quietly.

'You! Why?'

Gisela squeezed her hand. 'Listen to him, *meine Liebe.* Stefan will be safe with me until you find a way to get him across.'

'No. If I must go, he goes with me. And you, too.' She stood quickly and walked to the window, looking out onto the dark street.

'The only escape route with any measure of safety is through a tunnel from St. Sophia's Cemetery on Bernauer Straße,' Wolfgang said. 'It

37

is a difficult passage. You must crawl through a long, narrow space, and the contact man accepts no children, especially babies. If the baby made any noise, it could give everyone away.' He paused. 'One woman tried to smuggle her baby through and the child suffocated.'

Trudy pictured a tunnel of black earth, a mother emerging from the other end to find that her baby was no longer breathing. Her stomach rolled.

'Once you get to West Berlin,' Wolfgang said, 'you can send money back home. The DDR is hungry for West marks and will not intercept them. And I will help Gisela and Stefan any way I can.'

Wolfgang was taking a serious risk to warn her – unless his superiors had put him up to it. What if it was a trap, to get her admission that Rolf had escaped to the West? If so, he'd already succeeded. She turned to face him.

'If you know all this,' she said, 'you must also know if Rolf is safe.'

He looked at her a long moment. When he spoke, his voice was deliberate. 'I know that Rolf was not captured.'

'*Gott sei dank.*'

Trudy sank into her chair and Gisela clamped her hand again. No wonder Rolf hadn't sent word to her; the Stasi were watching. Was it possible she could cross over and find Rolf in West Berlin? Would he know how to get Stefan and Gisela across?

Maybe Rolf would already know she was coming, be there to meet her... She was too tired

38

to think. Tired of constant tension, of neighbors spying on neighbors. Some people claimed there was a Stasi spy in every apartment building.

'If you know about this tunnel,' she said, 'the Grepos must know, too.'

'Not yet, but they'll discover it soon. You must decide quickly.'

Trudy looked away, shook her head. 'No. I cannot leave Stefan. There must be another way.'

Wolfgang picked up his Vopo hat and stood. 'Gisela knows how to contact me.'

He settled the cap on his head and walked to the door. With one hand on the knob, he looked back at her. 'If you stay, Stefan might grow up without either his father or his mother.'

He paused a moment, then he was gone. She listened to the clunk of his boots down the stairs.

In the silent apartment, Gisela came to the window and stood beside her. They watched Wolfgang's straight back as he disappeared down the street.

'He's a Party man to the bone,' Trudy said. 'For all we know, he was the one who marked Rolf for arrest. Rolf could be in prison this very moment.'

Gisela sighed heavily and repeated Wolfgang's words. 'Rolf was not captured.'

Trudy turned to her. 'How can we be sure?'

For the second time tonight, there were tears in Gisela's eyes. 'Even as a boy, Wolfgang could never lie to me,' she said. 'I just looked at him and the truth popped out.' She turned away, her limp more pronounced than usual, and began to clear their cups from the table. 'Rolf is free at last.'

CHAPTER 3

Stefan awoke in the night fussing, with a hacking cough. Trudy lifted him from the crib and walked the floor with him until his breathing eased and he drowsed against her shoulder. Instead of putting him back in his own bed, she laid him beside her in Rolf's empty place and patted his diapered bottom until he slept soundly again.

But Trudy didn't sleep. She kept hearing Wolfgang's warning in her head.

Something stirred in the room, a hint of Rolf's scent like a presence. She reached her hand into the darkness, but nothing was there. Nothing but a familiar cold sinking and the bird-like fluttering of her heart.

Did he miss her the way she missed him?

But she knew that answer. She was the one who had fallen in love first and hardest. And she'd kept on wanting more than he could give.

When she was eighteen, a first-term student at the University of Berlin, Rolf was already a legend on campus. The *Sozialistische Einheitspartie Deutschlands* was the official party of the communist-controlled Russian Sector of Berlin, and open dissent was not allowed. Even the so-called opposing parties voted the way they were told. Rolf had heckled a speaker at an SED recruitment meeting and was threatened with expulsion from the university.

But he continued to take risks. Everyone knew of him, especially the few women who were students there during the 1950s. His dark hair and eyes – a legacy, she learned later, from a Hungarian grandmother – set him apart from the other students. He had an easy smile that took in everyone he met like an old friend. Even the devout SED members found it hard not to like him. He inspired both controversy and hero worship, especially among a fun-loving crowd of young men who liked to lift a stein at the local beer houses.

Trudy had no interest in politics. It seemed to her that political power struggles were at the root of Germany's troubled history. As a scholarship student in the Modern Languages program, she had plotted a future that was safe and secure. She studied English, Russian and Latin in hopes of working as a translator or perhaps a teacher. Nothing in that plan accounted for the reckless moment she accepted a friend's invitation to attend a secret political meeting off campus. It sounded deliciously subversive, and Rolf Hulst was to be the speaker.

That night Trudy sat with Erika among a dozen other young people and watched Rolf capture the small audience with his quick wit and a joke about campus food. Then he shocked them with open criticism of the SED. He said its leaders were puppets of the USSR, sycophants who were more interested in the approval of Russia than the progress of Germany. While Western economies progressed, he pointed out, Germany lagged further and further behind. He accused his own Christian Democratic Union of weakness, of constantly voting for the communist programs.

Some of the audience members shifted uncomfortably, but she could see that others agreed with him. When the meeting broke up, Trudy whispered to Erika, 'No wonder they meet in a dark basement. If he says these things in the open, he'll get the knock in the middle of the night.'

'Yes,' Erika whispered back. 'But he's right, isn't he.'

During the social time that followed, Erika disappeared to talk with a seriously thin man she'd been dating, leaving Trudy to find her way home alone. She was already on the sidewalk when she heard Rolf's voice behind her.

'*Fräulein,* please. I want to talk with you.'

She didn't suppose he was addressing her until a hand caught her elbow. She turned and nearly collided with him. Heat rushed to her face. 'Yes?'

Rolf's eyes swept over her. He was smiling. 'You haven't been to one of our meetings before. That makes you special.'

'Really? Why?'

He shrugged as if this should be obvious. 'Because you are the prettiest member of the group tonight.' A flash of white teeth. 'And you're my only chance for a convert.'

'Very flattering.' She turned to go. 'I don't care to be propagandized, thank you.'

He fell into step with her. '*Bitte.* Let me buy you a coffee or a beer. Otherwise my whole evening will be wasted.'

She was flattered, and reluctantly returned his smile. 'No, *Danke.* I have a history paper to write yet tonight. I only came out of curiosity. So you see, I am not a good prospect for your cause.'

'I'll help you write the paper.'

She frowned, but he waved away her skepticism.

'I've written dozens of them,' he said. 'I promise not to drag you into a heavy political discussion unless you force me.'

'Really, I cannot–'

'Of course you can. You shouldn't be walking alone at night, anyway.'

He took her elbow and piloted her down the dark street. She let herself be led, a moth sucked into the flame.

'Do you have your notebook?' he said. 'Good. We will go to the *Winegarten*. What is your name?'

'Traudl Reitz.'

'Hello, Trudy,' he said, nicknaming her instantly. His smile now had nothing to do with politics. 'You have beautiful eyes. I noticed them in the meeting.'

They sat at a private table and he ordered *bier mit Schuss* for them both. She opened her notebook on the nicked tabletop, but the history assignment was far from her mind. She asked about his speech instead.

'You seem to think that the Communists are no better than the Nazis.'

He shook his head. 'No, no, I didn't say that. Nobody compares to the Nazis. But the communist economic theory doesn't work. They pretend to champion the common people, the proletariat, but their methods oppress the workers, instead. There's no room for individualism, no reward for working hard or doing a good job.'

'They say such profit motives lead to class

43

stratification and decadence.'

'Hypocrisy,' he said, waving his hand again. 'Do you know how the Party leaders live, compared with the rest of us?' Then he smiled. 'But you see? You tricked me into talking politics, after I promised. You can't write on this topic for your history paper – it isn't allowed. That's *another* problem with the communists.'

A paper lantern cast amber light across the polished wood tabletop. She met his eyes. 'Actually, the paper isn't due until next week,' she admitted, closing the notebook. 'That was an excuse not to leave with you. Obviously, it didn't work.'

He held her gaze and his easy smile faded. His eyes grew intense, shining like black marble. 'I'm glad,' he said. 'I'd like to know everything about Trudy Reitz.'

She laughed. 'That's even more boring than politics.'

'Don't be modest. Tell me a story about Trudy as a little girl.'

She looked away. She understood his question as part of the dating ritual, an indication that his interest in her was personal. She didn't want to talk about herself, but if she wanted to cultivate his interest – and she did – she would have to play by the rules.

'All right,' she said, smiling. 'For my sixth birthday, my father gave me a mongrel puppy. He had black-and-brown shocks of hair that stood out around his face, so that he always looked surprised. He was my closest friend after my girlfriend and her parents disappeared. I still miss him.'

Rolf smiled. 'What was your dog's name?'

'Lavette. My father named him, and I didn't know until later that *lavette* is French for dish mop.' She was pleased that she'd made him laugh.

'Your father had a sense of humor.'

'Before the war, yes. He was drafted and never came back.'

'Mine, too.' His busy hands went quiet. 'And my brother. If it had lasted much longer, I'd have been gone.'

A waitress appeared with two more drinks she hadn't seen him order. Unwanted memories floated up like the bubbles in her beer.

Her mother had been ironing. Trudy smelled hot cloth as she pushed open the door and saw her mother standing with the letter in her hand, her face white as the linens on the ironing table. Tears had not yet formed in her eyes.

'Is it Vati?'

Her mother nodded. 'He was killed in battle. Near Paris.'

They looked at each other blankly. It seemed no more real to them than the thousand times they'd heard the news about other fathers, other husbands.

'What will we do now?' she asked.

'I don't know.'

The next time the air raid sirens awakened them in the night, Trudy was as terrified as the first time. In the tomb-like bunker, she prayed and clutched Lavette while her mother made meaningless conversation with the neighbors. Good Germans did not show fear.

'Lavette became my protector,' she said, to evaporate the memory. 'But then...'

Rolf watched her. 'You lost your mother, too.'

45

'Yes.' He seemed to know things she couldn't say. Maybe that's why she told him about losing her mother.

When the Allied siege of Berlin had begun in earnest, death and the news of it became a way of life – a cousin or an aunt, the brother of a friend. Trudy had felt strangely immune. They'd already lost her father, paid their dues in blood. Surely the bombs couldn't touch them. But one day when she was delivering the bandages her mother prepared at home for the hospital, the sirens blared and the bombs whined close.

She'd waited in the hospital shelter more than two hours. When she came out, the entire section of the city where she lived had been bombed to rubble.

Clouds of dust hung in a noxious fog in the streets. Trudy climbed over stones and broken timbers, coughing, calling out her mother's name. Only one wall of their house still stood.

The bunker where her mother would have gone was half a block away. Rescue workers were clearing debris from the opening, sealed up when the house next door suffered a direct hit. Frantically she helped throw boards and stones away from the door. She was eleven years old.

Somewhere beneath the rubble, a voice moaned, unrecognizable. The metallic taste of fear nauseated her.

She screamed into the wreckage. *'Mutti! Mutti,* can you hear me?'

But her mother did not answer.

A worker shouted, 'Over here!'

Two men rushed to his aid. They uncovered the

body of an elderly man Trudy recognized as Herr Kamp, their landlord. His head oozed blood and one arm hung weirdly askew. Trudy felt sick, lightheaded.

Another worker, his face blackened and sweating, appeared from the rear of the demolished building. 'The whole roof caved in. We need machinery to dig them out.'

The smoke-stained worker saw her standing there, tears streaking the powdery dust on her face. He picked her up in two arms, like a baby, and carried her away from the rubble, into the street where the elderly Frau Kamp was ensconced on a pile of debris.

The rest of that afternoon Trudy sat beside the silent landlady. Frau Kamp seemed frozen in place, her face the same gray as the wreckage around them. They watched men and trucks pull beams and concrete away from the opening to the bunker. Someone brought them hot soup and they held the bowls in their hands while the soup turned cold.

One by one the bodies were exhumed.

It was her mother's hair Trudy saw first, auburn waves tumbling over the end of a stretcher. Frau Kamp took a pair of scissors from her pocket and cut off a lock of her mother's hair. She placed the weightless curl in Trudy's hand.

She still had that lock of hair, in a wooden box in her dresser.

'I never found Lavette,' she told Rolf on that night in the *Winegarten*. 'I searched the streets every day. Frau Kamp and I stayed in a neighborhood church for three nights until my Aunt

47

Ingrid found me. She was actually the wife of my uncle, who'd been killed the year before. Ingrid and my mother were close friends.'

'She took you in?'

'Yes. But she had four other children, who thought I was strange because I spent so much time reading. They tolerated me, but they weren't my friends.'

The bravado had left Rolf's voice. They talked about the first wretched months after the Russian occupation, when people had scavenged for food and baths were a distant luxury. He knew; he'd been there, too.

Trudy's Aunt Ingrid had rented a room to a hulking man who was heavily into black-market trading. He kept the family in military rations and shoes. No one stole from them when he was there. But after Ingrid married him, he ruled the family with an iron fist. Trudy had escaped the house when she was sixteen by taking a job cleaning quarters for British servicemen. They gave her room and board and allowed her to attend school. Good marks had earned her admittance to the university.

Rolf's dark eyes glittered and he reached for her hands on the table. The heat of his palms was shocking.

'I am your new family,' he said.

They saw each other almost every day after that. With Rolf she felt safe in a way she barely remembered from before the war. She had been responsible for herself for a long time, but she began to put herself in his care for one evening at a time. It was a comfort to let someone else make decisions. And gradually she fell in love.

Rolf's feelings toward her were harder to discern. He took her hand when they walked together on campus, draped his arm across her shoulders when they sat in the beer gardens with his friends, laughing and debating. It seemed to be enough for him, but it was not enough for Trudy.

He never kissed her. Indeed, they were seldom alone. She coveted his raw excitement for politics; she wanted him to feel that way about her. In 1953 a major demonstration was planned against the communists, and Rolf couldn't wait to take part. She didn't want him to go, and they argued.

'If no one protests against a bully, his cruelty escalates,' Rolf insisted. 'We have to speak. The voice of the people is a powerful force.'

'You'll be arrested.'

'Perhaps. But there is strength in numbers.'

'Then go without me,' she said, turning away. 'I have to study.'

Some demonstrators were arrested, but Rolf escaped. When he came to see her that night, his eyes were brighter than she'd ever seen them. 'We are transferring to the *Freie Universität Berlin.*'

She stared at him. 'You're leaving?'

'*We* are leaving,' Rolf said. 'You will go, too, of course.'

'Where would we stay?'

'With my mother. She lives near the sector border, and she has a spare bedroom. We can commute to classes together.'

She stared at him as if he'd gone insane. He came to her and took her shoulders in his hands. His faced softened. 'What did you think? I would

49

never leave you behind.'

That was the first time he kissed her. She closed her eyes and felt the heat of his body, and at that moment it was hard to care whether the heat was for her or whether it was a carryover from the excitement of the rally.

When he spoke, his voice sounded husky. 'I can speak to a crowd of people on a minute's notice, but I can't seem to tell you how important you are to me.' He touched her face. 'Be patient. I have never been in love before.'

In love?

'I *have* been patient,' she said. 'Kiss me again.'

In the darkened bedroom where Stefan slept in Rolf's place beside her, Trudy blinked away her tears. Where was Rolf now, this moment?

Stefan stirred and rolled over, too near the edge. Trudy got up and carried him back to his crib. She leaned over him, rubbing his back, until she was sure he'd settled back to sleep.

'Your daddy promised he would never leave me,' she whispered. 'But right now it feels like he's gone.'

CHAPTER 4

On a January afternoon when ice crystals pelted the foggy windows of the textile factory, Herr Urban appeared beside Trudy's loom. Herr Urban was *Obermeister* of the government-owned plant, and a devoted Party member.

Trudy had just reloaded the weft threads and geared up again, bringing the loom to full speed slowly. The archaic machines required constant attention. Frau Ziemer swore the old looms were barely one generation advanced from ones invented by Jacquard in the nineteenth century. Everybody believed her because she was seventy-nine and had been a loom operator all her life. In deference to her age, Herr Urban had made a great production of bringing her a padded stool to sit on beside the loom. As soon as he left, Frau Ziemer kicked backward like a milk cow and knocked the stool over.

Trudy was thinking about Frau Ziemer while she guided the comb with her thumb. The friction felt warm beneath her cotton glove and the threads whirled off into the growing span of fabric. In the unrelenting racket, she did not hear Herr Urban approach, and his sudden presence by her elbow startled her. She had talked to him only once before, the day she was assigned to her job.

Trudy adjusted the machine's speed to lessen the noise but did not turn it off. She took a step backward, still watching the loom, and pulled out one makeshift ear plug – a wad of cotton cloth.

'*Ja, Herr Obermeister?*'

His face was stern and angular, colorless as white stone. 'I must speak to you. In my office.'

Her first thought was, *A message from Rolf?* But that was ridiculous. How would Herr Urban know anything about Rolf?

Perhaps it was a reprimand about her work.

51

She had turned out as many bolts as anyone on the floor last week and had met her quota, but by Herr Urban's reasoning, a reprimand to a good worker would make everyone else work faster. He had used this tactic before.

There was no avoiding his demand, and no appeal. She set her jaw and nodded. The loom was running smoothly now, the yarns spinning off in a monotonous rhythm. 'At the end of my shift?' she asked.

He shook his head. 'Now. Karl will run your machine.'

Trudy saw Karl, the foreman on her shift, making his way to her station across the concrete floor. Karl was all right; he understood the working conditions and did what he could to help out the crew of women. She looked at him as he approached, but he would not meet her eyes. Karl stepped to her place beside the machine without speaking and touched a callused thumb to the guide. Trudy backed away with a sinking feeling in her stomach.

Women at the adjoining machines snuck sidelong glances as she followed Herr Urban off the floor and up a flight of metal stairs to his office. He spent most of his time in the windowed cubicle that looked out over the machines. The workers called it the Eagle's Nest, a reference to Hitler's alpine hideaway.

Herr Urban entered first and waited until she came in. He closed the door behind her, blunting the noise of the looms, and took his place behind a broad desk. He sat with his back straight, both feet on the floor. Trudy remained standing.

A fine coating of lint covered the desktop, and

52

Trudy could see trails through the dust where he had moved paperwork from one place to another. The two walls not made of glass were painted cardboard brown and held only a hook where his black coat hung like an unstuffed bear.

'Sit down.' It was an order, not a courtesy. Trudy thought that he didn't like having to look up at her.

She sat.

He glanced at her through smudged glasses, then down at a paper on his desk. 'You have been summoned by the Grepo chief, Herr Schweinhardt, to report to an officer of the Stasi for questioning.'

At the word *Stasi*, Trudy's throat froze.

So it begins.

Herr Urban thrust the piece of paper across the desk. She looked at it but did not pick it up. For a week now, she had glimpsed a man watching her when she left work, felt a distant presence when she went out to do her shopping. At first she thought it was paranoia, her mind fulfilling Wolfgang's grim prophesy. Then the neighbor upstairs had been questioned about her activities.

Herr Urban was waiting for a response.

'Today?' she asked.

'Saturday. Ten o'clock in the morning.' He cleared his throat.

'Meanwhile, you are reassigned to the cleaning crew. Comrade Schweinhardt says they may require several meetings with you, and we cannot have a loom operator coming and going.'

A demotion. 'Herr Urban, my family cannot live on the wages made by the cleaning crew.'

53

'Perhaps you will need to work more hours,' he said, snappish. 'Be grateful you still have a job.'

He looked at her as if she'd done something despicable. Denials would be useless. 'Finish your shift today,' he said. 'Tomorrow you will report to Frau Gilderman at 5:00 p.m. to receive your cleaning supplies.'

The cleaning crew worked after hours, when the machines were still. She would be walking home in the coldest, darkest part of the night. Worst of all, she would not be at home in the evenings to rock Stefan to sleep. Her nose burned but she refused to cry,

Herr Urban picked up the paper and held it out to her. She couldn't move, her body weighted to the chair. Their eyes locked until, finally, she reached out and took the paper.

Then he looked away, and she thought she detected a slight softening around the stony eyes. 'If you cooperate fully with the authorities,' he said, 'perhaps further meetings will not be required and you can resume your former position. Go back to work now.'

There was nothing to say. She got up and left his office.

When she walked past Renate's machine, her friend looked at her with raised eyebrows, a question. Talking wasn't allowed during the shift. Trudy shrugged, but her expression must have given an answer, because Renate's face pinched shut as she turned back to her work.

Trudy stepped into position beside Karl and put her gloves back on. Karl moved away with the merest touch of his hand on her shoulder. For a brief second, she saw his eyes, sympathetic but shadowed, and wondered how much he knew.

Probably nothing. His job was no more secure than anyone else's.

When her shift was over, Trudy punched out and left the plant quickly before Renate could catch her. She didn't want to talk. Didn't want her friend to hear the tight fear in her voice. She wrapped her coat around her and walked home in a sharp-edged wind.

The sleet had stopped falling, leaving the sidewalks coated and slick. She had to step carefully. Her breath puffed out in clouds of steam. The paper Herr Urban had given her rustled in her pocket, a whispered threat.

What if the Grepo *Obermeister*, the chief of border police, decided to make an example of her? Rolf had breached the fortified boundary not just once but dozens of times, by helping others escape. Did the Stasi know everything, as Wolfgang claimed? What if they arrested her on Saturday and she couldn't come home to her baby?

She climbed the stairs to their apartment with heavy feet. Searching her pockets, she realized she'd forgotten her key. She tapped on the door. 'I'm home, *Mutti*. Let me in, *bitte*.'

There was no answer. Perhaps *Mutti* was in the bathroom. Trudy called out again, her hand turning the knob.

The door wasn't locked. She pushed it open and stopped, disoriented.

She must have come to the wrong apartment. Everything was out of order – books and clothing on the floor, sofa cushions upturned, exposing

55

the springs like bared innards. Then she saw Stefan's colored blocks littering the floor.

Trudy pushed inside, her breath jerking. *'Stefan? Mutti!'*

Near the dining table, Gisela sat in a heap on the floor. Her bad leg stretched out before her, the thick sole of her corrective shoe pointing upward, her skirt askew above the rolled top of her tan stocking. Her face looked empty. She was holding her mother's teapot on her lap, its broken spout in one hand.

Beside her, a straight chair sprawled sideways on the floor and Stefan was climbing through its legs. He shrieked a greeting and smiled up at her, showing his new teeth.

Trudy crossed the room in three quick steps and knelt beside Gisela. *'Mein Gott.* Are you hurt?'

Gisela's eyes turned small and hard. 'No,' *Mutti* said. 'I am all right, but our home has been raped. They searched everything. Touched everything with their filthy swine hands.'

Trudy looked into her face and saw a crone, suddenly unfamiliar, and she sat back on her heels. It took a moment to catch her breath.

'What were they looking for?'

'Names, I imagine. Rolf's friends in the underground. Somebody must have talked. They took Herr Geis away.'

The neighbor upstairs. He had gone to meetings with Rolf. 'The Stasi?'

'Who else?'

Stefan made an insistent noise. Bebe was trapped beneath the overturned chair and Stefan was yanking on the bear's leg. Trudy rescued Bebe and hugged them both before turning Stefan loose to climb again.

Gisela tried to fit the broken spout against the teapot's body and Trudy saw that her hand was trembling.

'We can glue it back,' Trudy said gently.

Mutti nodded. 'We can glue it, but it will never be the same.'

Trudy sank to the floor. She pulled the folded summons from her coat pocket and handed it over without comment.

Gisela read the words and her mouth compressed into a tight line. 'The bastards.'

'Not only that, I've been demoted to the cleaning crew at the factory.'

'So.' Gisela's head nodded. 'Just as Wolfgang predicted.'

For a moment they simply sat, looking around them at the mess. Finally *Mutti* said, 'Stefan will be hungry. I'll make us something to eat.' She shifted off her bad hip and struggled to get up. Trudy stood and helped her.

While Gisela went to the kitchen, Trudy cleaned up the mess. She moved in a slow silence like the rubble-pickers after the war. Fitting the cushions back on the sofa, picking up clothes to put back onto shelves, she was suddenly thirteen again, sifting through the bombed-out shell of a building with Aunt Ingrid, one day after the surrender. They were looking for unbroken dishes they might use, or linens not charred black with smoke. Things the soldiers hadn't already plundered.

Trudy saw a glint of silverware, still in a drawer though its cabinet was gone. She worked the drawer back and forth to dislodge it from the rubble. Ashes and dust sifted down from partial walls and powdered up beneath her feet where the broken straps of her shoes dragged the ground. With her left fist full of dinner forks, she was reaching for spoons when she heard a small noise under the debris.

She stopped, listening. The sound came again, like the mewing of a kitten.

Aunt Ingrid heard it, too, and together they pulled away fallen curtains and chair cushions in a corner of wall left standing. The last layer was the woven top of a basket, painted white. Aunt Ingrid lifted it away. But the living thing they found was not a kitten. It was a baby. A baby left behind in the rubble.

Trudy reached into the crushed basket and picked up the child, amazed by the warmth of the small body, its aliveness in her arms. The baby was wrapped in a lightweight blanket, white with tiny pink flowers. It wasn't even crying. The oil-colored eyes stared up at her, listless, without expression. She wondered if the baby might be blind.

'Where is its mother?' Trudy asked, as if Aunt Ingrid could possibly know.

'Probably dead,' Aunt Ingrid said. 'Or in a hospital somewhere.'

'Can we take her home?'

'For now. We'll get her some milk, someplace.'

Trudy carried the baby in her arms, leaving the silverware behind. She took care of the baby girl for three days before a doctor they'd contacted at the one working hospital came by to tell them the mother had been found. He wrapped up the baby and took it away. But in those three days Trudy had come to know that someday she would be a mother, and it was *the most important thing she would ever do.*

Trudy reshelved books and changed Stefan's diaper. Gisela had rewarmed yesterday's soup for their supper. She set Stefan in his highchair beside the table and tucked Bebe in beside him.

Neither Trudy nor Gisela had much appetite, but Stefan gobbled bites of bread and cheese from his tray, perfectly happy, his world complete.

In the middle of the night, Trudy arose and leaned over Stefan's crib. His breath purred through parted lips, his eyelids twitching with dreams. Trudy pressed a kiss onto his curly hair and carefully slipped Bebe from under his outstretched arm.

In the kitchen, she turned on a small light above the stove and laid the bear on the table beside Gisela's broken teapot. Bebe's glass eyes, amber against the brown fur, stared up at her. She poked her finger into his stomach and felt a telltale crinkling inside.

She turned the bear over and ran her finger over a row of crude stitching down its back. With a small scissors, she snipped the threads until a four-centimeter slit gaped open in Bebe's back. Trudy probed the stuffing with two fingers. There – a small flat object, cool to the touch. She worked the object out of the opening and laid it on the table.

The paper was folded four times into a hard square. She opened it and smoothed out the creases, tilting it toward the light.

'The names?' Gisela stood in the doorway in her nightgown, long gray hair loose around her shoulders.

Trudy looked back at the paper. 'First names only. And phone numbers.'

Gisela came into the kitchen. She eased herself into a chair and folded her hands.

Trudy swallowed, her throat dry and whispery in the quiet kitchen. 'If I give them this paper, they might leave us alone.'

Gisela said nothing for several moments. 'And they might not.' She took a deep breath. 'The guilt would eat us alive.'

'But to save Stefan...'

Gisela got up and took a box of matches from a drawer. She set it on the table beside the teapot. 'Stefan is not in danger. Only you. Once you cross over, we'll all be safe.'

Trudy closed her eyes and took a ragged breath. Finally she crushed the paper in her fist and dropped it into the teapot.

Flame leapt from the struck match and Trudy watched it a moment before she dropped the match onto the wadded list. The flame faltered and then caught one edge of the paper, curling it inward. Yellow streaks licked up above the teapot's rim and cast a flickering shadow on the wall. They watched it burn, two witches around a fire. In less than a minute, nothing was left of the names but a teaspoon of ashes.

'Wolfgang said you know how to contact him,' Trudy said.

'I already have.' The light over the stove reflected gold in Gisela's eyes. Dark eyes, from her Hungarian mother. Trudy wished she were more like Gisela, so wise and strong.

'Rolf and I will find a way to get you and Stefan

to the West,' Trudy said.

It was Rolf's last promise, too, before he'd gone. Maybe that's why Gisela looked away, her eyes shiny once again.

CHAPTER 5

Stefan stripped off his diaper and stood naked in the kitchen, his skin luminous in the creamy light from a single bulb above the sink. The burners on the stove warmed the room for his bath. Delighted with his nakedness, he patted himself on the tummy and danced around in a circle.

'Come here, my little exhibitionist,' Trudy said.

He held up his arms and she scooped him up, nuzzling his neck. He cackled and squealed, ticklish like his father. She lowered him gently into his plastic bathtub.

Stefan shivered and she smiled. 'That warm water feels good, *ja?*'

Her neck perspired beneath the weight of her hair. She fastened it into a ponytail with a few quick twists of a rubber band.

Stefan's knees stuck up like tent poles and the faucet poked his side. It was easier on her back to wash him here than to lean over the claw-footed tub in the bathroom, but before long he wouldn't fit into the sink. His bath would be quite a chore for Gisela when Trudy was gone.

...Mutti's eyes, fragile as an egg in the lamplight, her lips pressed into a hard line. 'Wolfgang has made

the arrangements.'

Wolfgang at their dining table again, one-thirty in the morning, this time in regular clothes instead of the Vopo uniform.

Trudy just home from her night shift cleaning floors and toilets at the textile mill. Her clothes reeking of bleach, fingertips numb, her resistance exhausted...

Stefan dipped the washcloth into the water and scrubbed his belly button, his face rapt with concentration. In the haloed light, she could see the fine peach fuzz that covered his back. She soaped her hands and smoothed them over the pearls of his spine, slid her fingers through the creases under his chin. Her hands memorized the dimpled elbows, traced the tiny cups of his ears that she was powerless not to kiss. How could she breathe without him, even one day?

She sang to him, her voice soft and fractured. 'Little froggie lives in a pond, loves to bathe and splash...'

Wolfgang had brought sugar. He watched her stir a spoonful into her tea, his calm, pale eyes a contradiction against the sharp angles of his face.

'Saturday morning, nine o'clock sharp. I have given Gisela the instructions.'

'So soon...'

'Yes. Before your appointment. Before the Stasi come looking for you.'

She took the washcloth from Stefan's mouth. 'Don't suck on the cloth, sweetheart. The water's soapy.' She gave him a measuring cup and spoon to play with. He slapped the cup on the water, mimicking a line of the froggie song, *hop, hop, hop!*

Trudy wrung out the cloth and washed his face,

the clenched mouth and puckered chin, the seven freckles across his nose. The bow tie birthmark on his shoulder.

At the hospital on the night he was born, the nurse had brought him to her rolled up in a blanket like a white cocoon, with a little blue cap on his head. The nurse roused her from an anesthetic fog. After twenty hours of labor, the doctor had feared the baby's oxygen would be cut off in the birth canal and so he had taken the baby by surgery. She would never have another child. But she had Stefan, and that was all she needed.

The nurse had laid him on the bed beside her. Trudy unwound the blanket until Stefan lay ruddy and naked as a baby bird, his thin arms jerking in alarm. She had inspected every finger and toe and fold of skin, the tiny sausage penis, the black stub of umbilical cord. And found the tiny birthmark on his shoulder.

The nurse leaned over them, smiling. She was almost Gisela's age and had helped deliver two generations of babies. 'It's an hourglass,' she said. 'A sign of long life. He will see many changes.'

Trudy soaped Stefan's foot and ran her fingers between the nubbin toes. He squirmed and kicked, dotting her blouse with water. 'That foot is ticklish, is it? Let's see if the other one is.'

It was. Steam rose from the bath water and fogged Trudy's eyes.

'If Rolf were here, he would say you should go quickly.'

'Yes. I am sure he would.' And could Rolf tell her why Wolfgang would risk his career to arrange her escape to the West?

63

But the reason was obvious, wasn't it? Wolfgang must have learned that Rolf was helping East Berliners defect, and he'd done his duty as a Vopo – he had reported his childhood friend.

Now, with perfect German irony, Wolfgang felt responsible for Rolf's family. It was the same twisted logic that allowed her to believe he was not laying a trap. If he wanted her arrested, he could simply do it himself and fabricate a reason...

She added warm water to the tub. 'Time to wash your hair. Close your eyes now.'

He sat patiently while she massaged shampoo onto his hair, the soft curls slick between her fingers. Because of his hair, strangers sometimes mistook him for a girl. Rolf had wanted her to cut it, but she kept seeing the locket of her mother's hair and she couldn't bear to use the scissors on Stefan's curls.

'Tip back now. Time to rinse.' She placed her hand behind his head.

He liked his shampoo but not the rinsing. When she dipped water with his cup, he began to whimper. 'I will be careful, sweetheart. Hold still.'

The sweet tea backed up in her throat. 'I hate leaving Stefan and Mutti alone.'

'I know.' His voice low, confidential. 'I will watch out for them. You have my word.'

She glanced up at the ice-blue eyes, and their coolness felt like the breath of a glacier. 'Your word, Herr Vopo? I am supposed to have faith in that?'

'Yes.' Without blinking. No hesitation. 'You have no choice.'

'That's the whole problem, isn't it? No choices.' It was exactly what Rolf would have said.

64

Stefan pointed his chin to the ceiling, his eyes squinched into slits. Water flowed through his hair and straightened the curls down his back. Puffs of shampoo floated in the tub.

'What a good boy. All done.'

She toweled his hair into damp ringlets and lifted him onto another towel spread out on the countertop. Wrapped up like an infant, he snuggled against her, shivering. She carried him through the living room where Gisela sat by the lamp with the television flickering, the sound turned low.

'Smell this clean boy, *Großmutter!*' She leaned down so Gisela could kiss his damp hair.

'He smells like a flower!' *Mutti* said, and Stefan giggled.

When he was powdered and pajamaed, Trudy played chase with him on the living room floor, his favorite game. They scrambled on all fours around Gisela's chair and under the dining table.

At 4:30, Trudy laced on her brown oxfords and took her coat from the closet. On this last day, she dared not call in sick and raise suspicions. Tonight *Mutti* would keep Stefan up past his bedtime, so he would sleep late on Saturday morning.

At 2:00 a.m., home from her shift, Trudy washed away the smell of the textile plant in the shower. She stood a long time beside Stefan's crib watching him sleep, storing up his sweet smell like bottled oxygen. She lifted a tiny hand and kissed his fingers.

Stretched out on the bed, her body was rigid, her eyes wide in the darkness. The weight on her chest was so heavy she thought her heart would stop and she would die before morning.

But she didn't die. She lay awake listening to the rhythm of Stefan's breathing. The hours were long – but not long enough.

It was still dark when she rose quietly and dressed in three layers of clothing – two dresses, then a skirt and blouse and sweater. No luggage was allowed. She put a small pouch of deutschmarks into a skirt pocket, along with her toothbrush and hairbrush. In another pocket, she put clean underwear and a picture of Stefan. She fastened the locket Rolf had given her around her neck.

Mutti was waiting for her in the kitchen, fully dressed. She had made tea and set rolls and jam on the table. They sat at the table, not speaking, watching the clock. They drank their tea but did not eat the rolls.

Finally Trudy returned to the bedroom where Stefan slept and leaned over him. Two tears spotted his blanket. *Daddy and I will bring you across the wall somehow. You and* Mutti. *We'll be together again soon, I swear it.*

She kissed her fingertips and placed the kiss on his head, another on his chest, for protection. Then she turned quickly and left the room.

She pulled on a long black coat and covered her hair with a dark scarf. Gisela handed her a spray of flowers wrapped in green paper. She was to be a mourner, attending a funeral. She would not have to fake her grief.

Gisela looked at her with tired eyes. Their common losses during the war – Gisela's husband

and older son, Trudy's parents – had forged a bond between them. This morning, Gisela's face looked ancient.

'Take care of yourself, *Mutti*. I love you.'

Gisela gave her a fierce hug. 'Go with God.'

Then Trudy was out the door and descending the stairs.

The winter sun rose sharp as an icicle above the rooftops. Her short breaths puffed white in the still air.

She forced a slow walk, like a mourner, and counted her steps to control the panic. The flower stems stained her fingers green.

Two blocks to Bernauer Straße, and there she turned right, toward the cemetery.

On a Saturday morning, East Berlin streets were deserted. Even so, she kept her head down so the scarf concealed her face. Her steps echoed on the pavement and her heartbeat battered her chest. But she did not second-guess her decision – too late for that. She would make it across and find Rolf.

Or she'd be caught and hauled to prison – the same result as if she stayed.

The stone Church of Reconciliation loomed tall and gray next to the cemetery, its ornate spire unaccountably spared during the war. The church sat on the border between East Berlin and West, and its west-facing windows and doors were bricked up, like dead eyes held shut with coins.

Gisela attended services here, but Trudy hadn't been inside for a long time. She pulled open the heavy door and entered the church, stopping inside an archway while her eyes adjusted to the gloom. The sanctuary was cool as a cave and smelled of candles. A spangle of stained-glass light angled across vacant benches. No one was here.

Beneath the heavy layers of clothes, sweat crawled on her skin. She walked down a side aisle, stepped into a pew and knelt as if to pray. She ought to be praying in earnest, but she couldn't find the words to speak to God. Instead she listened to the scraping of the wind, the chirping of sparrows in the steeple.

And waited.

How would she find Rolf in West Berlin?

If she was caught, what would become of Stefan?

Why was no one here? Had something gone wrong?

Suddenly a dark figure materialized from the gloom. The figure moved into a pew across the aisle. Trudy kept her head bowed, her face covered. One by one, other quiet shapes entered the church. They all wore mourning clothes, their faces obscured by hoods or dark caps. She counted five, six. They sat apart on the wooden benches, some kneeling.

Were they, too, twisted by regret for family they would leave behind?

From a hidden door at the front of the sanctuary, a priest entered the church, his hands folded. He checked a large wristwatch, incongruous beneath the loose sleeve of his black robe, and surveyed the assembled mourners, as if counting. When he spoke, the sound was startling in the still church.

'We are ready to begin.'

Now Trudy did pray, fast and fervently. She prayed that this man was truly a priest and not the secret police leading them to prison. She prayed she would not suffocate in the tunnel through which they would pass. She prayed for this nightmare to be over and for Rolf to be waiting for her west of the wall.

The priest walked down the aisle toward a side door and the shrouded figures filed out of the pews behind him, following like sheep. Suddenly she couldn't breathe; her vision shimmered like candle vapors. She stumbled, and a strong hand grasped her elbow from behind. The voice was a bass rumble.

'Take deep breaths, my sister. We are all mourning our loss together.'

She nodded and forced a breath, moving ahead, following the others outdoors into the sharp-edged light. The mourners formed a procession toward the cemetery.

Trudy saw herself from a distance, like a scene in an old film: the forlorn column captured in the double-barreled lenses of someone's binoculars. In the next scene a clutch of Vopos would storm the quiet street and arrest them, shoot the resisters. She felt no fear of it, only a breathless inevitability.

But no Vopos came. The group passed through a wooden gate and entered the graveyard. The priest led them to a fresh grave. Its opening was covered by a wooden slab carved with clouds and seraphim. Beside the slab sat a simple wooden coffin. Was there a real body inside?

The priest turned toward them and opened a

tattered Bible. 'Let us pray.'

He looked past their bowed heads toward the street while they stood in silence, waiting for the prayer. And they kept standing, until Trudy's knees began to weave again.

Finally she heard sounds the priest must have been waiting for – jackboots on the stone street behind them. She felt the group grow rigid, but all heads remained bowed. She held her breath.

'Father Almighty,' the priest intoned, his voice startling and strong. He launched into prayer.

Trudy prayed. *Dear God, take care of my baby.*

The clacking boots stopped by the cemetery fence not ten meters away. The priest began a eulogy of their departed friend. Trudy shifted her head just enough to see the officers from beneath the edge of her scarf. They were Grepos, the border police. They did not move. One removed his hat as if in respect, and Trudy thought he could not be more than eighteen. The other was older, his face hard. He examined the priest and each mourner, then looked over the rest of the graveyard and scanned the section of wall that bordered it on one side.

In a reverent monotone, the priest read a passage of scripture about the risen Christ. *'Und sie erschraken und schlugen ihre Angesichter nieder zur Erde. Da sprach der Engel zu ihnen...'*

The young Grepo reseated his hat and made some move to go on, but his partner remained rooted. Trudy listened past her own rough breath for the sound of more boots, but heard nothing. Her mouth tasted like dry metal.

The priest read on and on. *'Er ist nicht hier; er ist*

70

auferstanden. Gedenket daran, wie er euch sagte, da er noch in Galiläa...'

Finally the older Grepo grew bored. He nodded to his partner and the pair moved away down the street. Trudy felt the collective exhale of the group, but the priest never looked up or varied his tone. He read until the guards were out of sight, the sound of their boots only an echo in Trudy's head.

Then the priest raised his hands to heaven and his eyes to the western wall. He froze in this position, as if waiting.

Trudy caught movement by the grave.

There it was again. She glanced at the wooden slab that covered the fresh grave. *It was lifting.*

Her throat made a choking noise. Everyone else seemed engaged in prayer – were they blind?

The cover of the grave inched upward on one side like a door swinging open, then swiveled to the side. The group of mourners was positioned between the grave and the fence, concealing the grave from the street. When the opening had grown to twenty centimeters, a hand emerged from the darkness of the grave and beckoned.

This time Trudy gasped, her voice loud in the silence. Again the man next to her clamped her elbow, a warning. 'Shhh.'

She swallowed hard and looked toward the priest. He lowered his arms and checked the street in both directions. When he was satisfied, his voice and demeanor changed.

'Move quickly. One at a time, into the grave. *Move!'*

The wooden slab slid farther to one side and a

71

man's face appeared at the opening. He reached up and quickly helped one of the mourners into the cavern.

In seconds, the black hole swallowed them up one by one. Only Trudy and the tall man behind her were left with the priest in the graveyard. When she hesitated at the brink, her knees like water, the tall man lifted her into the open grave.

CHAPTER 6

Inside the grave, Trudy found her footing on trampled dirt. She blinked into a chilly darkness that smelled of fresh earth and something else she couldn't name, something foul and sour.

A hand grabbed her wrist. 'Duck your head!'

She obeyed and was pulled forward into a low tunnel, where the stale air felt warmer than the cold sunshine above. Crouching, she put her hands on the damp ground and crawled along the passageway on hands and feet, following blindly the sounds of someone ahead.

Her layered skirts fell forward and dragged the ground. She stepped on them and stumbled, yanked them loose and moved on. Soon her eyes adjusted enough to make out a bulky shape in front of her crawling in the same awkward way. Then the cover of the grave slid shut behind them, obliterating the last thin slice of light.

She had a vision of them all being gassed or suffocated in the blackness of that foul-smelling hole. Her chest tightened, but she crawled on. Her feet tangled again in the long skirts. She bundled them up and held them in one arm, but it was awkward going; she was falling behind.

Nothing met her open eyes now but complete blackness. Vertigo threatened. She forced deep breaths and moved faster. Behind her, she could hear the boot-scrape of the tall man who'd spoken to her in the church. Somehow that helped. She stopped thinking that her next step would lead her over the lip of a dark chasm, and concentrated on picturing the rocky ground, which was growing rougher and more uneven.

Her back ached and her neck burned. The pain helped clear her head and stop the scream that gathered like floodwater at the back of her throat.

Suddenly her breath came easier. The tunnel had widened slightly, and she saw a faint glow that outlined the shape of the hunched figure in front of her. Perhaps they would get out alive.

Ahead, a man with a lantern crouched to one side of the passageway, speaking words of encouragement to each person who crawled past and urging speed. When she struggled past him, the lantern man shook his head.

'Wrap up those skirts and stuff them into the front of your underwear.'

She squinted into the darkness. 'What?'

His face was hidden behind the light, the voice deep and gravelly. 'You are holding up the line!' He grabbed her three skirts into a wad in front of her. 'Either you stuff them in your underwear or I will.'

Trudy shoved the folds of material inside the

front band of her cotton panties. The man clapped a hand on her hip and pushed her onward through the tunnel.

She cursed him silently and scrambled to catch up with the person in front of her. But crawling was much easier without the dragging skirts, and that was lucky because soon the tunnel narrowed and the ceiling lowered even more. She had to drop to her knees and keep her head down.

Now she was grateful for the darkness. Her coat still covered her backside, but her legs were exposed and cold. Her knee struck a rock and she felt warm blood on her skin. After that she concentrated on groping for stones in the path, modesty forgotten.

Her hand touched the shoe of the person ahead; she was moving faster. Her knees throbbed and her fingers felt swollen. When she tried to raise her head to ease the pain in her neck, she bumped the ceiling and knocked dirt in her eyes.

The tunnel stretched on and on. They crawled through shallow, stagnant water on the tunnel floor. She heard gasping and it was several moments before she realized the sound came from her own open mouth. A strong odor gagged her – dead rat. She tried not to breathe until the smell faded. She shut her eyes but that made her dizzy and off balance, so she opened them again. Her heartbeat was an earthquake inside her head.

She was having a nightmare. Soon she would awake in her own bed with Stefan in his crib beside her. She prayed for that awakening, tried to make it happen.

The thick darkness was like breathing ink. Her

arms and legs felt fuzzy. Somewhere a dim voice cried out. 'Move faster!'

Or was the voice in her head? Was that a faint glimmer of light? Her body didn't belong to her; it moved in slow motion.

'You've taken too long. There's not enough oxygen for so many,' someone barked. She was too tired to care. She just wanted to lie down on the rocky floor and sleep.

Suddenly, hands seized her shoulders and hauled her out of the dark passage into light and space. For a moment she was blind. She squinted at the light, and dirt fell from her hair into her eyes.

She was inside a room, but not a house. She smelled root crops – potatoes or turnips. A bare lightbulb hung from the wooden ceiling.

She slumped against a concrete wall with the others and breathed through her mouth like a beached fish. Her head cleared slowly. Her legs were cold and bleeding, and she remembered to pull her skirts loose and cover them.

A young man in an American G.I. hat appeared before them, smiling. *'Willkommen in West Berlin.'*

'Gott sei Dank!' said one of the others. 'Long live freedom.'

'Let's get out of here,' the young man said. 'A van is waiting to take you to the aid station where a doctor or nurse will check you over. Someone will help you contact your relatives or friends in West Berlin.'

He held out his hand to Trudy, and she realized she was the only woman in the group.

'Up you go!' he said.

75

She took his hand and struggled to her feet. The American led her to a wooden ladder and steadied her as she climbed. She emerged into a shack with a dirt floor. Gardening tools hung on the walls and sunlight sliced through the cracks. The others climbed after her and they were led from the shack through a dormant garden to the waiting vehicle. Her knees felt like jelly.

The American helped her inside and spoke to the driver. 'Take good care of the lady, Paul. She is the widow of the famous Rolf Hulst.'

The driver removed his hat and nodded to her solemnly as she sank onto a bench seat.

Famous? Trudy sat forward. 'I am not a widow. Rolf escaped to the West.'

The driver and the young man looked at each other. She felt something awful and dark rising inside her.

'Rolf is here in the West,' she insisted.

The young G.I. looked stricken. 'I am very sorry,' he said. 'I presumed you knew.'

She tried to stand but her knees wouldn't hold.

He removed his hat and knelt beside her. His eyes were green and clear as glass. 'The bastards shot him,' he said, 'but he crawled to the West before he died.'

'*Nein.* You are wrong.' Her voice rose. 'He has to help me get our baby out of the East!'

But she saw the truth written on his face, the pity in his eyes. 'I am very sorry,' he said again. 'Herr Hulst is a hero to West Berliners. He helped dozens of people cross the wall. It is our honor to help his wife escape.' Then he stepped out of the van and closed the door.

Inside the vehicle, silent faces stared at her. Others averted their eyes. The man sitting next to her put his hand on her shoulder without speaking. His angular face was streaked with dirt.

The faces blurred before her, but she saw her situation with blinding clarity.

Rolf was dead.

She was separated from her child.

And if she went back now, she would spend her life in prison.

May God damn you, Rolf. Look what your politics has done.

Did Gisela know about Rolf? Surely Gisela would have told her, not sent her away alone. But Wolfgang must certainly have known. *God damn him, too.*

A keening rose inside her head but she clamped her jaws shut. She would not weep. Damn them all, *she would not weep.*

The van sped through the streets of West Berlin, and a blackness like dark waters closed in at the edges of her vision.

Stefan, my baby.

How will I get my baby?

CHAPTER 7

The West Berlin aid station smelled faintly of rubber and sweat, a legacy of the building's former life as a sports hall. Trudy drifted in feverish dreams that blurred the line between night and day, between sleep and consciousness. She wasn't sure whether she was dreaming or awake when a man's voice spoke her name.

'Frau Hulst? Can you hear me?'

Trudy opened her eyes. The room was suffused with a dusty yellow light that felt like morning. Her cot, positioned next to a cinderblock wall, was curtained by sheets on temporary metal poles. Between the curtains she glimpsed other cots in the huge, echoing room. Most were empty.

A white-coated man, nearly bald, sat on a metal chair beside her. A stethoscope hung around his neck, and he regarded her through rimless glasses. *'Guten Morgen.* Do you remember me today?'

Her mind felt thick as glue. *'Herr Doktor.'*

'Yes. Dr. Bauer. Your color is much better. How are you feeling?'

'Sticky.' Her voice sounded raspy and hurt her throat. 'My hair needs washing.'

Dr. Bauer smiled. 'A sure sign you're getting better. I will ask an aide to help you with that today. Do you remember where you are? Why you are here?'

The tunnel ... the awful darkness...

Rolf dead, Stefan lost.

She closed her eyes and wished she didn't remember. 'I got an infection in the tunnel.'

'And you were suffering from shock when you arrived.' He placed his stethoscope on her chest. 'A deep breath, *bitte.'* He listened, moved the cold disk and listened again. 'Your lungs sound much better, and the fever is gone.'

'How long have I been here?'

'This is the third day.' He patted her hand. 'You

78

will be fine.'

How could she ever be fine again?

'You have a visitor,' the doctor said. 'Would you like to say hello?'

A shadow loomed just outside the hanging sheets. Dr. Bauer motioned and a tall man ducked inside. His dark clothes hung loose on his thin frame. He held a shapeless hat, turning it round and round with spidery fingers.

The man bobbed his head. *'Guten Morgen,* Frau Hulst. I doubt you will remember me.'

She didn't remember his face, but the rumbling voice was unmistakable. 'You were behind me in the tunnel,' she whispered.

The man nodded, his eyes dark as oil in the dim room. 'My name is Henri. No need to talk now. I will come back when you are stronger.'

She tried to raise up on one elbow. 'My baby is still in the East.'

'I know.' He threaded the hat brim between his fingers. 'We will talk tomorrow.'

Her head dropped back on the pillow and she closed her eyes. The room turned like a slow carousel. When she opened her eyes again Henri was gone.

'Herr Henri has come every day to check on you,' the doctor said. He shined a tiny light up her nose, then touched her chin. 'Open wide, *bitte.'*

The doctor peered inside her throat, then probed the sides of her neck with thick, gentle fingers. His face was expressionless.

She closed her eyes and thought of Stefan. First his father had deserted him, now his mother. Gisela loved him like her own, but now that

79

Stefan was walking and climbing, how long could she manage him day and night, every day, with no help? Without Rolf, Trudy had no idea how to get them safely across the wall. Would the man named Henri know? He must have contacts here. If he did come back tomorrow, she must have her wits together and talk to him.

Henri kept his promise. The next afternoon, with the sheeting around her cot pushed aside, Trudy saw him crossing the waxed *turnhalle* floor in a giraffe-like gait. He walked past the other refugees who were scattered among the cots, sleeping or talking among themselves. He moved a chair next to her cot and sat down, worrying the battered hat with long fingers.

Trudy had slept most of the hours since his last visit and now she felt wobbly sitting upon the edge of the bed. But she had her questions ready.

'Did you know my husband?'

'Only by reputation. He is much admired here.'

'Why?'

He shrugged as if the answer should be obvious. 'Because he helped so many come across to the West.'

She could see her reflection in his dilated eyes. Trudy nodded, but she wondered how people here knew about Rolf's activities east of the wall. 'Why did you come across?' she asked.

Henri examined his hat. 'Political reasons.'

'Of course.' Her mouth twisted. 'What other reasons are there?'

'I have found a room for myself,' he said, 'and there is another in the same building. I explained your circumstances to the landlady. She will let

80

you have a room and meals on credit.'

She looked at him. 'I have to get back to my son. I cannot stay here.'

'Forgive me,' he said, ducking his head again, 'but you have no choice.'

No choice. First she'd heard it from Wolfgang, now from Herr Henri. A slow burning rose in her chest. 'Do you believe they would put me in prison if I went back?'

He bobbed his head. 'Without question. You are a defector, and so was your husband.'

Her stomach rippled. *What if Gisela wasn't safe? What would happen to Stefan?* Wolfgang had promised to help them – but how could she trust him after he'd lied to her, letting her believe Rolf was safe?

'You have no family or friends in the West?' Henri asked.

She shook her head. 'You are the only person I know here.'

His face grew even longer, weighted by sympathy or perhaps sadness.

'What about your family?' she asked.

He shrugged again, a gesture that was becoming familiar. 'I have no family left in the East. And only a cousin here, whom I have not seen in years.'

She took a deep breath and blew it out like a sprinter. 'My son is only a year old, and his grandmother is aging. There must be some way to bring them to the West.'

His rumbling voice dropped even lower. 'One day at a time,' he said. 'If you are well enough to leave the aid station tomorrow, I can take you to

81

the *Gasthof* and help you get settled. Do you have money?'

'A little.'

'Good. There are places where you can exchange East marks to West. At a loss, of course.'

'Do you have any contacts with the underground here?'

'There is no need for an underground here. It is not a crime for West Berliners to help their brothers out of the East.'

That was hard to imagine. 'Do you know anyone who can help me get Stefan across?'

'*Nein*. But I have heard that with enough West marks, there are ways to buy someone's freedom. As soon as you are strong enough, you should find work.'

She wondered how many West marks, and how long would it take to earn them. But it was a glimmer of hope, and she tried to smile. 'Thank you for your kindness, Herr Henri.'

He rose and set the abused hat on a crown of unruly hair. 'Just Henri, *bitte*.'

'All right. I am Trudy.'

Henri covered a smile with his hand, but she caught a glimpse of missing teeth. 'I will come back tomorrow and take you to your new home.'

Home is across the wall. But she nodded and said, 'Tomorrow. *Danke*.'

She watched his slouched shoulders as he crossed the floor. He slanted through the doorway and disappeared like a spook. She wondered about the missing teeth, and how he'd acquired the thin scar that angled across his left cheek. Perhaps Henri knew about East Berlin prisons firsthand.

The next morning Trudy bathed and washed her hair in the communal washroom. One of the nurses had kindly laundered the clothes she'd worn through the tunnel. When she slipped on her dress, the fabric smelled like perfumed soap. She lifted the hem to her nose and inhaled. The soaps she used in East Berlin smelled like lye.

By the time she had dressed, brushed her hair dry and packed her few belongings into a cotton bag an aide had given her, she was exhausted. Her head felt as hollow as a balloon. She lay down on the cot to wait for Henri, and dozed. In her dream he did not come, just disappeared as mysteriously as he'd appeared and she was totally alone. But soon a bass voice broke through the dream and she opened her eyes to see Henri standing beside her, twisting his hat.

'Guten Morgen.'

She sat up too quickly and something rolled behind her eyes. 'Guten Morgen.'

'You look much better today,' he said.

She smiled. 'A little soap and water works wonders.'

'Are you ready to see the Gasthof then?'

She took a deep breath. 'Ja. I am ready.'

'It is several blocks,' he said. 'If you don't feel like walking, we can take the U-Bahn.'

She pictured going down the long flights of stairs to the underground station. 'No tunnels, Danke. I will walk.'

Outdoors, the sky was the same mottled gray as the buildings that lined the street, the air leaden and cold. But the fresh air smelled good after the hollow gloom of the aid station.

Though it was the same city, the streets here bore two startling differences from those east of the wall. There, war rubble still lay in neglected piles that made her think of the awful photos from Auschwitz or Dachau, the piled skeletons of the dead. Here, the rubble was gone, with new buildings under construction everywhere. And West Berlin had much more foot traffic. People crowded the sidewalks and passed in and out of interesting shops. Some walkers carried briefcases, others toted parcels or walked their dogs. West Berlin was a precarious island of capitalism in the middle of communist East Germany, and yet the people here looked confident and prosperous. And they were better-dressed than workers east of the wall. She felt shabby in her old cotton dress.

They stopped at a store-front currency bureau and exchanged Trudy's money. The clerk was pleasant, and he apologized because Trudy's eighty East marks brought only eighteen West ones. She was practically destitute.

By the time they reached the building where Henri had found cheap rooms, Trudy's knees felt shaky. She hadn't walked very far for nearly a week. They stopped on the sidewalk so she could catch her breath before they went inside.

The building's exterior walls were stained dark by smoke and pollution, possibly left over from the war, but the inside hallway was clean and warm. Henri rang the bell for the landlady.

'Frau Weiss seems gruff,' Henri warned in a whisper, 'but she is a good woman.'

The woman who answered the bell wore her pale brown hair twisted up behind her head in a tight knot. She was middle-aged and sober. When Trudy thanked her for extending credit toward her room and board, Frau Weiss nodded without smiling.

'You will pay when you can.'

Apparently a renter on credit was better than no renter at all. Frau Weiss palmed a large ring of keys and led them up the wide wooden stairway. On the landing she pointed out the dining area, a pleasant room with white tablecloths, vacant at this hour.

'Breakfast comes with the room,' the landlady said. 'You can eat lunch or dinner here, if you wish, for two marks twenty-five pfennigs.'

Henri was right; she would need to find a job quickly.

Both Trudy and Frau Weiss were breathing hard from the climb. The landlady unlocked a door and opened it to a room that held dark, heavy furniture and a faded rug on a scrubbed wood floor. The faint odors of turpentine and stale tobacco smoke clung to the drapes. There was a wash basin, but the shower and toilet were down the hall. Two large windows overlooked the street instead of the alley, which Trudy counted as a definite asset.

Henri hovered in the doorway. 'The price is reasonable,' he said.

'It will be fine.'

Frau Weiss handed her a key. 'You know where to find me.' She disappeared down the dim, high-ceilinged hallway.

Trudy stood in the middle of the room, unable to imagine herself living here. Homesickness thickened like cold borsch in her stomach.

'My room is right above this one,' Henri said. 'If you need anything, you can bang on the heating pipes.' He pointed to exposed pipes that threaded from floor to ceiling in a corner.

She straightened her spine and faced him. 'I don't know why you adopted me, but I appreciate it.'

He looked at the hand she offered, then took it briefly in his rough palm, avoiding her eyes. 'I know what it is like to be alone,' he said. 'I will go now and let you get settled.'

When Henri had gone, Trudy shook out her two changes of clothes and hung them in the closet. She laid her hairbrush and toothbrush on the dresser, washed her underwear in the lavatory and hung it on a towel bar to dry. Then she sat on the edge of the bed and stared at the window.

That afternoon she went out on the street and found a shop where she could buy crackers and cheese and an apple. She ate them alone in her room, beside the window. Before it was fully dark, she hung up her dress and crawled into bed.

Traffic noise drifted from the street, and the unfamiliar scent of the bedding seeped into her sleep. But the bed was soft and comfortable, and for the first night since she'd been in the West, she didn't dream of crawling through an airless tunnel.

The next morning she felt stronger and grimly determined. She was also ravenous. She got dressed and went down a long hall to the dining room.

The aroma of strong coffee and fresh-baked bread reached her even before she stepped inside.

Only two other tables were occupied, and neither man was Henri. She chose a table by the window. The tablecloth was frayed at the corners but clean and pressed, and there was a yellow daisy in a miniature vase beside the condiments. Compared to her bedroom, the dining area felt light and cheerful.

A teenaged girl with shiny brown braids and skin like porcelain set a basket of fresh rolls on her table. *'Guten Morgen. Kaffee oder Tee?'*

'Kaffee, bitte.'

At home she rarely drank coffee, but today she needed something strong. She didn't wait for the coffee before pulling apart one of the fresh rolls and spreading it with butter. She ate without looking up, her hand shaking. When the girl returned with her coffee, Trudy took a second roll and made herself eat more slowly.

One of the other early risers finished his breakfast and tipped an imaginary hat in her direction when he left the room. He had abandoned a copy of *Der Tagesspiegel* on his table, and Trudy retrieved it. With her second cup of coffee, she searched for the employment section.

The paper listed an entire column of office positions available in West Berlin. In the East, despite her ability to type or her knowledge of languages, the state employment service had assigned her to the textile factory. Maybe here she could get a good job and save money quickly. If she could somehow buy Stefan and Gisela's safe passage, the three of them could start over, make a decent life for themselves.

She tore out the page from the newspaper and

folded it into her pocket, feeling almost hopeful. Then she thumbed through the rest of the newspaper. There was so much more to read in this paper than in the state newspaper at home.

On page three, her eyes froze on a headline: Widow Of Rolf Hulst Escapes Through The Wall. The coffee roiled in her stomach.

Widow.

Rolf's death still seemed unreal, her week in West Berlin a bizarre dream. But the headline destroyed any possibility of denial. The paper trembled in her hands. She couldn't pull her eyes away from the story beneath the headline.

The reporter had recapped the last moments of Rolf's life in brief and merciless detail. Rolf's face rose up from the words, the way he'd looked the night he left, intense and sorrowful. The story took her into the dark waters of the Spree; she flinched when the bullet struck, crawled with him up the glass-strewn embankment to the West. The article ended with an inscription he had scrawled in his own blood.

She dropped the newspaper and laid her head on her folded arms. *His last message was to me.*

Frau Weiss appeared beside her. 'Frau Hulst, *sind Sie krank?*'

Trudy lifted her head and blotted her eyes. '*Nein.* I am not ill.'

Two other boarders had come into the room and looked at her curiously. She whispered to the landlady, 'May I have this newspaper? I need ... to look for work.'

'*Ja*, sure.' Frau Weiss clapped her on the shoulder roughly, but her eyes were kind. '*Mehr Kaffee?*'

'*Nein, Danke.*'

Trudy folded the newspaper and hurried out of the dining room. Down one flight, she pushed through the heavy door that led to the street. The air was cool there, and she leaned against the building and took deep breaths. She pressed her spine against the gray stone and tried to erase the image of Rolf, bleeding and alone on a dark street. Calling her name.

People swept past her on the sidewalk, hustling to work. A few meters away sat a kiosk selling fresh fruit and flowers. The air smelled of diesel and oranges. It felt like a foreign land. *Who are these people?*

But they were Germans, like her. Eighteen months ago, before the wall, they were all neighbors who worked and traveled throughout the city. Trudy saw strength in their faces. The people of West Berlin had survived the Soviet blockade in 1948, when every road in and out of West Berlin was cut off and American airplanes had landed every three minutes, day and night, to supply basic needs like food and fuel. Perhaps West Berliners would destroy the wall, too, with their fierce disregard.

She scanned the street. At the corner, a sign on the cross street said Kürfurstendammstraße – and suddenly she knew where she was. The Kü-damm. She and Rolf had walked that main thoroughfare many times when they were students in the American Sector. She stepped into the stream of foot traffic, and when she reached the Kü-damm she turned eastward, toward the wall.

It was a long way to the place where the River

Spree intersected the wall, but her legs felt strong. She picked up her pace. Her pulse was rapid and she breathed through her mouth.

Where the Kü-damm ended, she turned up Gitschinerstraße and kept walking. Disconnected vignettes flitted through her mind – the *Winegarten* where she and Rolf had first talked; the late-night lovemaking in silence so Gisela wouldn't hear; the joy in his eyes when he first saw his baby son.

Had Rolf seen those same scenes as he died?

If he had stayed out of politics, if he'd gone to work and come home to his family like ordinary men, none of this would be happening. But Rolf was not an ordinary man. He was the kind of man who would save a young orphan living starkly alone at the university, protect her and love her.

Trudy turned down a side street that ran close to the Spree. At the river's edge, she looked across the slow-moving waters where they crossed from East to West and became part of the border. He must have crawled out of the river near here.

A light rain began to fall. Beyond the river on the East Berlin side, she could see soldiers at work reinforcing barricades with concrete and more barbed wire. The ground was being cleared and raked behind the first row of barricades, removed of any obstructions that someone might hide behind. They were erecting a second line of barricades parallel with the first, beyond the raked ground.

Trudy shivered in her too-thin sweater. Rain dampened her skirt and matted her hair.

To her left, the river angled into West Berlin

and shimmered away. A line of abandoned buildings faced the boundary, their windows boarded shut. Beside one of these, on the sidewalk, stood a wreath of flowers on a wooden tripod, its black ribbon sagging in the rain. She walked toward the wreath, her breath pinched in her chest.

On the banner stretched across the wreath, the words were written in gold. To Rolf Hulst, A Free Man.

She touched the black ribbon and her throat made a small, strangled sound. Water dripped from her hair. Who had placed this wreath? Unknown in his own half of the city, Rolf was a hero to someone here.

A dead hero.

She scanned the stone facade of the building behind the wreath. Her eyes stopped on a brown stain, about as far above the ground as a wounded man might reach.

She knelt beside the stain. The words were smeared and weathered, unreadable now. But she heard Rolf's voice quite clearly.

Trudy, finally free.

She laid her forehead against the stone. The sidewalk scraped her knees and the rain fell harder.

When she had cried herself out, she pressed her palm against the blood-stained wall and made a promise. *Whatever it takes, Rolf. Stefan, too, will be free.*

WOLFGANG

CHAPTER 8

Wolfgang Krüger squinted at his bedside clock in the milky darkness. Six o'clock in the morning. It was a Sunday, his day off, and he'd intended to sleep late as an antidote to the bone-deep fatigue that had dogged him for weeks. But he'd been awake since four o'clock, brooding over an incident yesterday at the wall. The whole city would be talking about it today.

It had happened in the Pankow District, where East Berlin bordered the French Sector of West Berlin. The details were reported to him by a young Grepo he had known for years. Hans Köhler had been a Vopo – a good one – under Wolfgang's supervision until two months ago. Then Hans was among a dozen men transferred from the *Volkspolizei* to beef up the *Grenzpolizei* who patrolled the frontier between East and West. Hans's face was grim when he'd described to Wolfgang the shooting of a teenager who was trying to climb over the barbed wire atop a concrete section of the wall.

The shooting itself didn't alarm Wolfgang. The youngster was breaking the law and he was old enough to know the risks and the consequences. But the boy was left hanging in the wire, bleeding to death in front of horrified citizens on both sides of the frontier, before his body was finally dragged back and handed over to his family. West Berlin

Schupos hadn't rescued him for fear of provoking more gunfire from the Grepos and setting off a major incident. And the Grepos didn't help the boy on orders from Albrecht Schweinhardt, commandant of the *Grenzpolizei*.

A sour taste rose in Wolfgang's mouth. It wasn't the first time he'd clashed philosophies with the overbearing little bowling ball who commanded the Grepos. When he took over the position, Schweinhardt had sworn in typically bombastic terms to stop the illegal exodus of East Berliners across the frontier. But people still managed to leave the DDR in creative and foolhardy ways – Western politicians called it voting with their feet. The defections were officially denied but privately humiliating to Schweinhardt. So he'd made an example of the hapless teenager.

It was exactly the sort of incident that fomented unrest among East Berliners. Schweinhardt was an idiot.

Wolfgang sat up on the edge of the bed, his bare feet seeking a small rug on the cold floor. He felt for his cigarettes on the night stand, lit one and exhaled his dark thoughts in a stream of bitter smoke. Why did East German cigarettes taste like burnt asbestos? Probably they couldn't get enough real tobacco and cut it with grape leaves, or something worse. Before the wall went up, he used to get Marlboros.

He reached behind him on the bed and rocked a mounded form beneath the blankets. 'Nadia. Time for you to go.'

Nadia groaned but she didn't move. He pushed her shoulder again.

'It's still dark,' she complained, her voice muffled by the pillow. 'Why should you care if somebody sees, anyway?'

He wouldn't answer that question again. He stood up and pulled on an undershirt. 'Get up. I'll make tea.'

He padded from the room, the linoleum like ice beneath his feet. A stream of curses in English followed him. Nadia spoke English when she was angry because she knew it irritated him. English was the language of capitalism.

In his tiny kitchen, Wolfgang lit a fire on the stove and set a teakettle of water over the flame. He retrieved his trousers from the back of the sofa and found his slippers. In the bathroom, he splashed cold water on his face, roughed it with a towel and ran a short-bristled brush through his hair. He needed a haircut again. If he didn't keep it cut short, it kinked up like sheep's wool.

From habit his eyes went to the bottom of the mirror above the lavatory, where a crack shaped like half a heart cut across the corner. Last night Nadia had noticed the crack and asked why he didn't move to a better apartment, take advantage of his rank and salary with the *Volkspolizei*. Perhaps because he was tired, the comment disturbed him. It echoed the Western disposable mentality he found so objectionable – if the mirror is cracked, get rid of the whole apartment. It was true he could afford a larger apartment, but that didn't mean he needed one. His one-bedroom flat was big enough for a bachelor, especially one who didn't spend much time at home. But he wouldn't explain himself to Nadia.

He told her the cracked mirror gave him something to contemplate while he brushed his teeth.

He rinsed and spit, glancing briefly at his hollow eyes, the angular jawbones shadowed by dark stubble. The best thing about his day off was that he wouldn't have to shave.

In the kitchen, he poured steaming water over the tea leaves and set the pot on the table. Nadia was dressed and stomping around the apartment looking for her shoes and handbag. She looked tired, too, he thought, and now he felt bad about the way he'd awakened her.

'Have some tea before you go,' he said quietly.

She rolled her eyes at him. 'Bastard. You have no heart.'

She stood on one foot and then the other to slip on her shoes. The shoes were black pumps with buckles on the side and narrow, impractical heels. They looked new, and he wondered where she got a pair of shoes like that. They certainly weren't accessible in most East German stores, even if she could afford them. Perhaps they were a gift. He reminded himself that the rest of her life was none of his business. And besides, he had no heart.

Nadia bent down to fasten the buckles, exposing a muscled curve of calf below the hem of her skirt. Her uncombed hair hung in thick strands across her eyes. It almost made him want her again.

Nadia's body was strong and graceful, but her face was severe until she smiled, and she didn't smile often. She was cursed with an intellect that left her disappointed with her circumstances. Watching her, he thought she would not turn thick and square in middle age like so many

German women. Nadia would be lean and fierce to the end. If it weren't for chronically ailing parents and a brother who'd been in trouble with the law, he suspected Nadia would be quite likely to vote with her feet. And she was tough enough that she just might make it.

He wondered if Trudy Hulst was tough enough.

The thought stung, and he rejected it immediately. He did not want to think of Rolf's wife while Nadia was here. He sat at the table and poured himself a cup of tea.

Nadia came out of the bathroom with her chin-length hair combed smooth and shining. She wouldn't look at him. She snatched her coat and scarf from a hook by the door. He thought of offering to drive her home, but he'd offered before and she always declined. When he wanted to see her, he had to meet her at the restaurant where she worked. He concluded that she didn't want a Vopo coming to her house, probably because of her brother. It was silly, of course; he could easily find out where she lived, if he chose.

'I enjoyed our evening,' he said, hoping to salvage something of the satisfying hours in his bed, their fervent, accomplished lovemaking. He'd come to appreciate these evenings a great deal in the past few months.

She cast a simmering glance over her shoulder and said nothing. He had insulted her by rushing her to leave, and she wouldn't be placated. She left the apartment without a word, slamming the door intentionally to alert his sleeping neighbors.

Let her go away angry then. She knew the rules. Wolfgang wasn't the only high-ranking Vopo who had a lover or a mistress, but he believed in being discreet. More than that, he chose not to form strong attachments. It was better for his profession if he was single-minded, not susceptible to compromise. He'd made this clear to Nadia from the beginning. And he knew that the next time he went into the restaurant where she worked six days a week, she would be ready enough to come home with him again. Nadia was not ashamed of enjoying sex; it was one of her best qualities. Once physical passion overtook her, the lines of bitterness dissolved from her face and she was fluid and alive, like an animal in its wild environment.

Wolfgang refilled his cup and slipped a bulky sweater over his undershirt. He passed through the living room and onto a tiny balcony that overlooked the street from two floors up. The balcony had room enough for two people to stand but wasn't big enough for a chair. The other buildings were still dark at this hour on a Sunday, the streets quiet. Nadia had already disappeared down the sidewalk.

He leaned his forearms on the railing and inhaled the smells of his city, the damp concrete and old rubber. He'd always been an early riser. The chilly morning air made each day seem like a fresh chance. This morning a certain foreign scent reminded him of Moscow, and his two seminal years at the academy there. The training had set a pattern for his rise in the Communist Party hierarchy, and thereby in the East German government. He could also see, in retrospect, that the academy was where a subtle separation had begun, between the Marxist philosophy he'd embraced as a teenager in his grandfather's book-lined study, and the Stalinist view of communism that prevailed in postwar Russia.

At the time, he'd had no idea how truly young he was. A decade ago.

Yesterday he'd turned thirty-five, and sometimes he felt like an old man. He hadn't even told Nadia it was his birthday.

He drank his tea, already going cold in the sharp air, and thought again about yesterday's incident at the wall, the teenager impaled on the wire. The young fool had brought on his own death, trying to go over the wall in plain sight of the border police. It shouldn't bother him so much; men died for their principles all the time, all over the world. During the war, thousands of teenagers died in the fighting, with or without ideals. Wolfgang might have been one of them, if his parents hadn't moved the family to his grandparents' house in Sweden during Hitler's rise to power. As academics, they'd objected to their son being coerced into the Hitler Youth.

But Germany wasn't at war now, and the dead teenager was somebody's son.

That was the crux of it, the reason the incident gnawed at him. He kept seeing the ruined eyes of Gisela Hulst when he'd told her that her last son, her youngest, had been shot and killed. The familiar face that had warmed his childhood collapsed inward, her body shriveling in the chair like a dried apple. She must have suspected it, Rolf had been gone so long, but the weight of certainty was almost too much to bear. For a moment he had thought Gisela would not survive the news, that it had opened her heart like the stroke of an axe. He'd had to look away.

But Gisela did not break. She'd lost a husband and an older son in the war, and her scars were tough and deep. While he stared at his hands and counted the seconds, she had pulled back from the brink. She'd composed herself and refilled his cup. And had enough *sang froid* to understand why they could not tell Trudy, not yet. Gisela Hulst was the strongest woman he'd ever known.

Gisela's family didn't have the resources to escape Berlin before the war as Wolfgang's had done. Nor could Rolf, two years younger than Wolfgang, evade induction into Hitler's child army. That was the stroke, Wolfgang thought, that had branded Rolf with the soul of a rebel.

Many youngsters in the Hitler Youth became mesmerized by the Nazi leader and succumbed to the brainwashing of Aryan superiority. But not Rolf. While Wolfgang was learning to hunt and fish with his grandfather in the forests of Sweden, Rolf became a political subversive by the age of twelve. Rolf never talked about the persecution he'd endured at the hands of those fanatical child recruits, but Wolfgang had heard the stories from others. After the war, Rolf channeled his indignation toward the Russian occupation forces, and then the communist government they imposed. By the time Wolfgang returned to Berlin and saw Rolf again at the university, rebellion was part of his nature, like athleticism or a love of music. And their political philosophies were poles apart.

While Europe had blackened under the scourge of all-out war, Wolfgang's grandfather tutored him through the works of Karl Marx. His grandfather was a college history professor, a brilliant man who could also laugh and show affection toward the grandson who adored him. *Opa* answered his naive questions without censure and encouraged Wolfgang to think in broader terms, what he called the big picture. *Opa* found much to admire in the theory of communism, but he distinguished between theory and practice. Marx's theories wouldn't work, *Opa* believed, because he didn't make allowances for greed and power lust, unfortunate but innate characteristics of mankind.

But Wolfgang, at seventeen, was innately idealistic. He embraced the ideal of a classless society where property and production belonged to everyone instead of the few. He grieved for his home country under Hitler's reign, and when the war ended, he returned to Berlin on his own. Germany had a chance to rebuild itself as that perfectly equitable society, and he wanted to be a part of it. 'From each according to his ability; to each according to his need.'

At the university, he'd tried to explain this dream to Rolf. They debated vigorously but carefully, for Rolf's open dissent toward the government was not allowed. But he loved to argue, and Wolfgang remembered those avid beerhouse nights as some of the best times of his life. Those, and the years he'd spent in the warm circle of his grandfather's love.

But *Opa* was gone now, and so was Rolf. Gisela was left to raise her grandson alone, and in helping Trudy escape arrest, Wolfgang had made contacts that could easily come back to ruin him.

Rolf's death had grayed the line between political ideals and reality, between what was right and wrong.

He lit another Caro and inhaled the caustic smoke. Ironically enough, Nadia had set off the whole chain of events, though she didn't know it. She wasn't aware that Wolfgang knew the man she'd offered up to save her brother.

Wolfgang tossed the dregs of his cold tea over the balcony railing. The sky had lightened, leaving a dull overcast typical of February. The gray light followed him inside, and for a moment he saw his apartment through Nadia's eyes – the linoleum floor curled up at the corners, the rust stain in the kitchen sink. At least the landlord made sure the plumbing worked and that he had enough heat. The man was a Party member and liked having a policeman in the building.

The annoying fatigue had returned, and Wolfgang felt its weight in his legs as he slippered into the hallway and down the stairs to the building's entry. A baby pram and a battered bicycle sat in the small foyer, beside a basket where newspapers for the building were delivered. He picked up his rolled newspaper from the basket, took yesterday's mail from his numbered box and climbed back up the stairs.

In the West Berlin papers, news of the teenager who'd died at the border would be splashed across the headlines today, probably with graphic photos of his body hanging in the barbed wire. The front page of his *Neues Deutschland*, however, carried nothing about the event, nor was there a report on the inside pages. For the East Berlin press, the incident had never happened. Maybe it was better that way. The wall was a bitter but necessary evil, an extreme measure to stop the bleeding of East Berlin citizens – many of them skilled people sorely needed here – into the West. The less people read about the wall, the better.

Unfortunately, East Berliners didn't need the newspaper to learn about such incidents. Someone would hear the story from forbidden West Berlin radio or TV stations, and pass it along in bars and on the street. The news would travel from neighbor to neighbor until everyone knew. They would learn the boy's name and claim to have met his relatives, shake their heads about the cruelty of the border police. Even after some other story flushed this one from the arteries of gossip, the people would not forget.

Gisela Hulst would hear it, too, and think of her son.

He ought to visit her today. And when he did, she would ask again if he had news of Trudy. On his last visit, he had assured Gisela that Trudy made it across the wall – or rather, under it – safely. But Gisela wanted to know where Trudy was staying, how she was doing. And he had promised to find out what he could.

If his source was loyal, there should be a message by now from West Berlin. But he'd have to go to Vopo headquarters to retrieve it.

He'd have to shave on Sunday after all.

CHAPTER 9

That afternoon Wolfgang put on his uniform and walked under overcast skies to the *Volkspolizei* headquarters. His little Trabant P50 didn't take much petrol, but unless the weather was bitter he preferred walking. He liked the exercise, and walking helped clear his head. In twenty minutes he mounted the stone steps of the building and pushed open the metal door.

The outer office, with its single window, felt dank and cloudy even on days when the weather wasn't. The building held offices for both the *Volkspolizei* and *Grenzpolizei*, and today Hans Köhler happened to be at the receiving desk.

The young man looked up from his paperwork and smiled. '*Guten Tag*, Comrade.'

Hans delighted in calling Party members comrade, though he wasn't a member himself. His tone irritated some of his superiors, who couldn't decide whether Hans meant to be courteous or mocking. Wolfgang knew quite well which it was, but he didn't take offense. Hans had been conscripted into service against his wishes, and it wasn't surprising that he used his wit as a form of passive rebellion.

'*Guten Tag*, Hans.'

'You are so dedicated you cannot stay away on your day off!'

'I have some research to do. Is Schweinhardt in?'

Immediately he regretted his slip. He should have said *Obermeister* Schweinhardt, or at least Comrade Schweinhardt; the last name alone sounded disrespectful.

The corners of Hans's mouth curved slightly, but he didn't let himself smile. 'Of course, sir. He's in his office. Comrade Schweinhardt does not recognize weekends.'

Just like me, Wolfgang thought. *How offensive.* 'No need to let him know I am here,' Wolfgang said. 'I wouldn't want to disturb him.'

Hans nodded. 'I never saw you come in, sir.' He returned to his paperwork.

Wolfgang gave a half smile and started to move on, then paused. 'How is your father's health?'

The humor melted from Hans's eyes. 'Much the same.'

'I'm sorry. I hoped for better news.'

'Thank you, sir. It's kind of you to ask.'

Wolfgang walked down a dim hallway to a large room that smelled of old books and dust. The smell reminded him of his grandfather's library, but the resemblance ended there. The Vopo book repository had tan walls with no windows, and a concrete floor painted brown. It felt like a cardboard box. Meter-long fluorescent lights hung on lengths of chain from the ceiling and illuminated the shelves of books with shaky, anemic light. There were books on German history, the USSR and volumes of SED Party convention speeches, mostly by General Secretary Walter Ulbricht. No Western literature was allowed, and even Stalin's books had disappeared some years ago.

Wolfgang passed through the main library to a

107

smaller room that held the newspaper archives. This area was kept locked. Wolfgang opened it with his key and switched on the light.

Every West Berlin newspaper printed since the city was parceled among the Allies in 1945 sat in stacks arranged by year, month and week on unvarnished wooden shelves. The old newsprint affected Wolfgang's nose like pepper. He tried to strangle his sneeze – Schweinhardt's office was directly above the library – but he was not successful and sneezed again. *Damn.*

He scanned the rows for the past week's issues of *Der Tagesspiegel* and removed them to a reading table. Western papers could not be purchased in the East and were forbidden reading for the average citizen, but Party officials used them to keep tabs on Western propaganda. Western television was also taboo, but the airwaves were harder to police. Every night thousands of East Berliners made a nightly emigration via television. During daylight hours, they had to make sure their antennas did not aim westward.

Wolfgang closed the door before he sat down. He was actually hiding from Albrecht Schweinhardt. It irritated him to take any action at all because of Schweinhardt, but he told himself that any sane man would avoid the Grepo commandant's company if he could, especially on his day off.

He opened the latest newspaper, which was two days old. Today's West Berlin papers, with their sensationalized coverage of the teenaged defector, wouldn't be here until tomorrow.

He scanned the headlines briefly, paged through

to the section that carried personal ads and ran his finger down the dense, narrow columns. Finding nothing, he refolded that paper, laid it aside and took another. Once he paused, thinking he'd heard footsteps on the floor above, but he heard nothing more and resumed the search. He'd gone through five newspapers before his finger stopped abruptly on a two-line notice.

Staying on Mühlenstraße.
Working Gasthaus zur Schwarzen Katze. HR

Wolfgang tapped the newspaper with his knuckle, gratified that Henri Bremmer had held up his end of the bargain. Bremmer had bought his safe passage through the wall by promising to keep an eye on Trudy.

Wolfgang wasn't familiar with a restaurant called the Black Cat. He had not been in West Berlin for a year even before the border was sealed. He wondered if Trudy was waiting tables, the same as Nadia did, both of them underemployed. The two lines of print gave no hint about Trudy's state of mind, and he tried not to imagine it. The separation from her child was most likely permanent, but at least she was alive and not in prison. And he could tell Gisela that Trudy had taken a room in the American sector and found a job.

Wolfgang stacked the papers and stood up, stretching the tight muscles in his neck.

Without warning the door behind him opened. He turned to face a middle-aged man with a protruding belly on a stick-like frame that made him look off balance. Thin brown hair was mostly concealed under his uniform cap, which he wore even indoors.

'*Genosse* Krüger!' the man boomed. He used the familiar title allowed only between two Party members, pretending civility. 'What brings you here today?'

Schweinhardt's voice was suited for outdoor stadiums, not a closed room. Wolfgang was careful not to flinch. '*Guten Tag, Genosse* Schweinhardt.'

He reshelved the newspapers, knowing that Schweinhardt would come back later and shuffle through the whole stack, speculating on Wolfgang's motives for reading the decadent Western press.

'Catching up on your reading?' Schweinhardt watched Wolfgang's eyes.

'In a way.' Wolfgang was a smooth liar when he felt justified. His training in the Russian academy had taught him this, indirectly. 'I heard that an old family friend in the French Sector had died recently, and I hoped to find out whether it was true.'

'And did you find anything?'

'No.'

'Perhaps, then, he is still alive.'

'I will write to my great-aunt Hilda in Wedding,' Wolfgang said, holding open the door of the musty periodical room. 'She knows all the family affairs. If the old gentleman has had so much as a cold, she can tell me.' Wolfgang smiled and waited for Schweinhardt to exit before him.

Schweinhardt looked at him with blank eyes and finally stepped through the door. 'You seem to have a number of family and friends in the West.'

'What Berliner doesn't? We were all surprised by the wall.'

'I was not surprised.' Schweinhardt straightened, his round belly bulging like a pregnant woman's. 'And if I had relatives in Berlin, I would see to it that they lived in the East.'

'Hmm. You must have uncommon control over your relatives.'

Schweinhardt trailed him to the outer office. Wolfgang replaced his hat and glanced at Hans. He could read the slight shrug of Hans's shoulders. *I didn't tell him you were here.*

Wolfgang gave an abbreviated salute. 'Have a pleasant Sunday, gentlemen.'

'I'm on duty all day,' Hans said glumly.

'*Auf Wiedersehen, Genosse* Krüger,' Schweinhardt said, his voice reverberating in the hollow space. 'I hope you find that your *friend* in the West is well.' He glanced at Hans to make sure he caught the implication.

What an ass.

Wolfgang stepped out onto the street, eager for fresh air and closed the door behind him. Schweinhardt was a petty tyrant, best ignored. But he hoped Schweinhardt's order to let that teenager bleed to death at the wall would come back to bite him someday.

Wolfgang lit a cigarette, replacing one bad taste with another. The sky looked like hammered tin and a sudden gust blew street dust into his eyes. A storm was brewing. He pulled his cap down and walked toward home, leaning into a strong west wind.

111

CHAPTER 10

After the rainstorm, Wolfgang changed into civilian clothes and went out again. The clouds had broken up and the sky was clearing. Tonight the wet streets would freeze into a thin skin of ice, but for now it was sunny and almost mild, a welcome break in a week of gray weather.

He carried with him a shopping bag containing tea, bread and sausage that he'd bought the day before. Most shops were closed on Sunday, but several blocks from his flat there was a *Konditorei* that was open a while in the afternoon. The chime of tiny bells announced his entrance, and a sugary aroma curled out to meet him.

Wolfgang was a regular customer here. Frau Hefke, the ample mistress, greeted him cheerfully while she tallied the purchase of another customer. *'Guten Tag*, Herr Vopo. One moment!'

'Danke,' he said. 'No hurry.'

When Frau Hefke had finished with her other customer, he ordered three small cakes, individual portions, to take with him. Frau Hefke slipped an extra one into the bag and winked.

'A small gift for Gisela's grandson,' she said. 'Tell them I said hello.'

Wolfgang thanked her and paid for his purchase. He put it in the bag with the good bratwurst he'd bought at one of the restricted butcher shops accessible to government officials and Party leaders. He rarely took advantage of the special outlets, but he knew that Gisela, on her widow's pension, bought meat for only two or three meals each week. She would enjoy a good bratwurst.

Back on the sidewalk with his purchases, he wondered whether little Stefan could manage to eat sausage. On Wolfgang's last visit, Gisela had proudly shown him the boy's two new bottom teeth. He'd felt silly trying to look inside the baby's mouth, but apparently such events were significant to a grandmother.

A block from the market he turned down a familiar street that led to Gisela's apartment building. He and Rolf had played along this street when they were bony little boys with nothing but fun on their minds. More than once Wolfgang had looked up to see Gisela's face in the second-story window keeping an eye on them, or calling them inside for milk and sweet bread fresh from her oven.

Rolf's home had been a gathering place in those days, full of friends and visiting relatives, noisy as a tavern. There was always something cooking in the kitchen. Wolfgang had managed to keep outside the sticky whirlwind of hugging and kissing in that house, but the familial exuberance was fascinating to a boy whose academic parents included him in discussions of Goethe at dinner but rarely touched him at all.

The neighborhood was quiet today, no sounds but distant traffic and the slap of his footsteps on the sidewalk. A shaft of sunlight broke through, and in its spotlight he saw a different Sunday afternoon, alive with the echoes of little boys shouting, running after a ball with their sticks. It was 1938, a year before the war began, the year before induction into the Hitler Youth became compulsory. Already Hitler's Youth Law had decreed his child army to be as important as school or home, but Wolfgang's parents had managed to keep him out because he was so young. By age ten, he was being pressured at school, even ridiculed, for not belonging. His father had managed to secure a post at a university in Sweden, where his mother's family lived, and later that year they would move.

But on that sunny Sunday in spring, he and Rolf ran amok down the sidewalks in front of Rolf's building, unaffected by the rumbling of world events. Ernst Klein was playing stick ball with them. Wolfgang stood half a head taller than Ernst, who was Rolf's age and even smaller. So when three other boys approached, swaggering with Hitler Youth entitlement, Ernst was the first to sense trouble. He backed up several steps, his freckles standing out in bas-relief on his white face.

Rolf and Wolfgang had stood their ground, sticks hanging from their slack arms, more surprised than frightened to see strangers in the neighborhood.

'We want to play,' the largest boy said. One of the others grabbed up the hard rubber ball that belonged to Rolf and tossed it from one hand to another.

The leader was at least thirteen, Wolfgang assessed, with a shadow of puberty on his upper lip and a good thirty pounds on Wolfgang. 'Give us

114

your sticks,' the kid said, and reached out his arm.

Rolf, more street-hardened than Wolfgang, took issue. 'Get your own sticks.'

'Why should we do that when we can have yours?' the big kid said.

He made a grab at Rolf's arm and Rolf jerked away. 'Get your own!' he yelled, and brandished his stick above his head. 'And give us back our ball.'

The boy with the ball stepped toward him. 'How come you don't have blue eyes, boy?' His own were lake-blue, and far too hard for a child's. 'Are you a Jew kid?' And in a quick, unexpected movement, the boy drew back his arm and threw the ball hard at Rolf's head.

It hit Rolf in the nose. He couldn't even scream. His eyes glazed and crossed slightly, and Wolfgang was pretty sure that for a moment Rolf didn't know where he was. He lifted one hand to catch the blood flowing down his chin. Ernst threw down his stick and ran.

Wolfgang still remembered the rush of fear and anger as he stepped forward on his left foot and swung with his right arm. He'd never been in a fight before, but he knew instinctively to go for the leader. Pain shot through his fist when it connected with the big kid's chin. He aimed his other fist for a softer spot in the boy's middle, and the kid folded over.

Immediately the two other boys were on him. One jumped on his back, the other swung his arms like a windmill, landing blows that missed as often as they connected. Wolfgang covered his head, but from the corner of his eye he saw Rolf running toward the door to his apartment building.

I'm on my own, he thought. *Against three of them.*

The boy on his back was trying to pin his arms. Wolfgang shook him off, but the leader had got his breath again and his face was ruddy with rage. He ran toward Wolfgang and butted him in the stomach, sending all four of them into a pile on the street. Wolfgang kicked and bucked, but he was overmatched and thought quite possibly they would beat him to death.

Suddenly Rolf was there again. Blood leaked from his nose and stained his teeth red. He held a long-handled garden hoe raised against the sky. Wolfgang saw the dull metal blade chop downward toward the boy who was straddling him. The kid screamed and fell away. The other two stopped pommeling him. Rolf swung the hoe in a horizontal arc and they scrambled away. The backswing caught Wolfgang on the forearm as he struggled to his feet.

Rolf lunged with the hoe at the astonished boys. 'Get off my street!'

Wolfgang stood beside him, his fists clenched, throbbing in a dozen places.

The three boys backed away and finally turned, casting glances behind them as they loped down the street. At that moment, Gisela and Rolf's father had come running out of their house, yelling threats at the retreating boys. *We're in big trouble*, Wolfgang had thought. But Rolf's face opened in a wide red grin.

On his forearm, Wolfgang still carried a small crescent scar from the garden hoe. It was shaped exactly like Rolf's bloody smile.

116

These days the street looked more run-down, Wolfgang thought, but perhaps it had always been this way and he was simply too young to notice. The building where Gisela lived had been damaged in the war but not destroyed, and she had not moved out even while repairs were being made. Wolfgang climbed the creaking stairs to her apartment and tapped his signature rhythm on the door.

He heard the child's voice from inside, then Gisela's heavy, uneven steps. She'd had the limp as long as he'd known her, but it never slowed her down. He stood in front of the peephole in the door where she could see him, and heard the latch retract.

The door swung open and Gisela smiled. '*Hallo*, Wolfgang. What a nice surprise.'

'I should have called first.'

She waved away his apology. 'Come in, come in. We are always glad for company.'

He stepped inside. Stefan sat on the living room floor, toy cars scattered around him. The boy looked at him with alert brown eyes that pricked Wolfgang's chest. *Rolf's eyes.*

'*Hallo*, Stefan,' he said.

The boy stared at him. 'Unh?'

Wolfgang wondered if a child that age would remember him from previous visits. He had no idea.

Gisela shut the door. 'Come and sit down. I will make tea.'

'I brought some tea, in fact,' he said, smiling. 'And a few other things I hope you can use.'

117

'You will have to quit spoiling us,' she said, but she took the bag from him and led the way to the kitchen.

'How are you getting along?' he asked.

'Fine, just a bit of arthritis. The rain aggravates it.'

Indeed, her limp seemed more pronounced today. She set the bag on the cabinet and moved to light a fire under the teakettle. Wolfgang set out the tea leaves he'd brought, the sausage and bread. 'I thought the little one might like a cake.'

'*Ach!* He'll love it. Then run around all day like a wild monkey.'

She laughed and called toward the living room. 'Stefan! Want something sweet to eat?'

A line of gibberish came in answer and Gisela smiled. 'Believe it or not, I can usually understand what he means.'

In seconds, to Wolfgang's astonishment, Stefan came toddling into the kitchen. He knew, of course, that the child could walk, but had not seen him do it. He seemed far too tiny, his feet no longer than Wolfgang's palm. Gisela pushed his highchair close to the table and Wolfgang picked him up.

Stefan's face grew still, watching him. The boy was solid as a stump, heavier than Wolfgang expected. No wonder Gisela looked tired. Wolfgang slid the boy's legs into the highchair and adjusted the tray. 'There you go,' he said.

The dark eyes fastened on Wolfgang's face. Suspicious. 'Unh?'

Gisela handed Wolfgang a small cloth with strings attached. He looked at it in his hand.

'Surely you know what to do with a bib,' she said, teasing.

'Of course.' Now that she'd told him what it was.

Stefan stopped wiggling while Wolfgang placed the bib on his chest and fumbled with the strings behind his neck. The child smelled like talcum powder and shampoo. When Wolfgang finished tying, he risked stroking Stefan's head, petting him like a puppy. The curly hair felt soft as spider webs.

Gisela cut one of the cakes in half and handed the saucer to Wolfgang. He set the saucer on Stefan's tray. *'Kuchen!'*

Stefan clapped his hands. *'Uchen!'* he echoed, and finally favored Wolfgang with a smile.

Wolfgang sat in a chair next to him. 'He is bigger every time I see him.'

Gisela nodded. 'And a climber, too. Just like Rolf was.'

She set the old Delft teapot on the table with two cups and saucers. His grandmother had owned a set almost like it. Gisela offered Wolfgang a cake but he shook his head.

'Just the tea, *Danke.*'

'This is a treat,' she said, sitting down. 'We don't usually have sweets.' She and Stefan took bites of cake and grinned at each other. Stefan sucked the crumbs from his fingers. 'Ach,' Gisela said. 'I forgot to wash his hands.'

'My mother used to say every child has to eat his pound of dirt.'

The teakettle whistled and he motioned her to stay put. 'Let me get that.' He poured hot water into the teapot and sat down again.

'Stefan,' Gisela said, in her teaching voice, 'this is Wolfgang.' She pointed to him. 'Wolf-gang.'

'Unh?'

She pointed to each of them in turn. 'Stefan, *Oma*, Wolfgang.'

'*Oma!*' Stefan sang, and crammed another bite of cake into his mouth.

She shrugged. 'Some things take time.'

When the tea had steeped sufficiently, Gisela poured. Steam curled up from the cups, and they watched Stefan demolish his treat. Finally she asked the question he'd known she would. 'You have news of Trudy?'

He glanced at the child, wondering how much a one-year-old understood. 'Just today. She is staying at a place on Muhlenstraße in the American Sector.'

Gisela nodded, sighed. 'So she knows about Rolf?'

'I'm sure she does by now.' Then he added, 'The message said she is working at a *Gasthaus*.'

'The poor girl must be miserable. Stefan was her reason for living.' Gisela shook her head, and her voice turned hard. 'First the Gestapo, now the Stasi. Tell me how we are better off.'

He would not talk politics with her. 'The afternoon has turned mild,' he said. 'If you feel up to walking, I thought we might take Stefan to the park.'

'He would love that. We did not go out this week because of the rain.'

She pushed herself up from the table and took a bottle of pills from a cupboard. 'Aspirin. To

120

loosen my joints.'

'Maybe you should see a doctor.'

She shrugged it off. 'You wait and wait and wait in line, and then the doctor tells you to take aspirin. I can do that by myself.' She drew a glass of water and swallowed two pills.

The park was three blocks away and they walked slowly. Wolfgang pushed the baby's stroller, but even so, Gisela's breath grated through her open lips. His grandfather had sounded like that, the year before he caught pneumonia and died.

'You should get yourself checked by a doctor,' he told her again. 'If there is no neighbor you trust to watch Stefan, I can take off a day.'

'Stop worrying. I have stiff joints because I'm sixty-four. And this one,' she flicked the tassel on Stefan's knitted cap, 'is a full-time job. There is a reason God made women my age unable to have children.' She chuckled, and her face looked content. 'I am lucky to have him. We get along just fine.'

A man leading a large reddish dog on a leash came down the sidewalk toward them. Stefan lurched forward in his seat, pointing. 'Wuff! Wuff!'

'Yes,' Gisela said. 'The dog says *wuff wuff.*'

The dog trotted past and Stefan twisted in his chair to watch it go. Then he looked up and pointed at Wolfgang. 'Wuff wuff!'

All three of them laughed. 'Close enough,' Wolfgang said.

While Gisela installed herself on a park bench with her knitting, Wolfgang pushed Stefan in a swing that had a safety bridge across the front. He started gently, but the boy was fearless. He

121

kicked his legs and squealed to go higher. They stayed at the swing a long time before he was ready to move on.

Wolfgang lifted him out and Stefan urged them toward a rocking duck mounted on a huge spring and bolted to the ground. The toy seemed precarious and there was no safety belt. But Stefan was insistent, so Wolfgang held him on the seat of the duck's back, while Stefan grabbed the wooden handles and gyrated dangerously, squealing.

So much energy, and no fear of getting hurt. How did Gisela keep up with him?

The rain had formed a moat around the merry-go-round, so when Stefan tired of the rocking duck, Wolfgang took him back to the swing. But the boy's eyes looked sleepy, and Wolfgang suspected Gisela had sat long enough on the hard bench. He stopped the swing and lifted Stefan out. Gisela enticed him into his stroller with a bottle of milk. She tucked a blanket in around his legs, and he was asleep before they'd gone a block from the park.

The sun hung low above the rooftops now, and the air had grown cooler. Gisela turned up the collar of her coat and held it closed at the neck where a button was missing. Wolfgang noticed the frayed edges of her sleeves. He would buy her a coat and have it wrapped as a gift. Otherwise, she wouldn't accept.

They walked slowly, each of them with one hand on the stroller. 'You must tell me if you need things,' Wolfgang said.

Gisela nodded. 'What I need is a letter from Trudy. Does mail come through from West Berlin these days?'

'It goes out more dependably than it comes in. Incoming mail from the West is opened at random, which slows everything down. But it's usually not intercepted.'

'Can you find out her address, so I can write to her?'

'I can try.' He had no way to contact Henri Bremmer now. 'But I'm sure she will send it to you soon.'

They were quiet then. The wheels of the stroller clattered rhythmically on the sidewalk. Wolfgang watched a flock of pigeons wheel against the sky, seeking shelter in an abandoned building.

Gisela took a labored breath, her gaze on the sidewalk ahead. 'And Rolf's body? What became of my son's body?'

Wolfgang's jaw clenched. There was something fundamentally wrong with a woman like Gisela having lost so much. He pictured a cemetery in the *Grunewald*, the sprawling greenbelt on the western outskirts of the city, and a newspaper photo of a flowered wreath atop a fresh grave. He wondered if Trudy had discovered where her husband was buried, and whom she blamed for his death.

'Rolf was given a hero's burial. Beside others who were killed at the wall.' He was glad this was the truth.

Gisela nodded slowly and the stroller clattered on. 'Good,' she said. 'Someday Stefan will be able to visit his father's grave. Even if I cannot.'

Perhaps, Wolfgang thought. Unless this wall outlives all of us.

123

CHAPTER 11

When Wolfgang first met Trudy Reitz, she was a scared rabbit tucked between Rolf and another college student in the booth of a noisy *Gasthaus*. Later he couldn't even remember her name, just the impression of a skinny girl with overlarge eyes in a pale face. He hadn't realized until he saw her with Rolf again that she was Rolf's girlfriend.

Then she turned up in one of his classes, an upper level course in Russian language. When he walked in, she was already sitting in a chair near the wall, close to the front. She wore her hair long and straight, pulled back loosely behind her neck and tied with a scarf. He wasn't sure it was Trudy until he heard her voice.

In the classroom, the scared rabbit was gone, her responses quick and confident. One day he spoke to her as they were leaving.

'You're younger than I am, yet you're in the advanced language class?'

Her face flushed. When she smiled, a light came on in her eyes. 'I've studied Russian for several years. My major is Modern Languages, so I'm taking Latin and English, too.'

He fell into step beside her. 'I can't imagine keeping that many languages sorted out in my head. I'm studying Russian only to prepare myself for the academy in Moscow.'

'You're leaving Berlin?'

124

'I've been offered an opportunity for advanced military studies. But my Russian pronunciation sounds like something from a bad film. Would you mind being my partner for the oral exercises?'

'Not at all, if the professor agrees.'

Trudy got the best marks in the class. Wolfgang learned more about the structure of the Russian language from Trudy than from the professor. Occasionally they studied together, with Rolf at the other end of the library table reading art history.

Wolfgang began to watch her, unconsciously at first, when she joined Rolf's late-night debate sessions. Wolfgang had no family in Berlin, and the grandfather he idolized had died that year unexpectedly. His grandfather's death gouged out a hollow place that he couldn't seem to fill, not even with the ambition to make his life count for something that *Opa* had instilled in him. Wolfgang thought he recognized in Trudy, an orphan of the war, a kindred sense of loss.

Sometimes on those occasions he tried to draw her into whatever discussion was underway. She would shake her head, her smile turning shy in Rolf's presence. If she had opinions, she kept them to herself. And finally Wolfgang saw Rolf looking at him curiously, so he cut it out. She was Rolf's girl, after all.

The night before he left for Moscow, a haunting loneliness drove him out of his Spartan room and onto the street. He was twenty-three and had been on his own for four years. But that night the unknown loomed before him like a child's fear of the dark space under the bed. Wolfgang had never visited the Soviet Union before, and he still felt inadequate in the language. Only because he loved Germany and wanted to make a difference in its future had he agreed to go. His selection for the Soviet school was an honor, but he dreaded spending two years in a country where Germans had so recently been the enemy.

If he'd been more of a drinker, undoubtedly he would have gotten drunk that night. Instead, he sought out the closest thing to family – Rolf and Gisela Hulst. Rolf had transferred to the so-called *Free University* in the American Sector of Berlin that semester, and moved back to his mother's house. Wolfgang hadn't seen Rolf or Trudy for weeks. But on this melancholy evening, he was struck with the need to say goodbye to someone who might care.

Wolfgang had no telephone, so he walked the two kilometers to the Hulst apartment in Prenzlauer Berg without calling. It was a cold spring evening, already dark but not late. A dusting of fresh snow laced the small patches of grass along the sidewalks and left the streets damp. He had not visited Rolf's old house since returning to Berlin after the war. Without working street lamps, the neighborhood looked much the same, and he found that reassuring. He climbed the stairs and rapped on the door. Even if Rolf wasn't at home, surely Gisela was, and it would be good to see her again.

But instead of Rolf or Gisela, Trudy opened the door.

'*Hallo*,' he said, and removed his cap.

'Wolfgang.' She looked as surprised as he was.

126

For an awkward moment, he forgot why he was there.

'I came to say goodbye,' he said finally. 'I leave for Moscow in the morning.'

'Oh!' She frowned. 'Rolf will be sorry he missed you. He has gone–' she hesitated '–to a meeting.'

'Ah.' Wolfgang nodded, shifted from one leg to the other. 'And Frau Hulst?'

'Still at work.'

She stood uncertainly in the doorway, and Wolfgang thought she looked different somehow, more mature. She had filled out since he'd last seen her, and her skin held the glow of good health. Suddenly aware that he was staring, he glanced down at his worn shoes.

'Do you want to come in?' she asked.

He did want to; he wanted to sit in the familiar house and warm himself in the shine of her hair. Perhaps he could ask if she ever felt like a hot-air balloon without sandbags, groundless and adrift.

'No, *Danke*,' he said. 'I should go home.'

But he made no move to go away and she leaned against the door, reading him with hazel eyes. 'I thought you wanted to go to Russia.'

'I do.' He smiled, wadding the knitted cap in his hands. 'But the winters there are cold and long.'

She shrugged. 'They are cold and long in Berlin, too.'

Yes, but you have Rolf. And Rolf has you. He has outdone me once again.

Wolfgang straightened, pulled on his cap. 'Please say goodbye to Rolf and Gisela for me. I wish all of you the best.'

'The same to you,' she said. 'Good luck in

127

Moscow. *Guten Nacht.*'

She was already closing the door as he turned away.

During the two years Wolfgang stayed in Moscow, especially when he lay awake on the narrow mattress filled with something that felt like dry corn husks, he often thought of that night and wondered what might have happened if he had accepted her invitation to come inside.

But the truth was that nothing would have changed. He still would have gone to Russia, and she would have married Rolf while he was gone.

The summer before Rolf was killed, a year after the surprise construction of a wall around West Berlin, Wolfgang had come to a crossroads in his career with the *Volkspolizei*. He was being mentioned for promotion to lieutenant-general, the second-highest rank in the entire *Volkspolizei*. When he'd returned from Moscow and accepted a job with the Berlin Presidium of the People's Police, he had viewed it as a stepping stone to the politburo. But the more he saw of the Russian influence on East German political affairs, the less he desired to become involved in Party politics. He wanted to serve the German people more directly, not to separate himself from the working class that was the backbone of society. He came to believe he could best serve his fellow Germans by remaining with the *Volkspolizei*.

Over a period of years, his political ambitions had drained away, but not his desire to rise in his chosen field. The lieutenant-general of *Volks-*

128

polizei functioned as the chief of staff who oversaw all police operations. Wolfgang wanted that promotion. As lieutenant-general, he would be in a position to influence decisions regarding law enforcement, and to suggest policy changes that would benefit the people.

To ensure his selection, he needed to demonstrate some special initiative – a small coup in the pursuit of state security. He was thinking about that on the night Nadia offered up Rolf's name to protect her worthless brother.

They were lying in bed late at night, smoking. Nadia had been quieter than usual all evening. She lay with one arm bent behind her head, the sheet covering her breasts just below the soft mat of golden hair under her arm. He watched the ash from her cigarette grow dangerously long.

'I have a piece of information,' she said, her eyes on the ceiling.

He was half listening, his blood still warm from lovemaking. He reached out and caught the cigarette ash in his cupped palm.

'I want to use it to shield Rainer,' she said. 'To make the police leave him alone. Can you make that happen?'

Her younger brother, in Wolfgang's opinion, wasn't worth saving. He had been in trouble for several minor infractions, and now he was suspected of belonging to an underground resistance movement. Nadia continued to protect him for her parents' sake. She'd told him her mother doted on Rainer, made excuses for him because he was charming.

'I don't know,' he said, drafting on the Caro, its

129

tip glowing red-orange in the dark. 'What kind of information?'

'A name. A man who's been organizing escape routes through the wall.'

And still he didn't realize the awful choice she was about to lay before him.

'The head of the underground?' he said, interested now. 'How do you know this?'

'Never mind how I know.'

From her brother, of course. Rainer had been questioned about the underground before and was probably still under surveillance. Wolfgang doubted Rainer would be involved in any enterprise that didn't benefit him personally; he was likely planning his own defection.

'Tell them this is a trade,' Nadia said, and he wondered who she thought of as *them*. 'I can give them the name, but I must have assurance that they'll leave Rainer alone. I need him to keep his job.'

Wolfgang retrieved an ash tray from the bedside table and set it on his chest. 'I don't know who is after your brother. If it's coming from the *Grenzpolizei*,' he said, thinking of Schweinhardt, the Grepo commandant, 'I can help. If it is the Stasi,' he paused, 'I can't make promises. You understand?'

'Yes. But will you try? Will you promise to try?'

He waited a moment before answering, thinking he'd rather not get involved in Rainer's problems, thinking maybe he owed it to her. And, of course, he was curious. Did she really know who had organized recent defections to the West?

'All right,' he said. 'What is the name?'

130

Nadia inhaled, expelled a stream of smoke toward the ceiling. 'Rolf Hulst. He worked in the American Sector until the wall went up. Now he's out of a job.'

He didn't hear anything she said after Rolf's name.

Wolfgang had suspected Rolf's involvement in the underground. But as long as he didn't know for sure, he could leave it alone. Nadia, un-knowingly, had forced his hand. She'd presented him a Faustian choice: a coveted advance in his career at the price of sacrificing his oldest friend.

The day after she told him, Wolfgang had phoned someone he knew who would do private inquiries and could keep his mouth shut. It didn't take much investigation to find evidence that Rolf had indeed helped arrange illegal passage of DDR citizens into West Berlin.

Wolfgang's duty was clear. Rolf was committing illegal acts against the state. Rolf was also the closest thing he'd ever had to a brother.

For three days he brooded, besieged by con-science and memories. Strangely, the image that recurred most often was of a girlish Trudy Reitz, framed in a doorway with lamplight on her hair. The memory was inappropriate; it had nothing to do with his decision. And yet he could not forget the bond of loneliness reflected in her eyes.

Finally, with time nearing for selection of the next lieutenant-general, Wolfgang planted an information leak. Through an internal source he suspected of subversive connections, he let it be known that the head of the underground was about to be arrested. He waited forty-eight hours for the warning to trickle through the tangled channels of underground communication. Then he reported Rolf's name to the outgoing lieutenant-general of *Volkspolizei*.

Like a clockwork god, he had set events in motion and let them play out on their own. Both the leak and the key information he supplied to his superior worked as planned. Rolf received the warning; Wolfgang got his promotion. The single flaw was Rolf's death at the wall. Wolfgang had expected him to get through the border unharmed, as he'd helped so many others to do.

Guilt was a poison he refused to ingest. And yet, on a cold day in February when Wolfgang left Vopo headquarters with confirmation of his upcoming promotion in his coat pocket, it occurred to him that turning Rolf in was the only action he'd ever taken that would disappoint his grandfather. Not because *Opa* would have defended Rolf's illegal actions, and not even because of the old friendship. But because Wolfgang used the information to further his personal ambition – exactly the kind of egotism *Opa* had cited as the reason pure communism would fail.

Wolfgang lit up a Caro and blew out a stream of smoke. Men and their governments were imperfect creatures, and he was no exception. But if ambition played a part in his choice to identify Rolf, so had larger motives. He had acted according to his sworn duty, and out of loyalty to his beliefs.

Ironically, he thought as he walked home, Rolf was the one man who would have understood.

CHAPTER 12

From the window of his second-story office, Grepo *Obermeister* Albrecht Schweinhardt watched Wolfgang Krüger light his cigarette and disappear down the quiet street. Krüger had been in the library again – twice in two weeks. That called for another entry in Schweinhardt's journal.

Albrecht turned away from the window and went back to his desk. From the bottom of a locked drawer, he pulled out a black notebook and placed it in the exact center of the vacant desktop. He took a black pen from its holder, leafed to an empty page in the notebook and jotted down the date and time.

Genosse Krüger continues his habit of reading the decadent West Berlin newspapers. He does this surreptitiously, hiding his actions from fellow officers.

Years ago the *Volkspolizei* had been purged of any man who had relatives or a former residence in the West. Schweinhardt thought it was time for another such purge. In recent years, recruiting officers in East Berlin had become so difficult that standards were relaxed, and sometimes men had to be conscripted. The result was a predictable dilution of discipline. And discipline was the only thing that stood between order and chaos.

Wolfgang Krüger wasn't conscripted, though.

133

He'd been handpicked by the Soviets and had volunteered for the *Volkspolizei*. The idiots around him thought his *Scheiße* didn't stink. Just yesterday Schweinhardt had heard a ranking officer in the *Volkspolizei* comment that Vopo Krüger would make an excellent lieutenant-general.

'I would not say excellent,' Albrecht had told him acidly. 'Excellent is a word reserved for very few. It is not a word to describe a man with divided loyalties.'

'What do you mean? Krüger is devoted to his job.'

'Genosse Krüger has sympathies for the West.' He didn't say more; let the dullard draw his own conclusions.

Albrecht was sick of hearing such comments, from supervisors and foot patrolmen alike. He added another sentence to his journal entry.

Krüger continues his weekly visits to the mother and son of the criminal Rolf Hulst – supplying aid and comfort to the family of an enemy of the state.

The last fact he had not observed in person. It was supplied by one of the myriad civilians who served as spies for the Stasi. Albrecht had comrades in the Stasi who were willing to share their informants. Some of the civilian spies were voluntary, but this particular informant was one of the reluctant ones. Nevertheless, under pressure, she'd been quite useful in the matter of Wolfgang Krüger.

Albrecht paused a moment, considering whether there was some embellishment he could add to his notes to make the facts more compelling. He decided against it. Better to let it stand as it was; everything here was true. He replaced the pen in its marble stand and leafed back through the pages.

Every time he made a new entry, he reread Krüger's complete record, assessing whether his book yet contained sufficient evidence to ruin Krüger's persistent rise through the ranks. Given Krüger's popularity among Party leaders, Albrecht couldn't risk bringing the information forward prematurely or it might backfire.

He himself had spent fifteen years as a Vopo and twice had been passed over for promotion. Only by effecting a transfer to the *Grenzpolizei* had he managed to keep his career from stagnating without the rank he deserved. Now young Krüger, the darling of the Kremlin, was to be the next lieutenant-general, second in command of the entire police force. Albrecht suspected that Krüger was being groomed for the top position, and the thought was almost too much to bear.

He took two antacid tablets from his desk drawer and popped them in his mouth. The pills tasted bitter and chalky, but they quelled the burning in his gut.

He should have transferred to the secret police, instead. One had to admire the thoroughness of the Stasi machine, which kept watch on every aspect of DDR life through its growing network of informants. His own skills might be better suited to being a Stasi officer than to remaining as commandant of the border police, where he was set up for dishonor by the continued breaches of the wall. His note-books could be the key to accomplishing a lateral transfer, if the need arose. He would not be disgraced again.

The first entry in his notebook dated back more than five years, shortly after Krüger had been assigned under his command. Comrade Krüger had objected when Albrecht severely disciplined a young Vopo. Quick and harsh punishment was the only way to maintain discipline; but Krüger thought the punishment was disproportionate to the infraction and had the temerity to challenge his superior officer.

It did him no good, of course. Rank has its privilege.

The next entry documented a time Albrecht had decided to mend the gap with Krüger and invited him for a drink. Krüger had refused. To decline the invitation of a superior officer was an insult and a flagrant breach of protocol. The notebook also contained details about Krüger's sexual habits, but those notes were too mundane to be helpful. Nobody cared if an officer had a mistress, as long as she wasn't some other officer's wife.

A click from the office wall heralded five o'clock, and a pair of painted cuckoos erupted from two wooden clocks. He paused a moment to enjoy the raucous music and the precision of their voices in unison. He had considered hanging another clock for a noisier chorus; but three was an odd number, and odd numbers worried him. At home, he had covered an entire wall with his collection of twenty-two cuckoo clocks, some of them exquisitely carved. But he wanted the spareness of his office to serve as a model of self-discipline to his coworkers. Other than the clocks, the room contained only a metal desk and filing cabinet, two wooden chairs and a coatrack beside the door. No pictures or personal mementos cluttered his workspace.

When the cuckoos stopped, he closed the notebook and removed his VS bag from beneath the desk. He slid the notebook inside the leather valise and closed the double latches. The VS bag went with him from home to work every day, even when it had nothing inside. Like his uniform, the valise distinguished him at a glance from lower-ranking Grepos.

Albrecht locked his desk and closed the blinds on the single window. He touched the tip of his finger to one slat of the blinds and felt the grit of dust between his thumb and finger. Tomorrow he would call the custodian to task.

He took his uniform coat from the rack and sucked in his stomach to fasten the jacket's buttons. He gave the cuffs of each shirt sleeve a firm tug and put on his topcoat. Adjusting his cap, he turned off the lights and locked the office door behind him.

In the reception area, the chubby-faced youth behind the desk snapped a salute and stood at attention when Albrecht walked past. That boy had possibilities. Albrecht returned the salute and walked out into the winter evening.

The temperature was unseasonably mild and he began to perspire almost immediately. He ignored the discomfort, because an officer should not remove his coat on the street. Albrecht walked briskly, looking neither right nor left, and by the time he arrived at the restaurant on Prenzlauer Allee, his shirt stuck to his armpits.

The *Gasthaus* was small and free of undesirable elements, probably because many Vopos and Grepos took their meals here. Albrecht walked directly to his usual table in a back corner and set his VS bag on an empty chair. He pulled off his topcoat, hung it on the back of the same chair and sat down.

At this hour the restaurant was nearly empty. He liked to arrive early so that he didn't feel he was on display while he ate. Albrecht glanced around the *Gasthaus*, looking for a particular young waitress. Instead, a fleshy middle-aged woman approached and laid a menu on the table. Her appearance repulsed him, and apparently the feeling was mutual. When he ordered his customary pot of tea, the woman's face looked as if she'd sipped sour milk.

When she brought the tea, he said, '*Fräulein* Fischer usually serves me. Is she here?'

The woman stared at him. '*Fräulein* Fischer is occupied.'

He looked away from her without opening the menu. 'I'll have today's special.'

'Who would have guessed.' The floor shook as she slouched away.

When the waitress was out of sight, Albrecht relaxed and poured his tea. He wondered if *Fräulein* Fischer had seen him come in and was hiding in the back to avoid him. No matter. He would deal with that later.

He leaned back in his chair and sipped the fragrant tea. His evening routine stretched before him, predictable and comforting. He felt almost content until the surly waitress appeared again, bringing out his dinner. She set the dishes before him without speaking and moved away.

The special that evening was a thick vegetable soup, flavored with meat broth. He considered whether he could eat it knowing the waitress might have touched the food, but he was very hungry. He tucked his napkin in the collar of his uniform shirt and added copious amounts of salt and pepper to the soup.

He ate without looking up. When the vegetables were gone, he cleaned the empty bowl with hunks of bread. The waitress brought unsweetened applesauce for dessert, but he sent it away and ordered a slice of pound cake and more tea.

It was hard to enjoy his cake with that repugnant woman hulking from table to table in the dining room. There was a callousness in her eyes that reminded him of his sister Karla, whom he hadn't seen in years. She was his only sibling, two years older. Karla wasn't heavy like the waitress – in fact, she was wiry and thin – but her body was filled with a corpulent evil. By the age of fourteen she was taking men into her bedroom regularly in the afternoons, before their father came home from work. If his father ever knew, he ignored the fact, and Albrecht knew better than to tell. His father never hit Karla – only Albrecht. He didn't want to know why.

When he was fifteen, Karla had tried to seduce him – her own brother. That incident had taught him the wickedness of the female sex, and he'd avoided them ever since. He avoided Karla by running off to join the army, lying about his age. In this way he escaped both his debauched sister and regular thrashings from his father.

In a twisted way Karla had done him a favor, he thought now, because in the army he had distinguished himself and found a home. Even the shrapnel wound in his thigh that kept him incapacitated for most of the war turned out to be lucky; otherwise, he might have been too closely identified with the Nazis and suffered the consequences. Even now he had to keep quiet about his former military service.

Albrecht finished his tea and trapped the last crumbs of his cake in the tines of his fork. The waitress came and laid his check on the table.

'Send *Fräulein* Fischer to me,' he ordered, keeping his voice quiet.

'I think she went home.'

'I think not.' He gave the woman a threatening look. 'I will not leave until I speak with her.'

The woman scowled and turned away. She disappeared through a doorway that led to the kitchen.

In less than a minute, *Fräulein* Fischer appeared. She approached his table, her face like stone. *Fräulein* Fischer was the opposite of the other waitress in every way, slim and pretty, her hair shiny as silk. The perfect little informant.

'What do you want?' she said.

'That is not a pleasant greeting, *Fräulein*,' he chided, but she said nothing else. 'What have you seen of our mutual friend recently?'

'I have not seen him.'

'Do not lie to me.'

140

'I'm not lying. He hasn't come in for two weeks.'

'When you do see him,' Albrecht said, glancing at his check, 'find out what he is looking for in the West Berlin newspapers.'

The girl frowned. 'I cannot ask that. I have never seen him read a Western newspaper.'

'He reads them at Vopo headquarters. He is looking for something and I want to know what it is.' He fished in his pocket and extracted a fistful of coins to pay for his dinner. 'You will find a way.' he said. 'For your family's sake.'

A quick glint of fear – or perhaps anger – lashed in her eyes. She turned and stalked back toward the kitchen, mumbling something under her breath. It sounded like *Schweinehunde*, but couldn't be sure. He chose to ignore it.

Albrecht placed three deutschmarks on top of his check on the table, leaving no tip for the surly waitress. He put on his coat and hat and went out.

At the corner, he bought a newspaper, then walked the six blocks to his apartment at a leisurely pace that was good for digestion. He inserted the key in the lock and checked his watch before pushing the door open. Precisely seven o'clock. Perfect.

His arrival was announced by a twenty-two-cuckoo salute. He stopped in the doorway, listening to the variant tones and muted squeaking of springs as the tiny birds poked in and out of their wooden holes.

Was one of them a fraction behind the others? He frowned, isolating the sound. When the chorus stopped, he flipped on the light and went directly to a small, intricately carved timepiece

141

imported from Switzerland. He removed it from the wall and, using a tiny screwdriver he kept in his pocket, made a minute adjustment to the mechanism. It would be an hour before he knew if the adjustment was accurate.

Albrecht hung up his coat and removed his boots in favor of soft slippers. He switched on a reading lamp and poured himself a cognac. In public he made a point to drink Russian vodka, but at home he savored a good cognac, rolling the amber liquor around the bottom of the glass to enjoy its bouquet. He gathered his newspaper, his drink and a fireproof metal box from the cabinet below his bookshelf and carried them to his favorite chair beside the lamp.

The chair's cushions remembered his shape. He settled in and lifted his feet onto the footstool. From a drawer in the end table, he took out his box of special cigars, an indulgence he obtained from a private source. He seldom watched television and he never had visitors. But he did enjoy a good imported cigar. He selected one, clipped off the tip and lit up.

For half an hour he smoked and read his newspaper. There was more Party doctrine than actual news in it, and that was good. He understood the need for controlling information made available in the public media; most ordinary citizens were not equipped to understand current events in the proper context. Albrecht read every word of his paper. When he'd finished, he laid it aside and set the metal box on his lap.

Inside the box lay a half dozen black notebooks like the one from his office. These were filled with observations on any Vopo or Grepo officer he disliked or distrusted. Tonight, though, he was interested only in the two notebooks devoted exclusively to Krüger. He started reading from the beginning.

At eight o'clock, Albrecht stopped to listen to the cacophony of the cuckoos. They were perfectly synchronized; his adjustment had worked. He smiled and went back to his reading.

Taken in one sitting, the records of nearly a decade proved more enlightening than he'd expected. He began to see Wolfgang Krüger in a different light. Krüger was more than an irritation; he had been a persistent obstacle to Albrecht's career. But if Albrecht could discredit the Kremlin's golden boy – show him to be a Western sympathizer and therefore a traitor to the Communist Party – Krüger might be Albrecht's ticket to the rank and influence he'd earned after so many years of loyalty to the DDR. The more impressive Krüger's fall, the greater its value to Albrecht's reputation.

At ten o'clock, his usual bedtime, he stopped his reading to wind his clocks. He began with the top row, as always, moving left to right. Number one was an Austrian-made clock of natural wood color, its cuckoo painted electric blue with an open yellow beak, a tiny pink tongue showing inside. It was the first clock he'd bought, when he was still in the army, and he'd managed to carry it home in his duffle when he was discharged with a cast on his leg. He grasped the sturdy chains that hung in a loop beneath the box of the clock, the two ends weighted with brass pinecones. Gently, he pulled on one chain to wind the clock, moving the brass weight upward almost to the clock's base.

Number two was made in Bavaria, somewhere in the mountains of southern Germany. It was much smaller, the carving so intricately detailed that it never failed to amaze. It was not painted at all, not even the tiny bird with its fountain of head leathers, each one detailed with incredibly thin veins. He admired the sharp fine tip of the knife that had made it, the steadiness of the hand. The chain weights were polished wood, carved with delicate fleur-de-lis.

Numbers three and four were Swiss, fine timepieces, and number five was actually carved in Poland. Six was German, seven was Swiss again, bought in a small shop in Lucerne on the only vacation Albrecht had ever taken, before the border was sealed.

He wound each of them with the pull chains, and that completed the first row. He moved on to the second row, starting again at the left and moving to his right, and then the bottom row. But tonight when he was finished, his mind felt too active to retire just yet. He returned to his chair, replaced the notebooks inside the fireproof box and relit the stump of his cigar.

He propelled a ragged smoke ring into the brown air. Collecting and reporting Krüger's minor deficiencies was taking too long. He needed to catch Krüger in a major mistake – or force him into making one – that was significant enough to knock him from his pedestal in the *Volkspolizei*. Perhaps get rid of him altogether.

144

AMERICA

CHAPTER 13

At the *Gasthaus zur Schwarzen Katze,* Thursday was *Wiener schnitzel* day. Customers crowded the entrance, and the lone busboy couldn't clear the tables fast enough. The aromas of fried veal and parsley potatoes hung thick as rope in the dining room. Amidst the clatter of silverware and occasional bursts of laughter, Trudy squeezed between chairs to deliver three more heaping plates. Strands of hair escaped around her pony-tail and stuck to her damp forehead. And always, just above the steamy redolence, she carried the image of Stefan in her head.

Sometimes she saw him asleep in his crib, his eyelids twitching with dreams; sometimes build-ing a tower with his blocks or toddling toward her with a pink-gummed smile. The ache of missing him was as constant as a phantom limb.

She scooped empty beer glasses from a table and went back for more. Once again she'd managed to get a job where she was on her feet all day, but it was better than cleaning toilets at the textile mill. Counting tips, the pay was better, too.

Verden, the other waitress, shouldered in beside her to pick up an order at the pass-through from the kitchen. 'What about my cigarette break?' Verden groused to the cook.

'That's on Wednesday,' he said, his grizzled face shiny beneath his white cap. 'On Thursday you have to work, for a change.'

The sniping between Verden and the cook had alarmed Trudy at first, until she realized it was simply a way to pass the time during long shifts. Verden and Franz had worked together for years, and they invented new ways daily to insult the other's work.

The lunch crowd spilled over into midafternoon. They barely had time to wipe down the wooden benches and sweep out the crumbs before the retirees began to arrive for early dinner.

'These people eat like pigs and tip like misers,' Verden observed, hauling an armload of dirty dishes into the kitchen.

'Watch out for her,' the cook warned Trudy, 'or she'll be taking the tips off your tables.'

'Are you kidding?' Verden said. 'She would chop off my fingers. She just *looks* innocent.'

Franz winked, and Trudy knew she'd been accepted. Now they'd probably start insulting her, too.

Despite her constant complaints, Verden had been a big help to Trudy during her first days on the job, covering Trudy's mistakes and making suggestions. She was about Trudy's age, slender, and with her hair in a ponytail, they looked enough alike that customers often confused one for the other. But Verden laughed easily – and loudly – and she had two small children at home. When she'd shown Trudy their pictures, the round, smiling faces brought tears to Trudy's eyes. It was two months since she'd seen Stefan, and she was no closer to being with him again than when she'd first arrived in West Berlin.

Waiting tables was hardly the office job she'd hoped for on her first day in the West. But office workers here wore tailored suits or stylish dresses. She couldn't even interview for an office job without new clothes, and clothes required money. At the restaurant, she wore a clean apron that covered her faded dress.

With her first paycheck, she had paid back-rent to Frau Weiss, keeping out only enough for a pair of slippers and a bathrobe, needed for walking down the hallway of the *Pension* to the common bathroom. When her rent was caught up, every spare pfennig would go into a sock under her mattress. Henri Bremmer had said it might be possible to buy Stefan, and Gisela's passage through the wall, and she held on to that hope. But Henri had moved across the city to be closer to his new job, and she hadn't seen him for several weeks. She kept an ear open to customers' conversations, hoping to hear something about wall-breakers, and saved her money.

By nine o'clock that evening, the dinner crowd gave way to the beer-and-snacks patrons, and Verden went home to her family. Trudy refilled salt shakers and wrapped clean silverware in napkins, ready for tomorrow. Herr Blauert, the restaurant owner, was pleased that she did these things without being told. In fact, the only hard part of her job was to keep smiling at the customers, but she managed it because smiling increased her tips.

Near closing, Trudy cleaned the tables and the coffee machine. She said goodnight to Herr Blauert and Franz and retrieved her coat from the back room. On the street, she cinched the coat around her waist and set off walking. She would not waste money on U-Bahn fares.

At midnight, thick clouds blocked out the stars and trapped the glow of city lights. Mounds of dingy snow lined the street gutters, and the cold air was sharp in her lungs. But instead of heading back to her room, she turned her tired feet toward the wall. It was a long walk from the *Gasthaus* to the barriers between East and West Berlin, but she made the pilgrimage almost every night. At the wall she felt closer to Stefan than when she lay awake in her rented room.

The streets near the wall were quiet at this hour, and her footsteps echoed from the shells of abandoned buildings. From one dark interior, an explosion of furious barking sent gooseflesh down her arms. She crossed quickly to the other side of the street, but the watchdog did not come out.

Walking along the ugly line of fortifications, she searched for some weakness, an unguarded link in the chain. Instead she noticed new antitank barricades, steel contraptions that looked like sawhorses with no back legs. Multiple strands of barbed wire looped around them. In some places concrete slabs blocked the view from either side, and these, too, were topped with spiked wire. In the places where she could see across to the eastern side, armed guards patrolled on foot or watched from elevated platforms. Every day the wall became more impenetrable.

Near Potsdamer Platz, a West Berlin Schupo approached. People on the west side didn't fear their policemen, but from habit her breath grew short. They were alone on the quiet street. When

150

he came closer, he touched his cap brim.

'*Guten Abend, Fräulein.* What are you doing out here at this hour?'

She looked at his shadowed eyes. 'My family is over there,' she said, and inclined her head toward the wall.

A muscle in his jaw tightened. For a moment, they both faced the concrete and wire, squinting toward the floodlight beside a watchtower on the other side.

'So is my sister,' he said.

Beneath the tower's angled roof, the barrel of a rifle protruded from the shadows. 'It is not safe to walk alone so near the border, especially at night,' the Schupo said. 'You should go home now.'

Trudy nodded and turned away.

The next night she would patrol a different section of the wall.

With her next paycheck, Trudy bought a hooded jacket for Stefan and warm gloves for Gisela. She was sure he would have outgrown his baby coat by now. Inside the gloves she tucked a message.

Bring Stefan to the wall at Bornholmer Straße at ten o'clock on any Sunday morning. There is a place where I can see you through the barbed wire.

Gisela usually went to church on Sundays, but it was also the quietest time on the East-side border, with fewer guards on duty.

The postal clerk said a package might take ten days to cross the few blocks from West to East. But at least mail went through; telephone calls were impossible for ordinary citizens. She mailed the package, walked the border and waited.

Snow fell again, cloaking the wall with a deceptive whiteness. On the other side of the barricades, the feet of East Berlin Grepos beat out a slushy line past which its citizens could not go. Sunday after Sunday she waited beside the barbed wire at Bornholmer Straße, but Gisela and Stefan were not there.

Trudy grew addicted to reading the newspapers, especially the daily reports on events or changes at the wall. According to the newspaper, more than fifty people had been killed so far trying to escape into the West. No one knew how many had actually succeeded.

On a clear, cold Sunday, Trudy dressed in layers and put on her warmest stockings. By nine o'clock she was pacing beside the barriers at Bornholmer Straße with another hour to wait. A Schupo passed her, clapping his gloved hands together in the cold. He smiled and spoke cheerfully. She nodded to him and walked on.

At ten minutes to ten, she saw through the barbed wire a woman carrying a small child. Her heartbeat vaulted and she raced to a section of chain-link fence. When they were still thirty meters from the east-side barriers, Trudy raised her arms and waved. They did not look toward her, and as the woman turned and walked down another street, Trudy realized it was not Gisela.

She sank to her knees. Perhaps Gisela had never received her message. She blinked to dispel a thin membrane of icy tears coating her eyes.

When she looked up again, she saw them.

This time there was no mistaking Gisela's slow, uneven gait. She was carrying Stefan, and he was wearing the blue jacket she had sent.

'*Mutti!* Stefan! Here!'

In the stillness of the morning, Trudy's voice echoed across the empty space. She waved her arms until Gisela caught sight of her. She saw Gisela speaking to Stefan, pointing her out. Then she set him on his feet, and he toddled towards her, a tiny snowman with a pink face. His childish shriek carried across the distance.

Trudy's gloved hands covered her mouth. *Stefan, my baby.*

She wiped her eyes viciously, her breath impaled by the remembered smell of his skin, the softness of his hair on her cheek. She pressed her face against the chain-link fence and laced her fingers through the wires.

Stefan teetered on the snowy ground and grasped his grandmother's hand. Gisela hauled him up and helped him wave. Trudy waved, too, her throat ragged with his name. A jet roaring toward Tempelhof Airport drowned out her voice.

Suddenly, an East Berlin border guard appeared beside them, ominous in his dark coat, a long rifle slung across his back. He grabbed Gisela's arm and placed his body in front of her, blocking Trudy's view.

'Leave them alone!' Trudy screamed.

Without looking at her, the Grepo marched Gisela and Stefan back the way they had come. Was he arresting them?

Trudy clung to the fence, helpless. '*Schweinehunde!* Leave them alone!'

153

In a few moments the Grepo unhanded Gisela and gestured emphatically for them to go home. Trudy breathed again as she watched Gisela plod away, laboring with the weight of her grandson, until they were lost from sight.

Trudy stood for a long time staring at the place where they had disappeared. Her face felt hot and she was sweating beneath her clothes. Why must the *Schweinehunde* drive them away? What harm could they possibly do?

The Grepo had noticed she was still there. He advanced menacingly and shouted something unintelligible to her. When she did not move, he pointed his rifle.

'Shoot me, you filthy communist pig!' she screamed, shaking her fist. 'Do you feel brave harassing old women and children? Have you no mother of your own?'

A West Berlin Schupo appeared beside her and took her arm. 'It does no good, *Fräulein*. Come away, before the bastard is provoked into firing at us.'

The Schupo's eyes were not unkind. She looked at him for several seconds, unable to move. 'What kind of place is this, where they threaten grandmothers and babies?'

He didn't answer. Somewhere in West Berlin, church bells chimed.

Winter weeks peeled away toward spring. Trudy visited the West Berlin aid station to hear stories of other escapes, hoping to learn how a grandmother and child might cross over. East Germans knew by now the wall was impenetrable, and only a handful of daredevils tried. Most were caught in the security strip; a few were shot trying to climb the last hurdle. Some tried the barbed wire barricades on the outer edges of the city where attack dogs were chained along the fence.

A group of teenagers had set up an escape route through the sewers and succeeded in smuggling out a few of their friends, one of whom was overcome by the acrid fumes and had to be dragged up through a manhole in the West. The Grepos saw them and threw teargas down the east-side opening. After that all manholes near the border in the East were sealed down.

'Harry Seidel is still digging tunnels,' one man told her. 'But they are on to him. Nothing is safe.'

No one knew how a grandmother and baby might get across.

Finally a letter came through from Gisela. She and Stefan had both had the flu but were fine now. Trudy thought *Mutti* wouldn't tell her if things were not fine. She had sent a snapshot of Stefan, smiling from the seat of a rocking horse Wolfgang had brought him. Apparently Wolfgang was keeping his promise to check on them. Trudy carried the photo to work and showed it to Verden.

She wrote a new location for Gisela to bring Stefan to the wall, and marked off the days on a calendar. In May she received a letter from Wolfgang.

I stop by to see Gisela and Stefan every week, he wrote. *Gisela seems completely recovered from her bout with pneumonia.*

155

Pneumonia! Who knew she'd had pneumonia?

Stefan is full of life and climbs everywhere, the letter went on. *He keeps Gisela busy. I hope you are well and learning to be content. Perhaps someday conditions will change so that you can be happy. Wolfgang.*

The tone of his letter chilled her – as if losing her son was not fatal, as if she might simply go on with her life. The man was so cold and unfeeling that it was easy to blame him for Rolf's death. She didn't doubt that if he'd learned about Rolf's activities, he would have reported him. If the situation were reversed, would Rolf have betrayed his politics to save his old friend? Not likely. They were both loyal to abstractions that ruined people's lives. And yet Wolfgang watched over her *Mutti* and Stefan with a degree of compassion that confounded her bitterness. How long would he continue to help them? Only as long as his guilt persisted?

She scanned the envelope but found no return address. Undoubtedly he had to be careful in sending mail to the West. She wadded up the letter and threw it away.

Trudy took up smoking, but only at work when Verden shared her cigarettes. Trudy wouldn't spend money to buy them.

The days grew warmer and the nights less chilly. In June the linden trees bloomed again, and the air was ripe with their perfume. The newspapers were full of the American president's planned trip to Berlin. Mayor Willy Brandt was crowing so about the impending visit, you'd have thought he engineered it himself.

More politics. She was sick of it. But she read with morbid fascination about the frenetic preparations to welcome the young U.S. president, John F. Kennedy, on his first visit to the Berlin Wall.

CHAPTER 14

On June 25, Herr Blauert hung a sign in the window of *Zur Schwarzen Katze*. Closed Tomorrow Until 5:00 p.m. He wanted to attend the speeches welcoming the American president to West Berlin, and to hear Kennedy himself talk. Herr Blauert was a fan of the *Amis* because of certain kindnesses after the war. Trudy wondered whether he'd feel differently if he lived in the East. People there had expected American tanks to overrun the barriers and knock down the wall. When the U.S. didn't act, they felt betrayed.

Trudy didn't care one way or another about the United States or their young president. She only regretted missing work, because she'd heard enough political rhetoric to last two lifetimes.

The next morning Trudy slept late and had breakfast, and then she had nothing to do. The June day smelled pleasantly of spring, and she was too restless to sit in her room. She tied on her brown work shoes and went out into the streets.

Walking had become her therapy. But today the sidewalks were so jammed with people that she had trouble moving along. The crowds thickened with every block, and they were all moving toward Rudolph Wilde Platz, the square in front of city hall. Some thoroughfares were already barricaded, and people swarmed behind the barricades hoping for a glimpse of dignitaries. The newspapers said Kennedy would bring an entourage of nearly two hundred.

Trudy let the tide carry her along. Excitement ran through the crowds like an electric current and the anticipation was infectious. Close to the square, people leaned out from upper-story windows. She could hardly push through the bodies on the sidewalk.

Sudden shouts rippled through the crowd. Trudy caught sight of a motorcade of long black limousines. The cars swept past and came to a stop in front of the beautiful *Rathaus Schöneberg*. She pushed and angled between bodies until she was close enough to see a platform festooned in red, white and blue. When the first car door opened, people began to applaud and cheer.

She recognized the first man to emerge from the cars – Chancellor Adenauer, the head of the West German government in Bonn. He was reported to be eighty-seven and he looked every bit of it, his face lined and tired. Then she spotted Willy Brandt, the dynamic mayor of West Berlin. His youthfulness was magnified by comparison with Adenauer. Many people expected Mayor Brandt would succeed Adenauer as federal chancellor.

Trudy had never seen such important people in person. She stood on her toes and peered between shoulders. Suddenly the crowd exploded in

158

cheers – much louder than their applause for
Adenauer or Brandt – and Trudy saw the
American president climbing the city hall steps,
surrounded by a clutch of sober bodyguards.

President John F. Kennedy smiled and waved
to the crowd. He looked tall and energetic as a
college boy, especially standing next to the
depleted Adenauer. President Kennedy shook
hands with Adenauer and Brandt while flashbulbs peppered around them. When Kennedy
took the podium, the clamor increased, and it
was a long time before he could begin his speech.

Finally the crowd quieted to hear him. 'I am
proud to come to this city,' he said, and the
applause drowned out the rest. He waited, then
his clipped voice echoed in the square. 'Two
thousand years ago the proudest boast was *"civis
Romanus sum."* Today, in the world of freedom,
the proudest boast is *'Ich bin ein Berliner.'* And
the crowd roared.

Trudy couldn't help smiling. In Berlin ver-
nacular, *ein Berliner* was a particular kind of
pastry. President Kennedy meant *Ich bin Berliner*,
but what he'd said was *I am* a *jelly donut*.

It didn't matter. The people understood his
meaning, and that he was trying to speak their
language. They cheered and clapped and waved.

Once again Kennedy's voice rang through the
square. 'There are many people in the world who
really don't understand, or say they don't, what is
the great issue between the free world and the
Communist world.' He paused. 'Let them come
to Berlin.' Again the crowd went wild.

Berliners loved a good speech, and Kennedy

159

was a good speaker. His thick hair ruffled in the wind and his confidence was compelling. Trudy strained to improve her view through the crush of people. She had heard many politicians when she'd attended the Free University, but Kennedy wasn't condescending or arrogant like so many others. His dignified presence was a striking contrast to the temper fits of Soviet Premier Khrushchev, whose red-faced speeches were broadcast on East Berlin television.

'There are some who say that Communism is the wave of the future,' the president went on. 'Let them come to Berlin. And there are some who say in Europe and elsewhere, we can work with the communists. Let them come to Berlin. And there are even a few who say that it is true that Communism is an evil system, but it permits us to make economic progress. *Let them come to Berlin.*'

From balconies, rooftops and streets, the cheers went up. A chant began. 'Ken-ne-dy! Ken-ne-dy!' Trudy climbed onto the stone base of a street light and clung to the pole to see over the heads of the crowd.

It was several minutes before he could continue. 'Freedom has many difficulties and democracy is not perfect, but we have never had to put up a wall to keep our people in, to prevent them from leaving us. I want to say, on behalf of my countrymen, who live many miles away on the other side of the Atlantic, who are far distant from you, that they take the greatest pride that they have been able to share with you, even from a distance, the story of the last eighteen years. I know of no town, no city, that has been besieged

160

for eighteen years that still lives with the vitality and the force, and the hope and the determination of the city of West Berlin. While the wall is the most obvious and vivid demonstration of the failures of the Communist system, for all the world to see, we take no satisfaction in it, for it is, as your mayor has said, an offense not only against history, but an offense against humanity, separating families, dividing husbands and wives and brothers and sisters, and dividing a people who wish to be joined together.'

Weeks of loneliness gathered hot in Trudy's chest. *This man knew. He understood what had happened to her family – and to hundreds of others.*

How many of the people pressing around her also had loved ones across the wall? For the first time, the ache for her own family deepened to include a divided Berlin and divided Germany; to all people who could not live and travel where they wanted, and be safe and at peace. She clung to the lamppost and to the hope in President Kennedy's voice.

'You live in a defended island of freedom,' he told the crowd, 'but your life is part of the main... Freedom is indivisible, and when one man is enslaved, all are not free... All free men, wherever they may live, are citizens of Berlin, and, therefore, as a free man, I take pride in the words *'Ich bin ein Berliner.'*

I am a Berliner.

If his German wasn't perfect, his sentiment was. The crowd erupted again. Rice and flowers rained from upstairs windows; streamers and homemade confetti showered Trudy's shoulders.

161

In the frenzied din, her throat locked tight.

If anyone in the world could get Stefan out of the East, the American president surely could.

When President Kennedy left the podium and was escorted back toward his car, Trudy fought her way toward the motorcade. Hands pushed and shoved. She stepped on someone's foot, lost a button from her coat. By the time she reached the curb, the first three cars had passed and the caravan was picking up speed.

A rampart of Schupos held people back from the limousines, but their determination was anemic compared to hers. She lunged under the arm of a policeman and threw herself into the path of the last black limousine.

Its horn bugled and tires screeched. The limousine's bumper struck her hip with a fleshy thud and pitched her forward onto the street. For one instant, the surrounding crowd hushed. Then the commotion erupted even louder than before.

Trudy looked up toward the sun. Uniforms and business suits swarmed above her like ants on a carcass. The suits spoke English – secret service men, she thought. For a few stunned moments she could not manage to tell them she wasn't hurt. At least she didn't think so, though her left hip ached dully. The ache wasn't important; her only concern was that the Schupos might arrest her. If they did, her chance to contact the President was lost.

Chaos swirled around her, with unintelligible shouts in both English and German. Then the sea of bodies parted and a man in an elegant gray suit crouched beside her, his face silhouetted against the sky. She squinted and moved her head so the

162

sun was behind him. He was sandy-haired and blue-eyed, a perfect example of Hitler's Aryan race. The thought made her shiver.

The man waved the others back and put his hand on her arm. His face was calm. A gust of wind caught his blood-red necktie and blew it up over his shoulder.

'Are you all right?' he said in German.

Trudy spoke in a rush. 'I'm not hurt. I only wanted to speak to President Kennedy. My baby is in East Berlin and I cannot get him out.'

Interest sparked in the blue eyes. 'Your child is trapped behind the wall?'

Ja. Stefan is eighteen months old and needs his mother. Please! I know the president can help me.'

The man's gaze traveled over her threadbare dress, the baggy coat and disheveled hair. Maybe he also saw her desperation. In one smooth movement, he stood and pulled her up with him, supporting her with his hand on her elbow.

'Can you walk?'

'Ja.'

'I am with the president's staff,' he said, his German flawless. He motioned her into the car. *'Steigen Sie ein.'*

A security man objected but he brushed it off. 'I'll take responsibility for her,' he said in English. 'Let's move.'

He urged her into the car, his grip emphatic on her arm. She stumbled onto the seat and he got in after her. The door clicked shut, muffling the noise in the street. The car rolled forward.

The interior of the limousine was cool and dim after the brightness of the street, and it smelled

163

like men's cologne. Her eyes took several seconds to adjust. She breathed through her mouth, her pulse hammering.

Several other men rode in the car. The one riding beside the driver turned and spoke. 'You're crazy, Garret. What did you put her in the car for? You could start a whole incident.'

Obviously, nobody thought that she might understand English. She kept quiet.

Her rescuer answered without raising his voice. 'Shut up, Dan. I know what I'm doing.' He looked out the window, smiled and waved at the faces that blurred past. Then he turned to her.

'Don't be frightened,' he said in German. 'My name is Garret Thompson. I will try to help you.'

There was silence then, while the queue of limousines passed the heaviest crowds and, with police escort, gradually picked up speed. The men inside the car sat stone silent. Trudy looked out the windows, her mouth dry as cinders. She had no idea where they were going.

After a while their car separated from the rest and in a few more blocks they pulled up to the entrance of an expensive hotel. The driver held the door open for Garret Thompson, who stepped out and offered her his hand. She hesitated.

'This is the hotel where some of the staff is staying,' he said. 'Please come in and tell me about your child. We will assess what can be done.'

She climbed out. With his hand on her elbow again, they followed the other men into a wide lobby. Thick carpet sank beneath her shoes. A chandelier the size of a small car descended from

164

the ceiling, ablaze with tiny lights. In each corner of the room, bronze cherubs held glowing orbs that dispelled the shadows.

All eyes followed them across the lobby and Trudy watched her brown shoes cross the floor. Thompson didn't seem to notice the stares. He ushered her to an elevator bay and opened a private lift with his own key. He motioned her inside.

The other men had disappeared. She was alone with Thompson as the elevator car ascended. She felt the weight of his eyes on her reflection in the polished brass walls.

'Are you all right?' he asked.

She nodded and said nothing. The scent of him filled the closed space.

The car stopped on the fifth floor and Thompson led her down a hallway. The floor was carpeted with a thick runner in a tiny floral pattern, a rich dark red. Thompson stopped in front of a numbered door. She watched his hands unlock it with the key he'd used for the lift.

This could be a terrible mistake.

The door opened on a private suite of rooms, and Trudy felt quick relief at the sound of a female voice. A small blonde woman in a tailored suit was speaking on a black telephone and taking notes. Two other telephones sat beside it on the desk. Trudy thought she heard other voices in an adjoining room.

Thompson waited for her to enter. She stepped inside and he motioned her to a chair. *'Kaffe, Tee? Wasser?'* he asked.

She responded in English. 'Water, please.'

165

His eyebrows lifted, and he smiled. He poured water over ice and handed her the glass. She wasn't accustomed to iced drinks; the cold hurt her eyeballs.

The woman hung up the telephone and Thompson spoke to her in English. 'Miss Shaw, please take notes while I talk with *Fräulein…*' He turned to Trudy.

'Trudy Hulst,' she said.

He loosened his tie and sat in a damask chair painted with roses. A low table sat between them. Thompson regarded her and she thought that his eyes were too blue; they looked artificial.

'Shall we speak English or German, *Fräulein* Hulst?'

'Your German is better than my English.'

He smiled. 'We'll see,' he said. 'Let me know if there's something you don't understand. Miss Shaw is with the American consulate here. I may need her to check on some things for us. It will be helpful if she writes down details.'

'I understand,' Trudy said, though her mind scrambled to keep up. It had been a long time since she'd spoken English.

'Let's start by spelling your name.'

Trudy obliged. 'It is *Frau* Hulst,' she added. 'I am a widow.'

'I see,' Thompson said. 'And you have a young son.'

He picked up a silver case from the table and took a cigarette, then held the case out to her. White cigarettes lay in flawless rows against a red velvet lining. Thompson's fingernails were perfectly manicured, the pads of his fingers pink and

166

smooth. She thought that his hands would feel softer than hers.

She looked from the symmetry of the cigarettes into the too-blue eyes and had a feeling that if she accepted a cigarette from those hands, she was sealing some kind of bargain.

Thompson waited.

Her hand barely shook when she reached out and lifted a cigarette from the case. He smiled, flicked a gold lighter and lit her cigarette, then lit his own. Smoke wreathed his head and he settled back in the chair.

'You're very young to be widowed.'

'My husband was shot trying to cross the wall.'

'My god. What a tragedy.' His face was somber but the eyes glittered as if this information pleased him. 'Tell me about it,' he said.

The cigarette made her dizzy. She held it without inhaling again, a thin ribbon of smoke curling into the space between them. In halting English, she told him everything she knew about Rolf's attempt to escape East Berlin.

She had never told the story to anyone except Verden at the restaurant. Speaking another language, her voice belonged to someone else, someone detached from the fear and heartache.

'I was warned that because I was the wife of a defector, I would be arrested and put in prison,' she said. 'I did not know Rolf was dead. I thought he was here, in the West. I crawled out through a–' she used the German word for *tunnel* and Thompson nodded '–but they would not let me bring my baby.'

Her voice cracked and Miss Shaw glanced up

with sympathy in her eyes. Trudy's face turned hot. She took a last drag on the cigarette and ground the stub in an ashtray on the table.

'Who is taking care of your child now?' Thompson asked.

She cleared her throat. 'My mother-in-law. But she is in her sixties and has–' she searched for the right words '–health problems. I must get them both to the West.' Trudy stopped, exhausted from the effort. She looked at Thompson and waited.

He stood and paced the sculpted rug that cushioned a polished wood floor. 'Does your mother-in-law want to leave East Berlin?'

She shrugged. 'She has no other family left. She will come if Stefan does.'

'I see. But otherwise, she would probably be content to stay?'

Trudy thought it a strange question. 'She has spent her whole life there.'

He nodded and was quiet for nearly a minute, standing beside the sheer curtains that softened a view of the city. Then he turned and met her eyes.

'I will help you get your son out.'

Miss Shaw looked at him quickly, her eyes wide.

'*Thank you,*' Trudy whispered. And again, '*Thank you.*'

Whatever doubts she had about this man didn't matter. He was in President Kennedy's private party, and there was power in association. A fantasy image flashed in her mind: Thompson crossing through one of the checkpoints at the border, delivering Stefan into her waiting arms.

'How long it will take?' she asked.

'Ah. That's a hard question. It must be done through diplomatic means. And those wheels turn slowly.'

She wasn't sure of his meaning. 'But how long?'

He shrugged. 'Several months. Maybe longer.'

She winced. *'Months.'*

He crossed to her chair, leaned down and put his hand over hers. The hand was rougher than she'd imagined.

He switched to German. 'It might be less, or more. You must have patience and not be discouraged. And you must cooperate with me completely, or we cannot succeed. Do you understand?'

The pupils of his eyes appeared almost vertical, like a cat's. She could read nothing in his expression. She eased her hand away. 'I will do whatever you say.'

This time he allowed the smile she had sensed him holding back. His teeth were white and perfect, his breath scented like shaving cologne. 'Good,' he said. 'I want you to come back with me to the United States.'

'Was?'

Again the shocked look from Miss Shaw.

'We will take your case to the American people,' Thompson said. 'They have a soft spot for mothers with lost children.'

Trudy pictured a roomful of chic politician's wives, but her understanding stopped there. 'I have no passport. And very little money.'

'Leave that to me. Make whatever personal arrangements you require this afternoon. We will leave tomorrow. Pack your things and come back

169

here by eight o'clock in the morning. Do you have a picture of your son?'

'Yes. A snapshot.'

'That will be fine. We will have some recent ones taken of you, too. The media will want pictures.'

He turned away. 'Miss Shaw,' he said, 'please see to the details of Mrs. Hulst's passport. She'll need a security clearance so she can travel with me on the support plane. We can't get her on Air Force One.'

'Yes, sir. 'I'll make the arrangements,' Miss Shaw said, but Thompson was already gone. He had disappeared into another room, leaving the two women alone.

Trudy was a few minutes late to work for the dinner shift at *Zur Schwarzen Katze*. But when she explained to Herr Blauert why it was her last night to work, he became misty-eyed and wished her well.

'Frau Blauert and I will pray for you,' he said, patting her arm. Then he added, 'You must send us a postcard from America.'

When Trudy's shift was over, Verden hugged her goodbye and wished her luck. 'Let us know if you get to meet the president,' she said. 'And when you have Stefan back, you must bring him in so we can see him.'

Herr Blauert gave her the pay she was owed, and at midnight she walked home. She laundered her clothes in Frau Weiss's basement and while the clothes dried, she wrote a long letter to Gisela. On paper, her explanation of what she was about to do sounded foolhardy. She was flying off across the ocean with nothing but the naive hope that this cat-eyed stranger would be good to his word.

But that hope was enough. It had to be.

CHAPTER 15

At Tegel Airport in the French Sector, the long black car skirted the terminal and swept directly onto the tarmac. The limo held three rows of seats behind the driver, all filled by dark-suited men, except for Trudy. She sat rigid in the center seat, between Garret Thompson and a beefy man whose shoulder brushed against hers with the motion of the car. Several of the men had glanced at Thompson with passive surprise when he'd ushered her into the car at the hotel. Behind his dark glasses, Thompson remained unperturbed. Trudy wished she had sunglasses to hide behind.

The airfield sat in an odd hush. No planes were taking off or landing, none circled in the sky. Apparently air traffic had stopped until the president's party took off. The limo drove toward two distinctive aircraft that sat apart on the tarmac. The planes were painted white over sky blue, with a horizontal stripe of gold separating the colors and an American flag emblazoned on the tail. Their stately beauty frightened her even more.

She hugged her arms and fingered the supple fabric of her new coat. When she'd arrived at the hotel that morning, clutching the cheap vinyl suitcase she'd bought yesterday afternoon, Miss

171

Shaw was there to meet her. 'Mr. Thompson ordered this for you,' she said, and held the coat while Trudy slipped into it. It was caramel-colored and rain resistant, with a hemline long enough to cover her cotton skirt. She had never owned such a nice coat. She understood that Thompson didn't want her looking like a street urchin when he took her on the plane. Still, the expensive gift made her uncomfortable.

The driver stopped the limo and men began opening doors and getting out. A nauseating quiver filled her stomach. What if the plane crashed into the ocean and she never made it home to Stefan?

Thompson offered his hand to help her from the car. Her own hand felt clammy inside his dry grip. He led her to stand behind a yellow line painted on the ground, where they waited to board while the driver unloaded their bags. The airplanes loomed even larger up close, and she felt inordinately small, her head barely level with Thompson's shoulder. She cinched the coat around her waist and shoved her hands into the pockets.

'If you pull that belt any tighter, you'll cut off your circulation,' Thompson said.

She glanced up at him and he smiled with perfect white teeth. She could see her tense face mirrored in his dark glasses.

He leaned close to her ear and spoke in German. 'Don't let these stuffy *Burschen* scare you. Just picture them in their underwear.'

She managed a weak smile.

'That one is the President's aircraft, Air Force One,' he told her, indicating the first of the two jets. 'Also known as Two-Six Thousand. Mrs. Kennedy commissioned the color scheme herself.' His voice was casual, meant to calm her.

She nodded, her breath jerky and shallow. 'I've never flown before.'

His eyebrows lifted, and he smiled again. 'Nothing like starting big.'

A final black limousine approached the group and rolled to a stop twenty meters from where they stood. A fluster of activity ensued, and then President Kennedy stepped out of the long car and walked briskly to Air Force One. He climbed the long steps to the door followed by a parade of dark-suited men. They disappeared inside, the staircase was rolled away and the door sealed.

Jet engines roared and Trudy flinched.

'Here we go,' Thompson said. He led her to the stairway positioned beside the forward cabin door of the second aircraft. 'Just follow me.'

She gripped the railing, whispered Stefan's name like a prayer and climbed the metal steps in her ugly brown shoes.

Thompson led her between long rows of seats. Finally he stood aside and motioned her toward a window. She edged in and sank into the cushioned chair. Thompson sat beside her. The back of the seat spooned in and the neck rest was too high, pushing her head forward. Her toes reached the floor but not her heels. She squirmed, and Thompson handed her a small cushion.

'Here. Put this behind your back.' He leaned across her and buckled her seat belt. 'All set?'

She nodded, her mouth too dry to answer.

'I hate flying,' he told her. 'But bourbon helps.' Then he turned away and began talking to a man across the aisle.

From the distorted, double-glass window, Trudy watched the luggage being searched before it was loaded. She spotted her cheap bag among the expensive leather ones and realized that a stranger's hands would paw through her shabby dresses and cheap underwear. Her face burned and she turned away from the window. She laid her head back on the seat and closed her eyes.

Rolf would have loved to make this trip, she told herself. *He would think it was an adventure.*

In a few minutes the aircraft began to move. Trudy glanced at Thompson, but he had opened a newspaper, the *Washington Post*. He was reading as calmly as if they were sitting in a café somewhere instead of preparing to cross thousands of miles of ocean. The jet taxied to the runway and swung into place for takeoff. Trudy's fingernails dug into the armrests.

The engines roared and the aircraft hurtled down the runway. The grayness of Berlin slid past her window at a dizzying speed. A heady, lifting sensation told her they were airborne, and the plane banked into a turn. Out the window, the ground sank away and she saw the meandering line of the wall. From the air, the raked earth between the parallel barriers stood out like a jagged scar across the city. The newspapers called it the death zone and said that land mines were buried there.

She tried to find the East Berlin street where at this moment Stefan and Gisela would be moving around the familiar rooms, but the plane curved away before she could orient herself. Flights from the West had to stay within specified air corridors to cross East Germany. Soon the city disappeared beneath a bluish haze.

Her head ached and she realized she had tensed every muscle, even her lips. She loosened her grip on the armrests, then relaxed her legs, her arms and shoulders. If she didn't think about the yawning space beneath the plane, flying wasn't so bad. Except for the popping and pressure in her ears, it was rather like riding a bus. She took a deep breath and surrendered herself to whatever came next.

A young man in a military uniform served Garret Thompson a highball.

'Something for you, ma'am?' he asked.

'No, thank you.'

'Bring her some water,' Thompson ordered. He shook a tiny white pill into his palm and offered it to her. 'It's an eight-hour flight. This will help you sleep and keep your stomach settled.' He pushed a button on the armrest and the back of her chair reclined.

After that she closed her eyes and practiced deciphering the American English of Thompson and a man across the aisle. She understood most of their words but not the context. Once she had wished for the opportunity to use her language skills; now her knowledge of English would be essential. What did Thompson have in mind to get Stefan out of East Berlin? Would she actually meet President Kennedy?

Out the window, the earth had disappeared.

175

There was nothing but brilliant blue sky above and curded, snowy clouds below. It was a different world, magnificent and peaceful, and she was very tired.

Thompson's white pill did its work. She slept most of the flight, rousing in time to feel the jet descend to the runway and touch down at frightening speed. Thompson looked amused as he turned her frozen gaze away from the window and held her hand until they rolled to a stop. Inside the airport, she endured a cursory search of her person.

She rode with Thompson in another limousine to a multistory hotel. It should have been evening, but the sun looked like midday, high and bright in a cloudless sky. Trudy's head buzzed; nothing felt real as he saw her upstairs to her room. The chamber was huge, with carpet so pristine that she removed her shoes before stepping inside.

Thompson set her bag beside the bed and used a telephone in the room to order a basket of fruit and muffins sent up. He placed the gold key on a table where fresh roses sat in a clear glass vase. 'Here's your room key. And here's another of those little pills. That will help with the jet lag.'

She nodded, standing stupidly in the center of the room.

'Get some rest,' he said. 'I'll phone later.'

The moment she was alone, she wrapped herself in the flowered bedspread and slept again, hoping that when she woke up, she'd be back home in Berlin.

Somewhere a telephone was ringing. Trudy opened her eyes and tried to make out the unfamiliar shapes that had figured in her dream. She was floating in an oversized bed. Heavy drapes dimmed the room and she had no idea whether it was morning or evening. On the table beside the door sat a linen-lined basket with enough fruit and muffins to feed a family. She hadn't even heard them delivered.

The telephone was still ringing. She pushed herself up on the bed and reached for the receiver. *'Hallo?'*

'Hallo,' Thompson's voice said, and then he switched to English. 'How are you feeling?'

'Groggy.' She rubbed her forehead and eyes. 'What was that tablet you gave me?'

'Only Dramamine. It's safe even for children.'

'Drugs have an exaggerated effect on me.'

'I'll have to remember that,' he said, and she could hear his smile. 'It's six o'clock now. Are you hungry?'

Her teeth felt scummy, but she was hollow as a cave. 'Starving.'

'I'll meet you in the hotel dining room at seven. I've had some things sent over for you. Call the front desk and the bell captain will bring them up.'

'What things?'

'Something to wear to dinner. Just call the desk. I'll see you at seven.'

She hung up the receiver and squinted at the fancy telephone until she deciphered the correct buttons. In a few minutes there was a tap at her door, and a young man greeted her with a large silver box and a shopping bag. With no American money for a tip, she thanked him and closed the door.

The dress was simple and black, very classy. Of course. The shopping bag contained high-heeled shoes, the same style in two different sizes and nylon hose. In East Berlin, nylons were a coveted luxury.

She ran a finger across the leather pumps and remembered the stories of Nazi officers who lavished expensive gifts on their families and mistresses. *It's not the same*, she told herself. She couldn't go to dinner in this fancy hotel wearing her wrinkled skirt and blouse.

She removed her clothes and slipped the dress over her head. The fabric poured over her skin, cool and shocking as a waterfall. She smoothed it over her hips and glanced in a full-length mirror on the bathroom door. Thompson had a good eye; the dress fit.

She'd never owned beautiful things, and it seemed wrong to enjoy the feel of them so much. She took off the dress and hung it carefully on a wooden hanger. In the bathroom, she ran water in the enormous white bathtub. There were bath salts in a small jar beside the tub. She sniffed them and poured some in. Did all Americans live like this? Surely not. Probably only government officials, the same as in Germany.

An hour later, a stranger looked back at her from the gilded mirror. She tried to see herself through Garret Thompson's eyes. In the black dress, her hair twisted into a knot on the crown of her head, she looked like a frail girl. When had she lost so much weight? Her cheekbones seemed severe, her neck too long and thin.

'He should have sent makeup, too,' she told the mirror.

The only jewelry she owned was her gold wedding band and the cloisonne locket Rolf had given her. She opened the locket and looked at Stefan's plump face, lit with a toothless grin. She'd taken the photo when he was six months old. Her eyes burned. *I wish I could hug you right now*.

And Thompson was her best hope to make that happen. She fastened the locket around her neck and blew her nose, set her jaw and stood up straight. The shoes were tight and she wasn't used to high heels. She practiced walking until she could cross the plush carpet without teetering. Finally she took a deep breath and slipped the gold key into her bra.

Stepping from the elevator into the lobby was like Alice dropping into Wonderland. When Thompson had brought her here, she was too paralyzed to notice the grand chandelier in the high-ceilinged foyer, the velvet chairs and polished mahogany tables. Even the hotel in Berlin where she'd met with Thompson paled by comparison. Crossing the grand room in clothes that didn't belong to her, she was someone else, a different person. Trudy Hulst would never be here.

The concierge greeted her. 'Mrs. Hulst. You look lovely. May I show you to the dining room?'

The woman was perhaps fifty, with a kind and well-tended face. She wore a tailored navy suit with a gold bar engraved with the name Marian. Was Trudy expected to call a woman she'd never met by her first name?

'Thank you,' she said. 'I am to meet Mr. Thompson.'

The woman smiled. 'He's waiting for you. Right this way.'

Thompson stood when she approached the table, and his smile looked satisfied. A white-coated waiter seated her in a carved chair with a cushioned seat. When the waiter had gone, Thompson poured wine in her glass.

'You are the prettiest woman in the room,' he said.

Trudy's face burned. 'I must be the *only* woman in the room. Thank you for the dress. It is beautiful.'

'I'm glad it fit.' He lifted his glass. 'To your future in America.'

She took a sip, then settled the glass on the linen cloth and met his eyes. 'You must understand, Mr. Thompson – I don't want a future in America. All I want is my son west of the wall.'

'Of course. And that depends on how well things go here in America.' His voice was patient, as if explaining to a child.

'What must I do? Are you going to speak to the president about Stefan?'

He smiled. 'The president has a cold war to worry about. The fate of nations. He can't be bothered with the problems of one person.'

'I'm sorry to hear that. When he spoke in Berlin, I felt that he cared about freedom, even for one small boy.'

Thompson nodded quickly. 'Certainly he would care. But it's not something I can ask him to become involved with personally. We'll use other channels.'

Trudy didn't understand other channels, but just then the waiter appeared again and looked at them expectantly. Trudy picked up her menu.

'Shall I order for you?' Thompson asked, and she agreed. When the transaction was complete, the waiter disappeared.

'Your command of English is impressive,' he said.

'I was a good student.'

'From now on, we'll speak only in English, so you can practice. Unfortunately, no one in America speaks *Deutsche*.'

'All right,' she said. 'I will practice. Especially the contractions. I think Americans use even more contractions than the British.'

He leaned back in his chair, regarding her with a look she couldn't read. 'You're so serious. Do you never relax?'

Her eyes traveled over the fine china, the lit candles, Thompson's manicured hands on the white tablecloth. 'Mr. Thompson, do you have children?'

'No. I'm not married.'

'I am sorry for that. If you had a child of your own, you would understand. I cannot relax until I have Stefan. I grew up without a father or mother, and I will not let that happen to my son.'

Thompson watched her for a moment. Then he drew a cigarette from a gold case, offered her one. She shook her head.

'I can't know how you feel, of course, because I've never been through what you have,' he said.

181

'But I understand how important it is for you to reclaim your son. I see it in your face every time I look at you.'

It occurred to her for the first time that Thompson was handsome – or would be, except for an occasional glint of something hard behind his eyes. It was a look that seemed familiar, like the name of an old acquaintance that she couldn't quite bring to mind.

He intended to gain something from helping her. What did he want?

It didn't matter – they each had their motives. They would use each other, and if her cost was greater, it was because she had more to gain. If sex was all he wanted, it was a cheap price to pay for her son. But she would have to make him wait. She sensed that once he had what he wanted, his interest in helping her would wane.

The meal arrived in well-seasoned waves. For a while they talked only of the food, but during the main course – some kind of fish with a rich cream sauce – she asked him again how he would go about getting Stefan out of East Berlin.

The waiter had brought a second bottle of wine and refilled Thompson's glass. Trudy was still nursing her first.

'I'll contact the German embassy right away to arrange an interview for you with the ambassador. We'll appeal for his diplomatic help. I'll also phone some influential congressmen who owe me favors, try to gain their support. Some of them might have contacts in Bonn. But our best weapon is the American people.' He punctuated this thought with his silver fork. 'The American public has a soft heart and a big pocketbook. We're going to schedule public appearances, put you on television programs all over the country.'

Trudy frowned. 'Why would anyone want me to be on television?'

'Because it's a great story – a mother wrenched away from her son by the evil communist government. The public will love it. And they'll love you.' He tipped his glass toward her, smiling. 'There will be national outrage.'

A waiter appeared and whisked their plates away. Another offered dessert, which they both declined.

Thompson leaned forward, his arms on the table. 'The power of this nation's private citizenry is amazing. They'll put more pressure on government officials than I could ever do alone. But you're the trump card.'

Her brain was tired from wine and too much English. '*Wie bitte?*'

'You're the key,' he explained. 'When the TV camera closes in, America must see that same longing in your face that I see.' He paused, his eyes narrowing. 'It will be hard work, but I'll be with you all the way. Can you do it?'

So that was his motive – he wanted publicity.

It was so simple she almost laughed. He would appear on those television programs as her hero, her protector. No doubt he planned to run for some higher office in the government.

'I can do whatever it takes to have Stefan with me.'

It was the right answer. This time even his eyes smiled, and he reached across to squeeze her

183

hand. 'That's my girl. Now if we're going to work together, we can't be so formal. In America, people call each other by their first names. Mine is Garret.'

'All right. Garret.'

'It's good to see you smile.' He checked his watch and laid his linen napkin on the table. 'Tomorrow I'll send my secretary to take you shopping and show you around the city. Her name is Sandra Fletcher.' He laid a business card on the table in front of her. 'The next day we'll set up an appointment with a good PR man I know.'

'What is *pee arr?*'

'It stands for public relations. He's in the business of building images for public figures and political candidates. He can get us on talk shows and network news. He's expensive, and worth it.'

'I have no money.'

'Don't worry. Funds will take care of themselves.'

She raised her eyebrows. How did money ever take care of itself?

But Thompson didn't explain. He signed the check and walked with her to the elevator. 'Shall I see you upstairs?'

'That isn't necessary. Thank you for the wonderful dinner. And for everything else.'

'You're very welcome.' He smiled, but he seemed distracted. His mind had already dismissed her and moved somewhere else. 'Good night then.'

As the elevator door slid shut, Trudy saw him check his watch again as he turned to go. The night wasn't over for Garret Thompson.

CHAPTER 16

Thompson's secretary spoke with an elongated accent that Trudy had never encountered. Perhaps English was not Miss Fletcher's first language, either. On the phone, Trudy had to ask her twice to repeat, but finally she was clear that Miss Fletcher would pick her up at the hotel at ten thirty.

Trudy was waiting in the lobby when a stunning woman in a business suit strode through the glass doors, ignoring the wake of stares that followed her entrance. She was petite but buxom, her features as flawless as a china doll's and she seemed to be looking for someone. Trudy felt certain this was Sandra Fletcher, but was she going to shop in those shoes? The heels could have punctured a tire.

Trudy felt like a street waif in her clumsy shoes and cotton dress. She glanced at the elevators, thinking of a quick escape before Miss Fletcher picked her out of the milling guests.

Too late. Miss Fletcher spotted her and the delicate face opened with a surprising flash of rampant teeth and pink lips. She approached quickly, offering a hand tipped with bright nail polish.

'You must be Trudy,' she said. 'I'm Sandra. Welcome to the good old U.S.A.'

Trudy shrank away, fearing the woman might hug her. 'I'm happy to meet you. Thank you for taking care of me today.'

Sandra's deep gold eyes made a striking contrast to the cascade of blonde hair, and Trudy thought there was something watchful about them, like tiger eyes.

'Your English is really good,' she said, still holding Trudy's handshake. 'I tried to learn French once, but finally gave it up. All I can speak is American.' Another dazzling smile. 'This *twang* you hear is a Texas drawl. I've lived in D.C. three years now, but I grew up in Texas and the accent won't go away. If I say something you can't understand, just say *whoa* and I'll try it again.'

Trudy nodded. *'Whoa?'* The word was new to her. 'Okay.'

When Sandra laughed, the copper eyes took on a light of their own. She was like a brilliant sunset, Trudy thought, too bright to look at directly.

'Are you ready? We're going on the world's biggest shopping spree at Garret's expense. We'll hit Garfinckel's first.'

Trudy didn't feel ready at all, but she nodded. They left the hotel in Sandra's oversized Ford car.

They started with her feet. Using a plastic card instead of money, they bought a pair of neutral pumps with a low heel, stylish but comfortable for walking. Trudy decided to wear them and put her old brown ones in the box. 'We'll get more shoes to go with your new outfits,' Sandra said, while the escalator whisked them upward.

The women's department was a fantasy of American capitalism. Trudy couldn't keep from staring at the glass cases of glittering jewelry, and

186

long counters laden with perfumes and pyramids of cosmetics. On a pedestal display, an eyeless manikin posed in a ridiculously lavish gown, one thin plastic arm reaching out to her. Who could afford such luxuries? And why would anyone need them?

She thought of the apartment in East Berlin, Stephan's secondhand playsuit and Gisela's well-worn dresses. How did America get to be so *rich?*

Sandra led her to an area where racks and racks of dresses hung in neat rows. An attractive woman who worked there greeted them like old friends. Sandra told the woman what they needed, and she sized up Trudy with a glance. 'You're about five-three, right? Let's look in petites.'

Sandra rummaged through the hangers of clothes as if she owned them. Trudy just watched, too overwhelmed to find anything on the crowded racks. The excess of goods seemed almost obscene – yet there was something thrilling about it.

'Is this a restricted store?' she whispered to Sandra.

'Restricted? I don't understand what you mean.'

'Can anyone shop here?'

Sandra grinned. 'Sure they can. As long as they have money.'

Sandra pulled out one dress after another for Trudy's inspection. She rehung the rejects and draped the others over the saleslady's arm. When they'd chosen five to consider, the lady installed her in a dressing room while Sandra went back for more. For an hour Trudy modeled clothes, standing before a three-way mirror in her stocking feet while Sandra and the saleswoman stood behind her and either approved or vetoed. When they'd settled on four outfits, Sandra paid with Garret Thompson's credit card.

'That's a start,' she said, and they moved on.

In another store, Trudy tried on business suits until three of them gained Sandra's approval. They bought skirts and blouses, jewelry and handbags, even slacks for casual wear. Sandra picked one outfit for Trudy to wear to lunch, and they folded her old dress into a bag.

'You look terrific,' Sandra said, the smile dimpling her cheeks. 'Now for more shoes!'

Trudy's guilt mounted along with purchases. 'Surely this is enough. Why would I need so many clothes?'

Sandra looked at her as if she were crazy. 'Why would you *not?*'

Trudy sat in a chair while Sandra pointed out various high-heeled pumps for the salesman to bring out. 'How can you walk in those high heels all day?' Trudy asked. 'Don't your feet hurt?'

Sandra glanced down at her slim feet and shrugged. 'I've worn high heels so many years they're part of my legs. This pair is really comfortable. Want to try them on?' She kicked off her shoes and pushed them toward Trudy. Without the heels, Sandra was even shorter than she was.

Trudy shook her head. There was something too personal about putting her foot into another woman's warm shoe. 'They're too small for me,' she said, smiling.

Sandra dropped into a chair beside her. 'This is fun, isn't it? Kind of like having a sister.' She glanced around at the scattered boxes. 'I think I'll try on those red ones I saw in the window.'

For lunch, Sandra drove to a restaurant with a view of the wide Potomac River. Sunlight sequined the water and a surge of homesickness flooded Trudy's stomach. How could she sit here lunching among the polished brass and ferns, while Stefan and Gisela were far away, rationing their meat and sugar?

She blinked hard and busied herself reading the menu. When they'd ordered, she asked Sandra to tell her about Texas.

'There's lots of wide open country,' Sandra said. 'I grew up on a cattle ranch and learned to ride a horse when I was four. Even before that, I used to sit on the saddle in front of my dad when he rode out to check on the stock.'

'What is *stock?*'

'The cattle. We had about two hundred head – that means animals – and that's a small operation in Texas. We also kept chickens and a milk cow, which my mother took care of. I loved the cattle – even the way they smell. But those chickens! Yuck. And it was my job to gather the eggs.'

Trudy pictured a flock of white chickens, herds of cattle with large benign eyes. Sandra was about Trudy's age, yet the war hadn't touched her childhood. 'Texas sounds like a wonderful place to grow up. Why did you leave?'

Their food arrived and Sandra peppered her tub-sized salad. 'I had dreams of a different kind of life. I loved the ranch, but it was lonely out there. I just have one brother, who's several years older, and he was always out with Dad. I spent a

189

lot of time by myself, and I envied my school friends who lived in town.' She stopped suddenly and looked at Trudy. Her face changed. 'I guess it *was* ideal. My dad didn't have to go to war, because he was raising beef to feed the nation and the troops. I'll bet yours did.'

Trudy nodded. 'Both my parents were killed.'

Sandra's gold eyes widened. 'I can't even imagine how awful that was. I'd really like to hear about your family and how you got out of East Berlin. But if you can't talk about it, I understand.'

'I need to get used to it,' Trudy said. 'I think that's exactly what Mr. Thompson has in mind for me.' She told Sandra about crawling through the tunnel to learn that Rolf was dead, and about the terrible guilt of leaving her son.

Sandra pulled a tissue from her purse and blotted her eyes. 'I can see why Garret wants everyone to hear your story.' Her tone hardened. 'Especially if he gets to be your champion, because that will make him look good to voters.'

Trudy remembered the feeling of humiliation when Miss Shaw, from the American consulate in Berlin, had looked at her with pity in her eyes. 'I dread it. But I'll do anything he wants if he can get the East Berlin government to give up my baby.'

A flicker passed through Sandra's eyes. She looked away quickly. 'Want dessert?'

'No, thank you. I have eaten too much.'

'Then let's hit the stores again!'

Trudy gaped. 'What else could I possibly need?'

Sandra just laughed. She added a generous tip for the waiter and charged the lunch to Thompson.

That afternoon, Sandra picked out lacy undergarments that Trudy never dreamed of owning. Her face steamed when Sandra held a sexy bra up to her chest.

'Honey, every woman ought to own at least one black lace bra and panties to match,' Sandra said, her smile wicked. 'It does wonders for your confidence.'

'I cannot imagine where I would wear something like that,' Trudy said.

'Wear it any day, anywhere. What do you think Mona Lisa was smiling about?'

They dropped off their shopping bags at Trudy's hotel, and Sandra hired the hotel car for a sightseeing tour. 'Trust me, you don't want me driving while I'm gawking and pointing out the windows,' Sandra said.

She kept up a running commentary as they drove by the domed Capitol Building and the White House where President and Mrs. Kennedy lived. They climbed the steps of the Lincoln Memorial, Sandra's high heels clicking like a dancer's, and they peered into the reflecting pool at the Washington Monument. The city was green and beautiful.

On the way back to the hotel, Sandra had the driver stop at a store called Woodward & Lothrop's, to purchase a respectable set of luggage for Trudy.

'It makes me uncomfortable for him to buy all these things,' Trudy said, watching Sandra sign yet another sales slip.

'I understand, honey. But don't worry about it. Garret comes from old money – that means his

191

family's rich. You can be sure he'll get his money's worth out of you. I just hope he can get your son to the West.'

Trudy's heart vaulted and she stopped walking. 'You have doubts, don't you?'

'Now, I didn't mean that.' Sandra stopped, too, and met her eyes.

'Well, yes, I did.'

She took Trudy's elbow and piloted her out of the store. 'Garret's a politician – I imagine they're the same in Germany. You've been through so much, I'd hate to see you get your hopes up and be hurt again.'

'But he does have influence with the president, yes? Connections to important people?'

Sandra gave a short laugh. 'He has friends in high places, all right. Enemies, too. As long as you're bringing him good publicity, he'll make an effort to get Stefan out of East Berlin. Just remember that Garret Thompson doesn't do anybody a favor unless he gets a bigger one in return.'

The look in Sandra's eyes said more than her words.

CHAPTER 17

The next day Trudy had nothing to do but wait on the promised phone call from Garret Thompson. The hotel left a newspaper outside her door, and she read the news section to practice her English. On the front page was an account of Soviet

192

Premier Nikita Khrushchev's visit to East Berlin, in response to Kennedy's speech on the other side of the wall. According to the *Washington Post*, Khrushchev had told the Party members who showed up to cheer him that he thought the wall was *a splendid idea.* She wondered if the American press was as biased as the communist newspapers in East Berlin.

She ate fruit and muffins from Thompson's gift basket, showered and washed her hair; she pressed her new clothes with an iron she found in the closet – and still Thompson had not called. Staring out the fifth-story window at the street below, she heard Sandra's warning in her head. *Garret Thompson doesn't do anybody a favor unless he gets a bigger one in return.*

By twelve-thirty the phone still hadn't rung. What if Thompson's promise to help her was nothing but a lie? What if he abandoned her in the United States – how would she get home?

Then the phone rang. 'We have an appointment with the German ambassador at two o'clock,' Thompson said without preamble. 'I'll pick you up in front of the hotel at one-thirty.'

The magnitude of her relief softened her knees. 'I will be ready,' she said.

She wore one of the new suits. Thompson zoomed into the driveway in a silver sports car and leaned to open the passenger-side door from the inside. He was a big man and the car looked too small for him. His hair touched the ceiling.

Trudy climbed in and Thompson mumbled a greeting. She noticed a red streak on the side of his neck, and his face looked like a headache.

Hangover, she diagnosed. He pulled away before she'd even shut the door.

'Thank you for the new clothes,' she said.

'You're welcome.'

He said nothing more. She kept quiet and looked out the window as they drove through traffic.

The German ambassador received them in a well-appointed sitting room off his office. He was plump and jovial, with a full head of silver hair.

'It is a pleasure to speak to a countryman in our mother tongue,' he said, shining a practiced smile at her and then Thompson. His secretary offered tea from a silver service.

Trudy sat in a peach-colored satin chair and explained her situation to Ambassador Veltman, stressing her desperation to remove her baby from East Berlin. The ambassador listened with a frown on his jowly face. She showed him a picture of Stefan and made sure to voice her appreciation for Thompson's generous help. Thompson was still silent, sipping his tea with a glazed expression in his eyes.

When she stopped talking, the ambassador nodded, his face solemn. She waited for him to say what he could do.

'It is a sad situation between East and West Berlin,' he said. 'The East German government is quite difficult to deal with. It's unfortunate that the United States did not take steps to stop the construction of the wall when it had the chance.' He mouthed a few other vague observations and said he would *make inquiries*, but he couldn't offer much hope. Trudy left the meeting bitterly disappointed.

In the car, she said to Thompson, 'He won't do anything, will he?'

'Probably not,' Thompson told her. 'But he was worth a try.'

From the Embassy, Thompson drove across the city to the office of RJM Public Relations Specialists, Inc. His mood had improved, and his forehead was not quite so pinched. Maybe the caffeine in Ambassador Veltman's tea had offset the headache.

'I want you to meet R.J. Maximilian,' he said, maneuvering through traffic. 'He's a fairy, but nobody in D.C. is a better PR agent.'

A fairy? Trudy decided Herr Maximilian must be quite small.

'I've talked to him about you,' Thompson said, 'and he's already setting up a schedule of television appearances.' He accelerated on a open stretch of street before braking again for a light. 'Max will have us on a different airplane every week,' he was saying. 'In a month your name will be a household word in America.'

Household word? Perhaps it was a slang expression; she didn't ask. But the idea of flying every week came through clearly and her stomach jittered.

R.J. Maximilian wasn't, in fact, small. He was average height with a bit of a belly, an expressive face and loose lips. She guessed him about fifty. He wore snug fitting slacks and a shirt painted with at least four colors in an abstract pattern.

'Aren't you *adorable*,' he said, smiling broadly when Thompson introduced them. He looked at

195

her as if he'd found a treasure. Then the smile disappeared and his expression turned earnest. He grabbed both her hands. 'I'm *so* sorry about your being separated from your son. That must be awful.'

'Yes. It is.'

'Just call me Max. Everybody does. May I call you Trudy?'

She nodded because he didn't stop talking long enough for her to respond. He turned to Garret, still holding onto her hands.

'She's adorable,' he repeated. 'She'll look great on camera. A little makeup, not too much, a nice simple hairstyle.' Then, 'Come sit down, sugar. What can I get you to drink?'

Sugar?

Max brought colas and they sat at a round table where a file folder and yellow tablet lay waiting. He took notes while she told her story once again.

'I know you'll get tired of telling the same thing over and over,' he said, reading her hesitation, 'but that's exactly what you have to do.' He leaned forward on the table and met her eyes. His expression was both kind and assessing. 'You'll be interviewed on TV programs, and you'll talk to women's clubs and political groups. They'll all want to hear what happened straight from you. Just keep thinking about your baby, how much you miss him. Make these people want to help.'

She nodded. 'I understand.'

'I'll coach you, before each event, so you'll know what to expect. Your English is quite good.' He glanced at Thompson. 'I was worried about

196

the accent, whether the audience would be able to understand her. But I think it's going to be fine.'

Max smiled at her and squeezed her hand. 'If you get confused about a question, Garret will be right there to help out.'

And that's what will keep him happy. He'll be the savior of the helpless German lady who's lost her son.

Max read off a list of planned appearances. 'Not all of these are finalized, but I think they will be.'

The names meant nothing to Trudy, but Thompson was impressed, and as the list went on, his smile widened. His eyes were bright now, the hangover gone. He clapped Max on the back. 'If you can pull off all of those, you're a magician. No wonder your fees are outrageous.'

Thompson got up and mixed himself a drink at a small bar in the corner of Max's office. He and Max began discussing some of the venues, but Trudy's mind had gone numb. She was a stranger in a foreign film, caught up in a chain of unreal events. A longing for Stefan, for home, settled over her like fog.

The first television appearance was in Baltimore. It wasn't far from Washington, D.C., Max said, so he drove them in his Lincoln Continental. He put Trudy up front in a leather seat that felt like a pillow, relegating Garret to the back. On the drive, Max coached her through a mock interview, and when they arrived he made sure she was introduced ahead of time to the woman who hosted the show.

Marla Deacon was olive-skinned, beautiful and confident. They spoke only a moment. Marla had intelligent eyes and seemed genuinely interested in Trudy's story. Trudy began to think this wouldn't be so hard after all.

During the commercial break before their segment came up, Trudy was placed next to Thompson on a sofa in a mock living room, with glaring lights and boom microphones that were anything but homey. A man in headphones stood beside the oversized cameras and signaled they were on the air.

Marla Deacon introduced her with a short background. 'Mrs. Hulst, tell us about your escape from East Berlin, and about your son.'

Trudy recounted her story smoothly enough, remembering to speak distinctly. Then Marla Deacon leaned forward, looked in her eyes and said, 'Do most Berliners blindly accept the communist regime, as they did the Nazis during Hitler's reign?'

The woman's dark eyes looked fierce and accusing. Trudy's mouth opened but for several panicky seconds, she couldn't think of a single English word.

Thompson rescued her. She heard his voice beneath the ringing in her ears, and his response was patient and politically smart. By the time he'd finished and guided the host back toward Trudy's lost family, her brain had unlocked. She was able to stumble through the rest of the interview on her own.

The segment ended with a close-up of Stefan's picture on the screen, and an appeal to American voters to let their congressmen know about Trudy's plight. Deacon gave an address where donations could be sent to help defray her expenses, and it was over.

Max led her from the set. 'You did great.'

'I was awful! My mind just froze.'

'She ambushed you. But Garret handled it like a pro. Deacon came off looking like the shrew she is.' Max gave her a one-armed hug. 'Don't worry, sugar. It will get easier after you've done a few of these gigs.'

A new word, *gig*. It made the appalling experience sound almost comical.

'Give us a smile,' Max said. 'You're going to be fine.'

The next week Max showed her the travel schedule for the rest of July and August. All those airplane flights. She asked Thompson if Sandra could go with them, but he said he needed her at his office.

Sandra did help her pack for the trip, and she saw them off at the airport. 'Call me if you need to talk,' Sandra whispered, hugging Trudy good-bye. 'And keep writing those letters.' She patted the carry-on bag where she had tucked a special folder of stationery.

Trudy thanked her and followed Max down the concourse, while Thompson disappeared into a bar to brace himself for the flight. Trudy's stomach thrashed like a cage full of birds.

In Philadelphia, the television appearance went well compared to Baltimore, though Trudy couldn't eat for twelve hours surrounding the show. Next came Chicago. Lake Michigan shone like rippled glass on their descent into O'Hare International, and crosswinds pitched the plane like a toy. Then Minneapolis and Denver, where the Colorado Rockies rose hazy and distant outside her hotel room. America became a geographical kaleidoscope from the windows of airplanes and taxis, tumbling through July and into August. The nation was diverse and immense, and often overwhelming.

Trudy gave herself over to makeup artists and sound technicians and she learned how to doze in flight. Her mastery of the language improved so that she began to dream in English, sometimes even to think in English phrases. She awoke in strange beds and spent anxious moments trying to remember where she was. She wrote letters to Gisela and wondered if they would get through to East Berlin.

Thompson often had to return to D.C. between bookings to meet his obligations with the president's staff. Trudy felt more relaxed when he was gone. She and Max spent free hours playing cards in hotel suites or wandering through museums and city zoos. But whenever she relaxed or enjoyed herself, she suffered a backwash of guilt.

'It's okay to have some fun,' Max chided, but gently. 'Do you think your family wants you to be unhappy all the time?'

'No. Of course not.' But the guilt persisted.

By San Francisco, Trudy felt like a veteran of *gigs*. And then they came to Los Angeles. Max warned her before they arrived that Barry Benson, the host of *L.A. Today*, was a *schmuck*.

Max assured her Benson's show was worth it; he pulled the largest audience of any program they'd done so far. In the preprogram interview, Benson lived up to his reputation. He was arrogant and suspicious, challenging her statements as if she'd made up the whole tale. With the floor manager counting down seconds to airtime, sweat trickled between her breasts and she dreaded what Benson might say on the show. The lights were too hot and too bright. She hadn't slept the night before, and her face felt like a mask in the heavy makeup.

Thompson sat beside her on the sofa, his legs crossed in careless ease. He thrived when the spotlights were on, and he handled rude questions as if the host's ignorance was amusing. The consummate politician. He might be a *schmuck*, too, but she was glad to have him there.

The manager signaled *on the air*, and the camera held Barry Benson in a tight shot that Trudy watched on the monitor. Suddenly he was a study in friendly animation – an intelligent boy next door. His face loved the camera.

'Good morning, Los Angeles! Welcome to *L.A. Today*. This morning we'll show you some radical new fashions from the House of Goddess, talk with the mayor of our fair city about the controversial Proposition 12 and meet a young mother whose family has been cruelly destroyed by that communist atrocity, the Berlin Wall. We'll be back with that story, right after this message from our friend Hugh Downs.'

They cut to commercial and Benson turned a warm smile on Trudy. 'You're up first, darling.

Just be yourself and they'll love you. All set?' Silky as Hollywood pajamas.

She nodded stiffly. She would never understand these people. Behind the cameras, Max gave her a smile and a thumbs-up.

They came back from commercial with the close-up of Trudy's snapshot of Stefan, while Benson narrated the basic facts of their separation. Usually they showed Stefan at the end of the segment. The surprise of his sweet face filling the monitor cracked her open. Her eyes filled, and the camera cut to her.

Benson's voice was gentle. 'Mrs. Hulst, thank you for being with us today. How long has it been since you've seen your son?'

Trudy blinked and cleared her throat. Even so, her voice sounded shaky. 'Six months and thirteen days. Except for a few glimpses through barbed wire.'

'Through *barbed wire?* Tell us about that.'

She had to clear her throat again. 'In the first months after I escaped, part of the wall was rows of fencing, made from barbed wire. You could see through to the other side. My mother-in-law would bring Stefan to the wall so I could see him. Now, it is concrete almost everywhere.'

'Tell us why you had to flee the East. It must have been very difficult to leave your son behind.' The *schmuck* was very good at his job.

Trudy retold the story, the same as she had in all the other cities, the way Max had coached. Her voice sounded tired and hoarse. At the end, looking directly at the camera, she made her plea for aid in getting Stefan west of the wall.

202

Then Benson introduced Garret Thompson. 'Mr. Thompson, how did you become Trudy's sponsor?'

Garret cleared his throat, and smiled. 'I met Mrs. Hulst in West Berlin when I traveled there with President Kennedy last month. She threw herself in front of my car and asked me to help her. I could see she was desperate. There was no way I could leave her standing there on the street and just drive away.'

His face was serious, full of compassion. Trudy watched him and thought that voters would believe everything he said.

'I listened to her story and knew I had to help in some way,' Thompson went on. 'So I brought her here – at my own expense – to see if something could be done. I knew if the American people heard what had happened to her, they'd get involved. Together I hope we can put enough pressure on the East Berlin government to force them to surrender little Stefan. It's inhuman and unnatural to separate a mother and child this way – and their government has already *murdered* the child's father.'

Trudy flinched at the word *murdered*. But that's what had happened, wasn't it?

'What can our viewers do to help?' Benson asked.

Thompson turned to the camera. 'Send your letters and donations to the Trudy Hulst Fund, P.O. Box 55515, Washington, D.C. The letters will be collected and sent to East Berlin and Soviet political leaders through the American embassy. The money, of course, will help defray Mrs.

Hulst's expenses while she's here in the States and on her return to West Berlin, where, we fervently hope, she'll be reunited with her baby.'

Stefan's picture came up on the monitor again. How many times would she repeat this scene before she could get through it unaffected? The lights buzzed under her skin; she was melting like a candle.

Benson's voice made the transition to the next segment and they cut away to a commercial. Trudy couldn't get up. Hands helped her from the set and into the cool shadows. Max's face swam before her.

'You were *spectacular*. Nobody could resist that face. I just talked with our agent in D.C. and she says money's already pouring in from the previous shows.' He stopped and looked at her closely. 'Are you all right, sugar?'

'I don't want their money, Max.'

'I know, but somebody's got to pay my bill. I'm very expensive.' He smiled and stroked her hair. 'Let's get out of here, get something cold to drink.'

In the studio break room, Max bought bottles of soda from a machine and gave her aspirin for a headache that spiked between her ears. Thompson found them there. His eyes were wild and his face flushed. At first Trudy thought he'd been drinking, but as he clasped her hand and squeezed her shoulder, his breath smelled like mouthwash instead of bourbon.

'That was great! You were terrific. Wasn't she great, Max?'

'Yup.'

'And next is New York City. Max has us on *The Tonight Show* next week.' He smiled as if he expected a big reaction. She looked blankly at Max.

'Just got confirmation before we went on the air here.' Max smiled. 'Carson's show doesn't mean squat to you, does it, sugar?'

She shook her head.

'I love this girl.' Then he explained. 'Johnny Carson is the host of *The Tonight Show*. He took it over last year when Jack Paar quit, and everybody thought the show was dead. Instead, he's probably got more viewers than all these other gigs combined. He usually books entertainment acts, but we got the grand dispensation. The producer owed me.'

Thompson toasted Max with his cola. 'You're the king, Maximilian.'

Trudy sank back in the chair. 'How many more?'

'Depends on the response to the Carson show,' Max said. 'But after that, we'll go home for a while. You have that Women's Coalition convention in September. It may seem small after the television stints, but those gals swing some power.'

Home, she thought. But Max meant D.C. 'I thought I'd be back in Berlin by September,' she said, more to herself than to him.

Max caught the look in her eyes. He lifted her hand and kissed it. 'Bless your heart, you've been a real trouper but you need some rest. I'll take you back to the hotel. You coming, Garret?'

He hadn't been listening. 'Huh? No. I'm too pumped up. I'll see you both at dinner. Meet you in the hotel bar at seven.'

Max shrugged. 'Whatever you say. Come on, sugar.'

They took a taxi through streets lined with glass-walled office buildings, and disembarked at their hotel. In the lobby, palm trees swept upward from an indoor courtyard. Trudy had never seen palm trees before this visit and still couldn't believe they were real. They rode the glass elevator together and went to their separate rooms.

In her suite – all blond wood and pastels, like a tropical beach – Trudy kicked off her shoes. They had arrived late the night before and arisen early for the rehearsal. What few hours she'd spent in bed were a jumble of events and places and people. Max was right; she needed sleep.

She closed the curtains and stretched out on top of the bedspread. But her nerves hummed like stretched wire and her hands fidgeted. She kept seeing the scenes she'd described so many times – Gisela and Stefan waving to her through barbed wire, and the blood-stained blotch that was Rolf's last message. *That* was real; everything here was an unearthly fantasy.

Finally she got up and slipped on the leather sandals Max had bought her – in *Southern California, you've got to look like* a *sun worshipper,* he'd said. She took the elevator down to the hotel gift shop and bought a package of American cigarettes the clerk assured her were not strong. With nowhere else to go, she took them back up to her room.

The terrace door let in a breeze that smelled faintly of the ocean. She paced in and out, smoking. Then she remembered the stationery and list Sandra Fletcher had sent with her.

'We have a slogan in America – write your congressman,' Sandra had told her. 'These are the names and addresses of every congressman and important government official in D.C. I'll take half the list and you take the other half. Let's write to every one of them and tell them about Stefan. Ask them to help.'

'Will they actually read our letters?' Trudy asked.

'I don't know. But somebody in their offices will. I hate to see you hang all your hopes on Garret Thompson.'

Trudy pulled the folder of stationery from her suitcase, placed it on the writing desk and switched on the lamp. She looked at the list of names, which meant nothing to her. She couldn't imagine that her letters would matter to these men; she wasn't even an American citizen. Nevertheless, on airplanes and in hotel rooms while others slept, she had written several letters. It was something to do with her hands, and it helped distract her from the ache of loneliness.

She sat at the limed-oak desk and looked over the list. Of the names that were left, she found only one that she recognized. She picked up the pen and hesitated over the blank page.

Her mind drifted back to the day she'd heard President Kennedy on the Rudolph Wilde Platz. *When one man is enslaved, all are not free.* In a moment of blind optimism she had believed he could help her. *Would* help her. Perhaps she'd been a fool.

But she had nothing to lose, and everything to gain. She gripped the ivory pen and began her letter with a firm hand.

Dear Mr. President.

CHAPTER 18

For Trudy, New York was the same as the other cities, except that the host of *The Tonight Show* treated her with respect both off camera and on. Mr. Carson seemed truly interested in her circumstances, and in Stefan. But her spot on his program lasted only five minutes, and the producer would not allow Garret to make a plea for funding.

'No problem,' Max told him. 'I'll see that people know how to contribute.' He arranged an interview with the *New York Times*. 'Even if they bury the article on an inside page,' he said afterward, 'with the readership of the *Times*, thousands of people will still see it.'

Trudy didn't understand Max or his job, but she had come to trust him. When she asked him a direct question, he answered her honestly – unlike Thompson, who circled around answers with a practiced ease. When she pressed Garret to know if anyone had actually contacted the East Berlin government about Stefan, his evasiveness was answer enough. But not the answer she wanted.

Thompson's slipperiness made her uneasy, and so did the constant push to raise money. She tried not to think about it. Her job was to keep from coming apart in front of the cameras until they finished the media tour. If she could do that, maybe somebody out there watching would do something, even if Thompson didn't.

When their jet touched down in Washington D.C. in early September, Max heaved a sigh of relief. 'Home at last,' he said. Trudy was just relieved to stay in one time zone for a while.

Max rode with her in the airport limo to the hotel, while Garret took a separate cab to his office. The limo smelled like aftershave and sour lemon. The weather was still hot and humid, autumn slow in coming to the nation's capital. Trudy struggled out of her jacket and laid her head back on the seat. She was dozing when the car rocked to a stop and a bellman opened the door.

It was the same hotel where Garret had first installed her, but Max had seen to it she was upgraded to a suite. He carried her bags into the elevator and stood patiently while she unlocked the door and pushed it open.

On a table in the living area of the suite, a bunch of balloons bobbed cheerfully above a basket of fruit and cheese and wine. Beside the basket sat a chocolate replica of the Empire State Building, where a few days ago she and Max had stood peering down over New York City. She looked at him, her mouth gaping.

Max grinned. 'Flowers remind me of funerals and weddings, two events I find equally repulsive. To cheer somebody up, I favor balloons and chocolate.'

She didn't know what to say, so she hugged him.

'Here, now. Don't cry over balloons,' he said. 'You haven't seen anything yet.'

Max set her bags next to a large cardboard box on the floor. The box was filled with letters.

'What is this?' she said.

'Your mail. From people all over America who saw you on television. My assistant has been depositing the donations in a bank account, but I thought you'd want to see the letters.' He smiled. 'You've made a lot of friends.'

Trudy tossed her purse and jacket on the bed and knelt beside the box. She lifted a handful of envelopes. Some of the postmarks named cities where she'd been, but many others she didn't recognize.

'Mail has been coming in from small towns all over the country,' Max said. 'Ordinary people who wanted to help however they could.'

Trudy sat down on the thick carpet, and the letters blurred into a mass of white before her eyes. Even Max, so often sardonic, looked a bit watery.

'I'll go now so you can rest,' he said, and placed a small leather folder on the desk. 'Here's your checkbook. It's a joint account in your name and Garret's. I've put a few hundred dollars cash here, too, so you can buy anything you need. Maybe a present to send Stefan. And the hotel has comped your room.'

'What is *comped*?'

'It's short for complimentary, which means they aren't charging us for it. When you eat in the restaurant downstairs, just sign your name and room number. It's on the house.'

210

Trudy shook her head. 'But why? I didn't earn any of this.'

'Sugar, you've not only earned it, you're not finished earning it.' He checked his watch. 'I need to get to my office before five. Call me or Sandra Fletcher if you need anything. And get some rest. You were snoring in the cab.'

'I was not!'

'How do you know? It only happens when you're asleep.' Then he laughed. 'I'm teasing, sugar.'

'Thank you for everything, Max.'

He hesitated at the door. 'Want me to pick you up for dinner tonight?'

'I'll be all right. I think I'd enjoy being alone for a while.'

'I can understand that. Bye-bye, sugar. In a day or two, we'll get together and practice your Women's Coalition speech.' He blew her a kiss and closed the door.

Trudy sat on the floor, weighted by jet lag and sensory overload. The room was silent except for the hum of the air conditioning and the rubbery whisper of colliding balloons. She kicked off her shoes and leaned over the box.

She couldn't believe all these people would take the trouble to write to her. She pulled one letter from the pile. The handwriting was tight and hard to decipher, but she persisted.

I know what it's like to lose a child, it read. *We lost our baby to a heart defect when he was only six weeks old.'*

The one after that was from a father separated from his little girl by divorce. She could hear the loneliness in his words. He wished Trudy good luck in regaining her son.

Not all the letters came from tragedy; some people had simply heard her story and wanted to help. But many told of losing children in accidents or husbands in war. One mother wrote of a stolen child.

Be glad your baby is with someone who loves him. We don't know where Robbie is or whether he's still alive.

After that one, Trudy got up and walked away.

She stood for a while by the window and watched cars sliding past on the street below, pedestrians moving down the sidewalks. But when the tightness in her chest had eased, the letters drew her back. She emptied the box onto the bedspread and kept reading.

Two hours later, her bags still not unpacked, she switched on a lamp in the darkening room. She freshened up in the gold-mirrored dressing area, put away her things and stretched out on the bed beside the pile of letters. Faces materialized with the words, and even more clear was their kindness and generosity. These people sounded different from Garret Thompson or the television hosts she'd met. Even different from Max. They were simple, hardworking people, each with a different story.

At midnight, she peeled out of her clothes and crawled between the sheets, blanketed by the

212

kindness of strangers.

She dreamed of Stefan and awoke the next morning feeling wounded. She phoned for room service and stayed in all day, reading the letters, missing her son.

For nearly a week she slept late, took long baths, ate alone in the dining room downstairs. She bought stationery and began writing thank-you notes for any of the letters that listed a return address. She wrote to Gisela, as well, as she had every week since she left Berlin. In every letter she had included the hotel's address, but she'd heard nothing from *Mutti*. Perhaps the letters didn't even get through.

Sandra Fletcher met her for lunch, bringing more letters from people who'd seen her on television. Max telephoned each evening. But she did not hear from Garret Thompson. Sandra said he'd gone to New York, giving no indication when he might return. Gradually Trudy's energy returned, and she grew restless.

'Nothing is happening,' she complained to Max. 'What can we do?'

'We have to wait, sugar. Wait for Garret to get back, wait to see if the American or German ambassadors get any official response to their inquiries. Wait for an answer from the senators we contacted.'

'This part is worse than the constant travel.'

'Waiting always is.'

Thompson returned to D.C. but was sent out of town again to help with logistics for an upcoming presidential trip. Trudy made a halting speech before the Women's Coalition, her mouth so dry she had to sip water to continue. Live audiences were even scarier than bright lights and cameras. She left the podium in a rush and considered it a disaster, but Max said they loved her.

More money poured into her fund. But what good was it? She was no closer to reclaiming Stefan than when she arrived.

In October the mornings grew crisp and the trees along the Potomac turned red and gold. Max booked several more personal appearances for her, but he had taken on the political grooming of a senator who was up for reelection, and she didn't see him as often. She saw Thompson even less. He had achieved his own objective – getting his face known nationwide – and the novelty of her cause had worn off. Apparently he had overstated his political influence. She wondered if she might as well go home.

Then one day when she was returning from a walk, the reception clerk waved to her. 'Mrs. Hulst, you have a letter from Germany!' He retrieved a crisp blue envelope from a pigeonhole behind the desk and handed it over.

The sight of Gisela's childlike handwriting filled her with joy. She thanked the clerk profusely, hurried to the elevator and jabbed the button. In her room, she snapped on a lamp and held the letter in its light.

Dear Trudy,

I am not good at writing, but will do my best. Stefan is well and growing every day. Several weeks ago I fell and injured my hip so that I could not move around. Stefan stayed for a few days with Wolfgang. They have become quite fond of each other. There is a good woman in Wolfgang's building who has a little girl for Stefan to play with. He stayed with them while Wolfgang went to work.

I am fine now, and Stefan is home again. He makes short sentences and his favorite toy is a set of farm animals. He sets them up in rows and mows them down with his toy tractor.

Trudy laughed aloud, her breath catching. She wiped her eyes and when she picked up the letter again, a snapshot fell from between the pages. Stefan was sitting inside a cardboard box, his plump arms resting on the edges. His hair was even longer now, and curls wreathed his head. His dark eyes stared up at her, unsmiling.

'You look so serious, little one,' she whispered. 'And so *big*.' She touched his face and pressed the photo to the ache in her chest. It was a long time before she could finish the letter.

I hope you are well and that you will come back to Germany soon. Even when you are across the wall, it is good to know you are close to us. With much love, Mutti.

Trudy laid her head back and stared at the ceiling. She could not picture Wolfgang and Stefan together, the sober Vopo and her vivacious son. Did Wolfgang talk to him, play with him? Was he always kind?

She stood and paced the room, which seemed suddenly alien. How had she gotten to this place, so far away from him?

215

Mein Gott, I must go home.

That evening she didn't go downstairs for dinner. She opened a bottle of wine and lay awake most of the night with the television playing, her heartbeat louder than the movie sound track. When she did sleep, she dreamed that she'd gone to the wall to see Stefan and Gisela, but Wolfgang appeared carrying Stefan on his shoulders. They were laughing together, playing a game. She called to them from beyond the fence, but they would not look at her. Stefan had forgotten who she was.

She awoke nauseated, her head throbbing from the wine. The room was bathed in cloudy light and a morning thunderstorm rumbled. She got up and drank a glass of water, then rummaged through a drawer for cigarettes and lit one with an unsteady hand. She leaned against the window jamb and watched the trees whip with rain.

She had tried to keep the promise she'd made to Rolf beside the wall, that his son would be free. She'd come halfway around the world trying to keep that promise. So far she'd failed. But if there was any hope that Thompson could get Stefan out of East Berlin, she couldn't give up yet.

He'd been avoiding her. Tomorrow she would confront him and demand to know if he could do anything more – if he *would* do anything. If not, she would use the checkbook Max had given her to buy an airline ticket to West Berlin.

Outside the window, the wind had stilled and the rain slowed to a steady drizzle. She opened the glass door to the balcony and felt cool mist on her face. Taxis whisked by, their tires sizzling

216

on wet pavement.

Somewhere in the hotel, a young child was crying.

CHAPTER 19

Sandra Fletcher was apologetic when Trudy called Thompson's office again. 'I'm really sorry, but he's not taking calls. He's got to finish a project for the chief of staff today, and he left orders not to disturb him.'

'Don't worry about it,' Trudy said. All she needed to know was that Thompson was in town.

'Want to see a movie with me tonight?' Sandra offered. 'My date canceled.'

Trudy smiled. 'Sure. Shall I meet you somewhere?'

'I'll come by your hotel after work. We can get something to eat first.'

'I'll leave a key at the desk for you in case I'm out. Come up and have some of the German wines Max keeps sending me. If I drank that much I would be crazy for sure.'

'Max likes you. He wishes he could be more help.'

'I know. He's been very kind.'

'See you later. I'll slip Garret a note to call you, but I wouldn't count on hearing from him today.'

'Thanks, Sandra. *Tschüss.*'

Trudy hung up and considered her options. She was determined to talk to Thompson today, one way or another, but she didn't want to make trouble for Sandra. Thompson often worked late; she would drop by his office after Sandra left.

That gave her the whole day *to kill*, as Max would say. She dressed for the cool morning and took a taxi to the shopping district where she and Sandra had gone before. At Garfinckel's, she bought play-suits for Stefan and a picture book about counting animals. Gisela couldn't read the English words to him, but the drawings and numbers were universal. For *Mutti*, she bought a knitted scarf that was soft as fur.

Lunch was a chicken salad sandwich back at the hotel coffee shop. That afternoon she wrapped the package for Stefan and Gisela and arranged with the concierge to have it shipped to Berlin, then she answered some of the letters Max had sent over. At five o'clock she was waiting in the backseat of a cab parked across from Garret Thompson's office.

When Sandra came out around five-twenty, the light was still on in Thompson's ground-floor suite. Sandra walked with two other women to an adjacent parking lot. Trudy waited until Sandra's car drove away, then handed the taxi driver twenty dollars.

'Please wait for me. I don't know how long, but I'll pay you if it's more than that.'

'Your time is my time.' He restarted the meter and switched on the radio.

She crossed the street and entered the building. The door to Thompson's suite opened quietly, and she stepped inside the darkened outer office. Light from his partially open door knifed across the carpeted floor. She heard his voice and stopped – he was talking to someone. But there was no response; he was on the phone. She crossed to his door and lifted her hand to knock, but hesitated when he spoke again.

'Look, Max, you're not my goddamned father and I didn't ask for your opinion. I asked you for facts.'

Trudy froze.

'We both know a married candidate looks more stable to voters,' Thompson said, 'so I've got to get a wife at some point. She doesn't know anything about politics, which is a plus. And she's damned good-looking, for a Kraut. All I want you to do is find out if voters are suspicious of a foreign-born wife. There's got to be some precedent.'

The arrogant bastard.

Thompson listened for a moment. 'Nah, it doesn't look good,' he said. 'The German ambassador's just an ass-kisser. The East German government won't even respond to him. I knew it was a long shot, but hell, stranger things have happened. Maybe public opinion really *will* move some senator to action.' He paused again, then gave a dry laugh. 'Oh, no, she won't. She's not going home until I say so.'

Trudy flinched and her handbag bumped the door.

'Hold on a minute, Max.' She heard his chair squeak. 'Who's out there?' he yelled. 'Sandy, is that you?'

A flicker of common sense told her to get out of there. But she was angry, and she shoved the door open.

219

'It's your little Kraut vote-getter,' she said.

Thompson sat behind his desk in his shirt sleeves. His expensive tie was pulled loose at the collar, the blond hair rumpled. His face registered shock, then a hard smile. 'I'll call you back,' he said into the receiver, and hung up the phone.

The ever-present glass of bourbon sat on his desk, nearly empty. 'Didn't anybody teach you it's rude to eavesdrop?' he said. 'You might hear things you don't want to know.'

He lolled back in the chair and swivelled to face her. Through the window behind him, the lights of the city winked on in the dusk. Cars passed silently on the street, headlights glowing. Inside, the building was eerily silent. A prickly feeling ran up Trudy's spine.

Thompson showed no remorse for his comments to Max, and no guilt for failing to keep his promise to her. His smile was sardonic. 'You look a little tense,' he said. 'Can I fix you a drink?'

'No, thanks.'

'Suit yourself.' He got up and refilled his glass.

Trudy had seen many men become drunk in her life, but Thompson was different. Over the weeks she'd traveled with him and Max, she'd seen Thompson drink staggering amounts of liquor but he never appeared drunk. His hand now was steady as he poured from the bottle. A slight glint of wildness in his eyes was the only visible symptom of alcohol.

He moved back to his desk and gestured with the glass. 'Have a chair and unload, then. You obviously timed your visit to catch me alone.' He smiled.

'Since you won't return my calls, this is the only way I could speak to you. I heard you tell Max that nothing was happening to get Stefan.'

He shrugged, sucked on his drink. 'Please sit down. You look like a tiger ready to attack.'

She moved to a wingback chair, keeping the desk between them.

She took a deep breath and delivered the speech she'd rehearsed in her head all afternoon.

'I did not object when you used me to help your political future. We each want something. I understand that. But if you do not keep your end of the bargain, I will no longer keep mine.'

'Is that a threat, Trudy?' He smiled crookedly, and she saw the wildness flicker in his eyes again. 'Do you think you're in a position to give ultimatums?'

She ignored his sarcasm. 'You have access to the president. I want an appointment to see him. I will give you two weeks to arrange it. If you've done nothing by then, I will announce to the press that you abandoned me, and I will fly back to Berlin.'

Thompson's face stiffened, and his smile turned dark. 'I'm afraid you can't do that, *Liebling*. I have your passport. You can't leave the country without it.'

'Then I will add that detail in my comments to the press,' she said, her voice flat. 'Not only did you lack the influence to help me get my son, you used our misfortune to your advantage and now refuse to let me go home.'

Thompson drained his drink without looking at her. 'And to think when I brought you over here, you could barely speak intelligible English.'

Trudy waited, her back rigid in the chair, while he stared into the empty glass for several stony moments. Then he sighed as if resigned, and got up slowly.

She did not cringe when he came around the desk and sat on the edge in front of her, their knees almost touching. It was too late to flinch. But at that moment – too late – she recognized the look behind his eyes, that dark, razor-edge she'd tried to identify since her first night in America. After the war, when she lived with her Aunt Ingrid, she'd seen that same threat in her step-uncle's eyes just before he beat her aunt nearly unconscious.

This was a man who liked to inflict pain. Trudy thought of the red scratches she'd seen on Thompson's wrists, a bruise like a bite mark on his neck.

But he still sat casually, his posture relaxed. 'What a coldhearted little Kraut you turned out to be,' he said, and smiled again. 'I'm impressed.'

Don't show him you're afraid. 'Just as cold as you, Garret. I'll keep my part of the bargain if you keep yours.'

Without looking away from him, she slipped her hand into the purse on her lap, searching for a weapon. All she found was her cigarette lighter. With deliberate movements, she pulled out one cigarette. Flicked the lighter. Inhaled.

There was no warning, no change in his eyes before he swung from the hip with his fist.

The blow caught her cheekbone with sickening force. The chair flew over backwards, somersaulting her onto the floor, her purse and lit cigarette scattering.

The world was nothing but black pain. She could not move, could not scream, could not see. When her vision returned, unfocused, she pushed herself up on her elbows and struggled to rise.

He was on his knees beside her. The flat of his hand smashed across her ear. She sprawled on her back and he straddled her. His face shimmered, but she could read the thrill in his eyes, the satisfaction. He smiled when he leaned close, breathing bourbon into her face.

'You want to come in here and threaten me, *Liebling?* You don't know who you're dealing with.'

He twisted her breast viciously. She screamed and his hand clamped over her mouth and nose, cutting off her air. He leaned over her, his breath hot on her face.

'Talk to the press and *I will beat you to death.* Do you understand me?'

She couldn't breathe.

'Do you? You are in this country *at my pleasure.* You'll do what I say, and leave *if* I decide to let you go. Do you understand?'

She tried to nod. Her arm flailed on the floor, searching for something – anything – and found the burning end of the cigarette. Her lungs bursting, she clutched the filter tip and drove the live end into Thompson's eye.

He shouted an obscenity and rocked back on his heels, grabbing his face. She shoved her foot into his stomach with all her strength, tipping him backward and off her.

She scrambled away on hands and knees. He lunged, swearing, and caught her shoe. She kicked at his face and the shoe came off in his hand. She scuttled toward the door and got to her feet, slammed the door behind her and ran.

The cab driver saw her stumbling toward the car and came out of his seat like a shot. 'What the hell....'

'Get me away from here!'

He helped her into the back seat, fired the engine and screeched away. 'Shall I call the cops?'

'No. Just take me to my hotel.'

As they swung through the streets, Trudy pulled her clothes into place. Her cheek bone throbbed and she found blood on her fingers when she touched it. Two buttons were gone from her blouse, one shoe was missing. How could she go into the hotel like this?

Would he come after her? He could easily bribe a desk clerk and get a key – perhaps he already had one. She had to get away, but where? She'd have to risk the hotel, get some money and a few clothes and escape before he could get there.

'Driver, please hurry!'

As soon as she crawled out the driver sped away, not even waiting for his fare. Head down, holding her one shoe, she hurried through the hotel lobby toward the elevators. The car took forever to arrive; the doors slid shut with glacial slowness. She watched the floor numbers flicker by, mouth breathing, her face blazing with pain. *Where could she go?*

When the door hummed open, she ran to her room – and realized her key was in her purse, still on the floor of Thompson's office.

'*Noooooo.*' She sagged against the door.

And heard music inside.

Sandra. She pounded on the door. 'Sandra, let me in! Hurry!'

The latch clicked and the door swung open. Sandra's beautiful face was smiling and she was holding up a pale envelope, her mouth forming words that turned into a gasp when she saw Trudy's face. 'Oh, honey! Were you mugged?'

Trudy pushed past her, slammed the door and shot the bolt. She leaned against it and her knees gave way.

Sandra sank to the floor beside her. 'What happened? Shall I call a doctor?'

Trudy shook her head. 'Thompson attacked me.'

Sandra made a sound like a gargle. 'God *damn* him!'

'He has my key. I have to get away from here.'

Sandra's eyes went wide. 'Is he coming after you?'

'I don't know. He was drunk and he threatened to kill me.'

'Let's go. I moved last month and he doesn't know where I live.' She touched Trudy's cheek where her eye had swollen nearly shut. 'You need ice on that, but let's grab a few things and get out of here first.'

Trudy caught her hand as she turned away. 'He has my passport. He won't let me go home. *I have to get my passport back.*'

'We'll worry about that later.'

Trudy watched through one eye while Sandy grabbed a suitcase from her closet and ran to the bathroom. Trudy heard brushes and bottles drop

225

into the bag. 'Which drawer for your undies?' Sandra called from the bedroom.

'The top one.'

Trudy hauled herself up and went to the closet. She pulled clothes from hangers and folded them double in a quick motion, stuffing them into the bag. She grabbed her checkbook from a desk drawer, the picture of Stefan and they were ready. As they hurried to the door, Trudy stepped on something and looked down.

'I forgot,' Sandra said. 'A telegram came for you while I was waiting.' She scooped it up and handed it to Trudy. 'You can read it later. Let's go.'

Sandra paid a bellman to bring her car to a side entrance. When the big Ford Fairlane pulled up beside the glass door, they pushed Trudy's bag onto the backseat and took off. Sandra kept to the side streets, watching the rearview mirror, for what seemed like an eternity. Trudy didn't ask questions, her swollen eye pounding. Finally Sandra turned a sharp right and came to a freeway entrance. She took the ramp and picked up speed.

'My place is in Alexandria,' she said.

Trudy nodded, though she had no idea.

They crossed the Potomac River and after a few minutes Sandra exited the freeway into an area Trudy had never seen. Huge trees lined the streets and multistory brick buildings squashed together like European common-wall houses. They passed small shops and restaurants with tables out front on the sidewalks, but tonight the diners sat inside behind lighted windows, safe from a chilly wind.

Sandra turned into a residential area and kept going. The distance was comforting; surely Thompson couldn't find her out here.

Sandra parked in an open lot beside an apartment building that housed four units. They climbed a flight of stairs to Sandra's flat and locked the door behind them. Sandra flipped on a lamp, flooding warm light into a cozy living room with beige-and-blue ruffled curtains. The furniture looked comfortably used.

'I even have a spare bedroom,' Sandra said. 'You won't have to sleep on the couch.'

Trudy followed her down a short hallway to a tiny room furnished with a daybed and night stand and one chair. Sandra scooped half a dozen colored pillows off the bed and tossed them in a corner. She pulled back the quilt. 'Why don't you lie down for a while,' she said. 'You're shaking like a politician on election day.'

'I'm sorry to get you mixed up in this,' Trudy said, sinking onto the bed.

Sandra waved her apology away. 'No, *I'm* the one who's sorry. I should have warned you – I just never thought... Well, I'll fix you an ice pack for that eye.'

Trudy slipped off her shoes and lay back. When she closed her good eye, the world turned eerily on its axis, so she stared cyclops-like at the nubby ceiling.

Sandra came back with crushed ice in a plastic bag, wrapped in a dish towel. 'Are you sure you don't need a doctor?'

'No. I'm just bruised.'

227

Trudy reached for the ice pack and realized she was still gripping the envelope Sandra had given her at the hotel. She laid it on the bed and placed the cold pack on her eye. The sting took away her breath. She adjusted it gingerly.

'Who would send me a telegram?'

Sandra sat on the bed, rocking the mattress. 'That's why I was so excited. This isn't a regular telegram. It's from the White House. Want me to open it for you?'

'Please.'

Inside the outer envelope was another, with a gold seal embossed into textured ivory paper. 'That's the White House stationery,' Sandra said. She undid the seal and handed Trudy a letter written in blue, feminine script.

The letters crawled in Trudy's one-eyed vision. 'Would you read it, please?'

'You bet. I've been dying of curiosity.' Sandra held the letter closer to the lamp. 'It's *signed Jacqueline Kennedy!* The First Lady!'

In her Texas accent, Sandra read aloud.

Dear Mrs. Hulst, I was touched by your letter to the president concerning your son in East Berlin. I would like to meet you and to discuss your situation. Please contact my appointments secretary to arrange a suitable time for you to come to the White House.

Sandra squealed and hugged her, sending a bolt of pain through Trudy's bruised jaw. 'Honey, you won't have to worry about Garret Thompson anymore. Mrs. Kennedy will ask the President to help you, and if anybody can get your baby back,

228

President Kennedy can.'

Trudy was afraid to believe it. An hour ago she had lost all hope. 'Are you sure this letter is real?'

'Let's find out.' Sandy grabbed a white telephone from an end table and set it on the bed. She began dialing numbers. 'It's after six and they might not answer. Then again, who knows what kind of hours the White House staff keeps.'

Trudy listened as Sandra reached the White House switchboard and asked for Letitia Baldridge. 'I'm calling for Trudy Hulst,' she said, and explained about the letter. 'Yes, I'll hold.'

She winked at Trudy, covering the mouthpiece with one hand. 'Miss Baldridge is the First Lady's chief of staff and social secretary.' Then she spoke quickly into the phone. 'She's right here. I'll put her on.' She handed the receiver to Trudy.

'Mrs. Hulst?' a woman's voice said.

'Yes. Mrs. Kennedy has invited me to make an appointment.' She glanced at Sandra, who was nodding encouragement.

'Yes, your name is on our list,' the woman said pleasantly. 'I can make a tentative appointment for you, then someone will call tomorrow to confirm the date.'

'Thank you very much.'

There was a pause on the other end. 'How about Monday, December second, at four-thirty in the afternoon? Is that all right?'

'Yes.' Trudy swallowed. 'But I hoped it could be sooner.'

'I understand. But Mrs. Kennedy wants the president to meet you, too. You can imagine how crowded his schedule is.'

The president? Her swollen eye throbbed. 'Of course.'

'Let me get a number where you can be reached during the day. I'll check with Mr. O'Donnell tomorrow, and call you to confirm or change the appointment.'

Trudy read the number from Sandra's telephone.

Before she hung up, the woman said, 'I saw you on television a few weeks ago. I hope the president can help. Good luck.'

'You are very kind. Thank you.'

Sandra sat breathless beside her, eyes wide. 'Mrs. Kennedy wants me to meet the President,' Trudy said.

For a stunned moment they just looked at each other, Sandra with her wide, tiger eyes, Trudy through a bloodshot haze. Then Sandra whooped and began to laugh.

'You're going to have one hell of a shiner, honey, but it'll be gone by December. And Garret Thompson can kiss your ass.'

CHAPTER 20

Wolfgang sped through the streets with the blue light on his Vopo car flashing. He arrived at the apartment building in Prenzlauer Berg district within minutes of Gisela's whispered phone call and used the key she had given him to let himself in.

He found her slumped in the rocking chair, Stefan playing at her feet.

'*Oma* sick,' Stefan said, looking up at him with large eyes.

Wolfgang knelt beside her chair. 'Yes.' He touched the boy's head, keeping his voice neutral. 'We will take care of her.'

Gisela's skin was the color of cold ashes. Her cheek drew to one side, pulling at her mouth and left eye. Her eyes were closed, but he could see the slight rising and falling of her breath.

'Gisela? I'm here.' He lifted her hand and felt dead weight. 'Do you hurt anywhere?'

'I am okay.' Her voice was hoarse and deep; he would not have recognized it. She did not open her eyes.

'Try to relax and breathe deeply. I'm taking you to the hospital.'

Stefan stood beside the rocker, his eyes fixed on his grandmother's face. The boy had no real experience with sickness, and Wolfgang hoped that innocence would shield him from the fear that rose in his own mind. *A stroke. She'd had a stroke.*

He massaged Gisela's cold hand. 'Can you open your eyes?'

She didn't respond. Perhaps she thought her eyes *were* open.

'Run and get your shoes,' he told Stefan. 'We must take *Oma* to the doctor.' Stefan took off toward the bedroom.

'I was telling him about his mother,' Gisela said. 'He always wants the same story.'

Her words slurred a little, but he was encouraged that her memory seemed intact. 'You were telling Stefan a story?'

'Your mother is beautiful and strong,' she said. 'Someday she will come for you.'

Wolfgang frowned. 'Try to rest now.'

Stefan returned with his shoes. 'Excellent,' Wolfgang said. 'Can you put them on? I will tie them for you.'

Stefan sat on the floor and began trying to pull his left shoe over his crumpled right sock. 'Here, try this one.' He left Stefan to work at stuffing his foot into the high-topped shoe.

A quilt lay across the arm of the sofa and Wolfgang retrieved it. An ambulance might take half an hour or more; he would transport her himself. He was assessing how to carry Gisela down the stairs and herd Stefan at the same time when she spoke again. He knelt quickly to hear the froggy whisper.

'Heinz was here.'

'Heinz?'

'To see his grandson.' One side of her face smiled. 'You missed him.' Her eyes remained closed.

'Heinz, your husband?'

'And Peter-Karl.'

Wolfgang's heart sank. Peter-Karl was Rolf's older brother, killed in the war.

He spread the quilt on the sofa and prepared to lift Gisela from her chair. She was not a small woman, but her weight had diminished in the past year. She startled and grasped at him with her right arm when he lifted her. The left arm lay useless across her lap. He transferred her onto

232

the quilt, straightened her dress and wrapped the edges of the blanket around her. Stefan had stopped to watch.

Wolfgang sat down beside the boy, straightened his socks and worked the left shoe onto his foot. It was hard to do; the baby feet were shaped like loaves, nearly as broad and tall as they were long. When both shoes were finally in place, he tied the laces. Stefan was watching his grandmother, wrapped up on the sofa. '*Oma* sleep.'

'We're going in the car,' Wolfgang said, 'all of us. Where is your coat?'

Stefan popped up and ran to the closet. He tugged on the doorknob but couldn't get it open. Wolfgang opened the closet and found the boy's coat, held it out while Stefan stuck his arms inside. Wolfgang fastened the buttons. 'Put up the hood,' he said. 'It's cold outside.'

Wolfgang squatted beside the sofa and secured Gisela's blanket again. 'I'm going to carry you downstairs to my car,' he said. 'Don't be frightened. We'll take it slow.' He couldn't tell if she heard him.

He worked his arms beneath her and carefully stood, shifting her weight to get his balance. 'All right, Stefan. You'll have to follow us down the stairs by yourself, like a big boy. Can you do that?'

Stefan nodded, his head sliding inside the coat's hood.

'Let's go.' He angled Gisela through the doorway and into the hall. Stefan followed, leaving the door open. *Let it go.* Wolfgang had taken three steps down the staircase when Stefan hollered from the landing.

'Bebe!' Stefan pointed back toward the apartment.

'Your bear?'

'Want Bebe,' Stefan said.

Wolfgang reminded himself he was dealing with a less-than-two-year-old, and a frightened one, at that. 'All right.' He steadied himself against the wall, not trusting the stair railing. 'Go back and get Bebe. I will wait for you here.'

Stefan hesitated, glanced back at the empty apartment.

'Go on,' Wolfgang said gently. 'You're a big boy.'

Stefan turned and toddled into the apartment. Wolfgang waited. He could hear Gisela's breathing in the silence, rough, like a mistimed engine. There was a rattle of toys inside the apartment, then more silence.

'Stefan?'

No answer.

His arms ached under Gisela's limp weight. 'Hurry and get Bebe,' he called. *'Großmutti* needs a doctor fast.'

Finally the boy appeared, his face beaming. In his arm he held the floppy bear wrapped in a piece of flannel that trailed behind. 'Bebe sleep!'

'Excellent. Now follow us down the stairs, and be very careful.'

Wolfgang turned and descended the stairs, not looking back. He heard Stefan bumping along behind them, coming down each step on his bottom.

His car was parked by the curb. He laid Gisela on the backseat, arranging her legs in the small car as best he could, and wadded a corner of the quilt beneath her head. He was backing out of the narrow door when her good hand grasped his arm.

'Where is Stefan?'

'He's here. He's just fine.'

The hand clawed at his sleeve. 'Take care of him, Wolfgang.'

He swallowed hard, the future rushing at him with heartbreaking speed.

'I will,' he said. 'I promise.'

Her hand dropped away and he thought he heard her sigh.

He put Stefan in front beside him and they sped through the streets toward the hospital. A thick cloud cover trapped the blare of the siren and magnified its volume. Stefan knelt, gripping the back of the seat, staring over at his silent grandmother. Wolfgang stretched one arm across the passenger seat to keep him from tumbling when they turned a corner. Stefan's eyes were wide, his face pale.

What will become of him if Gisela dies?

They stopped outside the emergency entrance to the hospital. Leaving the car doors open, he carried Gisela inside with Stefan and Bebe trotting behind.

Here the Vopo uniform worked its magic – two attendants rushed forward to help him. They strapped Gisela to a wheeled cart and rolled fast down a narrow hall. Wolfgang picked Stefan up and followed. The child made no sound, but his arm locked around Wolfgang's neck.

A doctor and another nurse took over at the door of the examination room. The room was tiny, and Wolfgang was left to peer in through a narrow window. The medical team leaned over Gisela, checking vital signs, pulling away clothing. Her body on the narrow table looked shrunken.

Wolfgang turned away. Stefan clung to him, fierce as a cat, and buried his face on Wolfgang's shoulder. His little body was tight as a spring, but still he didn't cry.

He knows, Wolfgang thought. *He knows this is serious, and he is afraid.*

Wolfgang hugged him, rubbed his back. But he had no words to reassure Stefan; he had seen the glance that passed between doctor and nurse.

Someone came and showed them to the waiting room. He sat stiffly, holding Stefan on his lap, both of them still in their bulky coats. They sat that way for half an hour until Stefan drifted off to sleep. Wolfgang made him a pallet of the folded quilt and covered him with his Vopo coat.

The doctor, a bald man with smeared eyeglasses, confirmed Wolfgang's suspicion that Gisela had suffered a stroke.

'The next few hours are critical,' the doctor said, standing just outside the room where she lay attached to plastic tubes. 'If she doesn't become more alert and responsive fairly soon, she likely never will, and things will get worse quickly.'

Twice that afternoon Wolfgang went in to see her. The first time she was sleeping and did not respond when he spoke her name. The second time Wolfgang stood beside her bed, she was lifting her right arm aimlessly, as if reaching for something only she could see. Her face looked tense

236

with concentration. Her eyes remained closed and she did not seem to know he was there.

At dinnertime, a pretty young nurse took Stefan to the cafeteria and got him something to eat while Wolfgang kept his vigil. When they came back, Stefan played for a while on the floor, putting Bebe in and out of a cardboard box the nurse gave him. Soon afterward he fell asleep again.

Gisela lingered a few more hours without regaining consciousness. After midnight, the doctor roused Wolfgang from a nodding sleep. The doctor's face looked apprehensive, as if he dreaded delivering his news. Wolfgang stood.

'I am very sorry,' the doctor said. 'She is gone.'

Wolfgang nodded.

'Do you want to see her again?'

Wolfgang rubbed his hands over his head and eyes, saw a vision of Gisela much younger, watching a group of rambunctious boys play in the street. He preferred to remember her that way.

'No. I need to take the child home,' he said. 'Will you make the necessary arrangements, *bitte?* I can stop by tomorrow to sign any necessary papers.'

'Of course.'

Wolfgang gave the doctor a card with his phone numbers. He put on his hat and coat. He lifted Stefan without waking him, wrapped in the quilt, and carried him down the long hall to the doors where they had come in.

It had started to rain. Wolfgang paused beneath the overhang and covered Stefan's head. The boy felt lightweight in his arms, an easy burden.

He stood a moment and watched the rain.

He thought of Trudy, thousands of miles away in the United States. Gisela had shown him a letter from her, and Wolfgang had gone to the Vopo library again to see what he could learn from the Western newspapers about Kennedy's visit to West Berlin in June. The effort was futile; he didn't even know the name of the man who had promised to help her.

Trudy loved Gisela like her own mother. And she should be here now, for Stefan.

Wolfgang drove slowly through the rain-soaked streets to his apartment building. He parked in a reserved space and carried Stefan into the building, shielding him from the rain. The boy whimpered in his sleep and Wolfgang held him close. He found it hard to swallow.

They climbed two flights and Wolfgang shifted Stefan to his shoulder while he unlocked the apartment and went inside. He pushed the door closed with his foot and carried Stefan to the bedroom.

When Wolfgang laid him on the bed and removed his shoes, Stefan made a snuffling noise and pressed Bebe to his face, but he didn't awaken. Wolfgang found an extra blanket and laid it over him, pulling it up to his chin.

He stood by the bed for a long time in the blurred light and looked down at the child. The boy's thick eyelashes made a dark fringe against his cheek.

How did one explain death to a two-year-old?

Wolfgang took off his boots and put on a dry shirt. He stretched out on his back beside Stefan and laid his arm across his eyes. His one-bed-

238

room apartment, comfortable enough this morning, felt small and stark and forlornly quiet. The radiator hissed and the kitchen faucet plinked its chronic drip.

He turned his head and watched Stefan sleep. The boy's face was untroubled, innocent of the tragedy that had just demolished his tender world.

May Gisela's God help us both.

CHAPTER 21

At his desk in the Vopo headquarters building, Wolfgang placed a sheet of blank stationery before him and picked up his pen.

I must bring you sad news, he wrote, with no pretense of a greeting. *Gisela recently sustained a serious stroke. She did not suffer, and died peacefully in the hospital. We laid her to rest at St. Sophia's Cemetery.*

In the week since Gisela's funeral, he had spent time helping Stefan settle into his new home and a new routine. He'd arranged for Stefan to stay with Frau Becker during the day so he could return to work, and he had cleaned out Gisela's apartment. All were necessary activities and good excuses to postpone writing the dreaded letter to Trudy.

*Gisela's life was never easy, yet she did not complain.
Her last request was for me to take care of Stefan, and
I will keep that promise. He is living with me, and
when I am at work, he stays with a nice family who
lives in my building. Frau Becker is a wonderful
mother and has a little girl named Sophie who's a
year older than Stefan. The family also has a puppy,
which Stefan adores.*

He did not write about the times Stefan grew
sad and cried for his *Oma*. Trudy would imagine
those painful details. Instead, he came straight to
his point.

*I will do everything I can for Stefan, but I cannot take
the place of his mother or his grandmother. I am
pursuing a plan that would allow you to repatriate to
East Berlin. Tomorrow I will be installed as lieutenant-general of the Volkspolizei, and that position
will afford me some influence. Tensions between East
and West have eased here in recent months. It might be
possible for you to return, under my sponsorship,
without major consequences.*

*I am certain your main concern is to be with Stefan.
I urge you to return to West Berlin immediately, and
try to contact me through the U.S. consulate. Since you
apparently have some connection to an American
political figure, perhaps their consulate will be willing
to help. I will alert my office to expect your call.
Meanwhile I will try to work out whatever details are
necessary to bring you home again. Wolfgang.*

He reread the letter and frowned. It sounded
formal and cold, and that was not his intention.

240

He considered for a moment, then added a line above his signature:

My deepest sympathy for your loss of Gisela.

It occurred to him he had never expressed his sympathy when Rolf died.

He sealed the letter in a *Volkspolizei* envelope. The official stationery should assure its passage out of East Germany. In Trudy's last letter to Gisela, he had found the address of a hotel in Washington, D.C. where she was staying. The letter might take weeks to reach her. Meanwhile he would execute the blizzard of paperwork required to apply for her repatriation to the East. At the end of the work day, he dropped the letter into the outgoing mail basket in the front office and headed home.

At six o'clock, Wolfgang knocked his habitual rhythm on the Beckers' apartment door and heard Stefan's shriek from inside. He smiled, removed his Vopo hat and waited.

The door burst open on a typical evening at the Becker household. Frau Becker greeted him warmly. Herr Becker was in the living room with the television playing. The beagle puppy, which they had named Stasi in a moment of black humor, zoomed into the hallway. Three-year-old Sophie ran after the dog, her ribboned braids flying. Sophie was a beautiful child, and Frau Becker dressed her like a little doll.

Stefan ran out and hugged his knees. Wolfgang leaned down and ruffled the toddler's hair.

241

'*Hallo, Schätzchen.*' He scooped up the beagle and handed him to Sophie, who dragged the gangly puppy back into the apartment.

The Beckers' home was always happy chaos, and Stefan seemed to thrive on it. He did not resist when Wolfgang dropped him off in the mornings, and for that Wolfgang was profoundly grateful. Even so, Stefan always seemed glad to see him when he returned. Wolfgang was surprised at how much pleasure that gave him.

He handed Frau Becker an envelope with her weekly pay for babysitting. 'I appreciate the good care you give Stefan. We will see you tomorrow.'

Frau Becker smiled. '*Danke.* They have so much fun together, I feel guilty for taking the money,' she said, nevertheless pocketing the envelope.

'And I feel guilty for not paying you more,' he said, smiling. 'So that makes us even.' He knew the family could use extra money. Herr Becker was a jovial but unambitious sort who would be content driving his milk delivery truck for the rest of his days. Not that he had many choices.

Frau Becker leaned out the door to call goodbye to Stefan, who was already running down the hallway toward the stairs. She handed Stefan's coat to Wolfgang and closed the door.

Stefan liked to climb the stairs by himself. The risers were knee-high for him, but he was a determined little sprout. He hung on to the railing and hauled himself up. Wolfgang climbed behind him, watchful to avert a fall.

'Good job,' he said, encouraging. 'What a big boy.'

'Big boy!' Stefan echoed.

When they reached the top of the stairs, Stefan held up his hands for the key to the apartment. Wolfgang selected the correct key and handed it to him. Standing on his toes, his tongue poking out, Stefan tried to fit the key into the lock. He was too short for the job, but he never tired of trying. Wolfgang was learning the importance of small rituals to a child. He let Stefan work at the lock for a while, then reached down and helped him.

Stefan ran into the living room while Wolfgang hung up their coats. The place no longer looked like a bachelor apartment. Crayons and storybooks filled the space on low tables where ashtrays once sat. By dinnertime, tiny cars and wooden pull toys would litter the floor. Clutter seemed to be a necessary part of a child's life. Nevertheless, after stepping barefoot on a metal fire truck in the night, Wolfgang had instituted a ritual of picking up all the toys before bedtime.

The hallway was lined with taped-up boxes from Gisela's apartment. More boxes sat under his bed and on the shelf in his closet. It had felt wrong to get rid of her things so soon, and perhaps Trudy would want them.

Wolfgang washed his hands, leaning over a step stool in front of the lavatory where Stefan stood each day to brush his seed pearl teeth. Wolfgang had to get up half an hour earlier now – there was simply no hurrying a child in the morning time. Thank goodness Frau Becker had offered to feed him breakfast.

Meals were the most difficult part of his assumed parenthood. That, and diapers. *Ach,* how

243

he dreaded hauling those smelly diapers downstairs twice a week to the laundry room, running
them through two cycles to expel the odor. Frau
Becker had begun to work with Sophie on potty
training, and Wolfgang encouraged her to include
Stefan, as well. Stefan, however, had expressed no
interest. Frau Becker said girls trained more easily
than boys, and Sophie was also a year older.
Wolfgang remembered his own mother saying she
had trained him using gummy candies – a bribe
for each time he *went* successfully – but Wolfgang
didn't want to promote cavities in Stefan's perfect
little teeth.

In the kitchen he took a pot of sausage and
beans he'd made last weekend from the
refrigerator. It was one of his staple dishes, and
luckily Stefan liked it, too. He set the pot on the
stove over a low fire.

When he lived alone, it had never mattered
much what he ate, or even if he ate. Now he rummaged through the refrigerator for vegetables.
Raw carrots and cabbage would do for tonight.
He rolled up his shirtsleeves and stood at the sink
to peel the carrots. He could hear Stefan's steady
patter of make-believe from the living room.
Some of his chatter was indecipherable, but he
was picking up new language fast from Sophie.

Watching strings of carrot peel sluff off into the
sink, Wolfgang had a vision of Trudy here with
them in the evenings. He pictured her moving
around his small kitchen, preparing real meals
for the three of them. In his new position as Vopo
commandant, he had applied for a house in a
nice neighborhood. He imagined a pleasant

living room with a Christmas tree and Stefan opening his presents. He even imagined laughter.

The illusion evaporated with a loud *thunk* from the living room and Stefan's voice in distress. Wolfgang dropped the carrot peeler and hurried toward the sound.

Only Stefan's feet were visible sticking out from the crevice where he was wedged between the sofa and end table. But he wasn't crying.

'*Vati!*' Stefan called.

Daddy. The unexpected name opened his chest. As he lifted Stefan from his predicament and set him on his feet, he felt he should correct him, tell him who his daddy really was. But he found that he couldn't speak.

'Bebe!' Stefan pointed behind the couch. Wolfgang retrieved the eyeless bear and handed it to him, and Stefan went back to playing.

At dinner Stefan finished his beans and a carrot stick but balked at the raw cabbage. Wolfgang cleaned up the dishes and wrestled Stefan into a clean diaper and pajamas. They made a race of picking up toys. Near bedtime, they sat in Gisela's old rocking chair and looked at picture books.

Stefan was good at naming animals, and he was learning his colors. The chair squeaked, and Stefan began to sing. Wolfgang thought perhaps he was remembering something his *Oma* sang. Or maybe even his mother.

Eventually Stefan fell asleep on his lap, and Wolfgang carried him to the crib in their shared bedroom. He tucked Bebe in beside him. The ragged bear was nonnegotiable. In their first week together, Stefan had screamed for half an hour

245

one night until Wolfgang finally found Bebe stuffed into the potato bin. Stefan had apparently put it there and then forgotten.

When Stefan was settled in bed, Wolfgang went back to the living room. He read his newspaper, and then switched to a Russian novel he'd been working on for some time. The novel was too romantic for his taste, and at midnight he laid it aside and went to bed.

At night, responsibility lay on Wolfgang like an overly warm blanket. Stefan made little noises in his sleep, and sometimes he awoke crying and had to be consoled. Wolfgang lay stiffly awake, trying not to toss and turn so much that he would wake his accidental roommate.

A longing arose in his chest. He imagined Trudy lying beside him, the three of them a family. It was impossible, of course.

But an idea had switched on in his head – a politically acceptable way to assure that Trudy could come back across the wall.

CHAPTER 22

On a November morning full of diluted winter sunshine, Wolfgang delivered Stefan to Frau Becker's door and drove the six blocks to Vopo headquarters feeling more optimistic than he had in a long time. Today he would initiate the paperwork to give Stefan back his mother.

He entered the station whistling and the young

officer on reception duty looked at him with alarm. Wolfgang saluted and walked down a long hallway to his office. He unlocked, hung up his coat and hat and sat down at his desk.

A stack of paperwork awaited his attention and signature, and he wanted to write a comprehensive statement of purpose and a list of suggestions to submit to the police colonel-general, the only man who now outranked him in the People's Police. But first he would prepare the application for Trudy's repatriation, and attach a personal note to expedite the application through required channels.

With Nadia, he had never considered the idea of marriage or a family. He liked Nadia, respected her in many ways, but he could not envision living with her. They had purposely kept each other at arm's length. This weekend he should talk to her and explain what he was planning to do; he owed her that much. She had to wonder why he hadn't come to the restaurant lately or invited her to his apartment. Or perhaps she'd already heard that he was now a surrogate father. She had an uncanny way of knowing things.

He had almost completed the application form, in triplicate, when a young clerk tapped on his open door. Wolfgang looked up. 'Yes?'

'A memo for you, sir.'

Wolfgang motioned him inside. *'Danke.'* The clerk handed him the note and went away. Wolfgang opened the paper and glanced at the signature. Here was the one cloud that could rain on his day.

Please come to my office at your earliest convenience for a conference on a matter of great importance. Grepo Commandant Albrecht Schweinhardt.

Mist. Wolfgang wadded the paper and threw it in the wastebasket.

He was tempted to ignore the request, but ignoring Schweinhardt only goaded him to greater annoyances. Besides, he couldn't ignore the man's rank. Eventually Wolfgang would have to see him; he might as well get it over with.

But he didn't rush. It was an hour before he climbed a flight of stairs and knocked on the door of a dreary office that so perfectly matched its inhabitant.

Schweinhardt's voice boomed from behind the door. *'Herein!'*

Albrecht's underlings had secretly nicknamed him Big Al, like the American gangster Al Capone. Wolfgang thought of that now when he saw Schweinhardt behind the nearly vacant desktop, his belly as round as the top of his balding head. Two cuckoo clocks adorned the wall, which Wolfgang thought ironically appropriate.

'Lieutenant-General Kruger,' Schweinhardt thundered. 'I appreciate your coming. I realize that since I no longer outrank you, you did not have to come at my request.' He smiled without grace, his eyes like iron pellets.

Wolfgang took a chair opposite the desk without waiting for an invitation. Schweinhardt sat abnormally high behind the desk, and Wolfgang wondered if he was sitting on a telephone book to make himself taller.

248

'So I am here, Genosse Schweinhardt. What do you want?'

'You are a busy man, I am sure,' Schweinhardt said. 'I shall come to the point.'

But he took his time extracting an oversized cigar from a wooden box and lighting up. He offered the box to Wolfgang as an afterthought. Wolfgang declined, but noticed that the cigars were imported. Big Al must have spent both money and influence to get those. No common citizen east of the wall had access to such luxuries.

Wolfgang almost smiled. Perhaps there was a worm in the flour – a tobacco worm.

Schweinhardt didn't notice. He leaned back in the chair and blew a smoke ring, then obliterated the ragged circle with a forceful puff. He put his elbows on the desk and fixed Wolfgang with a hard look. 'It has come to my attention that you are engaged in a stream of communications with someone in the United States.'

Wolfgang became very still and was careful not to change his expression. Schweinhardt must have pawed through the outgoing mail and seen his letter to Trudy. 'If you choose to call one letter a stream of communications,' he said.

Schweinhardt watched him closely, his lips pressed into a tight line. When Wolfgang remained unruffled, he tried again. 'It is a risky practice, this constant contact with the West,' he said. 'I feel it my duty to warn you that certain members of the politburo are looking upon it with disfavor.'

Ah. The oaf was only fishing.

Wolfgang drew a deep breath and relaxed. 'You know very well who it is I'm in touch with and

249

why. It's no secret I am the guardian of a child whose mother is in the West. Why have you suddenly decided to warn me about this?'

'As *Obermeister* of the *Grenzpolizei*, I can show no favoritism in performing my duties to stop the illegal emigration of our citizens. I hope you and this woman are not planning something foolish,' he paused, 'like trying to smuggle her child across the border.'

Wolfgang kept his face calm. 'Obviously you have not seen Trudy Hulst's application for return to the East.' Which he couldn't have, since Wolfgang had sent it through only twenty minutes ago. 'She will be repatriated, and we are to be married.'

The expression on Big Al's face revived Wolfgang's good mood. Schweinhardt turned the color of a fresh bruise.

'You are lying!' he said, his voice rising. 'It would be idiocy for an officer to compromise his career by marrying a known fugitive.'

'I am crushed that you disapprove,' Wolfgang said. 'I will try to struggle through my happiness without your blessing.' He stood to leave, then turned back, frowning.

'*Genosse* Schweinhardt, you worry me. You should know that the official position now is to welcome back defectors who have seen the light and wish to return to the DDR. Surely you would not disagree with official policy.'

Schweinhardt tapped his cigar ash into a pewter ashtray shaped like the Russian bear. His voice turned oily. 'Of course, we must welcome back our lost sheep. But we need not sleep with them. Your loyalty as an officer might come into question.'

If the game was intimidation, Wolfgang would not miss his turn. Against an opponent as paranoid as Schweinhardt, one need not have solid information – vague insinuations were enough. He opened the door. 'You should not concern yourself about my professional reputation. Instead, you might tell your runner to be more discreet.'

Schweinhardt scowled. 'What runner?'

'The one who delivers your contraband cigars.'

Schweinhardt's face reddened violently. Wolfgang thought blood might actually spurt from his ears. 'These were a gift!' he boomed. 'From a grateful citizen!'

Wolfgang nodded soberly, but the hint of a smile played on his lips. 'Of course, *Genosse*. But beware of careless contacts with the West. *Guten Tag.*'

He closed the door before the little tyrant had time to explode.

Stupid of me to taunt him, Wolfgang thought, but the man could hardly send more poisonous memos than he already did.

Nevertheless, he'd have to watch his back. He must not take shortcuts in the official procedures to sponsor Trudy's return. And he'd be wise to take a few measures that would cast doubt on the competency and loyalty of *Obermeister* Albrecht Schweinhardt.

Wolfgang walked back to his office with an ugly taste in his mouth. The petty business of internal spying disgusted him. When it was a matter of state security, he could accept the need for spying. But the suspicion and jealousy among high-ranking officials within the government itself was demeaning to them all.

They were supposed to be on the same side, for God's sake, working together for the progress of the state. Instead, men like Schweinhardt wasted time collecting meaningless details to use against a colleague if he should fall from favor. Schweinhardt epitomized everything that was flawed in the East German version of communism. Big Al and that wretched wall.

CHAPTER 23

Trudy awakened to the smell of coffee and the sounds of Sandra in the kitchen making breakfast. She sat up on the edge of the bed and something in her head rolled like a shot put, crashing behind her eye. She waited out the pain and stood up carefully, testing her balance. The bruised eye was swollen and allowed only a sliver of light.

On the foot of the bed, Sandra had laid out a frilly bathrobe. Trudy smiled and touched the silky fabric, then hung the robe in the closet. She had salvaged her yellow terry cloth one from the hotel. She pulled it from the suitcase and wrapped it around her like a security blanket, tying the sash. Then she followed her nose to the kitchen.

Sandra was frying bacon. She wore a cotton shift that looked as fresh as the sunshine angling through a window above the kitchen sink. Gingham curtains ruffled the window and a clock shaped like a cat swung its tail once per second.

Sandra looked up and flashed a smile. *'Guten*

Morgen!' It was the one German phrase she'd learned, and she seemed proud of it. 'How are the bruises?'

She stepped closer and examined Trudy's face. The smile faded. 'That son of a bitch. If he wants to beat up his hookers, that's their problem, but we should call the police about this.'

'He beats prostitutes?'

Sandy shrugged. 'There are rumors. I know he plays rough,' she said drily.

Trudy accepted a mug of coffee and sat on a stool at the kitchen bar. 'I don't want to involve the police. Thompson is an important man, and I'm not even a citizen. If I make him angry, he could ruin my chance to see the president.'

Sandra considered that while breaking eggs into a bowl. 'You have a point. Might be better just to hide you from Garret for the next few weeks.'

'As soon as the president's secretary calls, I'll find another hotel.'

'You'll do no such thing,' Sandra said. 'Garret doesn't know where I live. At the office I'll play dumb, like I haven't seen you and don't know what happened. I can find out if he's looking for you or not.' She pointed with the spatula. 'And maybe find your passport.'

The eggs sizzled into a skillet.

'What if he discovers you're helping me?' Trudy said. 'I don't want to put your job in danger.'

'Don't worry. Playing dumb is one of my best skills. But it'll be hard not to put poison in his coffee.'

'Don't hold back on my account,' Trudy said.

Sandra grinned and stirred the eggs. 'Thompson's a world-class jerk. I dated him for a while and found that out. I'd quit my job, but he won't give me a decent reference because I dumped him.' She sighed. 'As soon as I save up some money, maybe I'll just go back to Texas. Mom would love that. She could say "I told you so."'

She dropped two slices of bread into a toaster and turned to face Trudy. 'I haven't done many noble acts in my life – which is another thing my mom likes to point out. If I can help you, maybe I can go home with a little self-respect.'

Trudy thought if Sandra's mother couldn't see what a good daughter she had, something was wrong with the mother. 'My appointment is almost a month away. That's a long time to keep hiding from Thompson.'

Sandra dished up the eggs and toast and set the plates on the kitchen bar. 'I thought about that all night. I think we should tell Max.' She pulled up a stool and sat.

'Max? Why?'

'Max doesn't like Garret either. He charges him double, though Garret doesn't realize that. I can't tell Garret you're going to see the president because I'm not supposed to know, but Max could tell him. If Garret knows about it – and knows that Max knows – he won't dare harm you. There would be too much explaining to do. Besides, if it results in getting your baby back, Garret will want to take credit for it.'

'Can we depend on Max not to tell him where I am?'

'Max won't know. That way he can't tell.'

Trudy nodded. 'First we have to see if the presi-

254

dent's secretary confirms the meeting.'

'He will,' Sandra said, her eyes lighting up again. 'I just know he will.'

Trudy cleaned up the dishes while Sandra got ready for work. 'I won't call you from the office unless it's an emergency,' Sandra said before she left, 'but you can call me if you need to. Garret *never* answers the phone. It's beneath his dignity.'

'I wish I could repay you for all your kindness.'

Sandra waved it away. 'Just make yourself at home, and take care of that eye. If you need anything you had to leave behind last night, make a list and I'll shop for you. I don't think either of us should go back to the hotel.'

'I agree.'

When Sandra left and Trudy was alone, the apartment seemed foreign and quiet. She made sure the doors and windows were locked, then took a hot bath, leaving the door open so she could hear the phone. She applied another ice pack to the swollen eye and tried to nap on the sofa, but soon rose to pace the floor. She looked out the windows, wrote a letter to Gisela and Stefan; but mostly she waited for the phone to ring.

Near noon, eating a sandwich in Sandra's sunny kitchen, Trudy decided Sandra was right about telling Max what had happened. Max had been very kind to her, and she'd detected his dislike for Thompson. Even so, it was better for both of them if he didn't know where she was staying.

She was working on a crossword puzzle in Sandra's newspaper, listening to the relentless ticking of the cat clock, when the phone shrilled. The sudden noise startled her from her chair.

255

What if Thompson had somehow found her? Her mouth went dry, but she had to answer.

The voice on the line was female. 'Mrs. Hulst? It's Letitia Baldridge. I've co-ordinated with Ken O'Donnell and called to verify your appointment on December second.'

She gave instructions for Trudy to appear at a private entrance of the White House at 4 p.m. on that day. She would undergo a security check before meeting the president and Mrs. Kennedy. Trudy repeated everything to make sure she understood correctly, her heart racketing in her ears. As soon as she'd hung up, she wrote down the details.

Until she saw it written on a notepad, her good fortune had been hard to believe. Now her eyes filled. President and Mrs. Kennedy had small children; they would understand her urgency to be with Stefan. And there was no more powerful political figure in the world than the U.S. president. For the first time in months, she had real hope.

But how would she endure four weeks of waiting? If only she could talk to Gisela, tell her what was happening and that the three of them might be together by Christmas. She wanted to tell Sandra the news, too, but calling her seemed like a foolish risk.

She had to tell *someone*, so she dialed Max.

'Trudy, sugar! I've been trying and trying to call you. I heard you walk in on my conversation with Garret yesterday. Are you okay?'

'I will be. But I need to talk to you.'

'Would you believe I'm free for lunch? I'll pick you up at the hotel.'

'Um, no. I'm not at the hotel, and my appearance today would attract too much attention. Garret gave me a black eye.'

She heard the front legs of his chair hit the floor. 'Are you serious? That *asshole*. Have you called the police?'

'No, and I won't. But I need your help, Max. I have an appointment to meet with the President. He actually read a letter I wrote to him.'

'I'll be damned. That's fantastic!'

'But it isn't for several weeks and I need to stay away from Thompson.' She almost said *Sandra thinks*... but caught herself. Better if he didn't know Sandra had any part in this. 'I want you to let him know that I am scheduled to see President Kennedy. If he knows about the meeting, maybe he'll want to take credit for it, and he'll leave me alone.'

'It's worth a try. Are you sure you're all right? Where are you?'

'I think it's better if you don't know, Max, in case Garret asks. I'll call you to keep in touch.'

'You're probably right. Have you been to the bank yet?'

'What?'

'You'll need money, and Thompson can close that account, if he hasn't already.'

'I never thought of it.'

'First call the bank and see if the account is still open. If it is, don't go to the main bank. There's a branch on Massachusetts Avenue. Go there, and do it fast. Withdraw all but fifty dollars. If you don't close the account, they won't notify Thompson.'

'All right.'

'Get the money in cash and keep it hidden. I hope you're not in a bad area of town.'

'No. I'm safe here.'

'Good luck, sugar. I'll get the word to Thompson. Call me if you need anything. Call me anyway. I'll be worried about you.'

'Okay, Max. Thank you.'

Following Max's instructions, Trudy looked up the number for the bank and phoned. The account was still open. She camouflaged the darkening eye with makeup as best she could, found a pair of Sandra's sunglasses and a house key in a basket beside the kitchen phone and called a taxi.

Before Trudy's startled eyes, the teller at the branch bank counted more than five thousand dollars into neat stacks. She had no purse, so the teller supplied a zippered bag. The bag felt as conspicuous as a hand grenade when she hurried back to the waiting cab, her knees shaking.

On the ride back, the driver glanced at her several times in the rearview mirror. His was a face that had seen everything and said nothing. Maybe he thought she had robbed the bank. She gave him a good tip and he wished her luck before driving away.

She let herself into the apartment and locked the door. On the tiled kitchen counter top, she recounted the money, dividing it into stacks. She hadn't dreamed there would be so much. She could use it to buy her ticket home after she met the president. And she would pay Sandra's rent for the month she was here, maybe help her go home to Texas.

The stacks of money made her nervous. She hid one bundle under the night stand in her bedroom, others behind a Monet print and inside a spare roll of toilet paper in the bathroom. She tucked the last two under the sofa cushions and inside a vase, then made a list of where she'd hidden them and hid the list. After that she paced the floor, startling at every noise, until Sandra got home about six.

In the days that followed, Trudy secluded herself in the apartment. She cleaned and cooked, watched TV and worked crossword puzzles in English. The purple around her eye turned olive-yellow and began to fade. Twice she awoke in the night with a dark premonition of something terribly wrong. Was Stefan in danger? Gisela sick again? Was Garret Thompson planning to act on his threat? But each morning, in the light of Sandra's sunny optimism, the feeling of foreboding dissolved. She marked off the days before her appointment.

Sandra reported that Thompson never mentioned Trudy's visit to his office, nor her disappearance. In fact, he never mentioned her at all. He was making plans to establish a residence in his home state of Ohio and run for governor in the next election there. Apparently he wasn't the least worried that she would report his attack to the authorities. In Thompson's self-centered world, Trudy no longer existed, and she was thankful for that.

When her face had healed, Trudy occasionally went out during the day. Sometimes she window-shopped in the charming downtown of old

259

Alexandria, but her favorite haunt was a small park near the river. There, on warm days, she could sit on a bench and feed the pigeons. It reminded her of home.

Sandra made plans for a turkey dinner for the American holiday of Thanksgiving, and the department stores decorated for Christmas. Silver garlands draped light posts and gates. The lighted trees and glittering shop windows made Trudy miss her family even more. This would be her second Christmas without Stefan, unless President Kennedy could make magic happen. After all, it was the season for miracles.

She bought newspapers and read every printed detail about the president or his wife. The *Washington Post* reported that Kennedy would make a junket to Texas in late November. Sandra had relatives in Dallas and she wrote to them about his upcoming visit. The best news was that Garret Thompson would be out of town for a week to help make arrangements for the president's entourage before his arrival. In his absence, Sandra would search the office inch by inch to find Trudy's passport.

As soon as Thompson left town, Trudy called Max. 'Could you help me get the rest of my things from the hotel while Thompson is gone?'

'Sure. I'll go with you. I told them to hold the room, that you were traveling for a while.'

'I don't have my key.'

'No problem. Leave it to me.'

She took a cab and met him in front of the hotel. Max wore a topcoat that made him look like a tweed teddy bear. He hugged her and kissed the air by her cheek. 'You look great,' he said.

'I have nothing to do but eat and walk these days. I guess it agrees with me.'

'No trace of the shiner. I still can't believe the bastard hit you.' He shook his head. 'I'll get him for that someday. One way or another.' He took her arm and ushered her into the hotel as if she were royalty.

The concierge remembered her. 'Mrs. Hulst! Welcome back.'

'Hi, Marian,' Max said, so smoothly that it appeared he remembered her name instead of reading the name tag. 'We've managed to misplace Trudy's room key. Can you get us another, please?'

'Certainly.' Marian came out from behind her desk and ushered them to the reception area. She smiled at Trudy. 'There's a letter for you from Germany. I didn't know how to reach you while you were traveling.'

'Wonderful!' Trudy said. Thank goodness she'd come to get her things.

The concierge retrieved a room key and handed Trudy the letter.

The bold handwriting was not Gisela's and Trudy's heart sank. But she smiled at Marian and slipped the letter into her pocket. 'Thank you so much. I'll read it later.'

Max walked with her to the elevator. 'Is something wrong? Your face faded like a cheap shirt when you saw that letter.'

'It isn't from my mother-in-law as I hoped,' she said. 'It's from ... someone else.'

'Ah. A gentleman friend, maybe?' Max teased.

'It is a man,' she said. 'But I don't know if he's a friend.'

The hotel suite she'd abandoned in such a rush had been set aright in her absence. She snapped on a lamp and went to the closet. Her remaining clothes were still there, and so was the big box of letters. She packed her clothes in two suitcases while Max gathered her papers from the desk and put them into the box of letters. When they'd emptied the suite, Max called for a porter who loaded everything into the trunk of Max's Lincoln.

'I'll be glad to drive you wherever,' he said.

'I appreciate that, but I still think it's wiser if you don't know where I am staying. Could you store my things at your office for a while? I'll just take one bag with a few more clothes.'

'Sure. I'll lock them in the closet in my office. Nobody looks in there but me.'

'I don't know how long it might be. Everything depends on my appointment at the White House.'

Max smiled and touched her hair. 'I'll pray for a miracle. Nobody deserves one more than you.'

He signaled the doorman and a taxi pulled up to the curb. She thanked him again.

'Phone me if you need anything, or just want to talk,' he said. 'And for sure I want a detailed report after you meet the president and First Lady. I've been in this town for twenty years and *I've* never got to meet a president.'

Trudy smiled. 'I will phone you, I promise. Thanks for everything, Max.'

He hugged her goodbye. She climbed into the backseat of the taxi and Max shut the door.

'Where to, Miss?' the driver asked.

She gave him the address and leaned back on the seat. An Elvis Presley song played on the cab's radio. *Don't be cruel* – bump bump bump – *to a heart that's true...*

Trudy took a deep breath and pulled Wolfgang's letter from her pocket.

CHAPTER 24

The first sentence of the letter confirmed her premonition of bad news. *Please, no...*

But it was true. Stefan's beloved guardian, and her best friend, had died of a stroke. She didn't realize she'd made a sound until the taxi driver spoke. 'You all right, ma'am?' He glanced at her in the rearview mirror.

She could only nod and wave him on. She dropped the letter in her lap without reading further, her eyes blind. Dear Gisela. How could she be *gone?* Never once had she thought Gisela might die before her. *Mutti* was a fixture, always patient and strong. Trudy had thought she would live forever.

Poor Stefan! He must be so frightened and confused. She snatched up the letter again. Stefan was staying with Wolfgang. *God in heaven.* Her son was in the care of a dedicated communist who had quite likely betrayed his father.

I need to be there.

She looked our the smeared window of the taxi. Traffic blurred past on the street, but her eyes

263

saw a modest apartment crowded with aging furniture and the eternal mother who had taken in her son's young girlfriend and given her a home. She saw Gisela's lined face and heard the low-pitched laugh that had always made things right. *May God rest your soul, Mutti. It's too late now to tell you how much you were loved.*

Her heart ached for Stefan, and even a little for Wolfgang. He had cared for Gisela, too. She could not picture him as a surrogate parent. Yet the task had fallen to him to explain where *Oma* had gone, and why she wouldn't be back. No one was prepared for such a delicate responsibility. God knew what he might have told Stefan.

As the cab neared Sandra's apartment building, Trudy read the last half of the letter.

Tensions between East and West have eased here in recent months. It might be possible for you to return, under my sponsorship, without major consequences... I urge you to return to West Berlin immediately... Meanwhile I will try to work out whatever details are necessary to bring you home again.

Home, Trudy thought. Without Gisela, where was home?

The driver had stopped the taxi and was getting out to open her door. Quickly she dug in her purse for money. He retrieved her suitcase and she walked stiffly toward the apartment, the case in her left hand, the letter in her right. Her mind had gone numb; she couldn't think.

Sandra wasn't home from work yet, and the apartment was dim and quiet. Trudy didn't turn

264

on the lights. She set the packed bag in the closet and, without removing her coat, lay down on her borrowed bed.

'Are you all right?' Sandra asked that evening at dinner. 'You're sure quiet tonight.'

'I'm sorry.' She wanted to tell Sandra about Gisela, but if she did, she'd start crying. 'It's been a lonesome day.'

'You don't have to apologize, honey,' Sandra said. Then she brightened. 'I have some good news. I almost forgot.' She got up from the table and rummaged through her oversized handbag. She pulled out a brown booklet and waved it like a flag. 'Ta-da! I finally found it in his personal files.'

She laid Trudy's passport on the table. Trudy opened the cover and looked at the photo of a scared girl with stringy hair. How could she have changed so much in a few months?

That night Trudy couldn't sleep. She grieved for *Mutti* and for Stefan, and asked herself a thousand questions about Wolfgang's vague promise and his motives. She knew Gisela had trusted him. Trudy could take the money Max secured for her and buy a plane ticket to West Berlin. But what if Wolfgang's plan didn't work? If he couldn't use his influence to bring her back without imprisonment, what would she do then? She'd be alone in West Berlin again with no hope of getting to her son.

She was so close, so close to the purpose for which she'd come to America. It was her only chance to keep the promise she'd made to Rolf, and to herself. There was a chance President Kennedy might refuse to intervene, but there was also a chance he would make certain phone calls and induce the Pankow government to hand over her son. The two governments had traded spies before, why not a child?

Eleven days, Stefan. In eleven days I will beg the U.S. president for your freedom.

On the Friday before Thanksgiving, Sandra went to work as usual and Trudy stood at the sink washing the breakfast dishes. In the sudsy water, she saw Gisela's veined hands instead of her own, and she could almost smell the aromas of cabbage and strudel. Gisela had taught her how to cook, had listened to her complaints while she was pregnant. She wondered if Wolfgang had taken Stefan to the funeral. Did he remember his mother, who'd been gone so long?

Ten more days of waiting. The toast she'd eaten for breakfast felt like lead in her stomach.

She put the dishes away, straightened the apartment, read the morning newspaper and worked the crossword puzzle. And then there was nothing to do.

The apartment felt impossibly quiet. She couldn't stay there all day or she'd go crazy.

At midmorning, she put bread crusts into a paper bag, donned her coat and scarf and went out. She walked to the park by the river where she'd often gone before. In the cold November sun, she sat on a bench and fed bread crumbs to the pigeons. She pictured herself pushing Stefan in a stroller, like the young mothers she saw there

266

sometimes. Today the park was empty, and she closed her eyes and turned her face to the light.

When her feet got cold, she wandered toward a neighborhood deli that was run by an older German couple named Schneider. She had eaten lunch there several times. The Schneiders were plump and friendly and enjoyed speaking German with her. Herr Schneider liked to tell stories from his boyhood in the Old Country.

A brass bell clamored above the door when she entered. Frau Schneider was not in her usual place behind the cash register. Nor was Herr Schneider behind the counter making sandwiches. The shop was empty.

Trudy frowned. 'Herr Schneider?'

No one answered. The sound of a radio drifted from the back room. She walked behind the deli counter and peered through an open doorway, calling out again.

The storeroom was cool and dark. The Schneiders stood near the backdoor, hovered beside a black radio on a cluttered shelf. They looked up in unison, their faces grim and white in the shadows.

'Are you all right?' Trudy said.

Frau Schneider shook her head without answering. Her mouth was clamped tight and she wrung a kitchen cloth in her spotted hands.

The voice on the radio was a masculine monotone. Trudy couldn't make out the words, but there was no mistaking a tone of shock and sadness. She thought of the morning that the citizens of Berlin had awakened to find their city paralyzed by the wall.

A sick feeling rose with the image. '*Was is los?*'

Herr Schneider laid a finger to his lips and motioned her to come in. As Trudy approached, she heard the words *hospital* and *secret service* from the radio.

'What is happening?' she whispered.

Frau Schneider reached out to clasp her hand. When she finally spoke, it was in German, the language of tragedy. 'Someone shot the president.'

'*Mein Gott.*'

Implications burst like flashbulbs behind Trudy's eyes. She held her breath and tried to make sense of the announcer's words. 'Is he dead?'

'They do not know. He is in surgery.'

Trudy strained to hear through the static, her hands clenched in her coat pockets. The newscaster was talking to a witness who had been at the site of the president's motorcade through Dallas. Trudy heard the horror in the man's voice. The president had been shot in the head.

'We still have no official word from the hospital,' the announcer warned, 'but it looks bad. Very bad.'

Trudy hard never been to Dallas, Texas. She pictured it like the other cities where she'd traveled that summer, imagined the president on an operating table in a white hospital, the swirl and panic of masked figures beneath harsh lights. She thought of him standing in Rudolph Wilde Platz, so vigorous and young, his uncovered hair ruffled by the wind. Now he lay in an operating room while others fought for his life – if it wasn't too late already.

How could this happen?

268

Then the reporter spoke of the president's wife. Mrs. Kennedy usually didn't go on these trips, he said, but this time she'd accompanied her husband and was riding with him in the open car when he was shot. She was waiting in the hospital now, under heavy security, to find out whether her husband would live.

The days of waiting after Rolf made his escape crowded into Trudy's mind. She remembered the hours, days, weeks of not knowing if he was alive or dead. Then the awful knowledge.

Mrs. Kennedy already knows. Her husband is dead.

She pictured the slanted blue handwriting on the letter from Jacqueline Kennedy, and the two small children who would be fatherless.

What would happen to the United States without their popular leader? Would chaos reign? And what would happen in Berlin, where the freedom of West Berlin hung by its fragile connection with the United States?

Minutes ticked away and Trudy waited with the Schneiders. In the backroom of the deli, she heard their labored breathing, the monotone voice on the radio and the rapid-fire protest of her own heart.

Finally, it came. The newsman's voice was formal. 'Ladies and gentlemen,' he said, and paused a long time. 'We have just been handed an official announcement. The president is dead.'

For a few moments the airwaves were silent. Then the newsman regained his composure. He began rehashing details and consequences in a hoarse, subdued voice. Frau Schneider wept into her dish towel, her husband's arm around her.

Trudy put a hand on their shoulders, then turned away. She walked to the front window of the shop and looked out into an absurd November sky.

The world looked perfectly normal. But nothing was the same.

In a moment she heard Herr Schneider's quiet voice behind her. *'Fräulein,* can I make you a sandwich before we close the shop?'

She shook her head and thanked him. Squeezed his stocky hand and spoke to him in English. 'Goodbye, Herr Schneider.'

Outside the shop, she looked around the quiet street as if seeing it for the first time. Then she set out walking, back toward the park, heading home.

Trudy followed her feet, her thoughts splintered like the innocence of America itself.

Ladies and gentlemen ... the president is dead.

Sandra would be devastated.

What would come next? What should she do now?

She remembered reading that the First Lady had lost a baby, born premature, only four months ago. It was that thought, finally, that made her cry.

The park was empty except for a soiled vagrant who lay on an iron bench in the late autumn sun. He was grizzled and gray-haired, shielding his shoulder from the chilly breeze with newspaper. Trudy thought he was sleeping, but when she passed by his bench, he opened his eyes and looked at her. His gaze was vacant, red-rimmed.

'The president has been shot,' she blurted. 'He is dead.'

The watery eyes stared. She couldn't tell if he

270

understood, or cared.

The unshaven jaws worked as if chewing something. 'They shot the president?' His voice was like sand. He closed his eyes and turned his head away.

'We're all doomed,' he said. 'All doomed.'

She hurried on down the sidewalk.

When Trudy climbed the stairs to the apartment, she discovered Sandra at home from work. Sandra sat curled on the sofa, her swollen eyes riveted to the television. She did not look up when Trudy joined her, just reached over and squeezed her hand. A box of tissues sat between them.

They watched scenes of the hospital where the president had been taken, saw the street in front of the Texas School Book Depository where the shooting had occurred. There was a report that police were pursuing a suspect.

'Why did it have to happen in Dallas?' Sandra said, her Texas accent heavy. 'Why did it have to happen at all ... but I hate it that it was Dallas.'

They sat immobile, not wanting to watch the scenes on TV, unable to look away. 'Have you heard from Garret?' Trudy asked.

'No. The phone lines are jammed. He'll lose his job.'

Trudy glanced at her. 'Why?'

'Garret's job doesn't pass from one administration to the next. Besides that, he and the vice president have a long-standing dislike for one another.' Sandra blew her nose. Mascara smudged her eyes. 'And when Garret's job goes, so does mine. Not that I care.'

'What will you do?'

271

Sandra shrugged. 'I hate to go home broke, but that's probably what I'll do. My parents are there and I could stay with them until I can find a job.' She smiled faintly. 'My mother will love it.'

Trudy was glad Sandra had family to go home to. A sudden chill ran through her center. She got up and went into the bedroom.

From the closet she took out her suitcases, one large and one small. Anything she couldn't pack in these, she would leave behind.

She opened the closet and pulled clothes from their hangers.

Sandra yelled from the living room. 'They got him! They caught the son of a bitch who shot the president!'

'Thank God,' Trudy said, and folded a pair of slacks into the bag.

She retrieved bundles of cash from their hiding places. One thick stack went into an envelope, enough for plane fare to Texas with plenty left over.

'They're bringing him in,' Sandra called.

Trudy sealed the envelope and wrote Sandra's name on the outside. She propped it against the lamp on the nightstand.

'He doesn't look like a killer,' Sandra said. 'He looks like a wimp.'

Trudy tucked her yellow bathrobe into the suitcase and laid the letter from Wolfgang on top. The paper felt as cold as winter in Berlin.

THE WALL

CHAPTER 25

The highway toward Dulles International Airport was uncommonly quiet that Saturday morning. Neither Sandra nor Trudy could find anything to say. Sandra parked the big Ford Fairland and helped carry Trudy's bags to the terminal.

At the Pan American counter, Trudy bought a ticket on the first flight to West Berlin, via Frankfurt. The flight didn't leave for three hours. She checked her large bag and kept the small one. At an airport kiosk, she changed most of her cash into deutschmarks, and Sandra walked with her down a long concourse until they found her gate. It was time to say goodbye.

'What will you do now?' Trudy asked.

'Head for Texas. I don't want to be in the capital these next few weeks. It's just too sad.'

'I can never thank you enough. You've been a wonderful friend.' Trudy hugged her. 'Tell Max goodbye for me, will you?'

Sandra's copper eyes were shiny. 'Sure.' She found a scrap of paper in her purse and scribbled on the back. 'Here's the address where I'll be in Texas. Let me know what happens to you, okay? I'd love to meet your little boy someday.'

Trudy's nose burned, knowing it would never happen. There wasn't much chance she'd ever see Sandra again.

Trudy watched her walk away and suddenly her

275

body felt limp. She slumped into a row of plastic chairs that were welded together at the hip. Outside the tall windows, a silver jet waited on the tarmac and a cold drizzle had started to fall.

This would be her last view of the U.S.A., worldwide symbol of freedom and power, now shrouded in shock and grief. Was President Kennedy a victim of politics, or just of some crazed mind? Either way his children were fatherless, his wife a widow. And West Berlin had lost a powerful ally.

She fidgeted in the hard chair and finally rose to pace the concourse near the gate. The smells from the food stands made her stomach hollow, but she was too jumpy to eat. She ran her hand into the pocket of the coat Garret Thompson had given her and made sure her passport was still there.

When her flight finally began to board, she followed the queue down the Jetway and into the belly of the aircraft. People crowded the aisle, shoving baggage into overhead bins. How did something that heavy ever get off the ground?

She found her seat near the rear of the plane. No one came to sit beside her, and when it was time to leave, the aircraft was still half-empty. The jet rattled down the runway, gathering speed, and finally lifted off. In a few minutes she was looking out over a dark ocean.

Maybe the plane would plunge into the water and all her worries would be over.

Then she thought of Stefan, and changed her wish.

The wall had beaten her; Stefan would not grow up in freedom. Now she could only hope to be

276

with him by Christmas, on the wrong side of the wall.

Shortly before the jet arrived in Frankfurt, the attendant brought orange juice and a damp washcloth for each passenger. Trudy had barely dozed in the abbreviated night. She washed her face and prepared for landing.

In the Frankfurt airport she cleared customs and changed to a different airplane. The weather was rough on the short leg to West Berlin; the airplane bucked and yawed. She closed her eyes and wondered if Sandra was on her way to Texas yet, and what Max would do with all those letters and the rest of her clothes.

It was noon in Berlin when she arrived, but her body time was 5:00 a.m. She'd been awake for twenty-four hours. She followed the signs and collected her other suitcase.

Pewter skies and a stiff wind greeted her outdoors as she walked the short distance from the main terminal of Tempelhof to the U-Bahn station. She struggled onto the crowded train with her bags and stood clinging to a metal hand rail. At Hallesches Tor she changed trains and debarked at the Kürfurstendamm stop in the center of the city.

Lunch hour foot traffic crowded up the long flights of steps to the street and impeded progress on the sidewalks. Her bags bumped into other knees and after a while she stopped apologizing. On the Kü-damm, the air smelled of diesel and the sweet-pungent scents drifting out from a *Gasthaus* along the sidewalk. The signs spoke German;

277

it was good to be home. She stopped at a newspaper kiosk and bought a newspaper and a pack of American cigarettes.

Most lodging on the Kü-damm was expensive, but on a side street she saw a sign for a *Pension* that promised bed and breakfast at reasonable rates. She wanted to conserve her money in case she needed it to lubricate her repatriation. She lugged her bags up the steps of a stained gray building and pushed the buzzer outside a door marked Number One, Proprietor.

The landlady, Frau Hagen, was short and round with graying hair rolled up like a sausage at the base of her neck. She wore no makeup on a plain face, but her eyes were lively. 'I have one available on the third floor, if you'd like to see it,' she said. 'I keep my rooms very clean.'

A black-and-white dog stayed close to her heels as she labored up the stairs ahead of Trudy. 'I rent mostly to foreign students and middle-class tourists,' she said. Her heavy stockings and thick-soled shoes brought a lump to Trudy's throat. They looked like *Mutti*'s.

Frau Hagen stopped on the landing to catch her breath and Trudy bent to scratch the dog's head. The spaniel's ears were long and silky and its waistline was as plump as its mistress's. 'What's her name?'

'Schätzchen,' Frau Hagen said. 'She's even older than I am, as dogs go.'

Frau Hagen searched through a ring of keys while they climbed again. 'The room has a window that looks out toward the Kü-damm, so there is always something to watch. And the price is a bargain. Not everybody is willing to climb so many stairs.'

Trudy shifted her suitcases from one arm to the other. 'I don't mind.'

At last, they entered the third-floor hallway. Frau Hagen unlocked a door halfway down the corridor and Schätzchen pushed inside to inspect the room. The dog's nose made little popping sounds while she sniffed out traces of the last tenant.

Frau Hagen pulled back the heavy drapes. 'Breakfast is served on the second floor from six to nine. The bath is right down the hall, and so is the telephone. Local calls only.' She opened the door to a small closet. 'It is nice, *ja?*'

Trudy looked out the double windows. On a building across the street hung a billboard advertising an American film – *The Misfits*, starring Marilyn Monroe and Clark Gable. The landlady pointed to it like a tourist attraction.

'The man who owns that theater lives east of the wall. One day he awakened to find he could not go across the frontier to his place of business. The theater has been vacant ever since.' Frau Hagen smiled at the bit of trivia.

'The room will be fine.'

'How long do you plan to stay?'

'I'm not sure. A week, at least.'

'Good.' Frau Hagen bobbed her head. 'You can pay for one week now.' The efficient German businesswoman.

Trudy dug deutschmarks from her purse and Frati Hagen handed her the key. 'I will write you a receipt. If there is something you need, just knock on my door.'

'Dankeschön.'

The landlady went out and closed the door. Trudy pulled off her coat and hung it in the shallow closet. A well-worn rug covered most of the linoleum floor, and a damask-covered feather-bed floated like a cloud on the iron bedstead. There was a lavatory, a small table with two chairs and a slightly musty smell. All in all, the room seemed homey and warm. Maybe even too warm.

She opened one of the windows a few inches and cool air swept in, bringing with it the mingled smells of the street. Trudy stood for a moment looking out toward the busy Kü-damm, which looked more like an American street than any other in Berlin.

She had spent twenty-four hours in the same clothes and felt jet lagged and out of sync. She wanted sleep, but first a hot shower.

She took Wolfgang's letter from her suitcase and propped it and her worn snapshot of Stefan against a wavy mirror behind the bureau. Stefan's white face and serious eyes peered at her. Except for a glimpse through the wall, she hadn't seen her baby for almost a year. She felt heavy all over and dangerously close to weeping.

Too many time zones, too little sleep. She lifted her chin and sniffed, shaking it off.

Her gaze went to Wolfgang's forceful penman-ship, with its uniform slant and generous loops. A forgotten moment floated up from years before, the night before he left to study in Moscow. Wolfgang had come to say goodbye to Rolf, but she was the only one home. That night she'd seen a loneliness in his eyes that surprised her. When he'd come back from Russia, he seemed older, more somber, and he'd signed up with the *Volkspolizei*. Was anything left of the younger man she had studied and laughed with, who argued and drank beer with Rolf late into the nights?

Early the next morning she dressed in her least wrinkled suit and found her way to the American consulate, which was housed in the U.S. Embassy building. The structure looked like a grand old film star, its stately, age-stained facade rouged with bright flags. Trudy climbed the steps armed with the only name she knew – Miss Shaw, the woman she'd met in Garret Thompson's hotel room last June. She had rehearsed what to say – *an emergency; a death in the family; a Vopo commandant in custody of her son*. In America she had noticed that the person who made the most fuss got the most attention. But perhaps that was true only for American citizens.

The receptionist on the main floor, a young man in military uniform, was polite and helpful. He made a phone call and in a few minutes, Miss Shaw appeared. Trudy extended her hand and spoke to her in English. 'Hello, again. Trudy Hulst.'

Trudy saw recognition cross Miss Shaw's face. She smiled. 'Yes, I remember. How did things ... work out for you?'

'Not as I hoped. May I speak with you in private?'

'Certainly. Come up to my office.'

They took the stairs to the second floor. Miss Shaw ushered her into a room where a dark wood desk anchored an Oriental carpet. There were fresh flowers and an electric typewriter on a sideboard. One entire wall was lined with books, their spines lettered with several languages Trudy recognized and some she didn't. A placard on the desk said, Emily Shaw Linguist And Translator. Miss Shaw motioned her to a chair.

Miss Shaw listened intently while Trudy summarized her experience in the U.S. and Wolfgang's offer to help her repatriate.

'I need your help to contact Herr Krüger,' Trudy told her.

'I see.' Miss Shaw frowned. 'Will you wait here a moment, please?'

She left Trudy in the office and disappeared down the hall. Trudy watched a carved Bavarian clock tick off five minutes before Miss Shaw came back, smiling.

'Please come with me, Mrs. Hulst. My boss, Consul Osgood, wants to talk with you.'

Trudy followed her up another floor into an office twice the size of Miss Shaw's. Gilded maps hung on the walls. A lighted globe mounted in a wooden stand sat to one side of a mahogany desk that reflected her image in its polished surface. Behind the desk, a man of about sixty fixed her with arresting hazel eyes.

He stood when she came in and Miss Shaw introduced them. Consul Osgood offered his hand and a generous smile. He spoke in flawless German. 'A pleasure to meet you, Frau Hulst. Please sit down.'

'Thank you.' Trudy sat in a leather chair beside the desk, which held neatly stacked file folders and two telephones. Miss Shaw went out and shut the door.

Two gilded photo frames displayed a boy of about twelve and a smaller girl with missing front teeth. 'Are those your grandchildren?' she guessed.

'Yes.' He smiled, glancing at the pictures. 'They're in Ohio. I don't get to see them nearly enough.'

Good, she thought. *Then you'll understand how I feel.*

Consul Osgood offered something to drink but she declined. 'Miss Shaw filled me in on your situation, briefly.' His voice was modulated, like an actor or a newscaster, his eyes sharp and curious. 'I'm very sorry about your separation from your son.

She nodded. 'It appears that Commandant Krüger offers my only hope that we can be reunited.'

'Perhaps so,' he said, his forehead creasing. 'How well do you know this Commandant Krüger? Is he a man of his word?'

She explained their background, and Wolf-gang's role in her escape from the East. Herr Osgood listened with a thoughtful expression.

'He was kind to my mother-in-law and son this past year, and often helped them,' she told him. 'I have to trust that he cares enough about Stefan to bring his mother back home.'

The consul nodded. 'Then, too, he might not be prepared for his sudden parenthood. I imagine it is inconvenient to his career.'

'Another reason it wouldn't make sense for him to trick me.'

283

It took twenty minutes to convince Consul Osgood that she had carefully considered her decision and wasn't being coerced in some way. Finally, he agreed to put a phone call through to the Vopo headquarters in East Berlin.

Commandant Krüger was occupied, they were told, but would return the call shortly.

Again the consul offered coffee or tea, and this time Trudy accepted. It was something to do while they waited, and she could use the caffeine.

The consul was skilled at social conversation. He wanted to know her impressions of the U.S., and the various cities she had visited. He was either truly fascinated by people or a flawless actor. Her mind felt numb but she struggled to converse politely, while her eyes kept glancing at the telephone on the desk.

Finally the black phone warbled. He picked up the receiver quickly.

'Commandant Krüger? Emmet Osgood of the American consulate in West Berlin. I have with me Frau Trudy Hulst, who has requested to speak with you. Yes. I will put her on.'

He covered the receiver with his hand and spoke softly. 'I will step out to give you privacy. I should warn you these lines are usually monitored. If you wish to be advised on any matter, push this button and it will buzz on my secretary's desk.'

Trudy's throat was dry as he handed her the phone. 'Thank you.' Osgood left the room.

She drew a deep breath. *'Hallo?'*

'One moment please.' It was Wolfgang's voice, but distant and cold. Her shoulders tensed. She heard him speaking to someone and then there was a pause. When he spoke again, his voice had changed.

'Trudy? Forgive me, someone came in but he's gone now. How are you?'

'I'm all right. How is Stefan?'

'He is remarkably well. You received my letter, about Gisela?'

'Yes.'

She heard him sigh. 'Stefan is still quiet at times, but children are more resilient than adults, I think. He asks about his *Oma* often, and I explain again. He seems to be digesting what it means, on his own terms.'

Trudy's throat swelled. She closed her eyes. 'You said they might let me come back without punishment. Is that true?'

'Yes. There's been a softening of policy here. You will be allowed to return – with certain conditions.'

'What conditions?'

He paused. 'You'll need to return as my wife. That way I would be responsible for you.'

'Your ... *wife?*' She had expected to renounce her defection, confess her sins, make any number of humiliating apologies. But she had not expected this.

'Yes. I know it's a surprise, but it's the only way to be sure. I told them we would be married immediately upon your return.'

'This is more than a surprise. It's a shock.'

Wolfgang's voice sounded carefully controlled. 'I have applied for a house.' He paused again. 'With several bedrooms.'

'Ah.' So the marriage would be in name only, to

285

satisfy the government. 'I see.'

Another pause. 'It's the right thing to do, Trudy. For Stefan.'

She swallowed and heard the echo of it on the line. *No choice. Once again, she had no choice.* 'For Stefan.'

'Shall we proceed then?'

'I don't know. I'm too tired to think.'

'I have started the paperwork,' he said. 'Tell me where I can get in touch with you.'

She gave him the *Pension* address and the telephone number she'd written down.

'Wolfgang,' she said. 'I appreciate your taking care of Stefan. And of *Mutti.*'

'I came to think of them as my family.' He cleared his throat. 'Tomorrow morning at 8:00 a.m., we will visit Gisela's grave before I go to work. At St. Sophia's.'

She straightened in the chair. 'Across from Bernauer Straße?'

'Yes. I believe you remember the place.'

The cemetery where she had entered the tunnel. *He's telling me I can see Stefan across the wall.*

'I understand. *Danke.* Please hug Stefan for me.'

'I will be in touch soon. *Tschüss.*'

The connection went dead.

She replaced the receiver in its cradle and rested her forehead on the phone. A full minute passed before she straightened herself in the chair and pushed the button to summon the consul.

CHAPTER 26

Grepo *Obermeister* Albrecht Schweinhardt walked home from his office with an unaccustomed optimism livening his steps. His VS bag bumped pleasantly against his leg, and he pondered again the significance of the news that had swept through police headquarters like an induced virus. At home the evening before, he had not turned on his television, and he'd heard nothing about it until he arrived at work that morning.

At first he'd thought it couldn't be true. He went downstairs to check the state news channel. Several other officers were already watching the television in the library, where a news anchorman was reporting the story with a solemn face and a remarkable lack of Party rhetoric.

The U.S. president had been assassinated. In his own country.

It was a miracle.

John F. Kennedy had been a thorn in the side of the DDR ever since his election. Some Party officials were still amazed that he hadn't sent U.S. tanks to demolish the wall in its early days. But he hadn't; there was a weakness in the Western armor. Now that armor had split wide – Kennedy was dead, brought down by some unknown gunman, not even an organized coup. Shot in a motorcade at midday Friday, Friday evening in Berlin.

Who knew the real story? Perhaps the unknown

287

assassin was part of a well-organized plot. Perhaps the cunning Nikita Khrushchev was behind it. Everyone knew the Russians had a score to settle with Kennedy.

Schweinhardt suddenly stopped on the sidewalk. Absorbed in his thoughts, he had walked half a block in the wrong direction. He was heading out of habit toward the restaurant where he'd gone after work for several years. He glanced around him to see who might be watching as he retraced his steps. It was Saturday evening and the sidewalks were nearly empty. No one seemed to notice him. At the corner he turned right, toward home.

He had stopped going to the restaurant when it became clear he could no longer contact *Fräulein* Fischer there. She had quit her job, or so they said. Probably to avoid giving him information. It rather pleased him that he could influence her life so drastically.

He could find out where she was, of course, with one phone call to the Stasi. But so far he hadn't bothered. She hadn't been much help lately, anyway. And with *Fräulein* Fischer gone, he'd rather fix his own dinner than tolerate the presence of that walrus-like woman who had served his food the last time he'd gone in.

He arrived at his door on the half hour and regretted missing the chorus of cuckoos that usually welcomed him. He consoled himself that, by seven o'clock, he would be relaxing in his chair where he could truly enjoy their mechanical songs. He hung up his coat and hat, placed the VS bag beside the hall tree. It held only some minor paperwork, nothing that really required his attention on a Sunday. And he intended to take this Sunday off.

He collected his slippers and cognac, and turned on his television. Ensconced in his favorite chair, he settled back to watch the evening newscast. Again, the lead story was the assassination of the U.S. president. The suspected shooter had been apprehended almost immediately. It was an exact rerun of the report he'd seen earlier in the day.

Albrecht smiled. His luck was changing.

This was the second bright spot this month, after the mortifying news of Wolfgang Krüger's promotion to lieutenant-general of *Volkspolizei*. Albrecht knew the promotion was in the works and had filed a memo noting his objections. His protest was duly noted but not given enough importance to block Krüger's advancement. His stomach had required an entire roll of antacids the day he got that news.

The first bright spot was the last bit of information he'd gained from *Fräulein* Fischer, before she'd quit her job and disappeared. Under questioning she'd told him – with a peculiar twinge of bitterness in her tone – that Lieutenant-General Krüger had assumed guardianship of a small child. And not just any child – the son of Rolf Hulst, a recognized enemy of the state. Krüger hadn't even denied it. Apparently the child's grandmother had died and handed him off to Krüger.

A muted click announced the impending panoply of the cuckoos. He held on to his last pleasant thought and closed his eyes to block out the television's noise. He sipped his cognac. His mechanical menagerie heralded seven o'clock in flawless unison. They were his babies, his little wooden soldiers. He loved their orchestrated sound, their individual carved bodies and his complete mastery of their mechanisms.

When the chorus stopped, he resumed his train of thought. He had finally found the crowbar with which to pry Krüger from his pedestal.

Wives and children were always liabilities, an exposed vulnerability like the soft underbelly of an animal. This child wasn't actually Krüger's, but one could assume an emotional attachment, since he'd been visiting the child and his grandmother regularly for a year. It was stupid of him, and that part concerned Albrecht because Krüger was not a stupid man. Emotional attachment hardly seemed an adequate motivation to take on the responsibility of someone else's offspring. It made Albrecht wonder if there was something else going on with Krüger that he didn't know. Still, he had seen many rational men behave stupidly where children and women were concerned.

That had to be the explanation for Krüger's habit of checking the West Berlin newspapers over the past months. He must have been receiving messages from the child's mother through the press. And now he planned to bring her back and marry her, or so he said. It was a foolish scenario that seemed ludicrous to Albrecht.

With this new fact in evidence, he had convinced his friend within the Stasi to investigate Krüger. Sooner or later, almost anyone who came under surveillance would self-destruct.

And if Krüger didn't trip himself up, Albrecht would help things along, though he hadn't yet worked out how he would do it. He had waited years for this chance, and he intended to enjoy it.

Tonight he might have two cognacs.

Albrecht would be known as the man who brought down the Kremlin's golden boy, the lieutenant-general. Party officials would have to recall his warnings that they had chosen to ignore, and they would have to admit – at least privately – that *Genosse* Schweinhardt had been right. His promotion was a certain result. And the office of lieutenant-general of *Volkspolizei* might not be good enough now; perhaps he would demand a top position with the Stasi.

Albrecht blew a smoke ring toward the prattling television. His stomach growled with hunger, and he regretted again the loss of his customary dining habit. He would have to fix something for himself.

He got up and turned off the set. His refrigerator didn't offer much hope, and he didn't relish cooking. So he settled for canned soup, which he dumped into a blackened pan and set on the stove. While it warmed, he poured another cognac and went to the living room to perform the ritual of winding his clocks.

He took his time, moving from left to right in each row, from top to bottom. Occasionally he spoke to individual clocks that were his favorites. In the middle of the bottom row he had a strange thought. What would happen to his clocks when he died? He had no family he cared to leave them to, no friend who would appreciate such a collection. He pictured them abandoned on the wall, unwound and silent, coated with dust. Until someone, perhaps his landlord, came in and pulled them down and sold them.

The idea was disturbing. Perhaps he should locate a museum that would accept them when he was gone, where they'd be kept together and displayed with his name on a brass plaque. He imagined what the plaque might say: Donated From The Private Collection Of Herr Albrecht Schweinhardt, Minister Of State Security.

That thought made him feel better, and he went to the kitchen to eat his soup.

On Sunday evening, Albrecht did something he'd done only once before in all his career as a communist. He tuned his television to a West Berlin station, curious to see what the Western press had to say about Kennedy's assassination. His antenna wasn't positioned correctly to receive it, and so the picture was snowy and gray. He adjusted it as best he could and soon found a newscast that was reporting on events in the United States.

He was astounded to learn that the man who had been accused of the assassination had been shot as he was being transported to a different facility.

Ha! Just as he'd suspected, it was a nation of crazies.

Then the news program switched to local reaction in West Berlin. There were pictures of people weeping in the streets on Saturday while they watched televisions in shop windows. There were sentimental recollections of Kennedy's speech beside the wall that summer. The West Berlin mayor had proclaimed that the Rudolph Wilde Platz was to be renamed John F. Kennedy Square. Outrageous.

He saw men in West Berlin bars raise their steins and drink to the memory of a great man. Albrecht shook his head. But the most incredible image was yet to come. The camera panned down a quiet residential street, dark now except for an occasional street light and the pinpoint glow of candles in every window. Dozens of them. Hundreds! Every citizen of West Berlin, it seemed, had lit a candle for the slain U.S. president.

An eerie feeling crept over Albrecht's skin as he sat staring at those dots of light. He got up, switched off the television and walked to the window.

His living room had only one window that looked out toward the street, and it was covered by heavy drapes. He never looked out from here, and the invisible film of a spider web brushed against his cheek when he lifted back one curtain panel. He let the curtain drop and swatted the cobweb away, then tried again.

Now his skin crawled in earnest. Out the hazy windowpane, on his own street perhaps five or six houses away, he saw the flicker of a candle being placed on a windowsill.

And then he saw another.

Yes, another timid candle in a second-story window – there. He pulled the cord to open the drapes and stood watching. Every few minutes, up and down the street, another flickering light appeared.

The world had gone crazy.

East Berlin had gone crazy.

How could these citizens of the DDR mourn the loss of an espoused enemy? Ingrates! Sentimental idiots.

The lucky feeling he'd enjoyed all weekend melted like wax and pooled into an image of Lieutenant-General Wolfgang Krüger. Men like Krüger, with his spineless humanitarianism, were the cause of this madness. He was a weak link, a cancer on the state.

Maybe Albrecht couldn't set the whole crazy world aright, but he could do something about his own tilting city. Cancers could be excised, and Krüger had been foolish enough to supply the knife.

CHAPTER 27

Trudy walked back to her *Pension* with the phone call to Wolfgang roaring like static in her head. Early twilight gathered between the buildings, and she imagined curling up in a doorway and sleeping for days, maybe years. In her room, she peeled off her clothes and slept like the dead, not even dreaming.

In the darkest part of the night, she jolted awake. Was this the day Stefan would be at the cemetery? Was she too late?

She sat up and switched on a lamp, flinching in the light. She groped for her watch on the bedside table and squinted at the tiny hands. Only 3:00 a.m.

She fell back on the bed, her pulse gradually slowing. Plenty of time. The bed was cool and soft as a cradle, but she'd been there too many hours. Now she was wide awake.

Light from the street outlined the heavy drapes. She could hear traffic moving. Deliverymen and paperboys were out already, and bakers in their tiny shops, kneading dough. Life hummed on in West Berlin, plucky and independent.

Her insides felt as hollow as a manhole. Even more than food, she wanted black coffee. She got up and put on her yellow robe, padded down the hallway to the bathroom.

Back in her room, she dressed in warm slacks and a sweater, but the dining room didn't open until six so she stood at the window and watched the morning rituals of the Kü-damm. Yesterday her mind had refused to think, and now it wouldn't stop.

The Vopo commandant's wife.

Surely Rolf would turn over in his grave. Or maybe he would forgive anything she had to do for Stefan's sake.

What would Wolfgang expect of her? How long would he be content to live in the same house with a woman who slept in a separate bedroom? Or maybe he was truly cold and sexless, all Party rhetoric and no emotion.

And yet, he had arranged a way for her to see Stefan. In a few hours, if he kept his word, she would see her beautiful baby. She knew exactly the place where she could climb up and see over

295

the wall.

At six o'clock she stubbed out her cigarette and went downstairs to the dining room. Frau Hagen was serving her guests in person – fresh rolls, jam and cheese, coffee or tea, the universal *Pension* breakfast.

'*Guten Morgen*, Frau Hulst,' the landlady said. 'I hope you slept well.'

'Very well, in that wonderful bed.'

Frau Hagen smiled. 'You like it, *ja?* I am very particular about my beds.'

Trudy liked the breakfast, too, and fortified herself with two rolls and cheese for protein.

At seven o'clock, she caught the U-Bahn to Leopoldplatz Station and by seven-thirty she was pacing along the Western side of Bernauer Straße, that unlucky street that straddled East and West. The morning was clear and bone cold, the sun reluctant beneath the horizon. In the vague half light, the buildings and streets took on the grainy quality of an old black-and-white film. She'd worn wool socks, her heavy brown shoes and a scarf around her ears and nose, but the cold seeped through like ice water. Maybe that's why German soldiers goose-stepped – to keep from freezing when they marched in the cold. She kept moving, hugging her arms and walking fast.

Nothing had changed along Bernauer Straße except for rampant graffiti that now scaled the wall. She pictured indignant young political activists, with their spray paint cans and rebellious faces. Just like Rolf, except for the paint. Most of the words were illegible or expletives, but occasionally she deciphered a message: *Irgend-*

wann fällt jede Mauer. Every wall falls sometime. She wondered if that was profound or naive.

There were new memorials, too, honoring those who had challenged the wall and paid with their lives. A black feeling arose from the days just after the wall went up, a constant fear that wormed away the spirit. Soon she would go back into that world, where a knock on the door could destroy one's family with no warning. She had traveled backward in space and time, her months of freedom only a dream.

If she'd failed to keep her promise to Rolf, she would at least teach Stefan what his father believed in, and what it meant to live in freedom.

Where Ackerstraße dead-ended perpendicular to Bernauer Straße, the familiar spire of the Church of Reconciliation spiked up behind the wall. St. Sophia's Cemetery lay just to the right of the church, hidden behind a concrete barricade.

Trudy stood in the street and searched along the western side of Bernauer Straße for a high window that wasn't boarded shut. It wasn't hard to find, and she wasn't the first to find it. The wooden stairs were worn smooth by many feet. She followed the footsteps of others who had family across the wall.

On the third floor, in someone's long-abandoned bedroom, a glassless window overlooked the concrete barriers. She stepped over broken bottles and cigarette butts, a paper wrapper from someone's sandwich. From the window, she looked across the wall and into the cemetery.

Gravestones dotted the winter-browned grass, their corners rounded from weather and age.

Nothing moved among the silent stones. She scanned the rows until she found a fresh mound covered by wilted flowers. Gisela's grave?

If there is a heaven, Mutti, *I know you are in it.*

Mutti had spent her life taking care of her family, but she'd had none of them with her when she died. Except, perhaps, Stefan. Trudy wiped her eyes with the back of her glove and fished a tissue from her coat pocket. Her nose felt brittle as an icicle.

From this distance, perhaps a hundred meters, Stefan's face would be little more than a distant smudge. If they came at all. What if she had misunderstood? But there was no other reason for him to tell her they were coming to the cemetery this morning. It was kind of Wolfgang to think of this, and she would not forget it.

She checked her watch and scanned the cemetery again. No movement, no sound except the distant hush of car tires. Somewhere in that grassy field she had descended into a grave and been reborn as a different person. She searched among the stones but couldn't be sure of the exact place. The tunnel had been sealed shortly afterward; perhaps a real corpse now lay in the grave. The memory of her escape lay distant and hazy. Was the story she'd told a hundred times in English really true?

She checked her watch again – three minutes till. It was Wolfgang's nature to be punctual. She stomped her feet and rubbed her gloved hands together. Wished for binoculars and a cigarette.

At precisely eight o'clock, there was movement outside the cemetery fence. She leaned into the

298

window. A man in a gray topcoat and military-style cap entered the graveyard through the wooden gate. She recognized Wolfgang's straight posture, his measured walk. He was alone.

Where's Stefan?

Then, as he came inside the cemetery fence, she glimpsed a tiny figure walking beside him. Her mouth opened, soundless.

Stefan was holding Wolfgang's hand. They walked slowly toward the flowered grave. Trudy clung to the window frame, blinking fast, her breath jerky.

Come to this side, my baby, where I can see you!

As if in answer, Wolfgang stopped and lifted the child in his arms. Stefan's hair was covered with a dark fur hat above his white face. He wore a bulky coat and, she thought, mittens. *That's good. He shouldn't be out in the cold without his mittens.* Her arms ached to hold him.

They stopped beside the fresh grave, and Trudy saw that Stefan was carrying a long-stemmed flower. What went through his innocent mind when he came here, to his grandmother's grave? Had Wolfgang told him *Oma*'s body lay there, underground? She thought of the tunnel, its smell and the taste of dirt.

Wolfgang was talking to Stefan and she wondered what he was saying. If she went back to the East, this man would be her husband. Stefan's stepfather.

The two of them seemed comfortable together, familiar. A mean resentment knotted her throat. *She* should be the one to comfort Stefan, to answer his questions and make him feel safe. In that moment she hated Wolfgang, and loved him.

Wolfgang set Stefan on his feet close to *Mutti's* grave. Stefan tossed the flower overhand onto the mound and looked up at Wolfgang as if for approval. Wolfgang picked him up again, and they turned and faced the wall.

She saw Wolfgang searching. Trudy leaned out the window and waved her arms. 'Here! Here I am, Stefan!'

Her voice carried in the still morning. Wolfgang turned Stefan's head and pointed to her, but Stefan was looking in the wrong place. She saw Wolfgang put his face next to Stefan's, and the next moment shifted into slow motion: Vopo Commandant Krüger sighted down his extended arm and aimed directly at her heart. A vision of the future flashed like a muzzle in the dark.

The air froze in her lungs and her raised arm stiffened – but Stefan had seen her. He began to wave, and she thought she heard the chirp of his voice.

Her breath fogged in front of her. *'Kind, ich have Dich so lieb!'* She waved frantically, bouncing on her numb toes, laughing and crying.

Wolfgang waved, too, and then the moment was over. He glanced behind them, to his right and left. He gestured to his watch; time to go to work. They waved one last time before turning away.

Wolfgang carried Stefan out of the cemetery and out of sight, but Trudy stayed at the window, watching the place where they'd disappeared.

'Goodbye, *mein Schätzchen.'* She listened for their footsteps in the still morning. Finally she plodded down the sagging stairs.

That afternoon she went back to the American Consulate and sent a message to Vopo Commandant Krüger.

I accept your conditions. Please help me come home.

CHAPTER 28

She was in her old bedroom in East Berlin – Stefan asleep in his crib, the rocking chair beside the window. Mutti was moving quietly about the apartment just beyond her bedroom door – she could feel the vibrations of her uneven steps.

Home at last...

A sharp rapping evaporated the dream. Trudy opened her eyes to a darkened room and tried to remember where she was.

Again, the knocking, and recognition rushed back. She sat up, groggy.

'Who is it?'

'Frau Hagen. When you did not come out for lunch or dinner I began to worry.'

Trudy slipped on her robe and went to the door in stocking feet. The landlady's shocked face told her how she looked.

'I'm all right,' Trudy said. 'Still recovering from jet lag.' She pushed a tangle of hair away from her face. 'What time is it?'

'Half past eight. The dining room is closed.' Wrinkles bunched around Frau Hagen's eyes, and her face softened. 'You look white as a plate. Come down to my apartment and have some

Bratwurst and *Kartoffeln* with me.'

Trudy rubbed her face. 'That's very kind, but I could not impose.'

Frau Hagen dismissed the notion with a wave of her hand. 'I get bored spending the evenings alone. You get dressed and come down.'

Bossy as Gisela, Trudy thought, and she smiled. 'Are you always so good to your boarders?'

'Heavens, no. I am an old grouch – that way they leave me alone.'

Trudy laughed. 'I don't believe it. I'll clean up and come down in a few minutes.'

She brushed her teeth and her hair, then descended the long stairways to the first floor and tapped on the landlady's door. Frau Hagen and Schätzchen welcomed her inside. The dog gyrated circles at Trudy's feet until she'd given it a good ear rub.

Frau Hagen's kitchen table was spread with sliced bread and *Aufschnitt*, two kinds of cheese and a bowl of pears. The teapot sat steaming on the stove.

'This is a feast,' Trudy exclaimed.

Frau Hagen motioned her to a chair. 'Help yourself. I do not allow picky eaters at my table.' She went back to the stove, where she'd been preparing *bratwurst* with boiled potatoes, bacon and onions. The aroma was deliciously over-whelming, and Trudy took enough food on her plate for a field worker.

Frau Hagen brought the *Kartoffeln* and joined her. Schätzchen sat patiently at her mistress's feet and received an occasional morsel for good behavior.

302

'This sausage is wonderful,' Trudy said.

'I get it at the butcher's around the corner. You have to get there early on Tuesday morning, because by noon it is all gone.' Frau Hagen poured her another cup of tea. 'So. What brings you to Berlin?'

'I am from Berlin, actually. East of the wall.'

Frau Hagen's eyes opened wide. 'How did you get here?'

'Hmm. That's a long story.'

The Frau's grandmotherly face opened expectantly. 'Wonderful. I love long stories.'

Trudy had learned from Sandra Fletcher what a comfort it was to have a friend. So she told Frau Hagen her story.

'Um-um-um,' Frau Hagen said, serving them both a slice of pound cake with powdered sugar. 'That hateful wall! May Walter Ulbricht come to a gruesome end.'

Trudy talked about Stefan and Gisela and her failed trip to America, while Schätzchen snored gently at their feet.

'Um-um-um.' Frau Hagen shook her head and leaned forward as if imparting a secret. 'My nephew Fritz died at the wall. A boy of eighteen, my sister's only son. They shot him down like a rat.' She pointed a sturdy finger. 'You stay away from that border. They will shoot you, too – woman or not. And you will be no good to your little boy if you are dead, will you?'

Trudy sighed. 'I have agreed to marry the Vopo commandant so I can go back to the East safely.'

'*Ach du liebe Güte.* Are you sure you can trust this Vopo?'

'I have no choice. I will go back under his protection, but I will never get out again.'

'The wall cannot last forever.'

'I used to think that. Now I am not so sure.'

'If this Vopo is good to you, maybe you will fall in love with him.' Frau Hagen shrugged, patted her hand. 'And if not, marriages have been made for worse reasons than to give a child a proper home.'

'Yes. That's what I keep telling myself.' Trudy folded her napkin and sat back. 'I think I have gained five pounds.'

'You could use it. You're skinny as an Irishman's wallet.'

Trudy offered to help with the dishes, but the good Frau wouldn't hear of it. They said good night, and Trudy climbed the stairs feeling better about the future than she had for a long time.

By the next morning her body had readjusted to Berlin time and she felt rested. Renewed energy made her antsy. Wolfgang had promised to rush the paperwork, but what did that mean? It might be days, or weeks, before she heard from him again. Time yawned before her; she needed something to do.

She dressed to go out and stopped at Frau Hagen's door. 'I'm going for a walk and would be happy to take Schätzchen, if you like.'

'Bless you! Schätzchen could use the exercise.' Frau Hagen handed her a leash. At the sight of it, the dog made a diligent effort to leap for joy. Trudy could barely corral her to attach the lead.

For two blocks Schätzchen wagged happy circles, tangling the leash around Trudy's ankles.

Finally the spaniel calmed down and trotted along ahead of her, happily sniffing other dogs they passed on the sidewalk. Berliners did love their dogs. Trudy thought perhaps she could get Stefan a puppy of his own once they were settled in their new home.

On the way back, she stopped at a newsstand for a paper, and then at a café for coffee and pastry. She bought Frau Hagen a pastry, too, and delivered it along with Schätzchen to the landlady's door.

Walking Schätzchen became her morning routine. She helped Frau Hagen with chores and shopping. She located Rolf's grave in a cemetery near the *Grunewald* and laid fresh flowers beside the stone. One day she wrote a long letter to Sandra Fletcher and mailed it to the address Sandra had given her in Dallas.

The days floated like an island between the past and the future, neither happy nor sad. Ahead lay her new life and the scary-sweet task of regaining her son's love and trust. But in the interim she drifted in unmeasured time, like the hushed eye of a hurricane. Her patience surprised her. She was catching her breath, gathering strength.

The message came on a Thursday morning. She had just returned from her walk, the newspaper tucked beneath her arm, a pastry for Frau Hagen in a white sack. The landlady's face was somber when she handed over the envelope.

It bore the official stamp of the DDR. And it wasn't from Wolfgang.

Trudy took a deep breath and tore it open, allowing Frau Hagen to read over her shoulder.

In consideration of your application for reentry to the DDR under the sponsorship of Lieutenant-General of Volkspolizei Wolfgang Krüger, you are commanded to appear at the British crossing point, Invalidenstraße, at 10:00a.m. on 14 December, bearing your passport and only those belongings you can carry. Present this letter to the border official.

December 14 was the day after tomorrow.
'Um-um-um,' Frau Hagen said.

Fresh snow muffled Berlin. From her third floor window, Trudy watched vehicles creep along the streets shedding flurries of white from their fenders, drivers peering from ovals scratched in frosted windshields. Cottony flakes the size of deutschmarks thickened the sky and stacked up on ledges and utility wires. It was beautiful, and Trudy hoped that was a sign.

She let the curtain fall shut. She had laid out her clothes the night before – a skirt and sweater she'd brought from America, and the expensive boots with a warm lining that she'd bought the day before, after stopping by the American consul's office to keep him informed, as she'd promised. She wound her hair up beneath a fur hat and looped a thick scarf around the collar of her coat. She stood before the mirror and felt a perverse recklessness. If this was the day she married the Communist commandant, she would at least *appear* to know what she was doing.

She had packed a single bag. She squeezed it shut and snapped the latches.

At the door she glanced back at the cozy room, with its worn wool rug, the hand-carved frame on the cheap mirror. She had felt more at home here than anywhere she'd stayed for the past year. Someday, when she called up memories of the West, she would remember Greta Hagen and this room.

She pulled the door shut behind her and lugged her bag down the stairs.

Frau Hagen and Schätzchen were waiting at their door to say goodbye. Greta slipped a paper-wrapped bundle of cheese and bread into her coat pocket, as if there would be no food in the East. Trudy hugged her and let Schätzchen lick her chin. Then she went out into the snow.

Her bag bumped against her leg as she walked. Her breath came in short bursts that smelled of the cold. At the U-Bahn station, she descended the steps into the synthetic light that never quite reached dark corners. The trains were nearly vacant this early on a snowy Saturday. She stepped onto an empty car and set her suitcase in the aisle.

The train shuddered and squealed and began to move. Station lights flashed past the windows as the train picked up speed and then rattled into the darkness of tunnels. The U-Bahn line did not run as far as Invalidenstralße; she would have several blocks to walk in the snow.

When she exited the train, traffic was still sparse. She noticed only one other person on the platform, a well-dressed man in an overcoat who nodded to her from a distance. The brim of a hat shadowed his eyes. She climbed the stairs to ground level, switched the suitcase from one cold hand to the other and started walking.

Her boots made fresh tracks in the snow. Breathless flakes dotted her coat and caught in her scarf. Within a block she could see ahead of her the line of fortifications that was the wall, benign in a cloak of pristine white. Behind the first barricades at the crossing point, a guard shack sent up puffs of steam from a metal chimney. The shack must be the rendezvous point; there was no place else.

A young Grepo stood stiffly at the gate, both hands clutching his rifle. An unexpected gust whirled snow around her feet and sent her back a step, but she steadied herself and approached him. *'Guten Morgen.'*

He did not return the greeting. She set the suitcase down in the snow, withdrew the official letter from her pocket and handed it to him.

He looked at it briefly and nodded. *'Kommen Sie.'* He must have been told to expect her.

She walked behind him toward the guardhouse and stepped inside when he opened the door. He did not enter but snapped the door shut behind her, cutting off the cold.

After the brightness of the snow, she could see nothing inside the dim building. When her eyes adjusted, she surveyed a bare room no larger than a cell, empty except for one wooden chair where a man in uniform now stood up.

Lieutenant-General Wolfgang Krüger.

He looked at her a moment in silence. His eyes were unreasonably blue, as if nothing could hide there. His face looked tanned despite the season.

'I am glad you came,' he said.

'Did you think I would not?' He didn't answer. 'Where is Stefan?'

'With his babysitter. This is no place for a child.' He stepped toward her and offered her his hand, ungloved. 'It is good to see you again. Are you ready?'

She looked at the hand, and back at his eyes. 'For what?'

He let his hand drop. 'In the next room is Herr Heinrich Otter, an official of the DDR who processes immigrants into the East.'

'He must have plenty of free time.'

'Do not be flippant, Trudy. Herr Otter has the power to deny you entry if he sees fit.'

Her recklessness fizzled, replaced by a heavy feeling that made it hard to breathe. 'All right. I will behave.' The shack felt too hot. She loosened her scarf and coat, swallowed a dryness that tasted like ashes. 'Will you go in with me?'

'No. It is not allowed. He will explain the terms of your repatriation, and there are papers to sign. It should not take long.'

Cloak-and-dagger, like an old spy film. The dangerous giddiness rose up in her again. She clenched her hands in her coat pockets.

'I am ready,' she said, and thought in English, *Let's get it done.*

Wolfgang tapped on the door, then opened it. The space behind the door was hardly a room, no more than two by three meters. The floor, the walls and a small table were made of unfinished wood. There was no window.

A light bulb hung on a short cord from the ceiling, illuminating the bald pate of a fiftyish man in wire-rimmed glasses who sat at the table. He looked up at them, his eyes overlarge behind thick lenses.

'Herr Otter,' Wolfgang said, 'this is Frau Hulst.'

'*Danke, Genosse* Krüger.' He did not smile, but nodded to her and motioned to the vacant chair.

When she sat, her knees bumped the front of the desk. Wolfgang touched her shoulder and then the door clicked shut. Her heartbeat hammered.

Otter's voice was flat. 'Lieutenant-General Krüger has attended to most of the details for you. I need only to verify some answers.'

Trudy nodded. She saw a clean ashtray on the desk and fished a cigarette from her bag. 'Is it all right if I smoke?'

'I would prefer you did not.' His tone didn't change, nor did he look up from his papers.

'Ah.' She put the cigarette away but kept the lighter to occupy her hands.

'You have agreed to marry Lieutenant-General Krüger, and wish to live again in the DDR,' he said.

She paused only a second. 'Yes.'

'How long have you known Herr Krüger?'

Trudy frowned. But she should have expected this sort of personal questioning; the government liked to know everything. 'Since we attended the university. My son is here,' she added. 'I need to be with him.'

Herr Otter nodded, intent on his paperwork. 'You were married before to Rolf Hulst, a known criminal.'

She shifted in the chair but kept her voice level.

310

'Rolf was not a criminal.'

'He was engaged in the criminal slave trade of East Germans to the West.'

Heat rose to her face. 'They were hardly slaves. They wanted to go across. Rolf was not a criminal.'

Otter regarded her a moment through the distortion of his lenses. 'If you wish to be a citizen of East Berlin again, you will do well not to defend its law breakers.'

Trudy said nothing.

He glanced at his papers again. 'You left the DDR illegally in January of this year.'

The lighter snapped in her hands, the flame leaping up, disappearing. 'I did not know that Rolf had been shot. I thought he was in West Berlin.'

'And when you left, you abandoned a child who is now in the guardianship of Lieutenant-General Krüger.'

Abandoned. She looked down at her hands. 'Yes,' she whispered.

'*Was?*'

'Yes. *Yes.*' She flicked the lighter twice and caught an irritated glance from Otter.

He finished writing something on a form, shuffled it to the bottom of his stack and looked up at her for a moment. Then he began reading the next page and said nothing for a full minute.

To fill the silence she tried to calculate whether he was old enough to have had Gestapo training during the war. Probably not, but he was well-suited. Perhaps he was Stasi, instead.

Finally he spoke again. 'What was the purpose

of your recent visit to the United States?'

She hesitated. A trick question? What would be the proper answer? 'I am certain you know why I went.' Her tone was harsher than she'd intended and she thought of Wolfgang's warning. *Do not be flippant.*

Herr Otter seemed oblivious to her tone. He referred to his paper. 'You hoped to secure American interference and remove your son from East Berlin. However,' he said, and glanced at her pointedly, 'this effort failed.'

'Obviously.'

'You have been disillusioned by the false promises of the Western powers. You have seen the error of your judgment and are petitioning to return to your homeland.'

Trudy pulled a cigarette from her bag, lit up and blew smoke toward the bare lightbulb. 'Write it up any way you want to.'

Herr Otter waved smoke away from his face with a limp hand, a minor irritation, and smiled. His teeth had dark spaces between. 'We already have, Frau Hulst.'

He turned two papers toward her and placed them side by side on the edge of the desk. 'Everything is here, ready for your signature. I cannot say your attitude is appropriate for a citizen who is asking forgiveness of a crime and protection from the government she violated. But Lieutenant-General Krüger is not without influence and respect. We are confident that under his guidance you can be successfully repatriated.'

He placed a fountain pen beside the papers and sat back in his chair. 'If you will sign these, we

312

will remand you to the custody of *Genosse* Krüger, and your marriage will take place as soon as you cross the frontier.'

Trudy looked at the papers, then at his smug face. 'What are these?'

He tented his fingers and regarded her through the thick glasses. 'The first is your pardon for the crime of illegal emigration to the West. The pardon is subject to two conditions – your marriage, and your signature on the other document.'

Trudy glanced at the first document, then picked up the second, which consisted of three typed pages. She began to read silently.

I, Frau Trudy Hulst, acknowledge my crime against the Deutsche Democratic Republic and the governance of East Berlin and denounce my actions as illegal and traitorous...

'There is no need for you to read the entire document,' Otter said, motioning his impatience. 'We have worded it to show your rejection of your past actions, to encourage other East Berliners to profit from your unfortunate experiences in the West and to discourage similar foolish episodes among our citizens.'

Trudy read on.

I hold up my life as a personal example of the treachery and false ideology of the West and the intent of the Western powers to overthrow the People's Government of the Deutsche Democratic Republic and subjugate its citizens ... for immoral and capitalistic purposes...

She flipped the page and caught Rolf's name. Her chest tightened.

I reject and detest the actions of my deceased husband Rolf Hulst. His criminal and despicable actions aided the corrupt Western powers in the illegal slave trade of East Berlin citizens across the frontier ... or immoral and indecent purposes such as spying and prostitution...

Lies. They wanted her to endorse their lies.

...and I recognize the justice of his death for the protection of the People. I hereby authorize this document to be published in all East Berlin media for the edification of the citizens of the DDR, so that they will be warned against committing the crimes and misjudgments that I have suffered to redress.

Trudy bolted from the chair with the paper in her hand. Herr Otter's eyes filled his thick lenses. She jerked open the door.

Wolfgang stood up quickly. She waved the paper in front of him.

'Did you know about this?' Her voice was too loud in the small hut.

He hesitated. 'I...'

'Have you read it? *Have you?*'

He met her eyes, and she saw a tiny muscle contract in his jaw. 'Yes.'

'And you expect me to sign this? To let them print in their state newspaper that I denounce Rolf as a criminal – to dishonor his name by his widow spitting on it?'

314

'Trudy, think of Stefan–'

'I *am* thinking of Stefan! I will not brand my son with the stigma of a criminal father. I will not let him grow up thinking his father was evil, when we both know that what Rolf did was risk his life to help people who *wanted to be free!*'

Wolfgang grasped her elbow, his face like stone. 'This is the only way,' he whispered. 'It was a condition of getting you back safely, without punishment.'

She yanked her arm free. '*Mein Gott*, Herr Commandant. What kind of mother would I be if I did this?'

She ripped the papers in half and threw them at his feet.

Herr Otter now stood in the doorway. He spoke to Wolfgang as if she were not there. 'Perhaps we should keep Frau Hulst with us, to reconsider.'

Trudy looked at Wolfgang. She stepped quickly to the door but he was there, holding it shut. 'Wait, Trudy. Stefan needs you here. It is only a paper. Only words.'

'*Only words?*' She shook her head, disbelieving. 'Isn't it odd, how we have traded places, Wolfgang? Once, I would have said they were only words. Ideals meant nothing to me. But you were like Rolf – you loved ideals. Back then, you would not have said these were *only words*.'

A sharp knock rattled the door. It swung open to reveal a well-dressed man in a dark overcoat. The young guard hovered behind him, distraught, apologizing.

'I told him to wait! He would not stop. He has a diplomatic pass.'

The man tipped his hat. 'Emmet Osgood, American consulate,' he said, flashing his identification to Wolfgang and then to Herr Otter. He smiled congenially. 'Hello, Mrs. Hulst. May I be of service to you?'

'Yes, thank you. I want to leave now.' She glanced at Wolfgang.

'I would be pleased to escort you,' Consul Osgood said. He nodded curtly to Wolfgang and Otter. '*Guten Tag*, gentlemen.'

The consul offered her his leather-gloved hand. Trudy took it and stepped out into the dazzling snow.

CHAPTER 29

When Trudy didn't come out of her room for meals, Frau Hagen broke her own rule and brought food to her door. Trudy couldn't eat. She paced the dark perimeter of the rug, chain-smoking, stopping at times to stare out the window. The scene played over and over in her mind – the hard face of the man named Otter, the surprising pain in Wolfgang's eyes when she'd ripped the papers in half.

If she had signed the papers, she might be with Stefan now.

She must have been crazy.

But to publicly defame Rolf's memory and swear to their lies – *how could she?* She had been prepared to debase herself, to confess to cowardice or disloyalty or whatever they wanted. But how could she justify to Stefan, when he was old enough to understand, the shaming of his father's name?

And what would Gisela have thought of her then? Gisela would have spit on Herr Otter's boots.

Stefan had only one legacy from the father he'd never know: the courage to stand up for his convictions. She could not betray that gift.

Rolf had been right all along. All those years she'd resented his obsession with freedom, she hadn't even understood what it meant. But the last year had changed everything.

Pacing in her darkened room, she cursed Wolfgang for expecting her to betray Rolf. She cursed herself for being so gullible. She cursed the man named Otter and the cold fish Walter Ulbricht and the bloody communists and the goddamned wall. She paced and swore and thought of Stefan and wept.

On Monday morning when Frau Hagen knocked again, Trudy was slumped in a chair beside the windows, wearing her yellow bathrobe. She'd been there since before daylight, staring out at the street. She hadn't showered and her hair hung in strings.

The landlady used her key and opened the door a crack. 'Trudy? Are you all right?'

Schätzchen was not so polite. The spaniel pushed through the opening and bounded in. Paws landed in Trudy's lap and a wet nose nudged her chin.

Frau Hagen came in, too, shaking her head.

317

'*Ach*. You look terrible.' She switched on a light. 'Put on your clothes and take Schätzchen for a walk, will you? This group of Italian tourists is driving me crazy and I do not have time. All of a sudden I am a tourist guide besides the cook and the innkeeper.' She pulled the blinds all the way to the top.

Trudy squinted and rubbed Schätzchen's soft ears, but she didn't lift her head from the back of the chair. 'I don't feel like going out.'

Frau Hagen stood over her with her fists on her hips. 'Go anyway. The walk will be good for you. Nobody ever got over her troubles by feeling sorry for herself.' She dropped Schätzchen's leash in Trudy's lap and went out, leaving Schätzchen behind.

The dog sat on the floor in front of her, looking up with eager brown eyes. When Trudy didn't move, Schätzchen wagged and whined.

'Life goes on, does it, Schätzchen?'

The spaniel barked and licked her hand. Slowly she rose and dressed in slacks and warm layers.

Schätzchen led her down the same streets they'd walked the week before, and Trudy followed, block after block. At the park where Schätzchen loved to scare up clouds of pigeons, Trudy sat on a bench and watched the spaniel touch noses with a dog three times its size. The Great Dane stood with its legs spread, neck arched, but Schätzchen did not back away. A metaphor for something, no doubt, but Trudy was too tired to think about it.

She heard a child's laughter and looked up. On a circle of concrete that had been cleared of snow, a small boy was chasing a red ball that careened crazily when it bounced. He shouted and ran, and her breath locked in her chest.

The ball struck a crack and leaped sideways, rolling toward her. By reflex, she put out her foot and stopped it.

The boy came pelting after his ball but halted when he saw it caught beneath her shoe. His cheeks were rosy from the cold. His hair was auburn and curly, his dark eyes familiar...

The earth shifted beneath her feet. She felt herself floating.

The boy watched her, his eyes curious and unafraid. She could almost feel the softness of his tumbled hair and smell the powdery scent of his skin. Just beyond her reach.

Her voice sounded raspy and ancient. 'Stefan?'

Time had come untethered like a child's balloon. Her son was older now. She had sat on this bench for months, had been cloistered in her room near the Kü-damm for years.

Her hand felt separate from her, adrift in space, when she picked up the ball and held it out to him. 'Come, Stefan. Don't you remember me?'

The boy stared at her, his face blank. He didn't move, didn't smile.

A woman appeared behind him. 'Come away, Peter. She is *wahnsinnig.*' The woman tugged on his arm.

'Stefan?' Trudy whispered. 'Come get your ball, sweetheart.'

The woman stepped forward and snatched the ball. Trudy did not look at her; she saw only the child. The woman grabbed the boy's hand and pulled him away, scolding. *'Sprich nicht mit Fremden!'*

'I didn't talk to her,' the boy defended. 'She talked to me.' He looked back over his shoulder as he was hustled away.

Trudy watched him go. The bench stopped moving and Schätzchen tugged on her leash.

His mother is right. I am losing my mind.

It took great effort to haul herself to her feet and walk out of the park. Schätzchen paced along quietly, the slack leash dragging on the sidewalk, her energy spent on the pigeons.

Passing the entrance to the underground trains, Trudy caught a whiff of the warm, oily breeze ascending from the tracks. She felt the train's vibration beneath her feet, and for a moment she closed her eyes, heard the train's roar in her head. Did death beneath the wheels come instantly, or would it drag a body down the tracks, chewing up flesh and bone?

Schätzchen yanked on her leash, pulling Trudy toward home.

The next morning again Frau Hagen pounded on her door. 'Open up,' the landlady called. 'I have something to show you.'

Trudy was awake but could think of no reason to get up. 'Come on in.'

Frau Hagen entered and turned to frown at the latch. 'You should not go to bed without locking your door!'

Trudy shrugged. She sat up on the edge of the bed and rubbed her puffy face.

Frau Hagen tossed a newspaper on the bed beside her. 'Look what is in the papers this morning.' She drew back the drapes, showering Trudy with winter light.

Trudy squinted at the headline. *Agreement Reached To Open The Wall For Christmas.* She shoved hair from her eyes and tried to focus. *'Was is los?'*

'Read.'

Trudy picked up the paper. It was true; the governments of East and West Berlin had negotiated conditions for issuing passes that would allow West Berliners to visit relatives across the wall during the holiday season.

Frau Hagen smiled. 'Perhaps you can visit your son at Christmas.'

Trudy had been filleted by false hope once too often; she could not survive it again. But morbid curiosity made her follow the rest of the article to an inside page, searching for details.

She found it beside a small item that showed the American writer John Steinbeck visiting the wall. He said it made him sick. *Welcome to Berlin, Mr. Steinbeck.*

The front-page article continued in four columns of dense type that outlined the terms of an agreement between Walter Ulbricht's Pankow government and West Berlin Mayor Willy Brandt. West Berliners who had close relatives in the East would be allowed through the wall on twenty-four-hour passes – for a fee. East Berliners, of course, would not be allowed out. The visitors had to apply for each pass at least two days in advance. And any person who had left East Germany illegally or committed other crimes against the DDR would be denied.

'My name will be at the top of their shit list,' Trudy said, tossing the newspaper aside.

'Of course it will. But there are other names, *ja?* Are you so famous that all the border officials know your face?'

Trudy looked at her and frowned. False identification?

'Hope is the thing with feathers that perches in the soul,' the landlady quoted. 'An American lady poet said that.'

'You are a good woman, Greta.'

'Sure, but there's no market for good women.' She smiled. 'Get dressed and come down to breakfast. See there, you look better already.'

Trudy nodded, but she was rereading the newspaper story, possibilities already vaulting through her mind. Where could she get fake papers? She'd have to hurry – the crossover period would start next week.

And if she could manage to get a pass to cross over, could she somehow smuggle Stefan back with her?

'Save me a roll and some coffee,' she called as Greta left the room. 'I'm starving.'

Negotiations between the two sides dragged on for days before final details were announced. West Berlin was a flurry of excitement, old injuries at the hands of the Pankow government nearly forgotten in the optimism of the moment. Trudy waited like the others, alternating between wild hope and cold pessimism.

At last the announcement came. Passes would not be issued by West Berlin; instead East Berlin officials would come across, a fact Mayor Brandt had found difficult to swallow. Centers would be set up in twelve schoolrooms in the West. Only applicants with close relatives in the East were eligible, and permits would be valid for twenty-four hours only. But each person might be allowed three passes between December 19 and January 5. Crossings would occur at five checkpoints.

Trudy memorized the details. There was no time to lose.

That day she walked to the *Gasthaus zur Schwarzen Katze*, where she had worked before going to America. She timed her arrival for mid-morning, before the lunch crowd. Herr Blauert and Verden, her fellow waitress, were thrilled to see her. Even the grizzled cook came out to say hello. They pressed her for details about her trip to America. Herr Blauert had always wanted to visit there. She told them enough to satisfy their curiosity, but the ending of her story made them sad.

Finally the others went back to the kitchen, but Verden lingered at Trudy's table to talk. It was Verden whom Trudy had come to see.

Verden was about Trudy's age, with similar hair color and complexion. Her features were slightly larger, but in a bad photo the two of them would look much the same. Verden had three children, and no relatives in the East. She had viewed Trudy as something of a heroine after learning about her escape through the tunnel. Trudy counted on that romantic mentality.

'I need a big favor,' Trudy told her. 'And you are the only one who can help me.'

'That sounds serious.' Verden's eyes were

excited. 'What is it?'

A customer came in just then, and Verden went to serve him. When she'd taken the man's order and reported it to the cook, she came back and sat down again.

In a moment of conscience, Trudy hesitated. Verden could get in trouble if anything went wrong. But she took a deep breath and plunged ahead. 'I need to borrow your identification papers, and those for your smallest child.'

Verden blinked. 'What for?'

Trudy explained her plan. Using Verden's papers, she would apply for two passes to visit a nonexistent relative in Friedrichshain District. At the border, she would hide the child's pass in her undergarments and use only Verden's to cross over. She would find Stefan and bring him back across using the child's pass.

As Verden listened, her face went white. Trudy leaned across the table and clasped her hand. 'He is my only child. What would you do if little Jorg was over there, staying with a stranger?'

Verden's eyes watered. Trudy sat quietly while Verden looked out the shop window, considering the risk.

'My husband must never know I did this,' Verden said finally. 'He would go absolutely crazy.' She agreed to bring a birth certificate for herself and her youngest son to work the next day. And she would lend Trudy her driver's license.

She would also accept five hundred marks of Trudy's savings to buy a new refrigerator. Trudy wondered how she'd explain that to her husband.

The day before the first passes were to be issued, Trudy went to bed early and set her alarm for 4:00 a.m. The lines at the school buildings would be long and form early. She dressed in the darkness, layering on warm clothes. It reminded her of a similar morning many months ago, the day she had left her son.

She packed the identification papers into her pockets. She would say she had left her son at home because he was too young to stand in line in the cold. For a relative in the East, she borrowed the name of an old friend of Gisela's.

The school building to be used by Eastern officials was several blocks from a train stop, and at 5:00 a.m. the piercing cold burned her face as she walked. Snow lay in dingy drifts along the curbs and made icy patches on the sidewalks.

She saw the school from a distance. The lights were on inside but the doors were still locked. It was not a school day. People already had gathered outside, coated and scarfed, exhaling puffs of steam. Some stood around in small groups, talking in subdued tones and sharing hot drinks from vacuum bottles. Others paced silently, watching the doors.

A few minutes before eight, three cars swept up to the school and a man appeared from within to unlock a side door. The East Berlin officials were ushered inside, but the anxious customers were kept waiting in the predawn cold. Somehow people guessed which door was to be the official entrance, and a queue formed half a block long. Trudy fidgeted in the line, but the collective body heat kept them all warmer. There was no talking now, only anxious waiting.

When the school house doors finally swung open, the line surged forward as if the timid might be left out. Trudy moved with the group but was still outside the doors when the man and wife who'd been first in line came out. Everyone on the sidewalk stopped breathing and looked at them.

The couple turned to the crowd with disbelief on their faces. Then they waved their papers in the air, smiling broadly. Cheers and applause arose from the waiting line. Trudy's stiff cheeks stretched in a smile. Maybe this would really work.

The queue drew her closer until at last she stepped inside the double doors, which were propped open with chunks of stone that looked like war rubble. Now she could see the table where the East Berlin officials sat, predictably unsmiling. They took their time checking identification papers. She drew a deep breath and rolled her hunched shoulders, shook out her arms. If she looked tense and frightened, the officials might get suspicious and check her papers even more thoroughly.

From the front of the line came grumbling and muffled jeering. Someone had been refused. An old man in a worn olive-green coat turned away from the table and walked past the line of hopefuls. His shocked expression silenced them as they realized they, too, might be snubbed – with or without reason. The man had tears in his eyes as he walked away. What possible harm could he have done by visiting his family at Christmas? Trudy set her teeth and waited.

She'd been there two hours before it was finally her turn at the table. Behind her, the line snaked on indefinitely. She handed the official her two sets of identification papers. 'I need one for myself and one for my son, *bitte*. To visit his grandmother.'

The man took her papers and glanced over them, then looked behind her. His eyes were small and hazel-gray. 'Where is your son?'

'At home with a neighbor. It was too cold and the lines were too long to bring him.'

The official nodded contemptuously and began running his finger down a stapled sheaf of names, flipping pages. She shoved her hands deep into her coat pockets and tried to breathe normally.

The man scanned the list slowly, his expression blank. Then he closed the sheaf of pages, got up and walked into a backroom, carrying her papers with him. Others in the line glanced at her, then looked away. Her face burned as if she'd committed some crime.

She stood by the table fidgeting for several minutes before the official returned. He shoved her papers back across the table without looking at her.

'Pass denied.'

'*Was?*'

'Pass denied. Move on,' he barked.

Trudy didn't move. 'Why? What is the reason?'

He didn't answer or meet her eyes. 'Next in line!'

She leaned her fists on the table and put her face inches from his. 'I want to hear you say why I have been denied a pass.'

She could see the red veins in his watery eyes.

His breath smelled of menthol. A muscle in his jaw twitched but still he would not answer. Was he a robot? A machine?

Firm hands grasped her elbows. She was lifted from her feet and moved away from the table. Still she glared back at the official, daring him to blink or look away, but his eyes were unchanged. The two policemen moved her past the line of silent people and toward the door. They deposited her on the sidewalk and released her arms.

'Go home, *Fräulein*,' one of them said. He met her eyes with kindness, but spoke firmly. 'No one wins an argument with them. Just go home.'

She looked at him and realized these two wore Schupo uniforms; they were West police. Doing their jobs, distasteful or not. Finally she turned away.

Snow crunched under her boots. The sun was up now but hidden behind a bruise-colored sky. Instead of going home, she went to the wall.

She walked blindly along its jagged line, block after block. Cryptic graffiti scrawled on the concrete slabs gave voice to her impotent rage. Finally she came to the River Spree and could go no farther. Staring into the murky waters, she faced the fact that she might never see Stefan again.

She faced it, but she would never accept it.

The day the great crossover began, Trudy stood among the crowd waiting beside a checkpoint before daylight in the stunning cold. The barricades lifted at 5:00 a.m. and the stream began. Lines moved slowly, while every pass was scrutinized by border guards.

All morning she watched them cross through by the hundreds, maybe thousands. People carried fat ducks or geese for Christmas dinner and slim bottles of wine, delicacies hard to get in East Berlin. They carried brightly wrapped packages for families they hadn't seen in two years. The mood was jovial despite the long lines. Loudspeakers beside the wall that usually blared warnings not to approach the border now played Christmas carols. People standing in line sang the words.

The next day she went to a different checkpoint, and the next day to still another. She saw happy Berliners going, and tired, melancholy Berliners coming back home. An idea wormed into her mind that among the crowds and goodwill, she might somehow slip across.

But the Grepos were organized, and they carried their carbines.

On Christmas eve, Trudy went to bed early and tried to imagine what Stefan and Wolfgang would be doing that night. Did they have a tree, with presents? She hadn't even mailed a gift to her son.

Greta Hagen prepared a feast for her boarders on Christmas day, but Trudy went to the wall instead, this time to the checkpoint on Heinrich-Heine-Straße. The newspapers predicted that one hundred fifty thousand people would pass through the wall that day alone. The bells of St. Thomas Church pealed, and somewhere a loudspeaker played 'O Tannenbaum.'

Trudy mixed into the crowded line and moved toward the checkpoint where the guards examined passes. After a while her nerve failed and she dropped away, but she did not leave. When darkness gathered, she still stood among the dwindling crowd, a blinding ache inside her chest. She was tired and hungry but so were the guards, and she stepped into the line again.

Her breath made white puffs in the air.

Everything had gone so smoothly, the guards would not expect it. They weren't accustomed to people trying to slip *into* the East, only out. When it came her turn, she would bolt and run, zigzagging around the barriers. Disappear into the shadows before they caught her. What was the worst that could happen? If she was caught, they would turn her back to the West. All she could think about was seeing Stefan.

The line inched forward and the church bells chimed. She looked up toward the bell tower, silhouetted against an indigo sky.

And saw something else, as well. Two figures were climbing the barbed wire fence on top of the wall near the church.

They were hard to see in the darkness, and the border guards were busy watching the line of Christmas visitors pressing through. Trudy scanned the line of barricades for Grepos. One was posted in a guard tower less than thirty meters from where the two shadows struggled at the wire. She couldn't see into the shadowy tower, but the gleam of a machine gun protruded from under its tent-like roof.

She sucked in her breath and held it. The two figures had almost topped the barricade, ready to leap to freedom.

Then a loud, guttural voice barked an order. The guard in the tower whirled, and a spotlight flicked on. Trudy saw the guard lean out and aim the machine gun. He shouted a warning, quick and loud, but the two figures scrambled faster.

The rattle of the machine gun splintered the night. The crowd of Christmas visitors looked up in unison and saw one young man jump for the West, screaming.

The other crumpled like a punctured balloon and slid back into the death zone. His empty glove dangled from the top strand of barbed wire.

In the nauseating silence that followed, a Christmas carol echoed in the distance. *All is calm, all is bright.* Two West Berlin Schupos ran to kneel beside the jumper who lay still in the snow.

The echo of the machine gun rang in Trudy's ears. Behind the echo she heard Greta Hagen's warning. *You will be no good to your little boy if you are dead.*

Trudy turned away from the checkpoint and melted into the ringing darkness.

CHAPTER 30

Brita Becker answered Wolfgang's knock without the warm smile he was used to seeing every day. Her eyes were red-rimmed, her cheeks pale.

'Herr Lieutenant-General,' she said formally. 'Can you come in a moment, *bitte?* I would like to talk with you.'

'Of course,' he said and stepped inside, immediately worried that she would say she couldn't keep Stefan anymore.

He followed her into the living room and she moved toys from Herr Becker's accustomed chair so Wolfgang could sit down. Apparently Herr Becker was not home yet. From the kitchen, he heard Stefan and Sophie's voices, where they were absorbed with some activity at the table.

'They are making paper cranes,' Frau Becker said, 'so we can talk privately.'

She was always coming up with creative things for the children to make from paper or string or empty food cartons. She sewed all of Sophie's clothes herself, and had even made things for Stefan.

Wolfgang sat down, unbuttoning his coat in the warm room. 'Is something wrong?'

Frau Becker perched on the edge of the sofa. 'Two men came here today and insisted on looking through the apartment. They said it was routine, that they were counting how many people lived in the building.'

Wolfgang frowned. 'You let them in?'

'I had to. They were Stasi.'

His eyebrows lifted. 'Stasi? How do you know?'

'I asked to see their credentials. I was terrified. They looked in all the rooms, and asked what time Herr Becker came home from work.' Her eyes began to water. 'They wrote down our names, even Stefan's. What does it mean?'

Wolfgang shook his head, frowning. 'I have no idea. But I will find out.'

Frau Becker sat forward, her hands clenched together on her knees. She lowered her voice to a whisper. '*Bitte*, Herr Krüger. Can you protect us?

I swear we have done nothing wrong.'

Wolfgang leaned forward and put his hand over hers. Her skin felt clammy, the knuckles rough from housework. 'I know,' he said. 'Don't worry. I will find out what's going on and make sure you are left alone.'

She blew out a long breath. *'Danke. Dankeschön.'* She stood up quickly. 'I will get Stefan now.' At the kitchen doorway, she turned back and gave him a relieved smile. *'Danke,'* she said again. 'If all the *Volkspolizei* were good men like you, people wouldn't have to worry.'

In the stillness of the night, the rapid knocking on his front door sounded like machine gun fire. He'd been sound asleep, but he sat up quickly and glanced at Stefan's crib. The child still slept. Wolfgang quickly pulled on his trousers and padded to the door before the knock repeated.

He looked through the peephole and saw a man with his coat collar pulled up around his neck, his hands stuffed into his pockets.

Wolfgang opened the door. 'Hans! You look like a private detective from American television.'

Hans gave a lopsided smile. 'How would you know what is on Western television?'

Wolfgang grinned and clapped him on the shoulder. 'Come in. But talk softly. My little boy is asleep.'

My little boy. When had he started to think that way? Before or after Trudy had destroyed his ill-fated plans?

Hans lowered his voice. 'I am sorry to wake you. I had to be sure we had privacy.'

Wolfgang motioned to the sofa and Hans sat without removing his coat. A rim of wet snow edged the soles of his boots. Beneath his jacket, he still had on his Grepo uniform.

'You must have drawn the night shift this week,' Wolfgang said, and Hans nodded. 'Would you like tea? A beer?'

'*Danke*, no. I will not stay long.' He paused a moment, his hands still couched in his pockets, and met Wolfgang's eyes. 'I came with a warning.'

Wolfgang nodded. Good news never came at this hour. He sat in a chair across from the young officer and crossed one leg over his knee. A calmness came over him now, his dependable reaction to crisis.

'What is it, then?'

'*Obermeister* Schweinhardt,' Hans said.

'I might have guessed.' Wolfgang had suspected Schweinhardt would take advantage of his failed effort to bring Trudy home. Her refusal was a black mark on his name, and not with Schweinhardt alone. The little bastard must be delighted with this ammunition. 'What mischief is Comrade Schweinhardt up to now?'

'He has filed a memorandum with the central office regarding Stefan.'

'Stefan?' Wolfgang knew about Schweinhardt's continual memos defaming his service and his loyalty, but it did not occur to him that the man's spite would extend to a child. An ominous dread threaded up his spine.

'He has recommended that Stefan be taken from your custody and placed in the state home for children,' Hans said.

334

'An *orphanage?*'

Hans nodded. 'He sent the memo through channels today. I thought you should know.'

Wolfgang's jaw tightened. Schweinhardt had gone too far. 'I appreciate this, Hans. What was his justification for such an action?'

'He said the boy's mother is a fugitive – I think he said criminal – who refused an offer of repatriation. He said the state needs to keep its young people from being corrupted by Western values. Or smuggled out of the East.'

'Of course he did.' Wolfgang blew out a breath.

He got up and found an ashtray, offered Hans a smoke and then a light. Hans blew a hazy cloud into the quiet room.

'We all know Comrade Schweinhardt is a dedicated officer,' Hans said bitterly, 'who doesn't give a damn about the people he is supposed to serve. Do you think anyone will listen to him?'

Wolfgang shrugged. 'It is possible.' *They already have.* He thought of Brita Becker's frightened face, the visit from the Stasi. *And they know where Stefan stays during the day.*

Wolfgang picked up a yellow plastic fish they'd missed when picking up toys before Stefan's bedtime. A bath toy. He turned it over in his hands, seeing Stefan's round body in the bathtub, his hair in damp ringlets against his neck.

Hans stubbed out his cigarette. 'If I hear anything more, I will let you know.' He put on his hat and stood.

Wolfgang stood also, and extended his hand. 'Thank you, Hans. I owe you.'

'No. If we matched favors, I would be forever in

your debt.' He put on his cap and pulled the coat collar up again.

Wolfgang walked him to the door. 'How is your father?'

Hans pulled a deep breath. 'My father died two weeks ago. A heart attack.'

Wolfgang swore. 'I am very sorry. I didn't know.'

'My father was older than his years and suffered many ailments. Thanks to you, he got to die in his own home instead of in prison.'

Wolfgang placed his hand on the young man's shoulder and opened the door. 'Take care of yourself, my friend. And watch your back.'

Hans smiled wearily. 'The same to you, Herr Lieutenant-General.' He saluted. '*Guten nacht.*'

Wolfgang locked the door and went to the bedroom to check on Stefan. He was still sleeping, and his thumb had found his mouth. Wolfgang gently removed the thumb and slipped Bebe under his arm. Stefan snuffled in his sleep.

In the living room, he lit another cigarette and turned out the light. Standing beside the door to the balcony, he watched the wind toss leafless branches against a charcoal sky.

Ever since Trudy had left him at the checkpoint he'd been marking time, waiting for something to happen. Now it had.

He was angry when she'd refused to sign the papers, not because of the humiliation it would cause him, nor even the consequences. He was angry because she had seen the truth and called it by name: Wolfgang had betrayed Rolf for principles that were crumbling beneath him, principles he hadn't held sacred for a long time. He had crossed the line so many times that he didn't know where it was anymore. But Trudy knew, and she'd redrawn the line right at his feet.

He expected consequences for his failure – perhaps a loss of rank, a reprimand – and he deserved that. But he hadn't for one moment thought that Albrecht Schweinhardt might target a two-year-old boy.

Wolfgang had visited a state orphanage once. He remembered the smell, and the concrete walls that sweat in the summertime. Row upon row of miniature beds. One somber matron for each sixteen children. The children's eyes looked flat and dead, like caged animals behind thick glass.

Schweinhardt was a dung fly and he wouldn't rest. Herr Otter's report added weight to his accusations. If the decision to take Stefan away was made, it would come swiftly and without notice. A knock at his door and the boy would be gone – or they would pluck him from Frau Becker's arms while Wolfgang was at work.

He would have to act first.

He switched on a small lamp and dug in a drawer for writing paper and an envelope. He needed to get a message to Trudy, and it would not be safe to telephone the American consulate from his office as he'd done before. Schweinhardt could be monitoring his calls.

There were certain advantages for a Vopo commandant who kept his ears open and made friends among the men. He heard things from the rank-and-file officers, who heard things from their relatives or drinking mates. Wolfgang knew that four times every day, when the guard changed at the Soviet War Memorial just across the frontier in the West, an East German driver made the short run to deliver a brace of Russian soldiers and pick up the other watch. One of these drivers – maybe more than one, it couldn't be proven – was known to take messages across and drop them out the car window at a certain point along the street. After the car had returned to East Berlin, someone in the West picked up the messages and relayed them through a self-styled delivery service.

Obviously, Wolfgang was not supposed to know about the message deliveries, so he could not give the driver a letter himself. The man would play dumb, thinking it a trap. Once again, Wolfgang would have to count on Hans for a favor.

When the note was finished, he went into the bedroom and packed a bag.

Nadia came to the door in her bathrobe, her long hair tousled and wild. Her eyes went from his face to Stefan, bundled in a blanket in Wolfgang's arms.

He had not seen her since she changed jobs and moved into an apartment of her own. She looked good, he thought, her face a bit fuller than before but still fierce as a tiger.

'You have a lot of nerve, coming here in the middle of the night,' she said. 'What do you want?'

'Are you alone?' he said.

'That's none of your business.'

'We need a place to stay tonight, and maybe tomorrow.'

She looked at him, scowling, and glanced again at Stefan, who was awake now and staring at her with wide, sober eyes. Reluctantly, she stepped back and opened the door farther. 'Come in, then, before all the heat gets out.'

The apartment was even smaller than his, one bedroom with a kitchen and living area combined. She piled a blanket on a sagging sofa and didn't ask him anything.

'The baby can sleep with me,' she said. 'You sleep on the couch.'

She held out her arms to Stefan, and to Wolfgang's astonishment he went to her willingly. She parked him on one hip and gave him a smile that changed her face like sudden music. 'I like your bear. What's his name?'

'Bebe,' Stefan said, his voice barely more than a whisper.

'I sleep with my bear, too,' she said. 'Want to see?'

Stefan nodded, and she carried him off into the bedroom, leaving the door open.

Wolfgang stood there a moment, waiting for them to come back or Stefan to call out for him. When nothing happened, he folded the blanket in half and spread it on the sofa. He took off his coat and doubled it over in a chair, placed his cap on top and his shoes underneath on the floor.

He sat on the sofa and listened for several minutes but heard nothing from Nadia's bedroom. Finally he went to the door and peeked inside. Stefan was snuggled underneath the covers between Bebe and a larger stuffed bear. Nadia lay curved around him, with one arm across his body

339

on the narrow bed. Their eyes were closed.

Wolfgang returned to the sofa and covered himself with the blanket. He listened to the unfamiliar ticks and sighs of Nadia's apartment, thinking that she always managed to surprise him. What would she say if he told her the child in her bed was the son of Rolf Hulst, the man she had offered up to save her shiftless brother?

The rest of the night, Wolfgang lay awake and made his plan.

CHAPTER 31

At the end of her shift, Trudy straightened a table of ladies' underwear one last time and walked home from the KDW department store on aching feet. The day had been hectic, the customers impatient because she was new and didn't know the stock The job was mindless, but at least it forced her to get out of bed in the mornings.

At the *Pension*, the door to Frau Hagen's apartment was closed and quiet, Greta and Schätzchen already shut in for the evening. Trudy trudged up three flights and unlocked her room.

Paper rustled beneath her foot when she stepped inside, and she glanced down. Greta must have slid a note under the door. She picked up the small envelope, piled her coat and bag on the bed and switched on the lamp. She sank into a chair and kicked off her shoes before turning the envelope over in her hand.

At the sight of Wolfgang's handwriting, her breath caught. *What the hell...?*

She ripped it open. The message was choppy and urgent:

Things falling apart here. Come to the Friedrichstraße checkpoint noon Saturday. Wait for us.

Trudy looked on the back of the paper but there was nothing else, not even a signature.

Wait for us? Did *us* mean Stefan?

The envelope carried no stamp, no postmarks. How did it get here?

She knew all the crossing places by heart, and she pictured the checkpoint in her mind. Friedrichstraße was in the American Sector, the one nicknamed Checkpoint Charlie.

What did he mean by *things falling apart?*

Was he going to try to get Stefan across the border at the checkpoint? She rejected the idea immediately. Why would he do such a thing?

But he wouldn't risk sending a message like this unless something was drastically wrong. *Things falling apart here.* Either he was in danger, or Stefan was.

Pain like a knifepoint bloomed behind her eyes. She squinted at her watch, counting eighteen hours between now and noon tomorrow.

She bolted from the chair. But there was nowhere to go for answers, nothing she could do. She stood in the middle of the room rereading the note, heat rising in her throat. This was either terrible news, or it was miraculous. She had no idea.

She folded the paper and slipped it inside her blouse, as if it might disappear. Her hands shook when she dug a cigarette from her purse and cracked the window for ventilation.

She'd been smoking too much lately and had developed a cough. If Stefan came to live with her, she would have to quit.

Don't think like that. If you get your hopes up again and he doesn't bring Stefan, this time you'll die.

On her break at the department store that day, she had idled through the boys' clothing section, touching the little shirts and double-kneed pants, wondering what would fit Stefan. She wondered how tall he was now, how much he was talking. Every morning before she got out of bed she thought of him, and wondered what he was learning from his communist guardian.

What if, by some miracle, Wolfgang simply delivered him to her on Saturday? Stefan would have to sleep in her bed until she could find a small flat with a kitchen...

Don't do this. The note is too vague.

Damn it, what does it mean?

She remembered the world-weary shadow in Wolfgang's eyes the day she'd met him at the border. She thought of the two young men shot down beside St. Thomas Church on Christmas night, the empty glove hanging in the barbed wire. Was he disillusioned enough that he might try to cross over himself?

An icy wind swept down Friedrichstraße and the faded sky threatened snow. At half past eleven, Trudy walked down a sidewalk outside the check-

342

point, hands stuffed into her pockets, the tips of her scarf whipping around her neck. Across the forbidden zone, two armed guards stood rigid at the East Berlin side of the double line of barricades. On the Western side there were no guards, just a sign that warned in three languages: Attention! You Are Now Leaving The American Sector.

Between the two boundaries, a distance of perhaps thirty meters, concrete pylons created a labyrinth for vehicles that passed through. In the early days of the wall, people had crashed their cars through temporary barricades to escape. But no vehicle could speed through here now.

She walked half a block past the checkpoint, turned and retraced her steps. She saw no pedestrians on either side. She found a place to stand beside a building, partly sheltered from the wind. From here she could watch the checkpoint without making the guards suspicious.

Cold air snaked inside her coat sleeves. She rewrapped the knitted scarf around her neck, crossed her arms and waited.

On the West Berlin side, an official-looking black car approached the checkpoint. Perhaps a visiting diplomat, or an American politician. The car paused at the entrance, waited for acknowledgment from the Grepo guards across the restricted zone, then zigzagged slowly through the labyrinth between the two gates.

Trudy watched, frowning. Did the car mean something? There was still no sign of Wolfgang.

When the black car reached the East-side barricades, one of the guards signaled it to halt. The driver and a single passenger stepped out. The

343

senior Grepo examined their papers. Then the two guards, one on either side, performed a search of the vehicle. When they'd finished, the Grepo handed back their papers, the driver and passenger got back in and the car disappeared without incident into the streets of East Berlin.

Trudy huffed, her breath blowing away in steamy ribbons.

Fifteen minutes until noon. She tugged her fur hat down over her ears, stamped her boots on the icy patches beside the building.

Wait for us, the note had said.

She felt she'd been waiting all her life.

From the shelter of his private car behind the border crossing, Wolfgang sat with the heater running, watching. He had parked along a curb where his brown Trabant was inconspicuous from the checkpoint. The two border guards stood facing West Berlin, their backs to him. They hadn't noticed him there, and that was good. This checkpoint was not used by Germans, only Allied military personnel and diplomats, and it was quiet on a Saturday morning.

On the seat beside him, Stefan had finished his cheese snack and was dozing, one elbow hooked around the neck of Bebe.

At five minutes before twelve, a familiar figure in a Grepo uniform came out of the guard's shack near the eastern entrance to the checkpoint. He was tall and blond, and he walked with the slight slouch of an athlete. Hans stopped a moment on the pavement and lit a cigarette, flicked away the match deliberately, a signal. He did not look in Wolfgang's direction but walked toward the two guards on duty.

Wolfgang shut off the car's engine and got out, closing the door quietly. He moved closer to the crossing, using the narrow shadow of the guard shack for cover. From here he could keep an eye on Stefan but also watch Hans. A plain black overcoat concealed his commandant's uniform.

Hans approached the senior guard on duty. Wolfgang strained to catch his words on the wind.

'I will stand,' Hans told the guard. 'Go home and thaw out your bones.'

'*Hallo*, Hans.' The guard slapped his gloved hands on his own arms, shifted from one foot to another. 'I thought Kurt was on today.'

'He has a bad cold. I am substituting.' Hans glanced around the checkpoint area. 'Quiet this morning. Tell your partner over there he can go on, if he wants. I can handle it until his replacement comes.'

The guard saluted carelessly. 'I will tell him, but he won't go. He follows orders to the letter, scared of everybody who outranks him.'

Hans looked across at the other guard, his brow creasing. Then he smiled amicably. 'What is he, sixteen?'

'Eighteen, so he says. They get younger all the time.' The Grepo saluted briefly, then crossed the checkpoint to speak with his very young partner.

Wolfgang saw the teenager look toward Hans uncertainly. He said something and shook his head. The older guard turned toward Hans and shrugged, *I told you so*. Then he walked away

345

down the street.

Wolfgang stood behind the shack and waited for the boot steps to fade away.

Hans scanned the street and the empty buildings bordering the secured zone on the East. He waited a moment, then walked over to the young Grepo. They were far enough away that Wolfgang couldn't hear them talking. The teenager stomped his feet as if they were numb. Hans gestured toward the shack he'd come out of a few minutes before, casual, good-natured. Probably telling the kid there was something hot to drink inside the shack, that he should take a break.

The youngster smiled, then scanned the checkpoint and the street beyond. Nothing moved. Thin snowflakes had started to fall. He stamped his feet again, then said something to Hans – and stayed put.

Hans shrugged. He leaned his rifle against his thigh and lifted his cap, pulling down the ear flaps while he scanned the no-man's-land between the two lines of the border. Then he replaced the cap deliberately and walked back to his post.

Wolfgang would have to take care of the young Grepo himself.

He went back to his car and took off his overcoat, tossed it on the backseat. He'd worn his parade uniform beneath the overcoat, with every medal and distinction he'd ever earned displayed on his coat, for intimidation. He put on his cap and opened the passenger-side door.

'Wake up, Stefan. It's time to go see your mother.'

Across the secured zone, Trudy saw Wolfgang appear on the street as if from nowhere. In his dress uniform, he looked even taller than she remembered, his posture straight and assured. And walking beside him was a tiny replica.

Stefan wore a miniature uniform identical to Wolfgang's, down to the short-brimmed cap that shaded his eyes. Someone had made those clothes especially for him – who?

He walked like a tiny soldier, swinging his arms with each step, and Trudy's eyes burned. *No – he's just a baby, too tiny to wear a uniform.*

The wind had gone still and snowflakes thickened the space between her and Stefan. She moved from the shelter of the building into the open area in front of the checkpoint, where she would be plainly visible. Her eyes locked on Stefan; if he looked up she would wave.

But he did not look toward her. He was looking up at the blond Grepo who had just come on duty. When Wolfgang and Stefan approached, the Grepo saluted them both. Stefan seemed to know him, she thought. She stood at the edge of the restricted zone with her heart in her mouth, and waited.

Wolfgang returned the Grepo's salute and walked past him to the other guard, who looked incredibly young. The young guard hadn't noticed Trudy, his attention riveted on the senior officer's approach. The teenager stood ramrod straight and saluted Wolfgang.

She watched Wolfgang pull a cigarette from his breast pocket and search for a light. When he spoke his tone was forceful, and his voice carried

347

across the checkpoint in the snowy air.

'Comrade, would you happen to have a match?'

The boy looked nervous. 'No, sir. I do not smoke. I am sorry, sir.'

Wolfgang smiled at him. 'No need to be sorry. You will be healthier than the rest of us.' He glanced idly around the checkpoint. Trudy knew he saw her but he gave no sign.

'Go and get me some matches from the shack, then,' Wolfgang said. 'I will stand at your post.'

The young man shot a worried look at his partner on watch. But the blond guard wasn't looking at him; he was watching a car with an official insignia that was approaching from the East, driving fast.

The young Grepo saluted Wolfgang again and trotted off toward the guard's shack.

With the teenager out of the way, Wolfgang glanced over his shoulder and saw Hans jogging toward a car that had swept to a halt at the mouth of the checkpoint. It bore the official DDR insignia on its door.

Scheiße. Who is in that car?

Hans would do his best to distract them, but that wouldn't work for long. He had to act now.

Wolfgang knelt beside Stefan, smiled at him and straightened his cap. 'Look, Stefan. See that lady over there, waving?' He turned the boy's shoulders to face the West. 'That is your mother. She has come to see you.' Wolfgang swallowed hard. 'Run as fast as you can and give her a hug.'

And after that, I may never see you again.

Stefan looked across the restricted zone at

348

Trudy. She called to him. 'Stefan! It's *Mutti!*' She held out her arms.

But Stefan didn't recognize her. He didn't move. Wolfgang gave the puzzled boy a nudge. 'Show her how fast you can run. Go on!'

Stefan glanced up at him, then began an uncertain shuffle into the no-man's-land between the two gates.

Behind him, Wolfgang heard a car door slam and barked commands – the unmistakable megaphone voice of Grepo *Obermeister* Albrecht Schweinhardt.

Stefan was only a few meters into the forbidden zone when someone behind him shouted. He stopped and looked back.

Trudy froze in place as two men emerged from the staff car on the other side of the checkpoint. One was a Grepo with a rifle, the other wore the insignia of the Grepo chief. Trudy had seen his picture in West Berlin newspapers – they called him Schweinhardt, the pig man.

Everything happened at once.

Schweinhardt was yelling and pointing wildly toward Stefan. 'Stop him! Stop that child, you idiots! He is escaping!'

The teenaged guard Wolfgang had sent to the shack came running. He spotted Stefan entering the forbidden zone, looked from one commandant to the other and his confusion was plain. He hesitated, undoubtedly expecting Wolfgang to retrieve his child.

The blond Grepo, too, looked at Wolfgang and didn't move.

The Grepo chief shouted again. 'Get that child! Move, damn you!'

But both guards stood rooted, waiting for a sign from Wolfgang.

It was the pig man's driver who finally moved. He rounded the staff car, his rifle slung over his back, and sprinted toward Stefan. The blond Grepo took two quick steps and tripped him.

The driver fell headlong onto the pavement, his rifle clattering away, surprise flashing on his face.

Schweinhardt's face was a red balloon. 'You are finished, Krüger! I will see you rot in prison!' He turned toward the two guards still standing and bellowed, 'If you do not get that child back here immediately, I will shoot you myself.' His voice echoed from the abandoned buildings beside the wall.

Suddenly there was a great flurry of running.

Three men dashed into the restricted zone. The fallen Grepo scrambled to his feet and ran toward Stefan. The teenaged guard responded to Schweinhardt's threat and ran.

But the blond Grepo lowered his rifle and did not move. The third runner was Wolfgang.

Wolfgang reached Stefan first and grabbed him up, swinging him westward with the boy's feet skimming the ground. They had not covered five meters when a shot crackled through the cold.

Wolfgang pitched forward.

Trudy screamed.

The Grepo chief stood with his handgun in front of him, both arms extended. Wolfgang lay facedown on the concrete in a thin layer of snow, a red stain blooming on the back of his coat.

Stefan was knocked aside and began to cry. Trudy had taken three strides toward him when the second shot exploded.

Everyone froze.

The Grepo chief crumpled, the Luger dropping from his hands. He fell to his knees and clutched his shoulder, disbelief on his face. For a moment the blond Grepo who had fired the shot held his rifle limp in front of him, his face blank. Then he dropped his weapon and ran west.

'Shoot him!' the Grepo commandant ordered, and his driver obeyed instantly.

Wolfgang's friend stumbled but kept running. The guard fired again and the blond Grepo plunged forward and lay still.

An instant of silence followed. Citizens had appeared on both sides of the border, drawn by the shouting and gunfire. All eyes turned to the tiny boy in the center of the no-man's-land, who began to wail. He turned and toddled back toward Wolfgang's still body.

Before the two remaining guards could react, Trudy sprinted into the forbidden zone and swept Stefan up in her arms. She whirled and started back the way she'd come, zigzagging around the pylons.

'*Shoot her!*' the Grepo chief bellowed. '*I order you to shoot!*'

Stefan clung to her, screaming. Her boots slipped on an icy patch and she stumbled, nearly falling. Struggling to her feet, she glanced back and saw the two remaining Grepos level their weapons at her and Stefan.

The crowd of West Berliners gasped and jeered

at the guards. Trudy saw the teenaged Grepo lower his rifle, and his head drooped in shame. But the driver held his aim, and for two breathless seconds, his eyes locked with hers. The crowd jeered louder.

She turned her back and ran. Every step, she expected the rifle's crack, the jolt that would take her down.

It did not come.

At the boundary to the West, many hands received them into safety. People surrounded her; they thought it was over. Trudy knelt and set Stefan on his feet, hugged him and kissed him, wiped his tears with her scarf. Then she looked up into the stalwart faces of an elderly man and his wife. 'Keep him here. Please watch him.'

She turned and ran back into the restricted zone.

Kneeling beside Wolfgang, she carefully turned him onto his back and cradled his head. He was still breathing.

She brushed the snow from his face. 'Can you hear me, Wolfgang? Stefan is safe.'

The blue eyes flickered open, unfocused. In the distance sirens wailed, growing louder.

'Thank you. Thank you for my son.'

His lips moved and a red bead formed at one corner of his mouth.

Trudy got to her feet and hooked her arms under Wolfgang's shoulders. She began to drag him toward West Berlin.

Once again the Grepo chief bawled from where he knelt in the snow, clutching his bleeding shoulder. 'Give me my weapon, you gutless bastards!'

But on the western side, Schupos had appeared, and they held their rifles in front of them – a warning. The two Grepos only watched as Trudy dragged Wolfgang's body a few meters, caught her breath and heaved again.

Suddenly Stefan appeared beside her, pulling on Wolfgang's arm, trying to help. She looked at him and couldn't breathe.

Then the old man and his wife were there. And two West Berlin Schupos.

They dragged Wolfgang across the line, where other Schupos took over. They transferred Wolfgang's limp body to a stretcher and carried him to an ambulance that stood flashing in the street.

Stefan clung to her leg. 'Wolfie? *Wolfie!*'

Icy teardrops clung to his lashes, and she saw the terror in his eyes. She picked him up and followed the Schupos. The doors of the ambulance stood open, and a young medic bent over Wolfgang, preparing him for transport. Trudy and Stefan climbed inside.

CHAPTER 32

June 1964

The *Grunewald* was green again. In the park that bordered the cemetery, a row of linden trees sent up its yellow perfume, and Trudy breathed it in as she walked across the grass toward the cemetery gate. Sunlight sparkled in the water of a fountain. In the trees, birds courted and sang.

When she was small, before the war took her father, she had once come here with her parents to visit a relative's grave. Trudy couldn't remember who the ancestor was, but she remembered the broad lawn of the park, which seemed endless to her then, and the sense of safety and peace. It was hard to believe that spring had come again, and she was here with her own child.

Stefan ranged ahead of her, collecting wildflowers for a stubby bouquet that he gripped in his right fist. It was clear by now that he was going to be left-handed, like his father. He plucked a pink flower from the grass and added it to his collection. His fingers were stained with chlorophyll, and before they got home, the knees of his pants would look the same.

'Look, there's a blue one,' she said, and smiled as he pounced on a violet-blue windflower with a yellow center. Trudy carried a bouquet, too, red tulips bought from a street vendor, wrapped in waxy paper and tied with ribbon.

The cemetery was shady and cool and very quiet when they entered. But Stefan chattered like the birds. In the first few weeks, he'd been cautious and restrained. Now he talked constantly, and she never tired of hearing him. Sometimes, for no reason, he ran to her for a hug. Those moments always brought tears to her eyes. At home in their two-bedroom flat, not far from the downtown office where she worked as a typist, Stefan often sang while he played. She believed, as mothers will, that he might have a beautiful singing voice when he grew up.

Today they walked through the oldest part of the cemetery, where tombstones dated back to the turn of the century. Long before Hitler, before Germany was a divided country. The oldest stones tilted in the earth and were streaked with rusty brown. Then came a section filled with soldiers and other casualties of that era. Beyond that lay the new section they had come to visit.

Stefan knew the path. He skipped ahead, anxious now to place his bouquet. They came to a marble headstone by a grave that was still slightly rounded beneath the grass. Trudy knelt and laid her flowers beside the stone. For Stefan, though, that wouldn't do. She sat on the grass and watched him dig a hole to plant his flowers. He did his best to make the wilting blooms stand erect. When the stems were buried in the ground, he came and plopped on her lap, facing the gravestone.

'Read it, *Mutti*.'

She removed a strand of grass from his hair. 'You know what it says on the stone.'

'Read it again.'

His dark eyes fixed on the chiseled words, and she wondered what he was seeing in that bright little mind. She traced her fingers over the granite letters.

'In Loving Memory Of Rolf Hulst. A Free Man.'

Stefan was silent for a moment, and then he repeated what she had told him many times. 'He was my daddy.'

'Yes. And he loved you very much.'

'Tell a story about my daddy.'

She smiled. 'Tonight. At bedtime.'

The promise satisfied him. The ritual finished, Stefan's attention shifted away, following the line of gravestones in the direction they'd come. He stood up. 'Where is Wolfie?'

Trudy stood, too, brushing the grass from her skirt. She shaded her eyes and scanned the field of stones. Then she smiled. 'There he is.'

Near the gate where they'd come in, a man in a wheelchair rolled along the concrete path. He carried a picnic basket balanced on his lap.

Stefan's voice rang like a bell across the graves. '*Wolfeee!*'

Wolfgang looked toward them and waved.

'May I go, *Mutti?*' He was hopping like popping corn.

She nodded. 'Be careful of the stones.'

Stefan ran toward him, dodging among the tombstones, intent on the living instead of the dead. Trudy removed a faded bouquet from Rolf's grave and dropped it into a trash bin. Then she walked across the cemetery after Stefan.

Wolfgang was watching her approach, his eyes like a chipped summer sky. They were clouded with a certain sadness that never quite left him. She wondered if he saw a similar shadow in her eyes. When she came within hearing distance, he smiled and called to her.

'*Guten Morgen.* I brought lunch.'

'So I see. And you made it yourself, did you?'

'With the help of Gutzen's Deli.'

She offered her hand and he squeezed it, lifting it not quite to his lips before he let go.

Behind the wheelchair, Stefan strained to push

356

it along the sidewalk. Wolfgang turned the wheels with his hands, and Trudy walked beside him. His hands and arms had always looked strong, but even more so now that they were also his legs.

'Come live with us,' she had told him once. 'I can cook, and Stefan can fetch things for you.'

But he didn't want to feel like a burden. He had found a ground-floor flat and a job he could do sitting down. The bullet had shattered a bone in his spine, but he took physical therapy and believed that someday he would walk again. He had surprised her before; perhaps he would again.

Stefan's foot caught in the wheel and he tumbled. 'Here,' she said, righting him. 'Come around front and you can carry the picnic basket.'

Stefan grabbed the handle of the basket and trudged ahead of them on the sun-dappled path, but soon he was struggling with the basket's weight. 'I need to ride,' he said and handed the basket to his mother.

Wolfgang hoisted him onto his lap and they rolled on toward the park

'How is Rolf today?' Wolfgang asked.

She smiled. 'The same as last week. He says hello.'

'He does not!' Stefan piped up. 'He can't talk.'

'Ah, but he can,' Wolfgang said. 'The dead have stories to tell, if we know how to listen.'

Stefan had plenty of questions about that, and Wolfgang answered them. But Trudy was distracted by a sudden maverick breeze that shivered through the linden trees, raining blossoms on their shoulders.

EPILOGUE

November 9, 1989

Stefan saw it on the small television in his office at the university. He had tuned in to the nightly press conference from East Berlin to hear about the latest shake-ups in the DDR. Winds of change had swept through Eastern Europe in recent months, first in Poland, Yugoslavia, Hungary. Demands for reform were contagious. Soon the demonstrations had spread to Leipzig and eventually East Berlin. The head of East Germany, Erich Honecker, had resigned in October, and the new leadership was scrambling to make concessions that might save its crumbling government.

Stefan was only half listening to the newscast as he proofread a draft of chapter ten for his doctoral dissertation. Near the end of the press conference, Günter Schabowski, a Politbüro member and the Party chief for East Berlin, read an announcement he'd just been handed. Emigration would be henceforth allowed across all border crossing points between East Germany and West Germany and West Berlin.

Stefan looked up. The red pen in his hand went still.

What did the Party chief just say?

There was a follow-up question: When would this opening of the borders take place? The fumbled answer: As far as he knew, immediately.

It was stunning.

Stefan had the sense that Schabowski didn't realize the import of his own words. For more than a quarter century, East Germans had been prevented from traveling legally to non-communist countries – and suddenly they could? The implications rocked him back in his chair.

In his tiny office, shared with another graduate teaching assistant, he heard the hum of the heating system and the momentous ticking from an institutional clock above the door. It was 9:00 p.m., a Thursday evening. Stefan was alone on his side of the building, evening classes already dismissed. He abandoned his work and dug beneath sliding stacks of papers and books to find the telephone.

Marlina answered on the fourth ring. He could hear little Rolf in the background, screeching and laughing, probably roughhousing with the dog.

'Do you have the television on?' he asked.

'No, I couldn't tolerate the extra noise this evening. Should I have?'

He heard the clatter of dishes and pictured his pretty Danish wife in the kitchen, her stomach bulging slightly beneath an apron tied over whatever she'd worn that day to teach classes at the American University of Berlin.

'The chief of the SED in East Berlin just announced the opening of East German borders for private travel,' he told her.

He heard her turn off the water.

'Holy shit.' Marlina was addicted to American slang.

'I just heard the press conference,' he said. 'Nobody in the room knew how to react.'

'I guess *not*. This is huge.'

An explosion of barking came through the line. 'What's wrong with Elvis?'

'Nothing. He's hiding behind the sofa, and Rolfie's scrambling from one end to the other to stick his head over and look in at him.'

She held the phone away. 'Rolfie, did you put on your pajamas? Okay, go brush your teeth. I will be there in one minute.' She came back on the line. 'If the new one is another boy, I'm sending it back.'

'What makes you think a girl would be any tamer?'

'Good point.' She had grown up with two sisters, none of them timid.

'Go get him in bed. I'll be home soon,' he said and rang off. Then he dialed another number.

Trudy answered immediately. He imagined her in her big chair beside the phone, watching the evening news.

'Did you see it?' he asked.

'I saw. But it is hard to believe.'

'I guarantee we will find out tonight. I'm going to drive by one of the checkpoints on my way home and see if anything is going on.'

'Let me know. If people are coming through, I want to see.'

In his aging Volkswagen, Stefan turned on the radio. The news was on every station. He heard a report that a group of friends in an East Berlin bar had decided to test out the announcement. They walked to the crossing point at Bornholmerstraße, the one called Spy Bridge because of prisoner exchanges that had taken place there during the height of the Cold War. The drinkers had shown their identity cards to the Grepo on duty, who allowed them to pass. They walked across the bridge into West Berlin, then turned around and walked back. A reporter had witnessed the event and recorded a quote from one of the men. 'To walk across this bridge into West Berlin is the most normal thing in the world. But things have not been normal here for twenty-eight years.'

By half-past ten, people were streaming onto the sidewalks. Stefan drove down *Straße des 17. Juni* toward Brandenburg Gate. He parked some distance away and walked toward the wall.

Several hundred citizens had already gathered there. The historic Brandenburg Gate, the centerpiece of an undivided Berlin before he was born, stood just behind the wall, inside a forbidden area. The viewing platform that looked over at the gate and into the East was crowded with bodies, but Stefan waited his turn and climbed up.

On the eastern side, a crowd was also gathering. They stood beyond the Gate, held back by a line of nervous border guards. The crowd was getting noisier and braver, and larger. Much larger. Stefan waved and called across to them, and they waved back. On the West side, a chant began. *'Die Mauer muss weg! Die Mauer muss weg!'*

The wall must go.

Stefan climbed down and went back to his car. He drove toward Checkpoint Charlie. It was the same scene. Everywhere in the city people were pouring into the streets, flocking toward the wall. Stefan felt the weight of history pressing down on him.

He turned onto a side street to avoid the thickening traffic and drove fast across the city.

When Trudy opened her door, he heard the television playing. She'd been watching the scenes he'd just witnessed.

'Put on warm clothes,' he told her. 'It's cold out there.' He used her phone to call Marlina again.

'You two go on,' Marlina told him. 'Rolf is asleep and I am in my pajamas.'

'Wake him up. He should see this, too. I will pick you up in a ten minutes.'

The four of them packed into the wheezing Volkswagen, Marlina up front, Rolfie slouched across his grandmother's lap in the back, still groggy with sleep. Stefan drove as close as he could to the massive party that now stretched along the wall all the way from Brandenburg Gate to Checkpoint Charlie. He parked on the street and they joined the foot traffic.

Little Rolf was awake now, his dark eyes wide, tousled curls poking out from beneath a crooked stocking cap. Stefan hefted him up to ride on his shoulders. Rolfie straddled his daddy's neck and held onto his head, mesmerized by the night and so many people.

Old and young, the citizenry of West Berlin pressed around them. Car horns tooted, people shouted. A champagne cork popped and they were caught in the fine spray. People cheered and embraced each other, teary-eyed.

Finally Stefan and his family got close enough to a checkpoint to see the people coming across. Their papers were checked perfunctorily by Grepos who seemed overwhelmed. Most came on foot, but there were Trabants, too, the cheap little East German cars that gargled like lawn mowers with their two-stroke engines. East Berliners were received with hugs and cheers by perfect strangers, their brothers and sisters. Bottles of beer and wine passed from hand to hand.

On a four-meter section of wall that was painted solid with bright-colored art and graffiti, two young men hoisted up one of their friends, and then another. The youngsters stood atop the wall with raised arms and were cheered by the crowd. They reached down and hauled up several others.

Stefan and his mother and Marlina stood watching, smiles straining their cheeks, their eyes wet. They clapped and cheered with the rest. Stefan watched the young men who stood on the wall, his throat tight to bursting.

Unbelievable.

Trudy was watching him. She reached up and took Rolfie off his shoulders. 'Go on, then.' She nodded toward the wall. He looked at Marlina, who was grinning.

Stefan pushed forward through the crowd. He reached up toward the wall climbers and they grasped his hands. Other hands pushed him up from below. With a giant lunge he threw one leg over the rounded top of the wall and hauled himself up. It was wider than he'd expected; he had no trouble standing. Then he crouched and reached down to help someone else.

Radios played everywhere. Most of them were tuned to the news stations, but some played rock music at top volume. The people atop the wall began to dance. Stefan joined them. The air smelled of fireworks and sweat and wet wool. Someone handed him a bottle of wine; he swigged it and passed it on. He lifted his arms and danced; he couldn't stop laughing.

Behind and below him lay the death strip, the raked ground mined with anti-tank barricades and perhaps explosives. But behind that, he saw crowds of East Berliners. They were more subdued than on the West side, but their numbers were swelling. Huge lines had formed behind the checkpoint.

Stefan turned toward the West again, his face aching, heart racketing so hard he almost lost his footing in the jostling crowd now standing on top of the wall. He searched the faces below and found his family, looking up at him. His heart ballooned. Marlina, her blond hair blowing free and wild, her belly swelling with life, waved to him and blew a kiss. He had never seen her smile more beautiful. And riding her hip, their son – who bore the name of a man who had died at this wall, the father Stefan had never known. Rolfie was looking up at him, too, eyes spangled with lights, his mouth open wide with wonder. He was only three, but he would never forget this night.

And there was *Mutti*. Trudy's upturned face glistened with tears. What must she be feeling – she who had risked everything, more than once, to defy this wall?

For a few seconds, Stefan couldn't see, couldn't sing, couldn't even swallow. Then he shook it away and crouched on his knees. He pointed to his mother and motioned vigorously – *come here*.

She pushed through the crowd, closer. He lay on his stomach and reached down to her. 'Come up,' he yelled over the noise. 'I will help you.'

She laughed, shook her head. But he knew she'd already thought of it, had seen the image in her mind. At fifty-six, his mother was still agile and slim. She walked every day to her job at a huge import company downtown. When Wolfgang had begun to decline from complications of his paralysis, she'd taken care of him every evening, cooking his meals and arranging for daytime nursing care until he died two years ago. Now her greatest pleasure was her grandson and his expected brother or sister.

'Come up!' he yelled to her.

Others saw them and began to encourage. A burly man on the ground made a foot-saddle and knelt for Trudy to step up. Other hands made ready to lift her.

She looked at Stefan and smiled – grinned, actually. He grinned back. Then she lifted her arms to the ones waiting for her, and stepped with her small boot into the oversized clasped hands.

Up she came. They lifted her easily and Stefan grabbed her hands from above. With one more heave she was prone beside him, laughing, scrambling to get her legs on top. He held her steady while she caught her breath, then pulled her to her feet.

They stood together atop the wall, arm in arm. Marlina and Rolfie waved up at them, cheered and applauded. Rolfie wanted up, too, but Stefan saw Marlina tell him firmly *nein*.

Stefan put his arm around his mother and pulled her close to his side. Her shoulder fit just beneath his arm, and he could feel her heart pounding, hear the close rasp of breath through her mouth.

'Every wall falls sometime,' she said, and Stefan knew she'd once seen that written on the wall.

Fireworks sprayed the night. A song began to move through the crowd. *'So ein Tag, so wunderschön wie heute...'* It was a song of love, a song of freedom.

They stood together on the wall, swaying, and joined in the song.

The publishers hope that this book has given you enjoyable reading. Large Print Books are especially designed to be as easy to see and hold as possible. If you wish a complete list of our books please ask at your local library or write directly to:

Magna Large Print Books
Magna House, Long Preston,
Skipton, North Yorkshire.
BD23 4ND

This Large Print Book for the partially sighted, who cannot read normal print, is published under the auspices of

THE ULVERSCROFT FOUNDATION